"Do you wa gallows . . .

She had whispered the last part, indicating her intent to out him if he outed her. She had changed. She would never have threatened him in the past with betrayal. Her own father had been a pirate.

"Do you really want me to hang?" James inhaled the tangy scent of her perfume: a sensuous citrus fragrance that reminded him of the tropical island—and their heated affair. "A man tends to confess his sins when facing death. Would you like me to confess my sins, Sophia?" He dropped his lips to caress her ear with his breath. "Would you like me to reveal my transgressions . . . with you?"

She shuddered. "You belong in hell, Black Hawk."

In subtle strokes, he rubbed her spine. "With you at my side, sweetheart."

Romances by **Alexandra Benedict**

MISTRESS OF PARADISE
THE INFAMOUS ROGUE
TOO DANGEROUS TO DESIRE
TOO SCANDALOUS TO WED
TOO GREAT A TEMPTATION
A FORBIDDEN LOVE

ALEXANDRA BENEDICT

The Infamous Rogue

AVON

An Imprint of HarperCollinsPublishers

This is a work of fiction. Names, characters, places, and incidents are drawn from the author's imagination or are used fictitiously and are not to be construed as real. Any resemblance to actual events, locales, organizations, or persons, living or dead, is entirely coincidental.

AVON BOOKS
An Imprint of HarperCollins*Publishers*
10 East 53rd Street
New York, New York 10022-5299

Copyright © 2009 by Alexandra Benedikt
ISBN 978-0-06-168931-4
www.avonromance.com

First Avon Books paperback printing: August 2009

Avon Trademark Reg. U.S. Pat. Off. and in Other Countries, Marca Registrada, Hecho en U.S.A.
HarperCollins® is a registered trademark of HarperCollins Publishers.

Printed in the U.S.A.

10 9 8 7 6 5 4 3 2 1

To Suzy and Steve

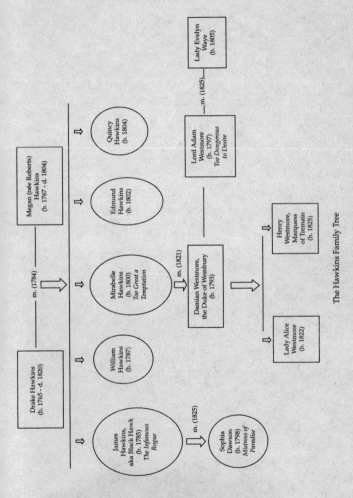

The Hawkins Family Tree

The Infamous Rogue

Chapter 1

London, 1825

Captain James Hawkins struggled with the cravat, slipping a finger between the stiff linen and his throat. The infernal noose! What he wouldn't give to be rid of it. But if he ripped the knotted material in public, it would only confirm the *haute ton*'s suspicion of him: he was a barbarian.

James maintained a distance from the revelry. He had arrived late to the ball, one of the last of the London Season. Hosted by Maximilian "Rex," the Earl of Baine, the tedious affair attracted the most affluent members of society, for the earl's "kingly" taste in decor was much gossiped about.

The ballroom was a glittering spectacle: smooth, white marble columns with soft gray veins, rich yellow drapery flanking each of the dozen windows, a pale blue fresco with gold filigree on the ceiling, gilded sconces on the walls, crystal chandeliers . . .

James considered it all garish rubbish, like too many sweets sitting deep in the belly, so heavy and uncomfortable.

Blood hastened through his veins. It was a subtle,

warm shift, too discreet for an unwitting mind. But two decades at sea stalking—and being stalked—had conditioned him to be more sensitive, and he scanned his surroundings in pursuit of the pair of eyes he was sure were watching him.

Slowly a creeping set of hands rubbed his calves, stroked the stiff, meaty muscles of his thighs before circling his hips in an intimate embrace.

James was sure no one had touched him, and yet the kneading fingers moved across his chest in a salacious manner, making his heart thud like booming cannon blasts. Sweat gathered between his shoulder blades. He pulsed with a long-forgotten energy . . . a yearning.

James slipped his hand into his vest pocket and removed the fob watch. He stroked the damaged timepiece, the glass face shattered. The hands didn't keep time anymore, but he still guarded the cursed piece of gold. He rubbed the bauble's underside, stroking the biting inscription: *May you rot in everlasting hell.*

He stuffed the watch inside his pocket again, expression grim. The ghostly fingers still traced the hard edges of his face in a sensual way. The movement was familiar, soft and stirring. But soon he cringed to feel the sharp nails dig into his cheeks.

The ballroom was alive with movement. He dismissed the glaring ensemble of skirts and black tails to search the miens of unfamiliar faces. Soon he lighted upon a quiet creature seated a short distance away from him.

His innards lurched. She was a spindly-looking thing, pale with fair hair: an ideal woman by the aristocracy's standards. He loathed her kind, so cold . . . cruel. *You don't belong here,* she said with her eyes.

He fisted his palms and folded his arms behind his back, sick with the thought that *her* creeping regard had aroused him in such a profound way. He was sure . . .

James dismissed the thought. He stared at her instead. She looked away from him. She appeared aloof, but her taut posture betrayed her anxiety. Did she fret the big barbarian might think she was flirting with him? That he might ask her to dance?

He noted the way her fingers trembled. He took great pleasure in her discomfort. She thought herself his superior. How quickly she would be humbled if she knew she disgusted him, that she made him ill with her superficial, scornful nature . . . however, she needn't be privy to the truth just yet.

She peeked at him once more.

He smiled.

James withheld a mordant laugh. She was flushed, a shine across her moist brow. He approached her. It was only a step, but the movement startled her. She wanted to skirt away, he could tell. But etiquette restrained her. She couldn't dash off without causing a potential scene. And rather than risk the stigma of a social blunder, she remained in her seat, sweating and twisting her fingers in her lap.

He took another overt step toward her, and observed with wicked delight as she flexed her fine jaw. But he wasn't satisfied; he wanted to disturb her even more.

He started for her.

"Is something the matter, James? Why do you look so murderous?"

William Hawkins advanced. He was thinking like a proper lieutenant, reading the captain's expression for warning of approaching danger. But the only prospective threat was that of James losing his temper and dragging that haughty bitch onto the dance floor for a twirl.

"Nothing's the matter, Will. I'm just having a shit time, is all."

The guests close enough to overhear the exchange gasped and moved off.

"Lower your voice, James. And curb your language! We're not aboard the *Bonny Meg*."

James bristled. More blasted constraints!

"Look at Edmund and Quincy," said William. "Can't you muster up some charm, like them?"

James observed his handsome brethren, dancing in step to the lively music. At ages twenty-three and twenty-one respectively, Edmund and Quincy were nearly half his age. He was already forty, William two years his junior, and indisposed to change.

"I don't belong here, Will."

"You don't want to belong here, you mean. You aren't even making an effort to fit in."

"I'm wearing a blasted noose!"

"You might dress like a gentleman, but you don't behave like one."

With considerable ire, James growled, "And just how should I behave?"

"Well, don't stand like that."

"Like what?"

"Like you're prepared to clobber the first guest who dares to speak to you. And your expression! Can you look more cross?"

James frowned. "I can try."

"Oh, that's very sporting of you, brother."

He sighed. "I'm not going to pander to the nobs."

"I'm not asking you to, but can you be polite?"

"No."

"Blast it, James! You really *don't* belong here, do you?"

No, he didn't. After four years of formal suppers and tiresome parties and posh maidens, James considered it more and more an encumbrance to feign interest in the customs of the *ton.* "I need air. Keep an eye on Edmund and Quincy."

"Aye, Captain," William said dryly.

James moved away from his kin, deliberately approaching the same woman who had treated him with such disdain, as if he might ask her to dance. He swaggered past her instead, her gasp of relief burning his ears.

He marched with purposeful strides through the ornate passageway, the shimmer a distraction. The more he glared at silk-paneled walls and fine wool rugs and hand-painted Oriental vases, the more the bile churned in his belly.

He escaped the palatial house at last. The moment the warm summer breeze greeted him, he cooled his heels. In a still leggy yet more leisurely gait, he wended through the well-manicured hedgerows and stepped into the blooming garden.

It was a small garden, for the earl's city home was in the heart of Mayfair. And so James glanced from side to side to ensure he was alone before he rent the noose from his neck and stuffed it into his pocket. The air was sweeter without the cravat, and he inhaled the perfume-fragrance of roses. It was not the tang of the salty sea, however.

James yearned to be back aboard the *Bonny Meg.* There he was in control and respected. There he was home. But instead he had to wear the dreadful manacles of "respectability." He had to try to fit in with the rest of the *haute ton* for the sake of his sister. He could not disgrace her with his sinful past. He could not shame her with his crude behavior. He had promised.

James stiffened.

A sharp blade pricked him in the back.

"Why aren't you rotting in hell, Black Hawk?"

Sophia Dawson pressed the tip of the knife more firmly into his spine. He was every bit as towering and robust as she remembered, and her heart fluttered at the hot stab of longing that welled in her breast.

She quickly quelled the spurt of unbidden desire. Her palms sweated, and she gripped the bejeweled knife with greater strength. "Answer me, Black Hawk."

Slowly he turned around. "Be careful how you address me in public."

The low drawl of his voice stirred her senses to arousing life, and she clenched the muscles of her midriff to tame the wild flutters in her belly.

The man's gaze lighted on her. Even in the shadows of the garden, those hard and commanding eyes struck her soundly, ensnared her. She knew they were a rich blue; she remembered. She remembered all the nights he had set fire to her passions with those sexy eyes.

"What *are* you doing in public, Black Hawk?"

He grabbed her wrist and hoisted it closer to his chin. The short steel blade shimmered in the moonlight, the silver light bouncing off the pools of his livid eyes.

"I'm not Black Hawk anymore."

The touch of his fingers burned her flesh. The heat

seeped into her blood, warming her arm, her breasts, sinking into her toes.

With a quiver in her voice, she said, "And who are you now?"

"Captain Hawkins."

"You joined the Royal Navy?"

The question riled him even more, for he gritted, "I'd sooner hang!"

The man had not changed in seven years: in opinion or manner. He still loathed the Royal Navy for pressing his father into service. And he was still boorish in behavior, befitting his rank as the most notorious pirate captain on the high seas!

His thumb brushed across the pulse at her wrist, thumping quick. "There are no accounts in the paper about Black Hawk. Did it ever occur to you I might not be a pirate anymore?"

Heartbeats swift, she dismissed the rising pressure in her skull to curl her lips into a sardonic smile. "I assumed you dead."

She could hear the breath rush through his nose. It warmed her fingers, stirring the fine hairs on her arm. "You have a cold heart, woman."

She angled the blade to fit snugly under his chin. "Release me, Black Hawk."

He let her go, and she took a shaky step back.

"You're right," he said. "Black Hawk is dead."

Dead? The wicked corsair wasn't dead. If he was dead, the man standing before her wouldn't have such a devastating pull over her senses. She would have the pluck to slice his gullet and walk away from him before he ruined all her carefully orchestrated plans.

But she didn't have the mettle to gut him. The rough sound of his voice, his sensual eyes and stalwart grip filled her head with potent memories. Memories of crisp, white bedsheets tangled together with limbs soaked in sweat.

She banished the pleasurable thought with a sharp breath and glared at her target. But the vim in her blood only swelled as she observed the faint flutter of black hair that caressed his temple.

He maintained an unfashionable long mane, tied in a queue. One wayward lock dropped over his temple and curled under his eye. The impulse to sweep back the rebellious tress gripped her. But she refrained from the whim, for the same dark curl emphasized the man's glower, bringing her back to her wits.

"You still look like a pirate," she charged. He had shaved his beard—hence his newfound role as Captain Hawkins. He was unrecognizable to the guests at the ball, whose jewels, surely, he had robbed at some point during his long pirate career—but he was still wicked and dangerous; she sensed it. "If you don't captain the *Bonny Meg* anymore, what do you captain?"

"I captain the *Bonny Meg*," he said slowly. "But she is a merchant vessel now."

"You retired from piracy to become a tradesman?" He had the heart of a pirate, the disposition of a scoundrel. Give up his wicked ways? "Why?"

"I had to protect my sister."

"Mirabelle? Is she here?" Sophia offered him a scornful look. "Will I make her acquaintance at last?"

Even the sinful Black Hawk had conformed to some traditional standards of behavior, for he had never introduced his sister to his mistress.

"Mirabelle is at home, nursing a new babe . . . she is now the Duchess of Wembury."

Sophia snorted. So that was why he'd retired from

piracy, to keep from besmirching his sister's respectable reputation. How very noble of him.

The hypocritical knave! He had once declared matrimony a sinister institution, a form of unfair imprisonment. It was called wed*lock* for a reason, he had contended. However, it was wholly proper for his sister to marry. Wedlock was only a sinister captivity if *she* wanted to be the bride.

Her blood burned with the haunting memory of taunts and snubs. She had suffered the stigma of being Black Hawk's mistress. She had struggled against the disdainful looks of the island's inhabitants. But she would suffer no more.

"If I had known you'd climb the social ladder," she said in a flirty manner, "I wouldn't have deserted you."

He took an ominous step toward her.

She lifted the knife to ward him off. "Stay back, Black Hawk."

"Damn you, woman!" He lowered his voice to impart, "Don't call me that."

"And what should I call you?"

"What the devil is wrong with 'James'?"

"Too sentimental . . . I only ever called you that in bed."

There was a plain shift in his posture; more rigid. His voice was a dark timbre, too. "What are you doing here, Sophia?"

He said her name with such heat, her bones trembled. "I'm about to be married."

"To whom?"

"To our host, the Earl of Baine."

He scoffed. "Maximilian Rex asked you to be his wife?"

She bristled at the derision in his tone. Slicing his gullet seemed a more tempting thought.

"The earl hasn't proposed to me yet, but he soon will."

If the black devil didn't foil all the progress she had made with the earl. She had deserted the pirate captain seven years ago. Cleary he was still miffed about the slight. And he wasn't the thoughtful sort, to keep their past affair a secret—or withhold her true identity as a pirate's daughter. She suspected him capable of ruining all her dreams in retribution.

"And what have you to offer the Earl of Baine, Sophia?"

He slowly ravished her with his eyes. He let the glossy orbs roll over her limbs in a sensual way, indicating she had only one thing to offer the earl.

"Money," she bit back.

She had to keep her wrist steady. The impulse to soundly strike the scoundrel across his sneering lips was appealing. But she maintained her composure. She wouldn't let him unsettle her with his biting contempt.

"Ah, yes, money," he said. "I forgot you had money."

"And I have more than enough to satisfy the craving of one greedy lord."

He smiled in a wicked manner. "What is your price, Sophia? Perhaps I can offer more than the earl."

The obtuse devil! She wasn't out to obtain even more wealth. All the pirate gold in the world wouldn't satisfy her. She wanted the respect the position of a wife offered. And not just any wife, but a titled wife: a countess.

The jeers, the cuts filled her head. She had suffered

for the pleasure she had found in the pirate captain's bed. But she was wiser now. She wanted more from life than passion. She wanted to have a noble rank, and the esteem it commanded. She wanted to make sure no one ever laughed at her again.

"I'm not selling myself to the earl . . . I'm buying *him*."

And she had enough coffers of gold to do it, too. After the death of her pirate father, she had inherited his treasures: sinful riches to tempt an insatiable lord.

"And why do you want to *buy* the earl?"

"For his title, of course."

He snorted. "You belong on the shelf."

She stiffened. "I'm only seven-and-twenty. I've not a single gray hair . . . unlike you."

He snatched her wrist once more and dragged her into his arms. Too late she regretted her clipped taunt. The black devil had ruffled her pique. But she was more furious with herself for allowing him to pester her so—and finding herself in his embrace.

"You witch." He dropped his lips to graze hers. "You think me too old, do you? Too old to be like a lover . . . and give you pleasure?"

His breath was hot. It tickled her mouth in the most sensuous way, making her shiver with delight.

The pulsing fury in Sophia's breast was choked by the handsome rogue's close proximity, a more arousing sentiment taking root. Her thoughts quieted. Even the stirring breeze and the distant cacophony of merry guests were hushed in her head. She was bewitched by the man's heady scent. He wasn't doused in perfume like the other men at the ball: there was only the softest trace of vanilla soap on his rough skin, allowing his natural musk to come through and tease her senses.

"Let me see if I remember what pleases you, Sophia."

Gently he sucked on her bottom lip. A surge of sensation quickly pumped through her veins, so strong she struggled in alarm. But he spread his fingers wide apart and gripped her lower spine, hugging her close.

Sophia's heart fluttered. The bone-ribbed corset holding her together was suffocating her, too. She was glutted with tantalizing kisses, so soft and steady.

"Do I please you?" he whispered, and nipped at her bottom lip.

Her pulse throbbed in her ears, her breastbone ached under the pressure of her pounding heart. She was caged between his strapping arms, pressed against his sturdy chest . . . and gripped with a dark need for an even deeper kiss.

He nuzzled her mouth. "Do I give you pleasure?"

She said in a quiet and shaky voice, "No . . . I feel nothing for you anymore."

He stiffened at the cutting remark. She was defiant. She didn't care for the bounder anymore. He still aroused her, though. But she wouldn't give him the satisfaction of hearing her capitulate, even if she yearned for another sultry buss.

"You feel nothing?" he said roughly. "Not even this?"

She swallowed a moan as he pressed his mouth hard over hers. Her resolve slowly weakened and she let him ravish her with his sinful lips.

The energy thrumming through him filled her in return. She had missed the man's dominant nature and robust vigor. The sensations welled inside her, a throbbing thirst.

The rustle of distant voices wrenched her from the

erotic encounter. She nicked him under the chin with the knife, drawing blood.

He pushed her away and reached for his face. He touched the blood. His expression hardened.

She stumbled backward, breathless. "Stay away from me, Black Hawk. If you try to foil my courtship with Maximilian, I'll reveal your true identity; I'll see you hang."

She tucked the short blade into the leather sheath between her breasts, where she always carried it. It had been a gift from James, the knife: a means of protection. Ironic that she now needed it to protect herself from him.

Chapter 2

James glared at the shapely figure skirting away. He reached for the wound on his chin and dabbed at the blood. One look at the dark stains smeared across his fingertips and his head throbbed, his limbs shuddered.

He started after her.

The pressure in his skull blinded him to the trumpery in the house. He moved through the elaborate passageways with brisk strides.

She had cut him, the viper. Did she think he would just curl his tail between his legs and sod off? Not bloody likely.

He reached the ballroom and scanned the frilly heads in search of Sophia. Blood pulsed through his veins; he could feel her stabbing stare. He glanced across the room, and bristled.

She was brilliant under candlelight. The lambent glow kissed the thick curls of her deep brown hair, arranged in a neat and sophisticated swirl. He imagined the long locks wild, spilling across a stark white pillow. He remembered weaving his fingers through the knotty tresses, twisting them in his hands in a moment of profound ecstasy.

His body thrummed with images from the past. He searched for the old Sophia under the layers of copper satin. The light played on the garment, giving it a lustrous sheen. Her clothes, her hair danced with life, but she . . .

She was prim in manner, poised next to the earl. James knew her true nature, though. He knew the passion she was struggling to repress, the fury—at him— she wanted to stifle to better fit in with the reserved members of the aristocracy. He could see her measured movements: a tight smile, soft brows low, fingers curled together and set neatly against her midriff.

Lies!

It was all lies! She was only acting the part of the traditional, meek lady. He wanted to expose her, to hear the gasps of the *ton* as they discovered there was another impostor in their midst; that he was not the only outcast at the ball.

He thundered toward her . . . but a hand grabbed him, dragged him back through the arched entranceway and into the quiet corridor.

"Let me go," James demanded.

"Like hell." William picked him over with his eyes. "Did you fall into the rosebushes and wrestle with the earl's dogs?"

With murder in his eyes, James growled, "I said release me."

"Not looking like a scoundrel. Where's your cravat?"

James fished for the blasted scrap of cloth in his pocket.

"Give it here," said William. He snatched the crisp material and set to work, lacing the noose around his brother's throat once more. "What happened?"

The thoughts in his head still spinning, James muttered an incoherent "She's here."

William fixed his eyes on the cravat as he tweaked it. "Who's here?"

He inhaled a rich breath. "Sophia."

William paused. "Dawson's daughter?"

"The very one."

The one who had deserted him seven years ago without so much as a note of good-bye . . . only a ticking timepiece wishing him to everlasting hell.

James gnashed his teeth at the dark memory.

"What is she doing here?" said William.

"Shopping for a husband . . . And she's set her cap on our host, the Earl of Baine."

"Shit." William glared at his brother with stern reproof. "Don't cause a scandal, James."

"Watch me."

William threaded his arm through the captain's and pinned him against the wall. "Think of Belle."

His sister's agonized cries filled his soul, the haunting wails still fresh and stinging. James shuddered at the morbid memory. What was the matter with him? He had never lost control. And yet he had come so close to making a spectacular stir, disgracing himself and every member of his family.

James took in a sharp breath. The fury surging through his bones weakened. William sensed it, too.

"That's better, James." He loosened his hold. "I know you're angry with Sophia, but you can't disgrace Belle. If you create a fuss tonight, it'll be in all the gossip papers."

With his unruly disposition back on kilter, James slowly headed for the ballroom doors again.

William stopped him. "I said—"

James pushed his brother against the wall and pressed his arm firmly under the man's chin. "I heard you, Will. I won't cause a scandal . . . but I'm not finished with Sophia yet."

He released his kin.

William rubbed his neck, flush from the assault. "At least wipe the blood from your face," he said hoarsely.

James eyed his brother briefly before he rummaged for the kerchief in his pocket. He swiped at the last drops of blood on his chin, and then shoved the napkin back into his coat.

After he had smoothed his hair and clothes to appear seamless, James stepped back over the threshold and once more searched for Sophia. He discovered her quickly; she was still with the earl. But two more ladies had joined their coterie.

He fisted his palms. He could not walk up to the four and engage in conversation. He needed to be formally introduced to the party by a mutual acquaintance.

James expressed a silent curse at the stupidity of the social custom before he turned to his brother. "Introduce me to the earl, Will."

William looked at him, dubious. "What are you going to do?"

"I'm going to greet our host. It's the proper thing to do, isn't it?"

The lieutenant remained quiet about the captain's sudden desire to respect social convention; however, his expression was clear: *Behave according to the rules.*

The two men appeared in the entranceway together, looking composed. One would never think they had just engaged in a heated exchange.

William started across the crowded ballroom first, James one step behind him.

Sophia was quick to detect their approach. She narrowed her dark brown eyes on James, burning with warning. He dismissed her fiery stare and advanced with confidence.

"Good evening, my lord," said William.

The earl returned the felicitation with a respectful "Good evening, Mr. Hawkins."

"I'd like to introduce my brother, Captain James Hawkins."

James was careful to keep his expression bland. "Lord Baine."

James had arrived late to the ball, so he had missed meeting the earl in the receiving line. He hadn't even glanced at the lofty lord during the course of the evening, but now knowing he was Sophia's intended groom, James regarded their host with the scrutiny of a pirate assessing his next target.

The fop was young. Thirty, perhaps. Fair, with pale green eyes. He had a polished manner about him, a refined speech. Ghastly taste in wardrobe, though. The man's brilliant green coat was a freakish blight.

James struggled to keep his composure. Sophia had picked a dandy to be her mate: a posh and sophisticated and noble dandy—everything her former lover was not!

"Might I introduce my sister, Lady Rosamond," said the earl.

The Hawkins brothers bowed.

The petite woman with honey gold locks curtsied. She eyed James with explicit interest. He might have been disarmed, even disgusted, by the overt gesture, but the heat stemming from Sophia attracted his senses, and distracted him from all other reflections.

The earl gestured toward the older matron. "And this is Lady Lucas." He then turned toward Sophia. "And her charge . . . Miss Dawson."

So that was how Sophia had seeped into the social folds of the aristocracy: she had hired a chaperone. However, James quickly dismissed the revelation from his mind.

The colors in the room blurred together as he watched the way the earl looked at Sophia. It was a besotted look . . . a lover's look.

A throbbing pressure mounted in his skull. James glared at Sophia, searched her fine features for the truth: Had she already bedded the earl?

Sophia's eyes darkened. The rich brown pigment pooled with fury and deepened to a near shade of black. She had guessed his thoughts . . . and she appeared piqued at the crude suggestion.

The throbbing pinch in his head weakened. The colors in the room brightened with distinction. She had not bedded the earl. James was familiar with that vexing look: the sort she offered whenever he had made a terrible blunder.

Lady Lucas glanced from her ward to the captain. "Captain Hawkins."

With reluctance, he shifted his gaze to the matriarch. "Yes, my lady?"

"Have you served in the Royal Navy for long?"

James curled his fingers into his palms. "I have never served in the Royal Navy."

"Then are you not too ambitious in your choice of rank, sir?"

James glanced at Sophia. She was stiff with apprehension. He was hard, too. Hard with indignation, for he had to confront yet another pompous female.

"I captain my own vessel, Lady Lucas."

"I see," she said with disdain.

It was like eating sand, the ignominious repartee. But James burned with restless energy to be alone with Sophia. And to get to her, he would engage the condescending company.

"It must be so dangerous at sea," said the earl's sister in a polished yet flirty manner. "Have you many adventures to speak of, Captain Hawkins?"

"Very few, I'm afraid." He swallowed the loathing he felt for her disingenuous regard. "But my ship is well armed, Lady Rosamond. No one gets the better of me."

Not even you, Sophia.

The quick, dark glance James leveled at Sophia did not go unnoticed by his brother.

"I must congratulate you on a successful evening, Lord Baine," said William, steering the conversation toward steadier ground.

James swallowed the distaste in his mouth before he formed his next words with tedious resolve. "Yes, the ballroom is a magnificent spectacle."

"Thank you, Captain," returned the earl.

"Lord Baine is accustomed to finery."

The harridan was quick to praise one man and slur the other. But James did not sour under the patronizing implication that he, a barbarian, was unfamiliar with good taste. He was much too engrossed with the tempting proximity of Sophia to submit to the vicious taunt.

James lifted his hand. "Might I have the next dance, Miss Dawson?"

Sophia's eyes glowed. He wondered she had curbed her tongue thus far. The spirited wench wasn't one to hold back her opinion—or her knife.

But she had to keep her true nature a secret from the *ton*. She had to maintain an amiable smile. Not too broad, though. Perish the thought she should appear vulgar in public. And she had to keep her brows low. Heaven forbid she should raise them and express a fiery opinion or too intelligent a thought. She had to keep her hands firmly together, too. An air of modesty was of the utmost importance. Imagine the outcry from the other guests if she reached for her blade and carved out his throat—which he suspected she very much desired to do.

He shuddered with disgust. Was this what she wanted from life? Was this why she had forsaken him seven years ago? To enter society and let a band of bloody nobs steal her spirit?

"I'm afraid Miss Dawson is feeling unwell and cannot dance." Lady Lucas fluttered her fan. "She needed air not a moment ago."

Air, indeed. She needed to slice his gullet.

"Yes, the room is stuffy," said Rosamond. "I must follow your example, Miss Dawson, and take a turn in the garden."

The young woman took a shaky step forward—and wobbled.

Quickly Lord Baine sidestepped Lady Lucas as Sophia and William reached for Lady Rosamond, but it was too late to stop her tumble. She seemed to sink into James's arms. He swiftly captured her wrist and steadied her before she dropped to the ground.

"Mondie, my dear." The earl patted her cheek. "Are you all right?"

The young woman pressed her palm over her bust. "I was a bit dizzy, but I'm fine now . . . Thank you, Captain Hawkins."

"Yes, my sincere thanks, Captain Hawkins," said the earl.

James offered a curt nod before he placed his hands behind his back, uncomfortable with all the accolades for such a simple gesture.

The matron slipped her arm around the girl's spine. "Come and sit, my lady."

"Thank you, Lady Lucas . . . Max, we must thank the captain in a proper manner."

"Yes, of course. Please accept our invitation to a country house party, Captain Hawkins."

James refrained from snorting. He would sooner hang than mix with such tiresome, frivolous company. "Thank you, however—"

"I insist," said the earl. "You must allow me to express my gratitude in a fitting way; you must accept my hospitality. Mondie and I are hosting an intimate country house party next week. There will be a few other guests, including Lady Lucas and her charge."

James was about to decline the invitation again . . . but one look into Sophia's murderous eyes told him she didn't want him to attend the party.

James offered his hand. "I'd be honored to accept the invitation, Lord Baine."

"Splendid!"

Once more James fixed his eyes on Sophia. "I trust

the garden air did you good, Miss Dawson." He admired the rose pigment in her cheeks. She had blushed so rarely in the past: the blooming color aroused him. "You seem well recovered. Shall we dance?"

He didn't wait for her refusal, but took her by the elbow and steered her onto the dance floor.

The harridan gasped.

William groaned quietly.

James dismissed their outrage. He slipped his arm around the arc of Sophia's spine and grasped her hand. Every part of him pulsed with vigor to feel her plump and seductive curves in his arms once more.

"Do you want to hang from the gallows . . . Black Hawk?"

She had whispered the last part, indicating her intent to out him if he outed her. She had changed. She would never have threatened him in the past with betrayal. Her own father had been a pirate.

But she wasn't the same Sophia anymore, was she? She wanted to climb the social ladder. She wanted to be a countess. Why? She had enough riches to live like a queen. What did she want with pomp and presentation, the snobbery of the *haute ton*?

"Do you really want me to hang?" He inhaled the tangy scent of her perfume: a sensuous citrus fragrance that reminded him of the island—and their heated affair. "A man tends to confess his sins when facing death. Would you like me to confess my sins, Sophia?" He dropped his lips to caress her ear with his breath. "Would you like me to reveal my transgressions . . . with you?"

She shuddered. "You belong in hell, Black Hawk."

In subtle strokes, he rubbed the low knob at her spine. "With you at my side, sweetheart."

She let out a loud huff of air through her nose. "Why are you coming to the house party?"

"I couldn't refuse the invitation. It would have appeared rude."

"And you have to refrain from being rude? To protect your sister's reputation?"

"That's right."

It sounded reasonable; there was no cause for her to doubt him. However, she did. He could tell by the way she narrowed her warm brown eyes on him. That fiery look meant she didn't trust a single word he offered . . . and she had good reason to be wary. In truth, he wasn't sure what he was going to do at the house party. But he wasn't about to let the witch dismiss him from her life again, that much was for sure.

The couple mixed with the other partners and moved to the swell of the music, but the stiff steps seemed so orchestrated, so restrained . . . unlike the slow and undulating movements of the erotic mento that they had danced on the island.

James searched his memory for the appropriate ballroom dance steps. Sophia twirled alongside him with more grace, yet little concentration.

The moment distracting, they bumped into another couple. After expressing an apology, the two twirled onward.

"We're making a spectacle of ourselves," she hissed.

"Shall we withdraw into the garden, then?"

He started to direct their dance steps toward the door.

She squeezed his hand. "If you drag me from the room, I will run you through with my knife."

He chuckled. She had the blood of her mother: a Portuguese wench with a fiery temper. Sophia possessed the ruthless heart of her pirate father, too.

"Does the earl know he's courting a viper?"

"I'm not a viper."

He dropped his gaze to the deep swell of her bountiful breasts. He imagined the short blade tucked between the mounds of flesh, suffocating. He envied the blade. "You sliced my chin."

Little bumps of desire spread across the tops of her breasts. He quirked a smile in carnal satisfaction, pleased to observe her own growing hunger. She was not so immune to him as she wanted him to believe.

Her voice was low, smoldering, "I only nicked it."

He inhaled a sharp breath at the sound of her husky voice. A pool of thoughts gathered in his head, sultry words whispered in passion: *Touch me, James . . . deeper.*

He dismissed the erotic dream with a brisk shake. "Missed my gullet, did you?"

She groused, "Unfortunately, yes."

Her lips whirred. He sensed the vibration, fixed his eyes on the full curve of her luscious mouth. So damn kissable. He had tasted her in the garden tonight. His every nerve pulsed with the memory . . . and one heated memory stirred others to potent life. Soon his flesh burned with the imprints of her lips. He had to bite back a groan as he remembered the cursed way she had brought him to come with her sinful mouth all those years ago.

He shuddered and missed a step.

She recovered her footing and glowered at him. "Are you foxed?"

"I should be."

He certainly intended to be before the night was over.

"Who does the earl think you are, Sophia?"

James caressed her warm spine. He desired to mop the moisture that had formed there, to slowly peel away the layers of satin suffocating her.

She quivered. "The earl thinks I'm an heiress, that my father once owned a sugar plantation in the Caribbean."

He hardened. She had used the plantation house—their home—as the covert means to enter high society. It had never belonged to her father. It had always belonged to them: an intimate hideaway filled with sweet blossoms and tart fruit trees. No slaves or sugarcane crops. Only two souls had dwelled within the quiet walls, free . . . and joyful.

"So you're supposed to be a rich and innocent maid from the colony?" he said stiffly, quashing the maudlin sentiment deep within his belly.

"That's right."

He snorted. "I must congratulate Lady Lucas. The Paragon of Virtue is worthy of praise. She convinced the besotted earl you're a charming prize."

"My money did that," she gritted, eyes alight. "Lady Lucas is a respectable widow. She accompanies me into society."

"To guard you against barbarians like myself?"

"Of course."

The muscles in his back firmed. "And I suppose she instructs you in the ways of etiquette, too? For a price?"

"Naturally."

He dropped his voice. "You might want to ask her to return your money. I can still see who you are,

Sophia. You cannot hide behind layers of satin and fool me."

She cut him again—with her eyes.

"What do you want, Black Hawk?"

He bristled. *Why did you leave me?* But he would sooner saw off his tongue than beg for an answer. Besides, it was clear to him now: she had no heart.

"Where have you been these last seven years?" he said darkly.

Her eyes sparkled in the candlelight, a bewitching shade of rich toffee brown. "In Jamaica. Where else?"

"Liar."

She stiffened.

"I stayed on the island for months after our affair ended." He would not confess he had spent the months searching the island for her—or that he had dreamed about her for the last seven bloody years. He whispered, "I would have spotted you."

She shivered; the tremors pulsed against his fingertips. "I was living with my father. You know he was the unreasonably suspicious sort. We moved away from his home in the mountains and went into hiding. I remained with him until his death before I sailed to England."

The stiffness in his jaw softened. "Your father was a good man."

"Only you and I would think so."

True. A black-hearted devil, Patrick Dawson wasn't the kind of bloke to make friends easily . . . but he had befriended Drake Hawkins, James's father—and saved him from a life of slavery. And for that James would be forever grateful to the man.

Sophia steadied her voice. It almost sounded cordial. "I propose a truce."

He about snorted with laughter. She had threatened him with betrayal, sliced his chin, and now she wanted to be friends? Horseshit! She only wanted him to keep her dark secrets. Her attempt to intimidate him with violence had failed. Now she hoped to persuade him to keep his distance with an offer of peace.

"You and I should not be enemies," she said in a measured tone. "We are both in society for the same reason."

He gritted, "I'm not searching for a wife."

"But you are searching for acceptance, aren't you? To protect your sister?"

She was a cunning witch. With grace she had paired them both as kindred folk, making their way through society to achieve similar goals. Whereas he needed to safeguard his sister's reputation, Sophia needed the approval from the superficial *ton* to become a countess.

But he was not so easily duped.

"In honor of our late fathers' friendship," she said, "surely we can forget about the past?"

Forget about the past?

Not in everlasting hell.

Chapter 3

"**H**ow dare he!" Lady Lucas crossed the fine patterned rug—and crossed it again. She twisted the lacy kerchief around her finger, and pinched her brows. "The . . . the beast."

It was a gloomy morning. A slow drizzle streaked the windows, dampening Sophia's mood even more. She missed the sun, missed feeling the warm rays touch her cheeks and lighten her heart. If only the shower would end and the clouds disband. She was convinced her disposition would then improve. The tedious pattern of raindrops slowly stripped her spirit, her sharpness of mind even. She wanted to slip back into her room, snuggle under the covers, and dream . . . about James.

She shut her eyes tight, willing away the vivifying image of him in her mind. She thought instead about the man's boorish behavior last night, his scandalous remarks. Quickly the heat in her belly weakened, replaced by a darker sentiment.

I can still see who you are, Sophia. You cannot hide behind layers of satin and fool me.

She opened her eyes and fisted the fabric of her leafy green day dress. He might destroy her. One word from his sensual lips, one whisper of impropriety, and her dream of respectability would be dashed.

Damn him to hell!

Lady Lucas touched her brow in a frantic gesture. "He'll ruin everything!"

Yes, James would ruin everything, she thought. He would stomp and maim all her hopes for a better future. The blackguard had a hard heart. He wasn't one to forgive a past transgression.

Would you like me to confess my sins, Sophia? Would you like me to reveal my transgressions . . . with you?

Sophia balled her fists. What did the devil want from her? To humiliate her publicly? Did he loathe her so much? Enough to put his own neck in a noose? For Sophia intended to keep her vow and see him hang if he ravaged all her hopes and dreams.

But if James outed her first, his neck in a noose would be poor comfort. She needed to convince the man to keep quiet *before* the murmur of scandal rounded the society pages. But how? He had rebuffed her proposal for a truce last night. Not in words, for he'd remained reticent about the idea. But she had recognized that "over my dead body" gleam in his eyes. He was such a stubborn, vengeful brute. Any other man might consider her proposal beneficial, even honorable . . . but not the pirate captain. She had to convince James some other way to keep her secret.

"We must spur the earl's affection for you." Lady Lucas collapsed in a nearby chair, her dark brow fixed in meditation. "He must propose to you at the house party."

A sound plan. Sophia didn't voice her sentiment aloud, though. She permitted the matron of nine-and-forty years to scheme in peace. She depended upon the counsel of Lady Lucas. Without her guidance, she was lost. The strict rules of etiquette baffled her, repulsed her at times.

But Sophia had learned to stifle her inappropriate impulses. She was not on the island anymore. The freedom to do as she pleased was a thing of the past. She didn't mind, though. Her reckless desires had only brought her misery. She was keen to be rid of them, to repress her natural tendencies. She intended to trade her wild whims for the respectability of a wife: a countess. It was a simple swap in her mind, well worth the effort and funds she had already devoted to the aspiration.

"We mustn't let the earl think another man is courting you." Lady Lucas stamped her fist on her knee. "Lord Baine is a gentleman. He might step aside if he believes the captain is interested in you . . . or he might search elsewhere for a bride if he thinks you are attached to the captain." She sighed loudly. "If only the barbarian had not asked you to dance!"

Sophia remained mum about her former, illicit affair with said barbarian. Lady Lucas would have an apoplexy if she ever discovered her ward's sinful past.

"If only the barbarian wasn't coming to the house party!"

Blood pulsed to Sophia's temples. Her fingers tingled. She imagined the scorn, the cold snubs if lurid word ever reached the ears of the *ton*. The vibrant sounds and flashes of color beset her mind, making her sweat.

"Don't fret about the earl, my dear." Lady Lucas softened her voice and composed her features. "I can repair any damage, I assure you."

Sophia had faith in the widow's matchmaking

skills. She was a highly regarded member of the gentry, albeit a poor one. After the death of her husband, Lady Lucas had slipped into the dreaded sin of poverty. Even her lofty name was not able to save her from the depths of ostracism and ignominy. But Sophia had offered the woman a considerable fortune to introduce her to society, to find her a respectable husband. Now each woman was dependent on the other for her happiness.

"You must write to Lady Rosamond." The matron slipped from the chair and took her by the wrist. She quickly escorted Sophia across the room to the writing desk. "You must tell the young woman you enjoyed His Lordship's ball. With each word of praise and adoration, she will suspect your attachment to her brother." Lady Lucas removed the quill from the inkstand and handed it to her. "I will dictate."

But Sophia only stared at the long, white feather, an uncomfortable shiver pressing on her spine. She could *not* write the letter. She was literate, however she possessed a disability. And if the matron ever discovered what it was . . .

"I think it better if you write the letter, Lady Lucas."

"Nonsense, my dear. Lady Rosamond thinks highly of your character. We will be far more productive if you write to her as a friend."

Sophia frowned. "I must insist, Lady Lucas. It might seem pretentious if I admit my feelings about her brother, even in a subtle manner."

"You will banter with her. Gossip. A young lady loves to share *on-dit* with a trusted acquaintance."

"Even so, she might take offense. She might consider the subject matter too delicate. However, she would not rebuff the compliments of a lady of your distinction."

Lady Lucas appeared to mull over the argument before she bobbed her head in brisk accord. "Your good sense does you credit, Miss Dawson. You should not risk upsetting the cordial bond between you and Lady Rosamond. I will write the letter."

As soon as the matron took a seat and flicked her wrist in a sweeping gesture, Sophia sighed. She had averted one disaster by refusing to write the letter. She was confident Lady Lucas would avert another by writing a fastidiously worded letter . . . now Sophia need only silence Black Hawk.

"Good morning, Sophia." James stroked the long curve of her spine with the tips of his fingers. "Did you sleep well, sweetheart?"

There was a sharp rap at the door.

James grimaced. The rapping resounded in his head, tender after last night's drinking binge. He growled, "Go away."

The door opened.

William sauntered inside the bedroom, looking cross.

"Get out, Will."

"We're not aboard the *Bonny Meg*, James. I don't take orders here."

James glowered. Aboard ship the captain had privacy. No one dared to enter the cabin uninvited. And no one dared to disobey an order. But here at the house in London, James was forced to associate with family, not crew. Here in St. James's, his sober and obedient lieutenant routinely transformed into an impudent and scolding sibling.

William slowly approached him. "You vowed not to cause a stir at the ball."

"I didn't cause a stir," he said in a sluggardly manner.

"So why are people whispering?"

James ignored his brother and continued to rub Sophia's back.

William rounded the table and paused in front of the window. He wasn't as big as James, but he was still wide enough to obstruct the weak, silvery light creeping in through the drapery. "Will you take your eyes off that damn creature and answer me?"

It was already a misty morning. William's shadow cooled the room even more, casting Sophia in darkness.

Gently James returned the iron lid over the glass case, securing the cold-blooded snake in her aquarium. "What the hell do you want from me, Will?"

"An oath." He folded his arms across his chest. "It appears Dawson's daughter is set to stay in society, so I want you to promise me you won't make an ass of yourself every time she appears in the room."

James bristled. The pounding impulse to strike his brother soundly in the teeth gripped him. He shrugged off the savage desire. Instead he moved toward the washstand.

James dipped his hands into the shallow basin, and slapped the cold water over his warm features. He rubbed his face, listless with fatigue and too much drink. But the memory of his stormy encounter with Sophia last night still burned in his head. Had he really made an ass of himself?

"I know you're angry with Sophia for leaving you—"

"You don't know shit."

"—but you have to keep a cap on your temper. You can't disgrace Belle."

James rubbed his throbbing brow before he snatched a towel. "Didn't we have this blasted conversation last night?"

"Fat lot of good it did. Gossip says you're smitten with 'Miss Dawson.'"

James wiped his face and gritted, "I'm not smitten with the witch."

"Then why are you going to the earl's country house party? You hate being in society."

"Go to hell."

James dropped the towel and stalked across the room. He was dressed in only a pair of trousers, and with the linens still rumpled, the bed looked very inviting.

He stretched across the messy feather tick with a loud sigh, and crossed his ankles. He closed his eyes, too.

"What are you going to do at the house party?" said William.

"Eat."

"Eat who?"

James humphed. "If you're suggesting I'm going to the house party to cause a scandal, I'm not."

But William sounded unconvinced. "Why don't you write to the earl and cancel the trip? Visit with Cora instead. Then you can get the frustration out of your blood and forget about Sophia."

Forget about Sophia? Did the man really think a roll in the sheets with a whore was going to satisfy the dark fire burning in his belly?

He remembered the sultry look in Sophia's fine

eyes, the sharp arch in her brows. He remembered the thrilling feel of her round and seductive curves pressed firmly against him, and the smoldering texture to her sassy voice.

James girded himself against the arousal slowly burning in his blood. No. A tumble in bed with Cora wasn't going to slake the lust in his belly . . . only Sophia could do that.

"No," said James. "I'm going to the house party."

William's footsteps drummed in his ears. He heard the chair legs scrape across the hardwood flooring as William swiveled the seat and sat down.

"I know you're having a wretched time attending parties, James. And Sophia's return only makes matters worse. But we've all had to adjust to the tiresome antics of the *ton* since retiring from piracy."

What did his brothers have to adjust to? They flirted and danced and charmed the society wenches with aplomb. The men even dined and gambled and snorted snuff with the rest of the peerage with considerable ease.

William suggested, "Look at Belle."

"Look at Belle?" He opened one eye to glare at his brother. "We're putting ourselves through this hell for her."

"Yes, but she had to adapt to her new life, too."

"How?"

"She had to start wearing a dress, for one."

James snorted and closed his eye again. "She should have been wearing one from girlhood."

"With four brothers, a father, and no mother for guidance?"

James stiffened at the mention of their mother. She had died in childbirth to Quincy, leaving a four-year-old Belle without a proper female example. But something more haunted him . . .

One thought about his mother was like losing his footing and slipping from a cliff. His thoughts tumbled backward with speed and he remembered the low sobs coming from her room when he was just a boy: sobs for his father, recently pressed into service by the navy.

Long before Mirabelle, Edmund, and Quincy had come along, Megan Hawkins had been alone with two small boys and no money or means of support.

You must help me, James. She had stroked his then four-year-old head with frantic regard. *You must help me now that Papa is gone. I need you, James. I can't take care of you and William by myself. You will help Mama, won't you, James?*

James dismissed the disturbing memory with a quiet shudder.

"Belle had to wear breeches," said William. "There was no way to avoid it with so many men afoot. But now she's more comfortable with her new position as duchess. And you'll eventually grow accustomed to being brother-in-law to a duke."

Why did that sound so ominous? James kneaded the pulsing spot at the crown of his nose. Trouble was, he didn't want to grow accustomed to such a stiff existence. He didn't want to pander to the nobs, to kneel before the pompous lords and ladies like a street urchin . . . but what choice did he have now that Belle was a duchess?

"Get out, Will. My head is throbbing."

There was no sound of movement.

James opened his watery eyes to see his brother still seated in the chair. "What?" he snapped, and regretted his clipped tone, for the pressure in his skull strengthened.

"There's one other matter I need to discuss with you."

James growled, wishing all his blasted relatives and their needs to damnation. "What is it?"

The door burst open.

Two strapping young bucks stomped into the bedroom, making all the furniture spin and dance.

James grabbed his head and stifled the roaring curse he was sure would do him in if he dared to voice it aloud.

"Did you see this morning's paper?"

Quincy flapped the newsprint, making James dizzy. He shut his eyes and tried to ignore his brethren, but the youngest fledgling refused to be rebuffed.

Quincy smacked the captain across the bare feet with the paper. "Wake up, James. We're famous—again!"

William quickly moved across the room and examined the paper. He sighed loudly. "Take a look at this, James."

The newsprint shoved in his face, James eyed the bold headline. But the letters only twirled together in quick fashion. "Why don't you just read it to me."

It was Quincy who snatched the paper from William and cleared his throat to impart: *"The notorious pirate Black Hawk strikes again!"*

James almost didn't give a damn, he was so bloody fagged . . . almost. "Read on, Quincy."

"The sea is once more plagued by the dreaded pirate Black Hawk and his wicked crew. After almost four years of unmolested travel, defenseless ships, like the Lorianne, *are again in peril. Last sennight, the passenger vessel was raided by the marauding rogues and stripped of cargo and*

personal possessions. The gentlemen aboard remained stoic and brave, the ladies terribly frightened and clinging to their sides." The pages rustled as Quincy theatrically performed: *"When will the Royal Navy bring an end to the infamous bandits' reign of terror? When will we have safe passage at sea? I call on you, faithful reader, to demand the pirate leader's head. Only then will justice triumph and the seas be secure."* Quincy beamed. "I've missed being in the paper."

William ignored the quip and said, "That's two reports in two months, James. First there was a group of miscreants bootlegging whiskey and rum in our names, and now there's another band attacking passenger vessels."

"They might be one and same," suggested Edmund.

"That's right," chimed Quincy. "Do you remember the duke's brother, Adam Westmore?"

James had coincidentally robbed the man as Black Hawk a few years ago—and Adam Westmore had maintained a grudge. He had hunted the *Bonny Meg* and its pirate crew for years, seeking vengeance. But once the two families had united in marriage, the lust for blood had ended and a tentative trust had formed.

Quincy scratched his chin. "Adam had stumbled upon a band of bootleggers while looking for us. Their leader was posing as you, James. "

"Rumor of our 'deaths' might have inspired the bold cutthroats to adopt our personas and take all the credit," said William.

"You mean blame," groused Edmund. He settled in a chair and stretched out his long legs, looking much too comfortable, giving James the distinct impression he wasn't going to get much peace that morning. "It hardly seems fair. Someone else gets all the spoils, yet we get all the fault."

William said grimly, "What are we going to do about the impostors, James?"

"Ignore them."

"We can't ignore them," returned William. "*We're* the ones being accused of the raid."

"So what?"

William frowned. "I know you're still drunk, James, but can't you see the pressing danger?"

James rubbed his aching temples. "I only see one pressing danger: three gutless brothers. Now get the hell out of my room. All of you."

Only Quincy budged—to straddle a chair.

James growled. The buzzing voices, the snapping thoughts of Sophia danced in his head, making him more and more irascible.

"What if the authorities go looking for Black Hawk?" wondered William.

"Then they're going to find the miscreant and hang *him*." James inhaled a sharp breath to soothe the spiking pressure in his head. He said with less bite, "I still don't see the bloody problem."

Cool even under the captain's fierce glare, William said in a reasonable manner, "The authorities might stumble upon the *real* Black Hawk and crew if they search for the impostors."

"That's not going to happen," avowed James.

"Are you sure?" William folded his arms. "There are those who know our true identity and might betray us in the wake of the recent report."

"Who? The duke?" James snorted. "He might be a bastard, but he loves Belle. He wouldn't betray us, if only for her sake."

Damian Westmore, the Duke of Wembury, was an infamous villain, dubbed the "Duke of Rogues" by his peers. James was still dumbfounded by his sister's choice of a mate. She might as well have married the devil.

Women made such odd selections in partners, he thought, disgruntled. His sister had wedded a rogue. Sophia wanted to attach herself to a simpering fop. It defied logic, their choices in husbands.

It was better for a father to pair his daughter with the right man. Drake Hawkins would never have agreed to let Belle marry a scoundrel, James was sure. And Patrick Dawson would have disemboweled the irritating dandy Sophia had picked. A pity the two men were dead. They would have saved their senseless daughters from misfortune.

"I'm not talking about the duke," said William. "I'm talking about Sophia."

The dull pounding in James's head surged. The hammering pulses blurred his dim vision even more.

Stay away from me, Black Hawk. If you try to foil my engagement with Maximilian, I'll reveal your true identity; I'll see you hang.

James gnashed his teeth at the foul memory.

"Sophia?" Quincy's eyes rounded. "Dawson's daughter is here in London?"

Even the grumpy Edmund appeared intrigued. "What is she doing in Town?"

"Husband hunting, of course." William offered the captain a pointed look. "James and I met her last night at the ball. She wants to marry the Earl of Baine."

"Who?" said Quincy.

"Our host last night, the Earl of Baine."

Quincy shrugged.

So did Edmund. "Too many parties."

"Never mind," said William. "About Sophia?"

"Now that's a bird." The flirtatious Quincy grinned. "Exotic, fiery, playful. I was still a pup all those years ago in Jamaica, but if I had the chance to meet her now—"

"You'd . . . do . . . what?"

Quincy bit his tongue and wisely didn't finish his lustful thought. Edmund smirked at his younger brother's misstep, for James's glower was murderous.

With the young upstart soundly muzzled, James fixed his eyes on William and said darkly, "What about Sophia?"

"Well, she didn't seem very happy to see you last night."

James stiffened. Blood hastened through his veins as he fingered the cut on his chin.

You belong in hell, Black Hawk.

"She might out us yet," suggested William.

"She won't."

James was adamant. The brazen witch might threaten him and brandish her knife, but she wouldn't betray his identity as Black Hawk. He sensed her heart was still loyal to her kind, even if she claimed otherwise.

There was a rap at the door.

The butler entered the bedroom without awaiting a proper invitation. He had learned long ago his four masters weren't men of etiquette.

"Good morning, gentlemen."

The group hushed as the old man moved across the room, arm outstretched. He stopped in front of the aquarium, lifted the lid, and dropped the thrashing mouse inside the glass case before he secured the trapping again.

James eyed the frightened rodent as it circled the enclosure in a frantic bid to escape. Sophia remained curled in an idle sleep, though. She would soon stir and devour the hapless creature . . . but not before she had tortured its senses.

The snake was very much like her namesake, James reflected with a grim smile.

As soon as the butler had departed from the room, William pressed onward: "We should still do something about the scoundrels roaming the seas in our name."

"Fine," snapped James. "We'll hunt down the impostors and thrash 'em—but not today."

"And not tomorrow, I assume," said William dryly. "You're going to a house party."

Edmund looked at his older brother. "*You're* going to a house party?"

The captain growled. "I am."

Quincy screwed up his lips. "Why?"

"Sophia will be at the house party," returned William.

"Oh," from both Quincy and Edmund.

James offered the lieutenant a look of murder. "I trust you three can take care of the matter while I'm gone? Start making inquiries about the impostors."

That seemed to mollify the lieutenant. The two bucks perked up at the news, as well. The restless fledglings had had the most difficult time giving up piracy. He and William had enjoyed the spoils of the sea for more than two decades, but Edmund and Quincy had only just tasted the pleasures of piracy before they'd had to "retire" as brigands to protect their sister's reputation.

That had been four years ago. And ever since that time, the two young men were always first to volunteer for any adventure.

Perhaps William had had a point, that he was not the only one struggling with their newfound positions as merchant sailors and society outcasts. Not that he was in any condition to acknowledge the point.

"Now get out," said James, his head ready to burst from the gnawing pressure.

William was already on his feet, and so headed for the door. Edmund and Quincy trailed behind him.

"Oh, Will, did you ask James about—"

Once again, Quincy faltered mid-thought. But this time William had curtailed him. He squeezed the back of the pup's neck and shoved him out the door. "No, I didn't, Quincy. Next time."

James was too disoriented to listen to the baffling exchange. He was only grateful for the quiet that followed the men's belated departures.

As soon as the door closed softly, James shut his eyes and breathed deep. He tried to hush the mesh of voices and sharp memories that crowded in his skull, but the damnable thoughts kept coming, hounding him . . . one thought more pressing than the rest.

How could Sophia do this to herself? To be a countess would crush her spirit. The restrictions imposed on a lady's conduct were brutal. He had only to attend a tiresome soirée to find dozens of timid maidens ruled by convention. According to his pestering brother, even Belle had struggled with being a duchess. However, she was in love with her bloody husband. What excuse did Sophia have for entering such a cold and passionless world? She wanted to be a countess, true. But was that all she wanted, the title? Was that why she had deserted him seven years ago? Because he didn't have a blasted rank? What did she want with it?

James furled his fingers into fists. Sophia wouldn't survive the wedding tour as a countess. Her spirit would wither under the merciless scrutiny . . . so what did he care? If she wanted to sell her soul, let her. He shouldn't give a damn. She had startled him with her unexpected presence at the ball. He had recovered now. He wouldn't let the witch twist his guts and warp his thoughts anymore. He wouldn't let her claim his mind and chain him to her like a slave. He had already made that mistake once.

His limbs pulsed with the memory of the empty plantation house, the wretched timepiece. She had walked away from him without even a niggardly thought . . . but she still desired him.

The blood in his veins roared with need. The fiery witch espoused her distaste for him, flourished her blade at him. But he had tasted the sweet desire on her lips last night. He had caressed her spine and sensed the tremors rolling along her quietly shuddering limbs. She had failed to hide her true self from him. She had failed to stomp out her burning passions.

She wanted to be one of *them*: a noble lady. But she didn't have it in her to conform to the strict rules of the *ton*. She was an outcast, like him. And he would prove it to her.

A dark thought sparked. He wanted to strip away her false mannerisms, her prudish ideas. He wanted her to accept her true, spirited nature, to admit she would never be happy with the tractable earl. He wanted her to end her courtship with the fop—and come to him.

James let the thought settle; he draped his arm over

his eyes. He imagined the lush feel of her thick hair wrapped in his hands. He imagined the salty taste of her moist flesh, her wanton cries in bed. He wanted one more night with her. He wanted one final—and proper—good-bye, to bring her to her knees in helpless desire before he walked away from her—as she had once walked away from him.

Chapter 4

Sophia skulked through the shadows of the St. James's district. A hired hackney coach had dropped her off a short distance away. She intended to make the remainder of the trip on foot.

She was confident she would not be recognized. It was late. The darkness masked her features. She was wearing a deep hooded mantle, too.

Lady Lucas would have her head if she ever discovered her midnight gallivanting. The bachelor quarters of London were no place for a lady, and Sophia was determined to obey convention. However, she first had to convince the damnable pirate captain it was in both their interests to be cordial and silent about the past. She couldn't risk another disastrous quarrel with the man, especially during the country house party. He might ruin her courtship with the earl . . . which might very well be the black devil's insidious plan.

She moved through the darkness, a small wooden box tucked under her arm. She eventually made her way to the address she had acquired through a few casual inquiries.

She descended the steps at the front of the prestigious townhouse, leading to the service entrance. She intended to slip in through the lower level, undetected. The staff was surely asleep at such a late hour.

She crouched and set the box on the ground before she removed the small blade from between her breasts. She squinted to better examine the lock. It was difficult to see in the dimness. The moon offered little guidance to an intruder in a sooty city like London.

Drawing on her late father's tutelage, she set to work on the door. All the while she mulled over the thought: Was her plan sound?

She had considered penning James a note, but she had quickly dismissed the idea. What if he didn't burn the letter after reading it? The incriminating missive might surface and ruin her. No. She needed to speak with him privately, to get him to agree to the truce in the only way she knew how . . . either that or she would have to slice out his tongue to keep him quiet.

She maneuvered the blade, blindly seeking the precise mechanism . . . when an iron key slipped between her eyes.

"Here," said the shadow in a low and teasing drawl. "Try this."

Sophia bristled. The blood in her veins quickened, the pulses in her head throbbed. She was parched, her tongue and lips like harvest oats.

Slowly she lifted off her haunches—and cradled the blade in her grip. She was prepared to strike at the figure to protect her identity. However, the flirty sound of his voice was faintly familiar, and she peeked at him instead.

"Quincy?"

She detected the white line of teeth as he grinned. "Hullo, Sophia."

The stiff muscles in her back eased, and she sighed. Quincy might be a pirate; he might share the same blood as his disreputable older brother, but he was no snitch. She suspected the young man would keep the secret of her midnight rendezvous from the rest of the *ton*.

As the pressure in her skull returned to a more steady beat, she tucked the short blade back into her bodice. "I'm here to see the captain."

"Are you sure?" The cheeky kid's grin broadened. "I'm much more charming than my older brother."

She was in no mood to banter with the scamp. But he had an easy manner about him that put her nerves to rest. She noticed he had blossomed into quite a presentable rogue. It was too dark to see his features, but he was tall and strapping, with fashionable short, wavy locks. He had always possessed an attractive charm. And with even more maturity, he was bound to become a distinguished rake . . . but right now he was still a pup.

Unlike James.

She dismissed the unwelcome thought with a quiet shudder, and stepped aside to allow Quincy to open the door. She sniffed the air as he moved beside her, the distinct fumes recognizable. He was doused in the smoke.

"Why are you sneaking into the house through the service entranceway?" she wondered.

He unlocked the door. "I could ask you the same question."

"I want to avoid detection."

"I want to avoid my older brother."

Quincy stepped into the dark room first. She scooped up the small wooden box before she followed him inside the kitchen. Once more she squinted in the dimness as he closed the door behind her.

"What do you mean you want to avoid your brother?" She lowered her hood. "Don't tell me the captain is so boorish he'd deny you a bit of fun?"

He chuckled softly. "James can be in a sour mood sometimes. I prefer to keep away from him."

She understood the sentiment entirely. "He's a brute, I know."

"A miserable brute."

She gathered her brow. "How's that?"

"James hates to be in society. I think it comforts him to make the rest of us miserable, too."

Her heart trembled. She suspected James wanted to make *her* miserable: a punishment for deserting him. At the troubling thought, she squeezed the box tight. It offered her redemption.

Sophia sensed the pup's eyes on her, pert and mischievous. She put a quick end to his ogling with a curt "Take me to your brother, Quincy."

He sighed. "This way."

He took her by the wrist and maneuvered her through the room and around the furnishings with ease. He didn't even need a candle. Clearly he had sneaked inside the house many times before and was now familiar with the design of the space.

As she trailed after the scamp toward the ground floor, she glanced around the slowly brightening passageway. The main part of the house was quiet, but candles still dotted the walls and tables, casting the dwelling in a smoldering glow.

The decor was deeply masculine. The wood furnishings were dark, the color palette was rich with shades of red and brown and touches of gold. She lifted a brow at the risqué paintings, the nude subject matters tasteful yet still shocking to a respectable lady's constitution. Lady Lucas would faint dead away.

Quincy escorted her to a waiting room. "Stay here. I'll go and fetch James."

"Thank you."

He winked. "Make yourself at home."

As soon as he had left the room, Sophia glanced around the formal parlor and spotted the model schooner perched on a long table. She approached the well-crafted structure and examined the fine detail. It was an exact replica of the *Bonny Meg*. She peered into one of the tiny windows astern—the captain's quarters.

Images quickly filled her mind: erotic memories of her nights aboard the moored ship with the black devil. She willed the dreams away and gathered her wits. She had more important matters to attend to, like keeping James from revealing their past.

She paced the room as the minutes ticked onward, her belly twisted in knots. There wasn't time to waste, she thought. She still had to return to Lady Lucas.

So where was Black Hawk?

He was wittingly making her wait. She understood the bounder's character well enough to suspect he enjoyed being in control of the situation. Well, she wasn't going to spend the entire night circling the waiting room. She had to see the pirate captain. She had to settle the matter of their truce *before* the house party.

Sophia left the room and explored the passageway. She searched the main floor for the sound of the man's voice, but the air was still . . . leaving her with only one other choice.

She didn't want to do it; it might put her at a greater disadvantage. But she couldn't shout the devil's name and demand an audience with him. She didn't want to rouse the servants or the rest of the Hawkins brothers. And yet she couldn't dawdle anymore, either. She had to return to Lady Lucas before sunrise.

With determination, Sophia lifted the hem of her skirt and mounted the sturdy steps at the end of the corridor.

Quietly she ascended to the next level. Her pulse tapped briskly in her ears as she stealthily made her way through the long passageway, searching for James's room. She didn't know which door belonged to the pirate captain, though.

She could just hear Lady Lucas exclaim in horror: *You're ruined*! She *was* ruined if she didn't convince James to keep her secret. With the alarming thought in mind, she was prepared to open random doors in her desperate search. However, a set of ornate pocket doors snagged her attention.

The sturdy panels carved with intricate jungle motifs confirmed she had found the captain's room at last. She skirted to the end of the corridor, convinced she had located the right room, for the doors were the most prestigious of the lot. She suspected only the high-ranking captain would get such a glorious bedchamber.

She stopped in front of the imposing doors. Her pulse rapped quickly. She steadied her breath and composed her features. He would not be pleased to see her in his bedroom uninvited. But she wasn't going to let the scoundrel rule her senses anymore. It was intolerable to think he might reveal her true identity, her sordid past. She couldn't stomach the twisting dread that he might oust her from polite society with one wicked word.

Sophia reached for the door latch, her hand shaky. She girded herself for a heated confrontation. She was disappointed to find the room empty.

Where *was* the devil?

She stepped inside the apartment. There were lit candles in the room. She examined her surroundings. Perhaps she was in the wrong space, after all?

But one look at the massive bed—and stylish, six-foot-high headboard—and she suspected she had the right room.

Softly she approached the bed. A disturbing longing gripped her heart at the sight of the rumpled bed-sheets: an improper desire to tousle the linens even more, soak them with sweat.

She arched her spine, pressed her lips to one of the pillows—and breathed deep.

She closed her eyes. She was in James's room, she was sure.

She rebuked herself for being so foolish, for feeling such trite emotions. Let the memory of his heady scent burn and rot—alongside him.

Sophia heard a soft rustle. She looked across the room and spotted the glass case. In the shadows she detected the slight movement, but otherwise failed to identify the creature.

In faint steps she advanced, and peered into the glass.

"I see you've met Sophia."

She gasped quietly. She searched for him in the room with her eyes, but he was elusive. She then sensed his stare coming from the adjoining dressing room.

He was in shadow, but his figure was still easy to make out, so tall and robust.

Her heart beat swiftly. She had to curl her fingers

more tightly around the box to prevent the rogue from seeing them tremble.

Slowly he approached her.

She quickly stifled the horde of unwelcome feelings that stormed her breast. The senses in her fingers, her spine, the tip of her tongue responded to the man's steady advance with characteristic delight. She tried to stomp away the treacherous desire. She failed miserably.

Why did he have to be so sinfully handsome? Why did he have to appear so bloody tempting in the candlelight?

It was sorcery, the way he snagged her every wit, making her dizzy with desire. She had no other word to describe the enigmatic pull he had over her senses . . . Sophia?

She glanced at the glass case once more . . . inside was a Jamaican yellow boa.

The blood throbbed in her head. He had named the snake *Sophia*?

The dark thought quickly doused her burning passions. She glared at the pirate captain with venom. The yellow boa wasn't poisonous—but she was.

James circled her before he paused and looked into the aquarium. "I found Sophia on the island seven years ago. She was wrapped around a branch outside our bedroom window."

How charming!

The pulsing pressure in her head worsened the more he gazed at the caged creature with tender regard.

She pinched her lips. She was here to negotiate with the bounder, to bring an end to their war of wills. She wouldn't let him tempt her into another doomed row.

"What are you doing here, Sophia?"

He looked away from the snake and set his eyes on her, his expression dark.

She shivered. "I need to speak with you."

She gasped as he pushed her against the wall. Not too hard. But he caged her firmly with his body—and his sensual blue eyes.

Dark locks framed his seductive expression. Loose from the queue, the long tendrils touched his shoulders. He had a smattering of silver at his temples, but he was still as sexy and fit as she remembered. She wanted to curse him for that.

An ache brewed deep in her belly as she stared at the man's lush lips, the memory of their heated kiss the other night filling her skull, making her other senses tremble in want.

She took in a deep breath to feel his long, thick fingers sink between her breasts. The hot strokes tickled, and she sighed inwardly as he rummaged through her bodice, searching.

At last she heard the soft hiss as the blade rubbed against the sheath. He removed the knife and pierced the wall high above her head.

"Now we can talk."

She glanced up to see the embedded blade, out of reach. She was dazed. Now they could talk? When she was defenseless? The beast!

She gathered her wits and noted the cut on his chin, the slight swelling around the wound. She took great pleasure in the mark she had made. But she could not afford to be vindictive anymore. He would only resist her request for a truce even more.

He let her go and she swiftly skirted to a nearby chair. She was breathless. Her skin still burned with the echo of his touch.

The man had a fierce hold over her mind. On the island it had attracted her, the distracting energy he possessed. Excited her, even. But here in London it was a dangerous game to be influenced by the wicked pirate. One simple look or gesture indicating an inappropriate attachment to the man, and her dream of becoming a respectable wife would fizzle away.

She took a seat and mustered a dignified pose. Lady Lucas had instructed her to keep her back straight and her shoulders down and her hands in her lap.

He appeared annoyed to see her acting in such a proper, ladylike manner, though. She noted the way his nostrils flared: a sign he wasn't pleased.

"Why did you come to my room, Sophia?"

He took a seat opposite her and stretched out his long legs. His bare toes came perilously close to touching her boots, and she tucked her footwear another inch under her seat.

"You left me waiting in the parlor," she said in a slightly flustered voice.

"I was getting dressed."

She withheld a snort. It had taken him a quarter of an hour to don a pair of trousers and a shirt? A shirt he had yet to button? A shirt that revealed his strapping muscles and dark chest hair?

"Well?" he said in a lazy manner. "To what do I owe the honor of your visit?"

She glanced away from the man's admirable physique, looked into his eyes with purpose. "We need to talk about the past."

He lifted a dark brow. "Do we?"

She clasped her hands more firmly around the box, resisting the impulse to quarrel. "I want you to promise me you will not reveal our island affair."

Slowly he laced his fingers together and rested them across his midriff. "And why should I do that?"

"So I don't out you as Black Hawk."

A small smile touched his lips. "You won't betray me, Sophia."

She ignored the sultry way he said her name. "Don't be so sure of that. If you ruin my plan to marry the earl, I *will* seek revenge . . . I've changed, Black Hawk."

He considered her thoughtfully. "You think to threaten me again? That did not work so well for you the other night."

Would you like me to confess my sins, Sophia? Would you like me to reveal my transgressions . . . with you?

She shivered again at the memory. He was right. She was letting the conversation get away from her. If she threatened him with betrayal, he would only threaten her with it in return. And what point would that serve?

She took in a deep breath, then slowly skimmed her fingers around the edges of the box. "Shall we play a game?"

He lifted a sooty brow. "Are you sure you want to play with me, sweetheart? You might lose."

She dismissed the tremors that rolled along her spine. She might lose, true. But what other choice did she have? It was the only way to settle their dispute. It was the only way they had ever settled a dispute in the past.

"I'm willing to take the chance," she said. But her rampant heartbeats belied her steady voice.

He pointed toward the empty table beside the window.

Quietly she approached the piece of handsome

furniture and set the elegant box in the center. She snapped the gold lock and lifted the lid, revealing the chessboard.

James took the seat opposite her and collected the players. He arranged the pieces in the proper starting positions. "Ladies first."

She removed her mantle and flexed her shaky fingers under the table to hide her discomfort. She had not played the game in years, not since she had parted from James. And sitting across from the blackguard now was a giddy distraction.

But one thought about her future, dashed to bits if she failed, and her scattered wits gathered in order.

She moved the ivory pawn one square.

He remained quiet, his eyes hot and hard—and centered on her. At length he pushed a jade piece forward. "I never did thank you for the beautiful timepiece." He lowered his gaze to the board and said in a blasé manner: "I still have the pieces somewhere."

Slowly she raised her eyes and said with an equal air of indifference: "You're welcome."

She noticed the man's chest muscles stiffen under his parted shirt. If he intended to intimidate her, she was prepared to stand her ground. She had no regrets in leaving him. Or even the manner in which she had deserted him. He had deserved the cold farewell, the biting inscription on the timepiece. Though she was sorry to hear it was damaged. It truly had been a beautiful watch.

"Does the earl know you're not a virgin?" he said in a low voice.

Her heart missed a beat. "No."

"Don't you think it wicked to deceive the man?"

"No."

He lifted his eyes and glared at her. "I think it very cruel of you, Sophia."

She set the ivory knight on the board with a distinct thump. "What is very cruel of me?"

"Fooling the intended groom." He moved another player. "Imagine the poor man's dismay to discover his bride's flower plucked by another man."

She snorted at the euphemism. "Imagine your crew's dismay to hear you refer to a woman's quim as a flower."

For the first time since their stormy reunion, he offered her a genuine smile—and it shook her to her bones.

"You're a lady now, Sophia. I didn't want to offend you with my crude language."

"Then be a true gentleman and forfeit the chess game; promise me you will keep our past affair a secret."

He captured a pawn. "I don't think so."

She curbed the impulse to slam her fist on the table. He'd nabbed a player already. She stared at the board. Her brain was starting to ache with dread.

"You're skirting the issue, sweetheart."

"Am I?" she said in a flippant manner. She eyed the opportunity and moved her knight. She captured his pawn with glee.

He didn't seem too disturbed, for the match was still young. "The earl likes treasures, after all. You've seen the gold and jewels and garish artwork in his house."

She shrugged. "He can have my money. That's treasure enough."

He chuckled softly. "Men like other things in life besides money."

She eyed him sharply. "Like flowers?"

He touched the top of his lip with the tip of his tongue. "Hmm . . . sweet-smelling flowers."

It was a faint gesture, but it captured her mind in a wicked hold. She stiffened, ached with the memory of his kisses, his tongue on her flesh . . . inside her flesh.

Her bones rattled with a hard quiver. "If it means so damn much, I'll fake my virginity."

"It's not the same."

"It'll have to do," she huffed.

His expression darkened. "It's the principle of the matter."

Damn the blackguard and his distracting prattle about principles! She wasn't a fool. Virginity in a woman was a prized commodity among the respectable members of society. Hence she intended to fake her squeamish cries, her maidenly airs.

However, she resented the deceit. She had no moral qualm with the treachery, but she believed the pretense unnecessary. Every day a woman exchanged her dowry for a man's title. It was a practical, fair trade in her opinion. Insincere professions of poetic love? Virginal blood? It was all a nuisance . . . but she couldn't admit the truth to anyone else but James. She had to keep quiet about her rebellious thoughts in polite society.

"You're one to speak of principle," she charged.

"I've retired my wicked ways."

"Not according to this morning's paper."

"A misprint, I assure you."

She humphed.

James moved another player. "What about an heir?"

Sophia frowned. "What *about* an heir?"

"I'm sure the earl will want one . . . and you're barren."

She twisted her lips, resisting the impulse to scratch out the black devil's eyes. "And this displeases you? My being barren never bothered you on the island."

He snorted. "*I* don't want brats . . . but do you really think the earl will be pleased to discover his wife is unfruitful?"

She quieted the swift, hard beats of her heart with a few measured breaths. She was barren, that much was true. She had never conceived a babe during her affair with James. She wasn't distraught at the thought of being childless. Far from it, in truth. She had no desire to be a mother. However, the pirate lord raised an exasperating—yet sound—point: What *would* the earl think to learn she was sterile?

"The earl has a sister," she said with confidence, quashing the tremors in her belly. "Lady Rosamond will marry well and produce an heir. The earl's estate will be secured."

"I see."

James nabbed her knight.

Damn him!

"Must you talk, Black Hawk?"

"Am I disturbing your concentration? My apologies. I won't say another word."

And the bloody cutthroat was true to his word. The remainder of the game was played out in silence. An hour later, exhausted, Sophia sensed her heart flutter as she spotted the weakness on the board.

Her brain throbbed. She scanned all the remaining pieces to make sure she wasn't imagining their positions before she moved the queen forward to corner the jade king.

"Checkmate," she whispered.

James frowned. He stared at the board for a few moments before he lifted his own somnolent eyes to meet hers. "You win, sweetheart . . . ask anything of me you wish."

She bristled at the expression. She remembered the last time they had played chess, the last time she had heard him say those words:

Ask anything of me you wish.

Marry me, she had asked him—only to be rebuffed.

She dismissed the smarting pain in her breast. "Promise me you will not reveal our past to anyone."

He looked at her for a good few seconds before he said, "I promise."

Her breastbone shuddered with relief . . . but the joy was tempered by one haunting thought.

"You seem uncertain," he said darkly. "Do you think the barbarian too dishonorable to respect a challenge loss?"

She looked at him pointedly. "You dishonored it once before."

His lips twitched. "My word is not enough, then? You really have changed," he said in a soft and chastising manner. "But so have I."

She ignored the contempt in his voice. Let him huff at the "change" in her all he liked, she didn't care. She had suffered enough hardship at the man's hands to feel indifferent to his pompous scorn. All she wanted was his assurance, his *real* assurance he would keep quiet about the past.

"Very well," he said in a rough whisper. "I promise on my father's grave I will not betray our past."

The oath was sufficient. He had adored and respected his father. He would not dishonor the man's name by breaking the vow, she was sure.

"Thank you." She collected the players and collapsed the board, locking the box. "I should return to Lady Lucas."

"I'll call for the carriage to take you home."

"No!" She lifted from the chair and adjusted her mantle before she took the box and approached the door. "I can't exit your carriage in the dead of night."

He stood, too. "But you can sneak into my house in the dead of night?"

She sniffed. "No one witnessed me steal into the house."

"Ever the wildcat." He perused her with a long and familiar stare. "You haven't really changed, Sophia. Lady Lucas would not be pleased."

She stiffened at the implication. "I *have* changed. I don't flout convention anymore."

He slowly lifted a brow.

She lifted a forefinger. "One time. And only because I needed to speak with you and settle this matter. Never again!"

"Fine." He crossed the floor and disappeared inside the dressing room. "I'll escort you home, then."

The idea sounded just as dangerous. "What if we're spotted together?" she called after him. "I'll just hire a hackney coach."

"Then I'll follow behind you and the cab at a reasonable distance." He returned from the other room. "But you are not going home alone!"

She snorted at the man's whimsical gallantry, but she didn't contest the point further. So long as he honored his word and maintained a sensible distance behind her, she would avoid scandal.

And just to be sure he honored his word, she strutted across the room and pushed a chair against the wall. She lifted her skirts and stepped onto the cushioned seat before she yanked the short blade from the wall and tucked it back into her bodice.

Chapter 5

I t was a warm summer day for a picnic. The tart lemonade was a cool and welcome refreshment. Sophia sat on the large white blanket purled with golden thread, admiring the bucolic landscape. She eyed the great house on the hill flanked by dense woods. The structure was two floors high, with rows of symmetrical windows and a sandy stone façade. The bright green turf stretched for acres in front of the house, the lazy countryside interrupted by a steady stream that cut across the rolling lawn and reached deep into the forest.

The air was thick. Sophia was sheltered under an old and gnarled oak. The wide canopy of leaves offered shade, but the heat remained. She removed the delicate fan from her reticule and swatted at the humidity. But it wasn't just the blistering weather making her uncomfortable.

There was a round of twitters.

Sophia was circled by pretty, spry debutantes fresh from finishing school. The Honorable Anastasia Bedford was the daughter of a baron. She boasted a fine pedigree that included foreign royalty. Miss Imogen Rayne wasn't so well connected; however, the banker's daughter was an accomplished singer, pianist, and multilinguist. Each lass possessed fine aristocratic traits, breeding and talent respectively. And both were Lady Rosamond's dearest friends . . . making Sophia feel like the senescent matriarch in the group.

The giggling quieted as the girls sobered.

Rosamond glanced around the terrain, making sure they were all alone before she whispered earnestly, "We must talk about the ball, Miss Dawson."

A spurt of alarm entered Sophia's breast. "What about the ball?"

"You created a stir," she said. "Even my brother is confounded."

Sophia swallowed a groan. She eyed Lady Lucas. She and the other chaperones crossed a small wood bridge, following the earl on a tour of the grounds. It was too late to summon the woman to return, so Sophia fixed her thoughts firmly on the matron's teachings and prepared to confront the dire matter herself.

"I don't know what you mean, my lady." The moisture between her fingers was uncomfortable, and Sophia flexed them in an effort to ease the discomfort. She had worked so hard to charm the earl, struggled to become a lady of manner and grace. Had one unfortunate waltz with the black devil ruined her courtship with Lord Baine? "How did I create a stir?"

"As the object of Captain Hawkins's affection!"

Sophia was nauseous. She wasn't accustomed to the wretched sensation. She had sailed aboard her father's pirate ship on more than one occasion. She had sturdy sea legs. However, she wasn't able to control the spinning images in her head, making her sick with vertigo.

"Are you all right, Miss Dawson?" Imogen pressed her palm to Sophia's wrist. "You look unwell."

"I'm fine."

But Sophia wasn't fine. She was breathing hard, moisture pooling between her breasts. She glanced at the circle of ladies. The looks!

Her head pulsed. The quiet chatter slowly evolved into a cacophony of laughter. The curious stares turned into cold and deliberate snubs.

"Well, we are all impressed with your charms, Miss Dawson," said Rosamond.

Sophia beat the fan in quick strokes, overwhelmed by giddiness. Had James betrayed her? It seemed impossible. Surely he wouldn't dishonor his beloved father's name by breaking his vow. And yet . . . "My charms?"

Anastasia wrinkled her nose, as if to dispute Rosamond's unanimous claim that they were *all* impressed with her charms.

"Oh yes." Rosamond reached for a scone and smeared it with strawberry jam. "After four years in polite society, the surly captain has finally danced!"

Sophia was dumbfounded. "What?"

"You managed to capture the interest of the coldest, most intimidating bachelor in London." Rosamond devoured the scone. "Brava!"

The blinding pressure in Sophia's skull weakened. She wasn't so sure she wanted the dubious distinction. Had the black devil really not danced a single dance since he'd entered society?

And then the throbbing pinch between her brows returned. It was just like the scoundrel to burden her with *that* distinction, bringing them both unwelcome attention.

We mustn't let the earl think another man is courting you. Lord Baine is a gentleman. He might step aside if he believes the captain is interested in you . . . or he might search elsewhere for a bride if he thinks you are attached to the captain.

Sophia had a biting impulse to gut the ruthless brigand as soon as she saw him. Did the earl suspect her smitten with the marauding rogue? He might have sensed the friction between her and Black Hawk on the dance floor. Had he mistaken it for passion?

"And yet I pity you, Miss Dawson." Anastasia sipped her fruit juice with poise. "To be the object of interest to such a barbarian? How you must suffer!"

"The captain *is* a beast," Rosamond was quick to assent. "I don't know why Max befriended him."

Sophia glanced at the pert chit. She wasn't accustomed to keeping her feelings, her ideas, even her impulses in check. But she didn't want to make a social blunder. She had already wooed disaster when she had danced with the pirate captain at the ball. She didn't want to make another faux pas. She didn't want to side with the brigand and make it seem like she was smitten with the rogue.

Sophia suspected the snooty Anastasia would jump on that tidbit of gossip and ruin her prospects before sundown. And the captain *was* a barbarian. Sophia wholly endorsed the claim herself. However, his invitation to the house party was at the behest of Lady Rosamond. What had provoked the girl's scorn? Sophia didn't know. And she didn't want to antagonize the earl's sister by making unsolicited inquiries. She might need Rosamond's support to win the earl's hand. She didn't want to make an enemy of the chit.

"Then it's true?" said Anastasia. "The barbarian is coming to the picnic?"

"Yes," returned Rosamond tersely. "And he's going to stay with us for a few days."

Anastasia made a moue before she shifted her cutting regard to Sophia again. "Why did you dance with the barbarian, Miss Dawson? I would have feigned an injury to my ankle."

Imogen lowered her gaze and stared at the picnic blanket in discomfort.

Sophia took in a firm breath. "He is the earl's friend, as Lady Rosamond remarked." James was nothing of the sort, but if Rosamond wanted to perpetuate the fib for some obscure reason, Sophia was going to let her. "It would have been rude to refuse him."

"That is just what I thought." Rosamond smiled. "You are too kind, Miss Dawson."

Anastasia sniffed. "Yes, very charitable."

Imogen lifted the plate of pastries. "More scones, ladies?"

Sophia was breathless and needed a moment to compose herself. She lifted to her shaky feet. "If you will excuse me, ladies, I think I'll go for a walk. The grounds here are so lovely."

Rosamond beamed with pride.

"You shouldn't spend so much time in the sun, Miss Dawson. You're positively brown!" Anastasia offered her something frilly. "Here. Take my parasol."

Sophia claimed the gift and mustered a courteous "You're too kind, Miss Bedford."

She quietly removed herself from the picnic. As she crossed the arched bridge and approached the woods, she resisted the impulse to toss the parasol into the bush. She jabbed the pristine tip into the dirt path instead, using it as a walking stick.

Sophia glanced down at her hands. She wasn't brown. She wasn't even tanned . . . She examined her fingers more closely. The skin looked a little dirty. She wiped her hand against her dress, but the soft glow was still there.

She grimaced. It might be the shade from the foliage making her flesh seem darker than it really was. But then she enjoyed the sun's warm rays. And she had deep brown hair and eyes. She wasn't fair like Rosamond and the other two ladies. Perhaps she wasn't so very pale, after all?

She intended to talk to Lady Lucas about the matter. There might be a cream or a powder she could apply to soften her complexion and make it more attractive. She had even heard lemon juice mixed with brandy and milk created a bleach for the skin. She would have to experiment.

Sophia needed to cool her temper—and her toes. The inviting pitter of the water lured her to the stream's intimate shores, and she paused beside the bank to enjoy the brisker air.

The glassy ripples looked so tempting; her sweaty toes twitched.

Sophia dropped the parasol. She crouched to peel away the laces before she slipped off her leather shoes. Mindful she was alone, she rolled down her white silk stockings and set them aside, too.

The cool grass between her toes was already a welcome treat, but she wanted a deeper soak. She lifted her skirts and tucked the fabric against her midriff to prevent the grass from smearing the soft, white fabric. With a hearty sigh, she settled beside the water and dipped her feet into the refreshing pool.

The water rushed over her ankles and calves, washing away the late summer heat, the irritation. For a quiet moment the world righted itself, and she flicked her toes, splashing spray.

The fine hairs on the back of her head slowly spiked. A shiver touched her spine as a pair of eyes summoned all her senses to obey.

Black Hawk!

Stay calm, she thought. *Ignore the barbarian.*

But she couldn't dismiss James's sharp stare piercing her spine. She had always been able to detect his eyes on her. She remembered tending to the orchids near their plantation house, and pausing because she had sensed him watching her. There had been nothing to indicate he had entered the garden: no sound or movement. And yet she had known he was there, silently observing her.

Sophia opened her watery eyes. She hadn't even realized she had closed them at the haunting reflection. It took her a moment to remember she wasn't in Jamaica anymore, but in England.

She steadied her uneven breathing. She tried to quiet her thoughts, too. Silence her thrumming senses. But the wicked corsair wasn't lifting his eyes from her. She didn't turn around to greet him. She refused to acknowledge him.

He was admiring her neck, she could tell. A sharp sensation at the base of her head pulsed. Was he thinking of ways to throttle her? . . . Was he thinking about the plantation house, as she was?

She removed a kerchief from her reticule, dabbing at the moisture across her brow and chin. The balmy climate mixed with the bounder's sultry gaze made Sophia faint. She took in a few measured breaths to clear her woozy mind, but she wasn't accustomed to the tight corset or the layers of linen in the hot summer weather. In the tropics she would wear loose attire, and less of it. But in England she had to endure the proper manner of dress at all times.

Again the fine hairs behind her ears stirred; he beckoned her. She took one wary peek before she smothered her inhibition and looked over her shoulder.

He was leaning against a tree. He had his arms folded across his strapping chest. Ankles crossed, the ball of his foot was braced against the sturdy bark. He was dashing in a form-fitted ensemble: soft brown breeches and a bronze waistcoat. The gold buttons across his chest neatly trimmed his well-manicured appearance. And with his unruly mane fastened in a queue, she could see every bit of his hard and masculine features.

He pushed away from the tree with his boot and slowly approached her. Her heart fluttered at the smoldering look in his deep blue eyes. The man's steady advance confused her senses. She wanted to dash back to the picnic grounds, to surround herself with the cold, strict rules of high society. The posh world wasn't a threat to her sensibilities. Yet another part of her was transfixed by the approaching pirate lord— and the wild cravings he stirred in the deepest part of her soul.

"You look warm, sweetheart." He settled beside her, thick legs raised, arms folded across his knees. "I think you're overdressed."

The stiffness in her muscles returned. The deep desire to strip away the layers of linen suffocating her was profound, alarmingly so. And the more James stared at her, the more the briny drops gathered and doused her burning flesh.

"I'm very comfortable," she said tersely. "What do you want, Black Hawk?"

"Do I disturb you?"

Her heart thumped with treacherous hunger. He was so close to her, she could feel the heat emitting from his torso. A deep desire to slip her hand under the man's tight coat and feed off his warm muscles gripped her.

"No, we have a truce . . . don't we?"

"I intend to honor our truce." The heat in his eyes was blistering. "I would never disgrace my father's name."

She had suspected as much. Regardless of his motives for being at the picnic, he would keep his word and guard her secret; he had vowed.

Sophia stretched the cords of her reticule and searched for the fan again. She snapped open the bone fingers and briskly swiped at the damnable heat. It did little to cool her, though. Under the brigand's scorching stare, the fluttering silk was scarce more than a drop of water on a parched and starving tongue.

"Then what are you doing, lurking in the woods?" she demanded, hoarse.

The thick fringe of his dark lashes lowered as he perused her form in an intimate manner. "I thought you wanted us to be friends? In memory of our fathers' friendship?"

The seductive look in his eyes sent her thoughts spinning. Her entire body pulsed with a wretched need, and she struggled to tamp the burning desire into the very bowel of her soul. "Can we be friends?"

"I don't see why not."

She snorted softly. She would rather have the bounder as her enemy. Friendship was too warm, too intimate.

Quiet stretched between them. If James moved a finger, hers jerked, too. If he shifted a leg, hers quivered, too.

"You're late," she said, eager to break the tense silence.

"I had to see to Sophia's needs. She doesn't like to sleep alone. I had to move her into William's room."

Sophia stroked the back of her neck, the muscles taut. He tended to that bloody snake with more tenderness and respect than he had ever tended to her.

"I was beginning to think you might not come at all," she said stiffly.

"Do I disappoint you?"

"Of course not. I don't care what you do or where you go. I was only making conversation."

"Ah, the trademark of a proper lady: mindless chatter."

She bristled.

"I have to keep my commitments," he said in an indifferent manner. "Otherwise my behavior would reflect poorly upon my sister."

Sophia snapped her brows together. "How *did* she marry a duke?"

The man's features darkened. "A devious quirk of fate. Our father should have whipped her as a child. She would have had more sense as a woman, then."

Sophia ignored the grousing remark. The man

adored his sister. She wondered instead, "You don't approve of her marrying?"

"I approve of her marrying . . . I don't approve of her husband."

The muscles in her belly tightened. She quickly scrambled away from the shoreline and started to slip on her stockings.

"Is something the matter, Sophia?"

"Nothing a'tall," she said brusquely. "I think it's time I return to the picnic."

She wobbled, pulling on the silk legging.

He lifted to his feet, eyed her closely. "Do you need help?"

"Not from you."

"I've upset you."

She wrestled with the other stocking. "The devil you have."

"I'll take you back to the picnic."

"No!"

"You might get lost."

"I won't get lost," she insisted.

"I wouldn't be a proper gentleman if I let you wander the woods by yourself."

She dropped the stocking and glared at him. A surge of heat ballooned in her breast, making her heart throb. The ruthless devil! He stood there with cold propriety, espoused the manner of a proper gentleman . . . a man who approved of marriage.

She struggled to quell the burning shame in her belly. Was that why he had rejected her seven years ago? She had always suspected that he didn't approve of her. She was the daughter of a pirate and a whore. She was good enough to be his mistress, but not good enough to be his wife.

She fisted her palms, her hands shaking. One silk legging hugged her leg and she took a mismatched step forward. "A proper gentleman wouldn't be *in* the woods with a woman, unchaperoned."

"Is that what the earl would do? Summon a chaperone? I'm not the earl."

No, he was not the earl. The earl didn't shake her senses and burn her blood and rattle her thoughts. The earl wasn't a senseless brute. The earl didn't *lie*!

Sophia snatched the other stocking again.

An echo of voices circled the air.

She paused. "It's the earl!" She recognized the man's sprightly laughter, followed by the natter of females. She looked at the pirate captain with alarm. "Hide!"

"Why?"

"We can't be alone together." She brandished the loose stocking. "I'm half dressed!"

"Then I suggest *you* hide."

She balked. "I thought you were a gentleman?"

"You just disabused me of that notion, remember?"

There was no time to quarrel; the voices approached.

Sophia cursed inwardly and cut James a dark glance before she picked up her shoes and moved deeper into the woods, squatting behind a bush.

"I can still see you," he said with a measure of snide humor.

Sophia gnashed her teeth and crouched even lower.

"Don't you feel ridiculous, sweetheart?"

She shushed him.

The voices more noisy, she also heard the sound of footsteps and swooshing skirts.

"Captain Hawkins!"

Sophia quietly struggled with the last stocking. She loathed the black devil for putting her in such a humiliating position. If only he would drown . . . no, she wished him shipwrecked, marooned on an island—inhabited by cannibals.

"Good day, Lord Baine," said James. "I apologize for being so late."

"Not a'tall, Captain. Let me see you settled."

"Thank you, but a footman already took my bags."

"Well then . . . You remember Lady Lucas?"

"How could I forget?" James bowed. "My lady."

"Captain Hawkins," the matron returned stiffly.

"And these are . . ."

The earl introduced the other chaperones as Sophia slipped on her shoes. But in such a cramped position with branches poking her body and leaves brushing her face, she wasn't minding her surroundings and—

A twig snapped.

The earl looked into the woods. "What was that?"

Sophia swallowed a groan and removed her foot from the cursed stick.

"A skittish creature, I suspect," said James. "The woods are full of mischievous nymphs."

The earl chuckled. "Fancy a game of archery, Captain?"

James eyed the target.

In the summer heat, the red center pulsed. He focused on the bright spot until it slowly morphed into a beating heart.

He released the arrow.

It struck dead middle.

"Good shot, Captain."

James lowered the bow, the earl's praise hollow. He never missed a mark. "Thank you, my lord."

As the earl nocked an arrow to the bowstring, James waited. A short distance away was a twisted oak with sagging branches—and a gaggle of females cooling in the shade. So stiff and formal and grotesque, the party seemed to guard their land, their house, their blood like stone gargoyles. They glared at James with warning, threatening him to keep clear of their closed circle of friendship.

The very thought that he wanted any part of their cold and foul cabal was repulsive, and he breathed deep through his nose to keep his fingers from crushing the bow in his hand.

James dismissed their snooty glances, maintained a taut posture, and fixed his eyes firmly on the ringed target.

The earl aimed. There was a soft whistle of air before the arrow struck the target one section below James's win. It earned the earl only eight points instead of ten . . . yet a crescendo of applause from the ladies on the picnic blanket rumbled.

"Bravo, Lord Baine!" they cheered.

Maximilian appeared sheepish under the pulsing ovation. He offered his hand in respect. "I concede defeat, Captain Hawkins. Well played."

James grasped his hand. "You are a worthy opponent, my lord."

There was a small equipment table positioned nearby. Maximilian returned the bow to the table before he confronted the captain again. "Shall we join the ladies for some refreshment?"

James's mood blackened even more. He would

sooner the earl shoot him with an arrow through the chest. He smiled stiffly instead.

"Perhaps the captain would be so gracious as to play a game with me?" said Sophia.

Slowly James looked over his shoulder, the stiffness in his muscles weakening as he spotted his fellow pariah.

Sophia pegged him with her stormy eyes. It was the first thing he had noticed about her upon her return, that livid expression. He had yet to determine what had set her off in the woods, but he supposed it didn't really matter when so much about her set him off in return. The woman's gait, for instance. She was approaching in a prim manner. She never used to walk like there was a carrot pinched between her buttocks. She used to strut with a sensual grace that reflected her passionate spirit.

So much of the old Sophia was buried under layers of ghastly stoicism and confining apparel and reserved mannerisms. And a deep-rooted darkness stirred in his breast, waiting for each right moment to come along so he could strip away one putrid, suffocating layer.

Sophia used a parasol as a walking stick. She handed the frilly accessory, speckled with mud, to a peeved-looking chit before she moved toward him with a smile that belied the fury in her eyes.

She then turned her smile toward the unsuspecting lord, and he, poor sap, looked so smitten, James almost sympathized with the dullard.

"How did you enjoy your walk, Miss Dawson?" said the earl.

"The grounds are lovely, my lord."

"I'm so glad you approve of them."

"How could I not? You have an impressive variety of flora. I even stumbled upon a rare cluster of *Hieracium lachenalii.*"

As she crouched behind the bushes? James reflected on the image with caustic humor. However, it begged the question: How long would she hide behind the metaphorical bushes before she grew weary of the restrictions imposed upon her, cast them off . . . and came back to him?

There was a mark of approval in the young lord's eyes. "Yellow Hawkweed? I didn't know you were an amateur botanist, Miss Dawson."

"I have a penchant for gardening."

That much was true. James remembered the wild and bright blooms that had covered the grounds surrounding their plantation house. He remembered the many fragrances that had soaked the air, the rich night blossoms that had teased the breeze with their divine scent. The breeze that had moved through the dark rooms and passageways, that had made the house alive in the evening . . . when he was alone with her.

"I think it a worthy attribute for a woman to be educated in botany," she said. "It means she can tend to the gardens of her husband's home."

The earl beamed. "I heartily agree with you, Miss Dawson . . . and the hawkweeds?"

"Oh, I plucked them and stomped on them." She cut James a biting glance. "You don't need the pests disturbing your pristine grounds."

James stroked the fine wood bow in his hands, a small, wry smile touching his lips.

"Are you not too tired for a game of archery, Miss Dawson?" wondered Maximilian.

"After a refreshing stroll? Not a'tall, my lord."

The earl's mooning was growing tiresome. James was having trouble keeping his breakfast in his belly. Sophia was a hardy woman. She might feign maidenly airs, but any man with half a wit could see the brilliant color in her cheeks and the luster in her eyes and the strength in her stance.

"Well, you have a fierce opponent, Miss Dawson," said the earl.

She didn't respond aloud, but James watched her lush lips move in rapid stokes, and he read the silent words: *So does he.*

"Do take care, Miss Dawson."

"Of course, my lord."

The earl motioned for a servant to clear the two targets of arrows before he moved off.

The last of the seemingly heavy manacles restricting James was lifted as soon as Lord Baine strolled away. The man joined the rest of the *haute monde* on the picnic blanket, leaving James unfettered from tedious social norms. The critical company still eyed him and Sophia with sharp regard. However, the party was far enough away to hear nothing of their exchange, and James took in a deep and refreshing breath to be apart from them . . . to be alone with Sophia.

She picked up a leather glove from the equipment table.

"What are you doing, Sophia?"

She didn't bother to look at him. She responded curtly, "I'm about to trounce you."

A heat smoldered in his belly. It was always a thrill to compete with her. In years past if he had won a contest the prize had been her submission in bed . . . and if he had lost a contest the forfeit had been no less pleasurable, for he had enjoyed submitting to her desires.

But there was no such award at stake now. There was only a test: a test of wills. Who would crumble first under the unnatural pressure imposed by the *ton*?

"No, I mean the glove," he said.

She looked at the leather. "What about it?"

"You're about to put it on the wrong hand."

She pinched her dark brows. "I have to shoot with my dominant hand."

"Yes, I know. But what will the earl think to learn you are left-handed?"

She balked. She had clearly failed to consider the matter when she had challenged him to the game— but he had not. It was an ideal opportunity for him to show her that acting like one of *them* was a fruitless effort; she would always fall short. To win, she would have to be herself.

He pressed on to underline: "What do you think the earl will do if he discovers you have a blemish, sweetheart? Do you think he will still ask you to be his bride?"

She fastened the leather glove to her right hand. "Go to hell, Black Hawk."

He smiled and gathered a projectile from the equipment table before he aimed for the target.

The arrow pierced the red mark.

"That's ten points for me."

Sophia glanced at him with venom before she nocked the arrow to the bowstring. The arrow quivered in her weaker right hand. She pinched one eye closed as she aimed.

The arrow cut through the air—and landed in the grass thirty paces off the mark.

She flushed.

James grinned inwardly.

Chapter 6

The ladies' drawing room boasted fine wood furnishings upholstered in rose fabric and marked with a faint harlequin pattern. Every well-crafted piece was curved and flowing: the bowed legs, the balled feet. Curved and flowing and feminine. Even the pastel colors in the room reflected tenderness. Together with the floral wall print and pink glass oil lamps, the space made Sophia's head ache.

"Well, I'm glad supper is over," said Rosamond.

The ladies had gathered in the drawing room for tea and pastries. Sophia was seated in a round-back chair in front of an inlay table. The table illustrated a couple courting: a gentleman pushing his sweetheart in a tree swing. Sophia pictured James pushing her in a tree swing and almost snorted at the absurd image.

"I very nearly lost my appetite," griped Anastasia.

Sophia smothered her fanciful thoughts. She glanced across the room to spot Lady Lucas seated with the other matrons, sewing beside the firelight. The woman's presence offered Sophia comfort. She had more confidence in her social abilities with her chaperone in the room. And Sophia was going to need all her skills, her poise to endure the uncomfortable conversation.

Rosamond served the tea. "Did you see his table manners?"

"Has he ever held a fork before tonight?"

As Rosamond and Anastasia complained about the captain's dining habits, Imogen and Sophia quietly sipped their tea in dainty cups with painted pink roses.

Sophia wasn't entirely sure what the two other women found so disagreeable about the pirate's eating habits. But she wasn't an authority on the matter of etiquette, either. If the man had made an error with his fork, the blunder was subtle, for Sophia hadn't noticed it.

"And his meaty hands!" said Anastasia. "The fork looked like a child's toy between his thick fingers."

Was that the man's mistake, having big hands? Sophia quickly glanced at her own fingers. Were her hands well proportioned to the rest of her body? She didn't want to have gauche fingers.

But then she remembered James's meaty palms, so strong and robust. Thick fingers had never hampered his swift movements.

She closed her eyes at the sharp memory that welled in her mind: James stroking her nipple to painful arousal. He might not be handy with a fork . . .

"The man is a barbarian!" said Rosamond.

Sophia opened her eyes and blinked a few times, her cheeks warm. The man *was* a barbarian. She had to remember that. She had to keep repeating the slanderous remark over and over again in her head until she stopped having wistful thoughts about the black devil.

Rosamond feasted on a raspberry tart with coconut sprinkles. "He doesn't even have the good manners to let a woman win at archery."

"Well, it was hard to let Miss Dawson win when she missed the target so often," said Anastasia.

Sophia swallowed a groan.

"That's beside the point," countered Rosamond. "If Miss Dawson missed, he should have missed, too. It's just common courtesy."

Sophia flushed. She didn't need the man to play with a handicap because she was a woman. She was a qualified markswoman—but only if she used her left hand.

She should not have challenged the brigand to a game of archery. But he had stirred her temper into a foul snit with his mocking remark about marriage. He had wanted her to suffer, the blackguard. He had wanted her to know he approved of marriage—but not with her. She wasn't good enough to be his wife.

Sophia set the teacup aside, her fingers shaking. If he had not riled her so with his brutal remark, she would not have confronted him in such a dander. She would not have asked him to humor her with a game of archery—and she would not have humiliated herself in front of the earl and the rest of the party.

"I hear his brothers are far more civilized," said Rosamond.

Anastasia sniffed. "I don't believe it. They all share the same blood."

"I met one of his brothers at the ball." Rosamond patted her lips with a white napkin. "He wasn't a beast like the captain."

"I'm astonished." Anastasia made a grimace. "I don't see why the captain insists on being in society."

"My dear, everyone *wants* to be in society," said Rosamond. "But the barbarian does not belong in it."

Sophia's heart cramped. The blood in her veins thumped with restless energy, as she pondered the dreadful thought: Did the *ton* believe *she* didn't belong in society, either?

"True, Mondie," returned Anastasia. "He does *not* belong in good society. Does he think we don't notice his wild hair?"

"Or how he casts his brow in a frown?"

"Or how he stomps his feet like a jungle boy?"

Sophia's heart started to pound.

I can still see who you are, Sophia. You cannot hide behind layers of satin and fool me.

The pirate captain wasn't fooled by her ladylike manners. Did the *ton* also see past her refined speech and rich wardrobe to the wild creature she used to be? Did they secretly whisper about her, as they whispered about James?

"Give us a kiss, Sophia!"

One drunkard grabbed his cock in a crude gesture and sucked on his bottom lip, making a loud smacking sound. "Kiss me, Sophia. I'm tastier."

"No, kiss me! I've got a prick you can ride all night."

Sophia dropped the basket, blistering heat coursing through her veins. She was about to draw her knife and cut off the foul men's cods, when the three hecklers quickly composed their mocking brows and sneering lips.

A young woman approached the rabble. She was pale, with curly locks, a fashionable flaxen blonde. She looked ridiculous in the tropical heat with her layers of linen, a bonnet and parasol to match. Sophia could see the sweat glistening across her wide brow and slim, aquiline nose.

However, she maintained the regalia with a chaperone to boot . . . and she commanded respect.

The governor's wife strolled past the vagrants.

"Good day, Mrs. Smith," the men murmured in unison and doffed their scruffy caps.

Mrs. Smith ignored the tramps. She walked past them with formal grace . . . offering Sophia a brief look of scorn as she went.

Sophia fisted her palms, staring after the prim and proper woman. Her heart thundered in her ears, her mind swelled with dark thoughts as shame billowed inside her breast. She struggled to tamp the roiling grief—the rage!—blustering in her head.

Mrs. Smith condemned her as a whore and treated her accordingly. The islanders' snickers and sneers had become commonplace, for Sophia was considered a trollop: no one of consequence, no one deserving respect.

The hecklers started up again, their jeers growing louder in her head. Sophia grabbed the basket and hurried through the lively street.

Sophia's heart smarted at the long-ago memory. The laughter still resounded in her head, the islanders' vulgar remarks still pierced her ears and jabbed her skull, the looks of scorn still filled her breast with shame. Would she have to endure the humiliation again? Would she have to endure the jeers and whispers and looks from the *ton* now?

Rosamond and Anastasia recognized the pirate captain as an outcast. They looked past his well-tailored coat and practiced mannerisms, and saw—and loathed—the beast that lay beneath the man's tidy appearance. He fooled no one with his true nature, his barbarian ways. Did the *ton* think her a pariah, too?

"And to think, Miss Dawson, the captain is fond of you," said Anastasia.

Sophia's heart pinched. If gossip spread that the captain was interested in her—or worse, that she was interested in the captain—she might lose the earl, so she quashed the rumor outright with a sharp "He's not fond of me, I assure you."

Anastasia gathered her lips in a sour expression. "I saw the captain look at you during supper—twice."

Sophia stiffened.

"And why shouldn't he look at Miss Dawson?" said Rosamond. "She is beautiful and charming."

And rich. Other ladies had breeding or talent or both, but Sophia had wealth. That was her one means to enter high society. And she would not let torrid tittle-tattle ruin her prospects. Lady Lucas was a shrewd and savvy chaperone. If Sophia was in social danger, if the *ton* suspected her an outsider, the matron would surely alert her, for she needed Sophia to flourish in order to restore her own standing in high society.

The stress in Sophia's bones started to ebb away. If the matron didn't warn her about pressing threats, then there were no threats to voice. Sophia was only letting her imagination get the better of her. And Rosamond's staunch support also meant she was accepted by the *ton*. Sophia needn't fear censure . . . well, apart from Anastasia. The woman looked piqued to hear Sophia described as beautiful and charming. But Sophia could tolerate the unpleasant chit's resentment, so long as it remained hers alone.

"I say let the barbarian admire you from afar, Miss Dawson." Rosamond winked. "It is the man's only means to associate with a respectable woman, for no woman of character would ever associate with him."

The door opened.

"Good evening, ladies."

The earl smiled as he entered the room with a cheerful gait. He and the pirate captain had retired to the sitting room after supper for port and cigars, as was customary.

"Good evening, Lord Baine," the party returned the greeting.

"We've come to join you," said the earl. He looked at Sophia and smiled. "There is nothing more disagreeable than to be without female companionship."

The ladies tittered at the general compliment.

Sophia smiled at the earl in return.

But her smile fell as soon as Black Hawk appeared in the doorframe, looking dour. No one greeted the grim-looking captain. In truth, the room fell quiet as soon as he entered it.

The cold stares indicated they had just been talking about him. James knew it, too, for his back stiffened and his eyes hardened.

She remembered Quincy's words: *James hates to be in society.*

A twinge of compassion for the pirate lord pinched her heart, but she quickly quashed the sentiment. It was a dangerous business feeling sympathy for the devil. Let the man suffer under the stinging censure . . . the way she had suffered in Jamaica.

James offered her a small gesture of greeting: a hot and stabbing glance before he moved across the room. His big body stirred the flames in the oil lamps to life, his heavy footfalls resounded in the silent space.

Sophia stiffened as he passed behind her. She sensed the restless energy thrumming through his muscles. Her heart beat at a swift tempo; sweat formed on her palms.

The pirate captain stopped beside the window and looked out into the blackness.

"Shall we play a game?" suggested Maximilian.

"What sort of a game?" said Rosamond.

The earl shrugged. "How about a guessing game?"

Rosamond set her tea aside. "I know . . . I will think of something, and you must guess what it is by asking me questions. However, you may only ask questions that require a yes or no answer."

"Sounds delightful!" said Anastasia.

Rosamond smoothed her skirt in quick strokes before she lifted her eyes heavenward. "I'm thinking of something . . . blue."

"The sky!" said Anastasia.

"No," returned Rosamond. "And you mustn't guess the answer unless you are sure of it or you will have to pay a forfeit."

Anastasia pouted. "Oh, very well."

Sophia remembered a contest she had played with James. He had challenged her to a fishing match. She had lost the game—he had caught the bigger fish: a mahi-mahi weighing two stones—and she had had to pay a forfeit.

"Give me your hands, Sophia."

"Why?"

"That isn't part of the forfeit, sweetheart, asking questions . . . give me your hands."

Slowly James bound her wrists.

Sophia shivered at the vivid images storming her head, images made more vivid with James standing in the room. She rubbed her wrists at the haunting memory, her pulse tapping at a rapid rate.

As the whole party gathered their seats to form a more intimate circle, the earl said, "Will you join us, Captain?"

"I'll participate in the game from here."

The dark timbre in James's voice was ignored by the rest of the company, too eager to engage in an evening of frivolity. But Sophia heeded the man's low tone and firm words. She tried to dismiss the shivers that pestered her spine. She tried to tamp down the burning desire to admire the brigand's physique beside the window. But even when he wasn't looking at her, teasing her senses, he was still *there*. And that was enough to distract her from the game . . . from the occupants in the room . . . from her mission to marry the earl.

Sophia closed her eyes and breathed deep to steady her wayward thoughts.

"Are you all right, Miss Dawson?"

Maximilian had set a chair beside her. She opened her eyes, distraught to think he had moved so close to her and she had not even noticed his presence.

"Yes, I'm fine, my lord."

Lady Lucas offered her a discreet smile from across the room before she returned to her sewing. The earl honored Sophia with his gallant and devoted attention. The matron recognized it. Sophia had to acknowledge it, too. She had to use it to her advantage if she wanted to be the next Countess Baine . . . if only Black Hawk wasn't at the party.

"Who will ask the first question?" said Rosamond. "Imogen, you haven't said a word. Why don't you start the game?"

Imogen offered an uneven smile. "Very well. Is it something small?"

"Yes."

"Is it alive?" said Anastasia.

"No."

"Is it made from wood?" wondered the earl.

Rosamond grinned. "No."

Lady Lucas looked up from her sewing. "Is it in this room?"

"Yes."

The guests searched the room, filled with myriad furniture and artwork.

"Is it the jeweled peacock beside the piano?" James said.

Sophia glanced at James. He had his hands behind his back, his features still turned toward the window. He was staring at the stars; she could tell by the subtle way he lifted his chin to better catch the glimmering lights.

She next peeked at the piano and squinted, searched for the jeweled peacock. She couldn't be sure in the hazy lamp light, but she assumed it the shiny ornament on the small table next to the piano.

Rosamond frowned. "Yes, it is." She looked disappointed that the captain had guessed her thought so quickly and ruined the game. "It is your turn, Captain."

James maintained his position beside the window. He didn't look at the other guests. "I'm thinking of something cold."

Sophia's heart boomed, the beats sound and firm and pulsing in her breast, making her bones throb. She folded her fingers in her lap and squeezed her hands together. What was the brigand doing?

The party wasn't too keen to play the game with the surly captain. The earl asked the first question to move the amusement along:

"Is it something large?"

"No."

Rosamond pinched her lips together and stared at her lap. Anastasia regarded the wall.

Imogen bravely filled the quiet void. "Can it fit inside your pocket?"

"Yes."

Sophia sighed to hear "it" was small enough to fit in his pocket. She wasn't the cold thing he was thinking about. But for a moment she had sensed he was talking about her.

"Is it made from metal?" said the earl.

"Yes."

"Is it made from gold?" said Imogen.

"Yes."

Cold? Small enough to fit in a pocket? Made from gold? Sophia was filled with another burning sentiment. "Is it a fob watch?"

James slowly looked over his shoulder. "Yes, Miss Dawson."

"Well done, Miss Dawson!" cheered Rosamond. "It is your turn now."

Sophia pinched her lips and formed a small smile. The scoundrel! She had sensed she was the cold thing he was talking about, and she had been right about it in a roundabout way. He had been thinking about the fob watch she had given him before she had deserted him.

But what about him, the blackguard? What about *his* cold disregard for her?

Sophia pressed her fingernails into her palms. She remembered coming home after her encounter with the drunkards and the governor's wife. She remembered storming the plantation house and dumping the basket of food on the kitchen table before she'd grabbed the chessboard.

Sophia took in a deep breath. She had won the chess game, too. But the dishonorable rogue had refused to honor his challenge loss. He had refused to wed her.

She wasn't good enough for him.

Sophia glared at the pirate captain. If she disarmed him in any small way with her piercing stare, as he disarmed her with his, then she would be satisfied. He truly deserved to rot in everlasting hell.

Sophia glanced at Rosamond and broadened her smile. "I am thinking of something . . ."

After an hour of parlor games, much laughter and merriment, the earl slapped his knees in a jovial expression. "What an enjoyable day! Let us end the evening on a high note . . . Miss Rayne, I understand you have a gift for music?"

Imogen smiled shyly.

"Oh yes, my dear," said Rosamond. "You must play for us."

Rosamond took the girl by the hand and steered her across the room toward the piano. The earl moved about the space, too. He gathered the lights and arranged the lamps around the piano so Imogen could read the sheet music, casting the rest of the room in darkness.

Sophia swiveled her chair to better see the performance. She ignored the black devil behind her. He remained at the rear of the room with the rest of the shadows.

As the company settled in their seats for a musical nightcap, Imogen flexed her fingers before she plinked the keys with aplomb.

The lyrical melody filled the room with its vibrato. Sophia wasn't familiar with the classical piece. She knew very little about music in general. However, she was moved by the grand sound coming from the fingers of an otherwise reserved and polite young lady.

But it wasn't long before the vexing brigand's stare took its hold on her senses again, and she found herself feeling his presence more than she was listening to the music.

Slowly the man advanced, his footfalls steady.

She bristled.

He took an empty seat behind her. The rest of the guests were seated closer to the piano, so she and James were alone in the shadows near the back of the room.

He moved his black leather boot. He softly bumped her chair leg, making her twitch. The music faded from her mind. She sensed only Black Hawk, the dark heat coming from his robust form.

He leaned forward.

Sophia twisted her ankles.

"She plays well."

James whispered the words against her naked throat, stirring the fine hairs there to arousing life.

Sophia suppressed a chill and maintained her eyes forward. She fixed them firmly on the young woman playing the piano. "She does."

The soft tickle of warm breath caressed the knob of

bone at the base of her skull. "Has the earl proposed to you yet?"

Her heart was booming in her breast. "No, we've yet to be alone together."

"Hmm."

The soft whistle of air kissed her sensitive skin, and she parted her lips in a quiet gasp of ecstasy.

"There are too many of us here . . . I wonder why?" he said in a smoldering voice.

"What do you mean?"

"Well, what makes you think the earl is interested in you . . . and not one of the other eligible females? After all, he didn't invite any other males to the party. I was offered a spontaneous invitation, remember? Perhaps the earl is selecting a bride from among his sister's friends . . . all three of them."

James moved off.

Sophia quickly looked at the earl. He was seated next to Anastasia . . . and the chit was whispering into his ear.

Sophia's head throbbed. The pounding music, the lingering heat from James, the startling image of the earl and Anastasia all muddled together in her mind, confusing her senses.

Was Anastasia looking to snag the earl, too? Sophia was certain Imogen wasn't interested in Lord Baine. However, Anastasia had lofty ambitions. And yet she was just a child! Seventeen? Eighteen, maybe?

Sophia watched as the earl smiled at Anastasia.

Was Maximilian interested in the girl?

The prospect seemed outrageous . . . and yet Anastasia had breeding, royal blood. She was young, but not too young to be married. She was handsome, too . . . and pretty girls with a good family name wed all the time. Anastasia would make any man a fine wife.

Sophia pressed her palm against her breast to steady her rampant heartbeats. She had come too far to lose the earl now. Anastasia might have a sound pedigree, she might make Maximilian smile with her sharp tongue, but she was still a child. And the earl was a man at thirty-two . . . and Sophia knew how to seduce a man.

Chapter 7

⌒⌒◦◦⌒⌒

Sophia inhaled the heavy scent of the woods. The fresh foliage and blooming wildflowers filled the air with the comforting breath of nature. Together with the trilling birds and the cool shade of leaves, it was an ideal place to stretch out and dream.

But she didn't have time to engage in the pleasurable pastime. She strolled the dirt path beside the earl, Lady Lucas tagging behind them at a respectable distance.

"I must say . . . that is a stunning necklace, Miss Dawson."

Sophia smiled. She touched the brilliant gems at her throat with her fingertips. The cold stones had no meaning for her. The sparkling rocks served only one purpose: to help make her the next Countess Baine. She would gladly trade every one of them for the earl's hand in matrimony.

"Thank you, my lord. The necklace was a gift from my father. The diamonds are from India."

She didn't really know where the diamonds were from, but India was a nest of treasures. She suspected the exotic setting sounded charming to the earl. The diamonds certainly looked charming. The man had admired the jewels at her bust for most of their morning walk . . . he had admired her bust, too.

Sophia made sure to keep her shoulders back. She didn't want to obstruct Maximilian's view of her bosom. She had chosen to wear the most dramatic piece of jewelry she owned, and she had positioned it to sit squarely across her chest, the heavy diamond center kissing the line between her breasts.

Sophia had learned an important lesson the other night: a lady had to exhibit her best qualities if she wanted to snag a man's interest. It was not enough to talk about her fortune, Sophia needed to *show* the earl her wealth, bedazzle him with gold and precious stones. To make the riches even lovelier, she had presented the necklace on her smooth skin and full breasts. Let the Honorable Anastasia Bedford compete with that!

"Ah, India," he said wistfully. "The jewel of the British crown."

Sophia gestured to the woods with her eyes. "Some might think so, but I feel the jewel you have here is far lovelier."

The earl looked at her thoughtfully. "Thank you, Miss Dawson."

She had stroked his pride with the compliment. She sensed the blush that singed his flesh beneath the layers of formal wear: the stark, white breeches and the stone gray, double-breasted coat.

He possessed everything she desired. He was sophisticated, esteemed by his peers. As the man's wife she was sure to be respected, even admired. She was sure to go through the rest of her life a part of high society . . . instead of standing at the fringe of it, being ridiculed.

"What do you think of mighty England, Miss Dawson?"

Drab at times. Too rainy. However, she had witnessed some lovely and haunting countryside in the north. She had docked there three months ago. It had seemed like a dream, the purple heather along the moors, the fog. So unfamiliar. It was not Jamaica. And she had suffered the loss, the separation from her homeland. But with her father gone, there was nothing for her on the tropical island. And so she had set out for the strange new world: mighty England. Everything was so different . . . except for James.

Sophia's heart swelled at the thought of the pirate. He reminded her of the plantation house. He reminded her of home. The image of him in her head stirred memories, longings for star apples and tender orchids and cool cedar planking under her bare toes.

But he also reminded her of darker times.

She swallowed the bitter memory inside her . . . the rejection . . . and returned her thoughts to the conversation at hand. "The company in England is very agreeable." She peeked at the earl to stress *he* was the agreeable company. "However, I have yet to see much of the countryside. Or London for that matter."

"Do you mean to tell me you haven't been to the races? To the theater? To the opera?"

"I'm afraid not."

"That's monstrous! Lady Lucas is remiss in her duty as chaperone."

Sophia touched his arm. "Oh no! Lady Lucas is very attentive. But it's taken me many weeks to get settled." *And learn the customs of high society.* "I just haven't had the time to explore the land."

He stared at her fingers.

Sophia sensed a muscle in his forearm dance. She removed her hand, brushing the bone at his elbow in a deliberate caress. It was a subtle movement, an innocent gesture. But it was also an intimate act . . . and it lighted the man's arousal.

She smiled inwardly. She had learned a hard lesson on the island: a respectable woman showed little emotion and had stiff mannerisms. It was deemed a virtue to be asexual, a purity of the soul to have no desires. Too much emotion was considered a form of mental illness; hysteria, she had heard. And she didn't want the earl to think her hysteric. No man wanted to sully his wife with his sexual cravings. No man wanted his wife to be passionate; it was a trait reserved for a mistress. And Sophia would be nobody's mistress— ever again. However, every man wanted his wife to be chaste and sensible. That was attractive. That was arousing.

"We must make things right, Miss Dawson."

"How so, my lord?"

"Will you permit my sister and I to expose you to every bit of culture before the season's end?"

"You are too kind, my lord."

He beamed. "Next week is the final performance at the opera house for the season. You must allow Lady Rosamond and I to take you to London for the production. We have a private box."

Sophia was filled with restless energy. The earl *was* smitten with her; she had suspected it all along. The pirate captain's insinuation otherwise was unfounded.

What makes you think the earl is interested in you . . . and not one of the other eligible females?

She snorted inwardly. If the earl had ever been interested in Anastasia as a potential bride, he wasn't anymore, Sophia was sure.

"I would be honored to attend the opera with you and your sister, my lord."

"Splendid!" He was quiet for a moment before he said, "I do hope you will allow me to escort you to many other functions, Miss Dawson?"

Sophia wanted to shake the man, make the proposal pop from his tongue. She'd do the bloody chore herself if it wasn't considered so scandalous. But she couldn't afford to lose Maximilian, to wait another year for another season and another suitor to come along. Very soon she *would* be on the shelf as the pirate captain had so boorishly expressed.

She suppressed a sigh. "I can think of no one I'd rather teach me about this great nation."

The couple walked in quiet.

The earl paused and crouched. "Look, Miss Dawson!" He snapped the blossom from its stem and handed it to her. "*Centaurea cyanus.*"

Sophia's heart beat swiftly. She accepted the cornflower, a mark of love according to folklore. She peered into the man's soft green eyes, keeping her features prim yet inviting.

Ask me, damn it!

But the earl only smiled and resumed the walk.

Sophia huffed quietly and fell in step beside him. She twirled the brilliant blue petals between her fingers, admiring the striking shade. It was such a rich, dark color. So intense, like the tropical sea . . . like James's eyes.

"I believe the cornflower originated in southern Europe," he said.

She pinched the bloom's underside, forcing the blossom to open even more. She peered into the deep blue center. "No, it was northern Europe."

"I see."

Maximilian fell quiet. A cramp gripped Sophia's breast. She quashed the reflection about the pirate's eyes. The blackguard disturbed her senses even now. He distracted her from the well-orchestrated seduction.

"Let us join the rest of the party for tea, Miss Dawson."

Sophia sensed the earl's withdrawal. She had wounded his male pride by correcting him about the cornflower. Oh, curse James for upsetting her thoughts! She quickly searched her brain for a way to bridge the sudden distance between her and the earl.

"Ouch!"

Sophia grimaced and crumpled.

Maximilian crouched beside her and grasped her hand. "Miss Dawson, are you all right?"

Lady Lucas skirted toward her charge and knelt, too. "What happened, Miss Dawson?"

Sophia reached for her foot. "It's my ankle."

"Oh, my dear!"

The earl glanced at her foot. "Might I examine it, Miss Dawson?"

Sophia pinched her lips together as if in agony. "Yes, please."

Gingerly the man pressed his fingers to the bone at her ankle. She eyed him closely. He kneaded the joint in slow and circular movements, searching for a breakage.

"I don't think it's broken, Miss Dawson."

"Oh, thank heavens!" said the matron.

Sophia thanked the heavens, too. The man was aroused again, his wounded pride forgotten. Sophia could tell; his fingers quivered as he touched her ankle.

She struggled to stand.

"No, my dear!" The matron pinched her wrist. "You might make the injury worse."

"Lady Lucas is right, Miss Dawson. I will fetch help."

"Did someone call for help?"

Sophia cursed in her native patois under her breath.

James quirked an inward smile. The remaining company didn't hear the whispered expletive, too engrossed with the woman's ankle. But even if the earl and harridan had heard the word, only James understood its meaning.

"Miss Dawson is injured," said the earl. "I was just about to fetch the servants to bring her back to the house."

James glanced down at the prostrated Sophia. A garish string of diamonds choked her throat. He resisted the impulse to snap the necklace and scatter the rocks across the woods, the unnatural beauty so distracting. He was blinded by the stones, so much so that the harridan sensed his lingering gaze. She removed her shawl and draped the diaphanous material around her charge's shoulders.

James lifted his gaze. He detected the acrimony in Sophia's handsome brown—lying!—eyes.

He crouched. "Might I be of assistance, Miss Dawson?"

Sophia's features darkened; her eyes narrowed with warning.

James scooped the dishonest witch into his arms. "I'll take you back to the house, Miss Dawson."

Sophia glared at him. She slipped her arms around his neck. She looked like she wanted to strangle him. He rather admired that fiery stare. It suited her temperament.

The harridan parted her lips to protest the jostling. The earl appeared consternated.

James ignored the tongue-tied couple; he started for the house.

Sophia rested her cheek against his shoulder and whispered tightly, "What are you doing, Black Hawk?"

A quiver kissed his spine. He sensed the woman's hot breath against his throat, her lips so close to his skin, her brow pressed against his ear. The tenderness disarmed him. It was such a contrast to her cutting words.

James's heartbeat quickened. The deep boom in his breast was in sync with each heavy step he took. He tightened his fingers around her back, under her knees.

"I'm taking you back to the house, sweetheart."

She slowly exhaled through her nose. The air roused the fine hairs at his nape. He closed his eyes for a moment: just one moment to better feel her warm presence in his embrace.

James dismissed the tread of footsteps behind him. Instead, he centered his thoughts on the woman curled in his arms.

Sophia's thick, dark hair was gathered in a tight swirl, the layered locks pressed close to his nose. He took in a deep breath, the spicy scent of bay rum shampoo filling his lungs. He sensed the woman's natural musk, too. He bathed in it, absorbed it. It had been so long since he had been so close to her: close enough to smell her . . . taste her . . . touch her.

James opened his eyes. He sensed soft petals brushing his skin just below his ear. She had a flower in her hand. He had seen the bloom just before she had wrapped her arms around his neck. Had she picked the blossom herself? Or had the earl given it to her in courtship? . . . Had the man proposed?

James firmed his back muscles at the dark thought. He imagined the earl slobbering as he asked the witch for her hand in matrimony. And he imagined Sophia's cheerful response.

James wanted to pluck the flower from her fingers and stomp on it. She was teasing him with the earl's sign of affection, and the twirling petals at his neck were making his head throb.

But then he thought the witch might only be tormenting him. It was in her nature, after all. If the earl had proposed, surely he would have objected to another man embracing his fiancée? The harridan would definitely have voiced a protest. But the couple remained silent. Begrudgingly so. But silent.

Sophia moved her fingers. It was a faint shift. She burrowed the long and slender appendages into his hair.

James stiffened. He continued walking, but his every muscle was taut and alert. Sultry fingertips wove through his tight tresses, tied in a queue. Soon he sensed hard nails slip down his collar and stroke the back of his neck in a stirring motion.

The movement was fine, slow and steady. She teased

the muscles, the bones with her tender touch, lighting his blood. But then the heady ministration turned rough, and he gnashed his back teeth as she dug her fingernails into his skin.

Did she think to cause him discomfort, even pain with the biting assault? She didn't know true pain. She didn't know the hell he had already suffered because of her, the anguish he had endured upon returning to the plantation house after a raid at sea—and finding it empty.

James breathed deep to quiet the storm in his breast. He slowly turned his head, dropped his chin, and whispered roughly, "You're not the only one with power here, sweetheart."

He sensed her muscles bristle. Her fingers quickly skimmed his throat in withdrawal. But it was too late to mollify him now. He was filled with a savage desire to make her suffer, too.

He was holding her, so he had little movement with his hands. Still he worked his fingers under her knee, groped under the layers of fabric until his hand was against her stocking.

She started to breathe in short, loud gasps. The moisture condensed on his throat, making him shudder in ecstasy.

He was careful to keep his movements concealed beneath her overflowing skirts. He didn't want the meddlesome couple behind him to see what he was doing.

With the same deliberate touch she had tortured him with, he pinched her silk stocking and yanked it down a tad.

She twitched and moved her knee away, closer to his chest. But he only cupped her again, and grasped the stocking between his thumb and forefinger, dragging the silk legging another inch down her thigh.

She quivered in his arms. Her breasts swelled. He could feel the heat, the sweat starting to seep through the thin fabric of her faint yellow day dress and dampen his palms.

James glanced at her, but she had buried her face in the nook between his ear and shoulder, so he couldn't see her features. But he could still feel the softness, the warmth of her cheek against the underside of his chin, and feeding off her growing arousal, he trained his eyes on the road ahead and maintained his steady assault on her senses.

Once more he fingered the delicate stocking, and once more he yanked the supple material, wrinkling and clumping it together at her knee, exposing her smooth and rounded thigh.

There was a burning sentiment inside him to carry her into the shelter of the woods and set her on a leafy bed for a more thorough seduction, for in tempting her, his own need thickened.

But he ignored the impulse. He remained firmly fixed on his desire to bring her to a pulsing want. He wanted her to feel the promise of fulfillment . . . and the agony of unquenched passion.

He had always tended to her needs during their affair. He had never denied her her deepest wish or her wickedest desire on the island. Let her endure the discomfort of unfulfilled longing now. In time she would come to him for sexual release, for freedom from unnatural bondage . . . and then he would have his revenge.

James pressed his fingers against her bare leg—and stroked it. Slowly he skimmed the soft underside of her thigh. She was shaking in his arms, and the shudders rolled across his chest and belly. She weakened him. He sensed his legs waver under the pressure of her arousal.

But he didn't stop. He didn't stop touching her. The trees, the woodland creatures, even the hounding couple at his heels were barred from their intimate encounter, their secret struggle against the heat ballooning in their blood.

James was restrained by Sophia's weight. He couldn't run his fingers across the length of her body as he desired. Still he reached the sensitive part of her thigh, the hollow of her knee, and rubbed his fingers back and forth over the small patch of skin until he sensed the goose pimples spread across her flesh.

There was a deep, dark satisfaction in the pit of his soul. He raked his trim fingernails over her leg before he removed his hand from under her skirts. "You see, sweetheart. I can make you suffer, too."

She was warm. His own body was doused with sweat. He maintained a firm hold on her as he stepped out of the woods and into the bright sunlight.

He headed toward the back of the house. There was a white tent pitched in the wide and open yard, a gaggle of females hiding beneath the canopy and lazily sipping tea or lemonade. As soon as he and Sophia were spotted, the fuss ignited.

"What happened, Miss Dawson?!"

The supercilious chit, Lady Rosamond, was the first to make a ruckus as she glanced at the approaching troupe without rising from her padded seat.

"Miss Dawson's injured her ankle," said the earl. "She needs to rest."

"Take my chair, Miss Dawson."

Imogen Rayne presented her seat, and James set the witch down before he backed away from the rabble.

He was stiff, his muscles twisted with longing for Sophia. But he would gladly endure the crippling spasms to see the viper succumb to him once more.

James eyed Sophia closely. He studied the wayward tresses escaping from her sophisticated bun. He wanted to shake the chignon, set the wild locks free. Pinned down, the hair looked tight and uncomfortable. *He* was tight and uncomfortable watching her.

Sophia was breathing in quick, hoarse gasps. She didn't glance at him. Not once. She was flush, too. A half-dozen white and lacy kerchiefs fluttered in front of her, and she snatched the first one in reach, pressing it to her brow.

Imogen filled a glass with lemonade. "Drink this, Miss Dawson."

Sophia set aside the blue flower in her hand and downed the cool tonic in one unladylike gulp. James twined his wrists behind his back and steadied his own irregular heartbeat. He wasn't standing under the tent, so he was exposed to the roasting sunlight. But he maintained a good distance from the females pinched together in a tidy circle. He preferred the baking sun to their cold company.

"I'll fetch the doctor," said the earl.

"No!" Sophia hiccupped. She quickly pressed her fingers to her lips to suppress the undignified gesture. "I'm fine. I just need to rest, that's all."

She could sleep for a hundred years; it wouldn't do her any good. And a doctor? A healer couldn't cure what ailed her . . . only James could do that.

"You don't look well, my dear." The harridan fanned her fingers. "I agree with Lord Baine. We should summon the physician."

Sophia dabbed at the moisture on her chin. "Really, I'll be all right."

"I insist," said Maximilian. "I'll go to see Dr. Crombie at once."

"You mustn't be headstrong, Miss Dawson," said Rosamond.

It isn't ladylike, thought James. He watched Sophia quickly wilt under the dire implication. She swallowed her protests and quieted.

The earl nodded in accord and strutted off.

Anastasia sniffed and sipped her tea in an easy manner. "Perhaps we should put her in the house?"

"Yes, that's a good idea." Rosamond turned to James. "Take her into the house."

James bristled. He wasn't a bloody servant. He glared at the impertinent chit as a muscle in his cheek twitched.

Sophia quickly interrupted: "I'd much rather rest here, my lady. I prefer the outdoor air."

"Oh, very well." Rosamond sighed. "However, if the doctor orders you inside the house, you will follow his advice."

"Of course she will," said the harridan. "Miss Dawson is a sensible young woman."

James dropped his stiff shoulders. He was dismissed once more; he preferred it that way. He preferred to remain in the allegorical shadows.

"Would you like a glass of lemonade, Captain Hawkins?"

He glanced at his side. Imogen was holding a cup of the concoction, her fingers shaking.

"No, thank you," he said curtly.

"You looked parched." The glass still rattled in her hand. "Won't you reconsider?"

James stared at her, wondering what the devil was wrong with the woman. He wanted to be left alone. Surely she sensed it. The glass looked ready to crumble in her trembling fingers.

He took the lemonade from her.

She offered him a small smile before she returned to the tent and immersed herself in the hoopla still surrounding Sophia.

James ignored the lemonade in his hand. He eyed the witch instead. He watched her fingers dance across her features as she attempted to cool her face. But the frilly napkin wouldn't absorb the heat stemming from her pores. James would, however. Soon he would press his tongue to her flesh and take in every drop of briny sweat that tormented her.

Chapter 8

There was a merry din coming from inside the house. Sophia wanted to squelch the laughter, so sweet and lyrical. The gay atmosphere grated against the turmoil churning in her breast.

She fixed her eyes firmly on the brilliant sunset, a blushing rose. She let the quiet night embrace her. It slowly stretched across the heavens, shrouding the sleeping earth like a blanket.

She closed her eyes. A set of thick and robust fingers gingerly rubbed her thigh, her knee. She parted her lips at the teasing movements. Air filled her lungs, pushing her breasts, her bones outward. In contrast to the deep swell in her bosom, the muscles in her belly clenched. Blood warmed and stirred her heart.

Sophia folded her arms across her chest and squeezed her shoulders in comfort. She swatted at the flames in her belly, crushed the rising pressure in her breast. But the heat still spread and strengthened; it consumed and ravaged her.

You see, sweetheart. I can make you suffer, too.

She shuddered at the diabolical words. The black-guard hadn't changed in seven years. He had made her suffer on the island. He still made her suffer. She suspected the man's touch, even his memory would always twist her insides and curl her toes.

"Are you all right, Miss Dawson?"

Sophia opened her eyes and gasped. She quickly composed her features, smoothed the pinched lines across her face. "I'm fine, my lord."

The earl stepped between the wispy curtains. He was so handsome, with honey gold locks and light green eyes. He had an amiable disposition, too. The man would never torment her, she thought. He would never inspire wicked reflections or whisper cruel words into her ear. She would be happy with him, safe. Safe from Black Hawk's bewitching hold. Safe from ridicule and despair.

He strolled across the terrace. "You seem distressed."

She struggled to keep her poise as he approached. She struggled to tame the restless storm inside her. "I'm well, I assure you."

The earl stopped. "Let me fetch Dr. Crombie."

Sophia dropped her arms at her side, took in a deep breath to steady her rampant heartbeats. "It isn't necessary, really."

The physician had already examined her ankle. He'd affirmed she was fine. And Sophia didn't want to spend the rest of the evening in bed, nursing a phantom injury. The country house party would soon be over. She needed to spend every available moment wooing the earl.

Perhaps she should not have faked a wounded ankle. But in a panicked state of mind, she had thought it a savvy ploy to get the earl's affection. She had failed to anticipate the drawbacks, however. That the earl would fret, encourage her to rest in seclusion . . . that a notorious pirate lord would come along and gather her into his strapping arms.

She inwardly cursed the black devil for upsetting her soul.

"Let the good doctor enjoy the party," she said in a whimsical voice.

The earl had invited the healer to stay for supper. But Sophia didn't want the doctor to fuss. If the man suspected she was ill, he would order her confined to her chamber. She would lose the opportunity to engage in courtship with the earl. She would stalk the bedroom endlessly . . . thinking about James.

Sophia stared as the shadows on the green lengthened and reached for the house. She eyed the dark shapes creeping across the rolling lawn and quivered.

Even the pirate lord's name evoked mighty sentiments . . . sensual memories. The man's handprints were still seared on her flesh. His sultry breath still teased her cheeks and aroused her nerves.

"It's only a headache," she said in a shaky voice. "The cool night air is so refreshing; it chases away the discomfort."

"Your headache might be the result of your ankle injury. Perhaps you should come inside and sit down?"

"Thank you for your concern, my lord. But a light breeze will do me good, I'm sure."

The earl frowned. "Our walk was too long this morning. You must forgive me, Miss Dawson. It was thoughtless of me to take you so far. I just wanted to show you the grounds. But I failed to think the journey might be too exerting for you."

"I enjoyed our walk today, truly. Please don't blame yourself for my condition."

"It's my fault," he insisted. "You must allow me to express my sorrow and shame."

It was not the earl's fault she was so frazzled . . . it was Black Hawk's.

Sophia took in another sharp breath. She wanted to pound the ruthless devil with her fists, cut off his sensuous fingers with her knife. She wanted to choke him, maim him . . . ravish him with her lips.

She started as the earl slipped his fingers through hers and lifted her hand. "Will you accept my apology, Miss Dawson?"

Sophia stared at the man's tender fingers, so clean and crisp and well manicured. He stroked her knuckles softly, cooled the fiery blood coursing through her veins with his steady words and unmoving inflection.

He wasn't James.

Sophia gathered her wayward thoughts. The earl wasn't James. The earl didn't stir the longing in her soul. He was everything she needed in a respectable partner: quiet and upright. A man with scruples and good sense and polite manners.

She would be cold sometimes. But she would gladly endure the formal, even indifferent relationship between a wife and a husband if it offered her prestige. She didn't need passion. She had endured enough hardship under its tight hand, suffered the sneers and crude jokes as Black Hawk's mistress. She would not put herself in another position to be mocked; the pain was too great.

"There is nothing to forgive, my lord." She smiled. "I'll be inside shortly."

After a short pause, he kissed the back of her hand. "Very well, Miss Dawson."

Sophia stared after his departing figure. He had

kissed her! Not on the lips, true. But the affectionate gesture was a sure sign he was ready to propose. She was so close to her goal. She was so close to making her dream come true.

Sophia imagined being the next Countess Baine. She pictured a faceless gentleman as he doffed his hat in deference, a lady as she curtsied. The impression was vivid, the longing in her heart profound.

She turned away and looked at the sunset again. Soon. Soon she would be free of the ignominy, the fear of censure. Soon she would be free of James.

Something stirred at the back of her neck. She swatted at it, rubbed her skin. But there was nothing there. It must have been the wind, she thought. But once more the pressure rested on her flesh, her bones.

She bristled.

"Where are you, Black Hawk?"

"Right here, sweetheart."

She glanced over her shoulder. He stepped out of the shadows and pressed his shoulder against the wall, locking his arms together. He had been hiding in the garden. Listening to her exchange with the earl?

Her heart started to pound. He had tucked his fingers under his arms, out of sight. But she still sensed their arousing touch at her thigh.

She quelled a shiver. "I'm not your sweetheart anymore, remember?"

"No, you're not my sweetheart anymore," he said softly. "I've replaced you in my bed."

Her pulse quickened. The balmy heat that had blanketed her just a moment ago vanished, replaced by a vicious need to bite his damnable finger. She dismissed the unwelcome spurt of jealousy, choked it quiet.

"What do you want, Black Hawk?"

"I told you not to call me that in public."

Sophia quickly looked inside the house. The curtains served as a shield, guarding them from the other guests. But the glass was parted, allowing the merriment to seep outside.

She lowered her voice and hissed, "Then keep your distance."

He approached her instead.

She turned away from him, nerves thrumming. The sun was gone. A soft chorus of chirping crickets filled the dark stillness.

She shuddered as the pulsing heat from his torso nestled behind her. She inadvertently licked her lips.

"What's the matter, sweetheart? Have you overexerted yourself today?"

He *had* been listening to her conversation with her earl. He was tossing the man's words back at her in mocking reverberation.

Sophia bit her bottom lip with a savage pinch. "I'm fine."

He didn't touch her. She could feel him breathing, though. He stirred her hair. And then his breath caressed her ear.

"You're not fine."

Slowly he fingered her ear in a feathery stroke, brushing aside the stray curls, making her shiver.

"What will you do when you're hungry, Sophia?" He skimmed the rim of her earlobe with the tip of his tongue. "What will you do when you're married and your bones throb in the dead of night? Who will you turn to?"

Not you.

She fisted her palms as the ache welled deep inside her.

"I don't need passion," she repeated the mantra. She was in a daze, a trance. There was a deep echo in her ears, her heart beat wildly. "I don't need you."

"No, you don't need me . . . you have everything you need in the earl."

She gasped. "Yes."

Touch me!

No! She didn't want the beast to touch her. She didn't want the black devil to soil her with his wicked hands.

"How will you live, sweetheart?"

He moved his lips to the back of her neck. He didn't touch her with his mouth, but he touched her with his sultry breath.

Sophia swallowed a groan, tamped the feral impulse into the pit of her soul. She was shaking. It was a faint quiver, but it sapped her energy and made her feel weak.

"What will you do when you want to dance in the moonlight—or swim in the nude?"

She shuddered at the erotic memory. She closed her eyes and willed away the enchanting dream.

He moved to her other ear, tortured her with more whispered words. "What will you do when you lose your temper? Do you think the earl will play a game of chess with you?" He grazed her hair with his nose. "Do you think you will ever win another argument once you're married? He will be your husband then. He will always be right in all matters."

He was chipping at her resolve, the blackguard! She remembered Quincy's words again: *James hates to be in society. I think it comforts him to make the rest of us miserable.*

Was that what the rogue was doing? He sensed the earl was about to propose, he sensed she was about to be happy, so he wanted to make her miserable?

Sophia gathered her strength. She opened her eyes and confronted the scoundrel. "I will gladly submit to my future husband . . . but not to you," she said tartly. "Never again to you."

The man's lips firmed.

"Supper is served," the butler announced from inside the house.

Sophia abandoned the brigand in the shadows and entered the drawing room. The glowing candlelight warmed her already flushed features.

Imogen stepped beside her and offered support. "Are you all right, Miss Dawson?"

"Yes, I'm fine."

"Let me escort you to the dining hall."

Sophia simpered at the young woman. "Thank you, Miss Rayne."

"Imogen, please," she whispered back with a genial grin.

The earl took his sister by the hand. He smiled at Sophia from across the room. She returned the affectionate gesture before the whole party filed out of the room.

Sophia still burned with desire for the formidable brigand's sensuous lips. But the passion inside her would wither and die with time. And once she was married, she'd bar the black devil from her house—and soul. She would never suffer the pangs of longing again.

James was slow to cut the roasted duck, for it was like carving his own flesh. The surreptitious scrutiny from the other guests hampered his movements—and stoked the fire in his belly.

He thought about dropping the gold fork and grabbing the meat with his fingers, chewing the cooked fowl like the barbarian that he was . . . like the barbarian they all believed him to be. But he refrained from the whim. He wouldn't disgrace his sister in a moment of thoughtless passion. And he wouldn't give *them* the satisfaction of being right about him.

"Mr. Dibbs." Rosamond summoned the butler. "Please tell Cook to delay the next course. Captain Hawkins is still eating."

The haughty bitch was still miffed with him, it seemed. He had ruined her stupid game the other night by guessing her shallow thoughts too quickly. So petty and immature, she had fixed her eyes on the peacock ornament: the most sparkling decoration in the drawing room. It was too easy to suppose she would pick the brightest treasure in the space.

"There's no reason to delay the next course on my account," said James. "I'm finished."

Rosamond pursed her pampered lips as a footman collected the dishes. He had insulted her by leaving most of the meal untouched, for she had designed the menu. He had unintentionally insulted the cook, too. But James wasn't about to give the arrogant chit the satisfaction of calling him a slow-witted barbarian.

"I saw the loveliest great spotted woodpecker in the woods today," said Imogen. "It had a brilliant red crown and vibrant underside."

James glanced at the woman seated to his left. He sensed her discomfort, her distaste for confrontation. She wasn't one to let an awkward moment stretch or a silent void go unfulfilled, he supposed. She wasn't like the other wolves at the table.

As the assembled company commented on the bird sighting, James glanced at Sophia. She was seated across the table from him, prim and proper in a rich agglomeration of silk and linen. The quiet, lily white frock was a stark contrast to her deep, earthy brown tresses. And the lavish diamonds at her breasts winked in the candlelight, blinding the guests. But then that was the stone choker's purpose, wasn't it? To blind the guests and keep them from seeing who she really was?

The earl was hoodwinked for sure. One look at the simpering mooncalf confirmed the man was smitten with Sophia; he considered her a great treasure. But poison seeped from the viper's lips and cruelty flourished in her cold heart.

Sophia ignored him with commendable resolve. She sensed him watching her, he could tell. A pulse throbbed at her throat. But she resisted the temptation to meet his gaze. Instead, she smiled and engaged in light table conversation with the doctor seated beside her.

Dessert was making its way around the table. Sophia was served after the earl and she dipped into the bowl of sugared plums.

James watched as she lifted the glazed fruit to her lips with a spoon. A smidgen of frosting rested near the corner of her mouth, and she patted her lips with a napkin. He imagined the sweet icing dripping from her lips and pooling between her breasts. He imagined slipping his tongue into her bodice and licking the sugary syrup off her tender flesh.

He stiffened at the erotic image. He heard the woman's wanton sighs of pleasure in his head. Blood and muscle and bone ached under the pressure of the lusty dream, and he gnashed his teeth to do away with the haunting reflection. He had come to the country house party to seduce Sophia, not to be seduced by her. He needed to bolster his seduction if he wanted to get the witch into his bed and foil her courtship with the earl.

"Dr. Crombie, I understand you champion a new form of treatment to cure all types of illness," said the earl.

The distinguished physician was senior in years, his soft brown hair speckled with gray. He was a rotund man with a brusque manner. But he enjoyed the pleasures of country dining and feminine companionship, for he had consumed two of everything and eyed all the ladies with interest.

"Yes," said the healer, "it's called mesmerism."

"Mesmerism?" Rosamond quirked a brow. "What is that?"

The doctor wiped his lips with the napkin. "Mesmerists believe the mind, if properly focused, can cure any ailment."

"No surgery or medicine?" said Lady Lucas.

"None a'tall," returned the doctor.

The company appeared both skeptical and intrigued by the claim. James half listened to the unfolding conversation, too engrossed with Sophia's subtle movements as she savored the sugared plums with almost licentious delight.

"Doesn't the treatment involve magnetic irons, too?" said the earl.

"Under the teachings of its founder, Dr. Franz Mesmer," said the physician. "Mesmer had his patients place their feet in a pool of water while holding magnets. However, the practice has evolved to exclude all external forces. Today we focus solely on the mind."

"And how does one focus solely on the mind?" said Sophia in a soft and measured voice. The tip of her tongue darted between her lips. She licked the icing from the corner of her mouth, making James's head throb.

"The patient is placed in a trance," said the doctor. "The presiding physician then offers instruction and therapy to cure the individual."

"My goodness!" from Lady Lucas.

The earl leaned forward. "Have you had success with the procedure, Dr. Crombie?"

"Great success, my lord."

"Can you cure a headache, for instance?"

"Certainly, my lord. I can treat both minor and serious afflictions."

Rosamond glanced at her brother. "Do you have a headache, Max?"

"Not I, no . . . But I was thinking about Miss Dawson."

The harridan dropped her fork and turned to her charge in alarm. "Are you ill, my dear?"

"I'm fine, really." Sophia quickly squelched the fuss. "I had a little headache earlier in the evening. I feel much better now."

"You don't look well, Miss Dawson," said Anastasia. "You look sickly."

Sophia soured under the implication. James almost snorted with laughter. She wasn't suffering from a headache or an injured ankle. She was suffering from unfulfilled lust. The woman had a hard heart; she had dismissed him earlier in the evening. However, she had not dismissed the stirring feelings inside her. Not entirely. He sensed her arousal. And with steady encouragement, he intended to get her to admit those feelings aloud.

"Well, if Miss Dawson is agreeable, I will gladly perform the mesmerism," said the healer.

Sophia looked cornered. It seemed every guest at the table considered it a good idea that she undergo the treatment to cure her "headache." If she resisted, she might be classified as unreasonable or even reckless for putting her well-being at risk. And perish the thought she should be considered as anything other than perfectly agreeable.

A few minutes later they were all cloistered inside the drawing room. The ladies gathered around Sophia, who was seated in a chair opposite the physician. The earl stood behind the doctor, looking on. Meanwhile, James remained in the shadows beside the window.

The healer removed a luminous bauble from his coat pocket. "I want you to look at the timepiece, Miss Dawson."

Sophia sighed. She folded her hands in her lap and gazed at the watch as instructed.

James shifted his eyes to the timepiece, too, thinking about the fob watch Sophia had gifted him seven years ago.

"Concentrate," said the doctor. "Look into the watch . . . fall deeply into the watch."

James glared at the radiant timepiece in the firelight. He remembered the ticking sound coming from the watch Sophia had given him on the island. He remembered returning to the empty plantation house, the small box sitting on the windowsill. He remembered admiring the fine timepiece, the polished glass face, the sleek hands . . . and then reading the elegant inscription on the back of the watch: *May you rot in everlasting hell.*

"Close your eyes," said the doctor.

James closed his eyes.

"Take a deep breath."

James breathed in a slow and heavy breath.

"Concentrate on the pain."

He gripped the cold gold between his fingers, knuckles white, blood pounding in his ears. He let out a robust cry before he smashed the watch against the wall.

"Think deeply about the pain. Let it fill your mind, your soul."

He glared at the damaged timepiece on the ground, imagined grinding it into the floorboards. But he crouched beside it instead and started to pick up the pieces.

"Now I want you to stop thinking about the pain. Think about a pleasant memory instead."

James watched the woman from afar. So lovely. More lovely than any of the delicate blooms in the garden. She was kneeling, her bare toes buried in the moist soil. She cared for the garden, for him with such passion. And it welled inside him, the profound and stirring sentiment . . .

I love you, Sophia.

"I want you to feel at peace . . . now open your eyes."

James opened his eyes, bewildered.

"How do you feel?" said the doctor.

"Wonderful," said Sophia. "My headache is gone."

James thought the bones in his breast about to snap. Blood throbbed in his head under the crushing pressure of the haunting memory. He pressed his fingers to the desperate pounding at his temples, crushing the pulsing nerves into submission.

The pain was alive and deep and burning in his belly. The old wound bled without mercy, filling him, drowning him.

A crescendo of applause.

"Bravo, Dr. Crombie!" cheered Rosamond. "That was magnificent."

"Yes, well done," praised the earl.

The doctor beamed. "It was my pleasure to be of service."

James swallowed the bitter bile that was churning in his belly, rising in his throat. What service? The blasted healer had ripped him apart. He was in greater agony now than he had been on the night of the earl's ball—on the night he had reunited with Sophia.

James glared at the coterie swarming around the "cured" Miss Dawson, and he vowed the witch would not get the better of him—ever again.

Chapter 9

"**M**esmerism is so fascinating . . . is your headache truly cured, my dear?"

Sophia eyed the steam rising from the bath in the adjoining room. She longed to slip under the balmy water and let the heat ease her stiff muscles and sore temperament. But Lady Lucas was filled with vivacious energy. Sophia suspected she might not reach the warm pool before it cooled.

"Yes, Lady Lucas." She sighed. "I'm fine."

Sophia was wearing a silk wrapper, her hair pinned. She was sitting on the bed as the matron strutted across the room in quick and lively steps. But Sophia wasn't really fine. She wasn't suffering from a headache . . . but a throbbing in her bones that refused to cease. A pity the physician's performance hadn't put her in a trance and cured her ailments. Perhaps the hot bath would fare better in that regard—if she ever reached it.

"The earl shows you great affection, my dear."

Sophia's heart swelled. "Do you really think so?"

"Oh yes. Do you see how he cares for your needs? He went to fetch the physician as soon as you injured your ankle. And tonight he even urged the doctor to heal your headache." The woman eyed the bright patterned rug as she paced. "Mark my words, Miss Dawson. The earl is very much in love with you."

Sophia had thought the same thing. It was a comfort to hear the matron express a similar conclusion. It proved she was not imagining the whole courtship . . . as the black devil had wanted her to believe.

The dark and striking image of Black Hawk filled Sophia's head. She remembered him standing on the balcony, strapping arms folded. He had concealed his fingers from her. The fingers that had caused her so much anguish earlier in the day. The fingers that still disturbed her senses and tortured her mind.

She dismissed the man's mesmerizing features from her thoughts. She reflected on the earl instead.

Sophia sensed the tingling sensation in her fingertips. There was a thickness in the air, making it hard to breathe, and she took in a deep breath to satisfy her greedy lungs. Soon she would be the next Countess Baine. The thought put her in a near tizzy, for she was so close to achieving her dream. She even tasted the air of respectability in the opulent setting surrounding her. The lavish drapery and fine furnishings and bright carpeting reflected the tastes of a proper lady: one she was very much determined to become.

"If only the barbarian wasn't here," griped the matron.

Sophia's heart cramped. What about the barbarian? He was a wicked soul, irredeemable. Had he misbehaved? Had he said something foul to Lady Lucas?

"How dare he force his attention on you, Miss Dawson. And right in front of the earl!"

Sophia was alarmed. Had the earl witnessed her

exchange with the captain on the terrace? Had he observed the ruthless brigand whisper into her ear?

"What do you mean?" she said, parched.

"He handled you like an ogre this morning." The matron sniffed. "It was so distasteful. You must have suffered sorely, my dear."

Sophia sighed. She had suffered, yes. She suffered still. It was seared in her memory, his adroit fingers working under her skirts, teasing her flesh until she trembled with need. But she would endure the discomfort, the restless energy teeming inside her. She would not risk betraying him as a rogue; the truth might expose her own infamous past.

"But I suppose we must be cordial with the captain," said the matron. "The earl's befriended the barbarian."

An oddity, that. But Sophia supposed the earl was just being hospitable. The captain had saved his sister from a disgraceful fall, after all. It stood to reason the man would be so affable and courteous.

"Let us forget about the barbarian, Miss Dawson."

A sound idea. She was fagged. The day had boasted both successes and setbacks. She was one step closer to becoming the next countess. However, each step proved more troublesome with Black Hawk at her heels. She wanted to rest in the warm and inviting water and forget about her grueling ordeal for a few blissful minutes.

"The earl will propose to you soon. I can sense it."

But the matron's assured words piqued Sophia's interest once more. She put aside the thought of a bath and relished the humming joy swelling in her bosom. "He will?"

"Oh yes."

"When?"

"Patience, my dear. The earl is a prudent man." She muttered, "Perhaps too prudent."

"How do you mean?"

"Prudence is a virtue . . . but it can lead to an indecisive nature. The earl might be struggling with the right thing to do: to marry you or not to marry you. We must plan our next move carefully. We must encourage the man to propose. What are our plans for tomorrow?"

"I think the party is going to the park for an afternoon of boating. The earl's sister is organizing a waterside picnic, too."

"Hmm." The matron twisted her lips in thought. "We will all be at the picnic, so there isn't much chance of him proposing to you there . . . but a boat ride sounds romantic. We must get you and the earl alone in a rowboat. He will surely ask for your hand then."

There was a quiver of doubt in Sophia's breast. "I was alone with the earl tonight. We were together on the terrace. He did not propose, however."

"Drat!" But then the matron paused and eyed her charge. "You were alone with the earl tonight?"

"Briefly." She was swift to impart, "He was a perfect gentleman."

The older woman's lips puckered. "I trust he was; the earl is not a rogue."

Unlike Black Hawk. The pirate lord had come upon her shortly after the earl. And he *was* a rogue, with his sinful touch and wicked words. She was woozy just thinking about their encounter.

"You must never put yourself in a questionable position, Miss Dawson."

Sophia's sensual thoughts snapped. "Yes, Lady Lucas."

"It is one thing to sail with the earl during the day and in full public view. However, you mustn't be alone with him in the dark, even for a moment. It might ruin your reputation."

Sophia's heart started to thud. What then would being alone with Black Hawk do to her reputation? Smash it beyond recognition, she supposed. The very thought was chilling, and she shuddered.

"I understand, Lady Lucas."

The matron nodded. "Lord Baine is an honorable man. Even if a scandal had resulted from the encounter, I suspect the man would've immediately proposed to save your good name. He is not the sort to take initiative, but if pushed . . ."

"What is it, Lady Lucas?"

"That's it!"

Sophia pinched her brows. "What's it?"

"We will push the earl."

"Off the boat?"

The woman looked aghast. "No, my dear. We will push the earl to propose."

"How?"

"We will use Captain Hawkins to make the earl jealous."

Sophia's heart dropped. She trembled at the thought of using the captain. She trembled at the thought of what he might do to her "good name" if he ever discovered the ploy. "But you said scandal will ruin—"

"Yes. Yes. Scandal *will* ruin a young lady's reputation. But we will not cause a scandal, my dear."

"Then what will we do?"

"It's obvious the captain is smitten with you."

Blood throbbed in her veins. "It is?"

"He admires you all the time."

Sophia did her utmost to ignore the brigand in public. Did he really admire her "all the time"? Something stirred in her heart at the thought. Something suspiciously akin to sentimentality. She quickly stomped the feeling dead. The blackguard wasn't smitten with her. He just wanted to make her miserable with his piercing stare, unnerve her.

"Do you remember what Lady Rosamond said the other night?"

Sophia's head was unfortunately filled with thoughts about Black Hawk; there was room for little else. "No."

" 'Let the barbarian admire you from afar,' she had said. And so you will. The more the captain admires you, the more the earl will see you are worthy of admiration. Jealousy can be a powerful motivator."

Sophia wasn't so sure it was a good idea. She pressed her fingers to her breast to quiet the quick bangs of her heart.

"Come." The matron took her by the hand and dragged her off the bed. "We must prepare the dress you will wear tomorrow. We should pick another sparkling jewel to match the outfit, too. Baubles capture a man's interest."

After another few minutes the matron had decided upon the proper attire, and Sophia had consented to the garb and jewels selected. At last she was alone in the bedchamber.

She rubbed her brow, thinking about tomorrow—and using Black Hawk to make the earl jealous. The matron was adamant the scheme would work. But she wasn't privy to the past between her charge and the captain. The woman would balk if she ever discovered Sophia's sinful affair with the pirate. She would do everything in her power to keep her and the brigand apart then. The matron might even dismiss Sophia from her sight entirely. But she would not suggest Sophia cross swords with the devil, that much was for sure.

Sophia closed her eyes. She really *was* getting a headache now.

She moved toward the adjoining room. The ceramic tiles were cold beneath her warm feet. A sharp memory returned: cool cedar planking under her bare toes.

Sophia shrugged off the reflection as she shrugged off the silk wrapper. The garment slipped silently to the floor.

She dipped her hand in the water, testing the temperature. It was warm, but not hot. She made a grimace. Still, she resigned herself to a tepid bath and stepped into the tub.

Quickly her bones sighed. Stiff muscles loosened, too. She watched the dreamy candlelight dance across the wall and lull her senses . . . but soon a distinct throbbing distracted her from the respite.

Sophia glanced at her leg. The water was still, and she looked at the marks on her outer thigh.

Her leg surfaced. She pressed her knee just under her chin to better examine the scratches.

The skin was flushed, the nail marks a deep red and glossy from the water. She eyed the wound, stinging. Her thoughts pounded in her head, her mind crowded with sensations and memories.

The tub quickly morphed into James; it cradled her as he had cradled her. The water kissed her skin in every place, embracing her.

Sophia skimmed her fingertips lightly across the scratches. Back and forth she stroked the swelling marks, thinking about James. Thinking about the man's touch in the woods . . . on the terrace. Such small touches, so short in pleasure. But the impressions lingered afterward.

Sophia slipped her leg beneath the water's pristine surface again. She rested her head against the tub, breathed deep to quash the heat stirring in her belly. But the pirate lord's damnable caress still haunted her thoughts, her flesh. His fingers still moved over her body and tortured her senses.

Sophia pressed her hand against her belly. The muscles bounced. She was tight. Even the warm water failed to soothe her, to douse the fire in her blood.

Slowly she slipped her hand between her breasts. She rubbed the bone there. Softly at first. Then with more vigor.

She splayed her fingers . . . reached for her nipples. There she ached. There the nerves thrummed with need and begged for satisfaction.

Sophia brushed her nipple with the pad of her thumb. Her heart beat wild and sure under the ministrations. The sore nub puckered and stretched under her quick and hard strokes. She rubbed and rubbed, searching for release. The tip of her breast was so tender, painfully so.

She bit her bottom lip hard to quell the groan rising in her throat. She moved in the water, undulated her buttocks in the pool. Small waves appeared, lapped against her swelling breasts.

She gasped as the pressure and tenderness settled

between her thighs. She cursed the brigand for putting her in such a raw and burning state. Cursed him to hell.

"Oh, James!"

James stood beside the window, transfixed.

He braced his hands against the frame, arms outstretched. The glass was open. The breeze whisked inside the room. Curtains quivered. Candlelight flickered.

But he remained still.

Perfectly still.

Across the courtyard was another window. Inside the candle flames danced. Something else danced, too.

Shadows.

James watched the shadows . . . he watched the naked woman inside the room making the shadows.

He had aroused her. And the satisfaction in his blood was keen. The pain was also intense. The pain he had for her. The ache.

She slipped her hand between her breasts. It was the only part of her he could see from his vantage point. But then . . .

The hungry growl in his belly slowly turned into a howl as he observed her hand dip below the water.

He imagined her as she tickled her quim. She gasped his name; he heard the begging words in his head.

James touched the scratches at the back of his neck. He spread his fingers apart to match the spacing and stroked the wounds, the marks she had made on him.

"Sophia."

He breathed the name like a spell, a curse. She was a witch. She ensnared him with her need, called to him with her desire.

But he would not come to her. He would not give her the pleasure she craved. If she wanted his touch, she would have to come to him—and beg for it.

Chapter 10

S ophia strolled between the rows of great oak trees lining the thoroughfare. It was a quaint park, well manicured. The cooing birds, the soft patter of the water were idyllic. The sounds quieted the fierce storm in her breast.

She had searched for satisfaction last night, searched for pleasure. But her own fingers hadn't smothered the passion in her blood. Not all of it. Embers of longing still burned in her belly.

"Isn't it a lovely day, Miss Dawson?"

Sophia moved through the unnatural beauty of the landscape, so symmetrical and tame. She moved through it like a shadow in a dream.

"Yes, very lovely."

She was exploring the grounds with Imogen. The earl and captain had yet to join the party. The men had gone horseback riding. And Sophia wasn't prepared to endure the company of so many ladies alone. There was a harmony in the air when the gentlemen were present. The ladies tended to keep their sharp tongues somewhat dull.

"I'd like to think we're friends, Imogen."

The woman smiled. "So would I."

"Then please call me Sophia."

Imogen appeared sheepish. "I must admit, I don't make friends easily."

Sophia glanced at her. The young woman wasn't like the other ladies. She didn't have a quick tongue. How had she befriended such a posh brood?

"How long have you been friends with Lady Rosamond?" said Sophia.

"For three years."

"And you met her at finishing school?"

"Oh no! I didn't have the means to attend the best finishing school in Switzerland. I still don't. Mondie and I met through our parents. My father offered the late earl financial advice."

"I see."

"Mondie befriended me."

Sophia heard the indifference in the young woman's voice. "You didn't return her affection?"

"Not at first." She shrugged. "We are . . . dissimilar in so many ways. Perhaps you've noticed?"

"Well, I don't mean to pry."

"It's all right." The girl chuckled. "It's very simple, really. Every young lady needs friends . . . but Mondie is very selective."

"How so?"

"She doesn't want anyone to outshine her."

"Imogen!" Sophia gasped, feigning outrage. "That was very frank."

"Forgive me."

"Nonsense. I appreciate it. You can be frank with me all you like."

She smiled again. "I have a gift for music, Anastasia is well-bred, and you . . ."

"I have money."

"Yes." She laughed. "Meanwhile, Mondie has all three traits."

"I see."

Was that why the earl's sister had befriended her? Because she had *one* desirable aristocratic trait and no more?

Sophia made a moue.

"I accepted Mondie's friendship at my parents' behest." Imogen folded her hands behind her back. "Mondie's patronage raises my own social standing, so I can make a more respectable match."

Sophia lifted a brow. "And have you made a respectable match?"

The girl fell quiet.

"Pardon my intrusion." Sophia dropped the banter in her voice. "I should not have inquired about something so personal."

"It's not that," she said quietly. "I want to tell you . . . I sense you're an honorable woman, Sophia."

Some might not think so, she thought. Black Hawk considered her a coldhearted viper. But she dismissed the devil from her mind.

"I trust you won't betray my confidence," said Imogen.

"I can keep a secret."

Sophia had so many of her own that one more seemed a trifle.

"I've met someone," whispered Imogen. "He's wonderful. Handsome and kind . . . I love him!"

Sophia listened to the young woman's heart, bursting with passion. She had once guarded such romantic ideas in her head, too. But that had been a long time ago.

"I'm happy for you, Imogen."

The girl's features fell flat. Tears appeared in her eyes.

"What's the matter?" said Sophia.

She sniffed. "I can't be with him."

"Why?"

"He's not the sort of man my father would approve. He isn't suitable."

An image came to mind: an image of a rogue like Black Hawk. The impulse to protect Imogen from such a man welled in Sophia's breast.

"Perhaps it's best if you listen to your father's counsel," she said gently. "If the man isn't suitable—"

"You don't understand. He is respectable. But he is . . . Jewish. I'm afraid my father would disown me if I married him."

"I'm sorry, Imogen."

"It's so hard to be apart from someone you care about!"

Sophia listened to the woman's suffering. It was romantic rubbish. The wound in Imogen's heart would heal with time. The girl was naïve. It was better to make a respectable match than to live in ignominy. She would learn the truth one day. Love wasn't real. Desire ensnared the senses, fooled the heart. But desire wasn't worth the pain of disgrace.

"Listen to me blather." The girl wiped her eyes with her fingers. "I'm souring your good mood with my melancholy."

"Rot." Sophia slipped an arm around her waist and hugged her. "I cannot help you, but I hope I can offer a sympathetic ear."

"And that you have. Thank you."

Sophia smiled. The two women walked the length of the thoroughfare and returned to the riverside picnic.

"There you are, ladies," said the earl. He bounded up to them in greeting. "The captain and I had prepared to search the park for you. We feared you both lost."

Sophia's heart quickened. The captain was positioned beside a tree. He stood under the canopy of leaves, arms folded. He watched the quiet river with a thoughtful expression—and for the first time since their reunion she desired to know his thoughts.

The man was detached from the party in both proximity and regard. He still emitted an unfriendly aura . . . but he also emitted a seductive one. That lazy stance belied a maelstrom of feeling.

Sophia sensed his restlessness . . . and the sentiment inspired fretful feelings in her own breast. She was supposed to make the earl jealous. She was supposed to use the captain to encourage the earl to propose. But their truce was so tenuous. If she flirted with the black devil, even in jest, she might get the earl's attention—but she would also get Black Hawk's.

Sophia quieted her wild heartbeat with a few measured breaths. "How was your ride, my lord?"

"Spirited, Miss Dawson." He eyed the emerald bauble at her bust; it matched her rich green frock. "Come and sit, ladies. You must be parched after your long walk."

Imogen approached the picnic blanket and settled beside Anastasia. Sophia was prepared to take a seat, too. However, the cool breeze coming off the river was so inviting, she approached the shoreline instead.

"I've procured a boat for the party," said the earl. He stepped beside her and gestured toward the raft staked in the ground. "We shan't all fit inside, but the captain and I will take turns ferrying each of you across the river. The scenery is marvelous."

"Oh yes, I long for a boat ride," said Sophia.

The earl beamed. "Well, then—"

"Perhaps Miss Dawson will accompany me in the boat?" The man's voice was low yet commanding. "She is keen to see the scenery and I would be happy to take her."

Sophia gulped. A dry heat closed her throat. She stared at the glassy water. She ignored the barbarian. But the man's deep and penetrating glare was impossible to snub.

She glanced at Lady Lucas. The matron bobbed her head in accord. She even smiled.

"Your parasol, my dear," said the woman.

There was a feeling in Sophia's gut that stirred with each shaky step. She crossed the lawn and took the parasol from Lady Lucas before she approached the captain.

The brigand was formidable. The restless energy inside him strengthened with each step she took, she sensed it. He was calling to her, beckoning her to approach.

Come to me.

Blues eyes, so mesmerizing. A strength so pulsing and raw . . .

Sophia licked her lips. She was trapped. He was watching her keenly, summoning her. The rest of the party was watching her, too. She had to restrain the restive impulses inside her. She had to remain composed.

"Thank you, Captain."

He eyed her with the care of a hawk. The man's lips twitched into a handsome smile.

She shuddered.

James helped her into the boat before he removed

the stake from the ground and pushed the craft into the water.

He stepped inside, his boots wet.

Sophia chewed on her bottom lip. She glanced at the shoreline slowly fading away. The earl was still standing beside the river. He was looking at her differently . . . possessively.

Lady Lucas had been right: jealousy *was* a powerful motivator. The earl would soon propose, she was sure. However, Sophia would have to suffer plenty to get the man's title.

She lifted the parasol and quickly blocked the party from her sight. If only there was a way to blind the black devil from her eyes, too. The man's glare was making her blood burn.

Sophia stared at the scenery: well-hewed grass, brilliant wildflowers, majestic trees. But it wasn't easy to ignore the brigand. He always commanded attention with his presence. Even if she averted her eyes, her other senses obeyed the man's call . . . robust musk filled her lungs . . . the soft splash of water danced in her ears as he powered the boat's movements with his meaty hands.

He shifted his boot, bumped her toes. She quickly tucked her feet beneath the bench, her pulse thumping.

After a few quiet minutes, the brigand set the oars aside . . . and caressed the brass buttons of his coat.

She watched, transfixed, as he removed the fresh-pressed garment, shrugged it off his wide shoulders in a slow and teasing manner. He was dressed in a clean white shirt and tight gray vest. She could see . . . nay, she could feel the man's strength thrumming through the crisp apparel.

Sophia's heart quivered. A longing stirred in her breast . . . a longing to see more . . . to feel more.

She curled her fingers around the parasol.

He next set to work on his cravat, stripping the material from his neck with an almost eager resolve.

Sophia's heart pulsed as she watched the sinewy muscles in his neck throb. Sweat gathered between her fingers. He slowly reached for his cuffs and rolled up his sleeves, revealing stalwart fists and thick forearms. He was starting to look like Black Hawk, the pirate. He was starting to look like the lover she remembered from the island.

"Are you going to take off *all* your clothes?" she finally snapped.

He picked up the oars again and rowed with more agility. "Is that a request, sweetheart?"

"No!"

Flushed at her erroneous—and erotic—assumption, she returned her gaze to the tranquil landscape. There were other couples strolling the shore, even children frolicking. Sophia might be trapped in the boat with the black devil, but she was safe. She was in full public view. There was nothing the bounder could do to her—except set her senses afire.

"The harridan didn't seem too worried about our boat ride together." Without a cravat, the man's collar parted. The muscles at his neck and chest strained as he maneuvered the oars. "I wonder why?"

Sophia was bewitched by the beads of sweat that formed on his skin, glistening in the sunlight. She imagined pressing the tip of her tongue to the salty drops in ravishment.

"Are you thirsty, sweetheart?"

She inadvertently licked her lips. There was a smoldering look in the man's eyes. She swiftly gathered her wayward thoughts.

"You heard what the earl said." She looked at the bucolic countryside again . . . but something tugged at her eyes, forcing her to gaze at the brigand once more. "You'll each take turns rowing one of the ladies across the river, remember?"

"Yes, I look forward to it . . . Let's hope the boat doesn't turn over."

There was a wicked gleam in his eyes. Sophia wondered if the man would really capsize the craft with one of the other ladies aboard.

She wouldn't put it beneath him.

"You still haven't answered my question. Why didn't the harridan make a fuss?" he said. "I am a barbarian, after all. It's her duty to protect you from me."

Sophia snorted. "I can protect myself."

"Yes, I know. It was I who taught you, remember?"

He had gifted her with the knife she had tucked between her breasts. He'd instructed her how to wield it, too. But the steel blade and leather sheath seemed so heavy to her now: a burden rather than an asset. "Then what's your point, Black Hawk?"

She shifted, her buttocks sore. The wood planking was hard, and the moisture forming beneath her thighs and posterior was making her uncomfortable.

"I was sure the harridan would've preferred the earl show you the scenery instead."

The frilly parasol offered little comfort and shade under the man's blistering glare. He was clearly prodding her for an incriminating answer.

"If you thought that," she said, parched, "then why did you offer to take me on the boat ride?"

He shrugged. "For the same reason you so readily consented . . . to make the earl jealous."

Sophia took in a sharp breath through her nose. Her heart started to pound with more vigor.

"What's the matter, sweetheart?" The man's lips curled into a sinful smile. "Did you think the barbarian too stupid to figure out your ploy?"

She was quiet. She didn't know what to think. The man always disturbed her senses, tossed her wits overboard, as it were.

"If you want to make the earl jealous," he said in a low and seductive voice, "there are other ways besides the boat ride . . ."

The dark and sensual look in his eyes was so inviting, Sophia's heart pinched. "I have my knife, Black Hawk."

She was breathing hard, her fingers moist. But another heat was gathering inside her, too. A deep and familiar heat.

He lifted a black brow. "You'd attack me in full public view?"

"I'd sink you and the boat if I had to."

"And yourself?" he said with amusement.

"I can swim."

"So can I."

The roasting sun was almost suffocating in strength. Sophia eyed the cool water and ached to slip beneath the tranquil waves, to douse the fire raging in her belly.

"Why don't we turn back now?" she said quietly.

"Not yet. There's a beautiful bit of scenery I want you to see. I think you'll appreciate it."

She flitted her tongue across her upper lip. "What scenery?"

He fixed his eyes on her mouth, so intent. A savage hunger burned in the deep blue pools. His balmy expression made her own lips thirst.

"I spotted it during my horse ride," he said tightly. "We're almost there."

He was taut. Sophia sensed the stiffness in his posture. The wild, booming beats in her breast drowned out nature's other sounds. The lapping waves, the twittering birds, the children's laughing cries all faded from her mind. She was captivated by the man's strong and swift movements as he rowed the boat. Enchanted by the dark need in his eyes: a need that matched her own.

She was strangled for words. She should order him to return to the picnic. She should jump from the craft . . . but she refrained from either deed. She let James take her away. She let her thoughts and good sense drift away with the current.

There was a bend in the river. The shoreline was higher—and more desolate. The park goers steered clear of the rocky embankment.

The air was thick. Sophia gasped for breath. Her corset seemed so tight. All her summer wardrobe seemed heavy, in truth. Even the delicate parasol was bearing down on her.

An old willow tree appeared, its gnarled body leaning to one side. It rested beside the shore, the escarpment crumbling. Knotty roots reached into the water like a squid's tentacles. Sagging vines lilted softly in the breeze, grazing her cheeks as she passed beneath the enormous canopy. There was a gathering of boulders, too. And James effortlessly slipped the boat into the dark grotto.

The craft bumped against the rocks. It was a tap. But she was so tight inside, the light movement made her jump.

He rested the oars inside the boat. With a slow, even lazy regard, he moved his eyes across her figure in a thorough assessment.

Sophia sighed inwardly. He touched her with his eyes. Every patch of skin stirred and trembled under his searing stare.

The linen fabric hugged her moist flesh. She was imprisoned, the material sticky. She breathed deep and hard, stretching her lungs, the garment.

She dropped the parasol behind her.

He lifted his eyes.

Such haunting eyes.

She looked at his fingers.

The appendages twitched.

He seized her ankles and forced her feet apart. She grabbed the bench seat for support, her limbs thrumming, her pulse throbbing.

He thrust her legs upward and positioned her feet on each side of the boat, her skirts pooled at her waist.

She was open to him.

Wide open to him.

He knelt between her splayed thighs, rocking the boat with this heavy movement. She could hear his ragged breathing; it matched the tempo of her own wild heartbeat.

He pressed his great body against her torso, and she shuddered to feel his weight between her legs. She had missed him. She had missed his delicious touch, his captivating presence. He ensnared her senses like no other lover. And she relished the intense feeling once more.

His tongue darted between his teeth and licked the center of her throat. It was a slow and sensuous caress. He was taking in her scent and leaving his own mark behind.

She closed her eyes. She dropped her head back and parted her lips in a silent groan. She was so vulnerable, trapped. She had no sway over her legs, her arms. She had to hold the bench seat to keep from falling. And he still gripped her ankles, keeping her legs spread apart.

But she cherished it.

She cherished submitting to him.

He moved his hands along her calves. Thick and sturdy fingers scraped her silk stockings as he scaled her knees and groped her thighs.

He rasped, "Is this what you were searching for last night in the bath?"

She cried out at the pressure between her legs. He splayed her quim with his fingers and rubbed the tight, throbbing nub of nerves in quick and fluid stokes.

She trembled and gasped. "You watched me?"

"Through the window, sweetheart." He smiled against her throat. "It was a delightful show."

She lifted her head and pressed her sweaty brow against his. "You son of a bitch."

He slipped a long finger deep inside her. He crooked the appendage and rubbed a spot, so sensitive she had to bite her bottom lip to keep from moaning. She whimpered instead, the stress between her legs swelling. She undulated against his thrusting hand, seeking release.

"And this is just what I have to give you in my one finger," he whispered.

The conceited blackguard!

"I'm glad you enjoyed the show." She flicked her tongue over his hot lips. "Did I make you jealous, Black Hawk?"

There was a dark fire in his eyes.

"Did I make you angry?" She nipped his lower lip. He tasted so bloody good, the salty sweat on his mouth intoxicating. "I don't need you anymore. I don't need you to give me pleasure . . . I can give myself pleasure."

He stabbed her quim with his finger; his lips thinned.

She groaned at the man's hard and steady assault. The muscles in her quim pulsed with need.

The pirate lord removed his hands.

Sophia's senses reeled. "What are you doing?"

She was panting, so taut and poised for pleasure. She ached to feel the orgasm pour through her blood, her womb.

"You don't need me anymore, remember?" he said hoarsely.

He returned to the opposite bench seat, trembling.

She glared at his stiff cock, the erection pressing against his trousers. "But *you* need me!"

He offered her a wicked, even cruel smirk. "I can give myself pleasure."

A cold, dark impulse gripped her heart. She was so very tempted to slice his gullet.

He took up the oars again.

The boat's jerking movement upset her balance. She quickly closed her legs, still quivering with unresolved lust.

She wanted to disembowel him.

She wanted to drown him.

She wanted to beg him to give her satisfaction.

As only you can.

Urgh! She was such a ninny. She was letting the brutal cutthroat torment her, make her miserable . . . but she could make him miserable, too.

The rest of the boat ride was quiet.

Sophia gripped the parasol again and stared at the landscape, searching for a distraction. But with the black devil so close, the pressure between her legs remained.

She crossed her ankles and squeezed her thighs together. The damnable pirate captain worked off *his* frustration through vigorous exercise, but *she* had to suffer in silence.

She would make him suffer, too.

"Ahoy!" called the earl.

James steered the craft toward the embankment. The earl bounded to the boat and assisted Sophia from the bench seat.

"How was the scenery?" said the earl.

She gathered her composure. "Lovely, my lord."

James picked up his coat. "It was a pleasant trip."

He was breathing hard. It might seem to the rest of the party he was suffering from fatigue after an exerting boat ride, but Sophia knew the truth. He was suffering from unquenched lust—like her.

"Would anyone else like to go for a ride?" said James. "Miss Rayne?"

"Oh thank you, I'd—"

"No!" snapped Sophia.

The party looked at her, bewildered.

"Miss Rayne is still eating lunch," Sophia said with

more aplomb. She wasn't about to let Imogen inside the boat with the ruthless brigand. The craft might "turn over." "A boat ride will make her queasy . . . take Miss Bedford instead. She's finished her meal."

Anastasia blanched.

So did Black Hawk.

Chapter 11

James gazed at Sophia from across the dining
table. The room was dim. The candlelight
warmed her features, darkened her complexion. He
admired the shadows. She looked tanned . . . as on
the island.

The table rustled with guests. He ignored the tiresome company and fixed his eyes firmly on the cold-
blooded viper. In truth, she looked more and more like
the old Sophia he remembered from the island. She
was attired in a white dress, so similar to the cotton
shift she used to wear in Jamaica. And there was no
garish bauble choking her throat. Instead, she revealed
her full and tempting bustline.

Slowly she lifted her eyes; firelight flickered in the
dark brown pools.

A sharp sensation welled inside James; it crippled
him. He thought about their heated encounter in the
boat, so intimate. He had pressed his pulsing body
against her. He had tasted the briny sweat at her throbbing throat. Still he burned for her. Still he trembled
with need. But he would not come to her. He would not
give her what she wanted—what they both wanted—
until she begged him for it.

Servants bustled inside the room with platters of freshly cooked fare.

The earl sniffed. "Hmm . . . what's on the menu tonight, Mondie?"

The chit beamed. "Pork loins glazed with applesauce and honey."

Honey.

James closed his eyes.

"Are you hungry, Black Hawk?"

He looked at her, blood and bones throbbing. She had made a mess, smeared the honey across her breasts, her belly. The glaze glistened in the firelight. It glowed like liquid gold over her sun-kissed skin.

James opened his eyes. He stiffened at the haunting memory. He still tasted the warm honey in his mouth, his belly. He had sucked and lapped it off her nipples . . . her breasts . . . her midriff. The witch had even smeared the sweet syrup on her quim . . . and he had feasted there with great pleasure, too.

He shuddered.

Sophia was watching him closely. She was flushed. She was thinking about the same erotic memory, he could tell . . . and it stirred the blood in his veins to know she was dreaming about him—about being ravished by him.

She stroked her throat. It was feather-light, the touch. She moved her fingers just under her ear before she skimmed the breastbone.

She wanted him to look at her bustline. She wanted him to stare and . . . what? Imagine the honey slathered across her voluptuous breasts? Long for her? Ache for her? Suffer?

James lifted his gaze to meet hers. He had already suffered. The witch had already scraped and sliced and drained the blood from his heart. But she wanted more, it seemed. Was that why she had dressed like her old self? To tease his senses with thoughts about the past?

She wanted to punish him. She had purred in the boat, voice thick—and sweet—like honey. She had gasped wanton cries of pleasure. But she had not begged him for more. She had dismissed him instead. And so he had dismissed her. And she had yet to forgive him for it. The loathing, the scorn burned bright in her eyes even in the dim room.

She wanted to give him pain.

Go ahead, sweetheart.

James dismissed her and cut into the meal. The party was merry. Even the harridan wasn't glaring at him anymore. For a few minutes, he enjoyed the food in peace.

He stilled.

A dark expression slowly crossed his features as a toe moved up his leg, caressed his shin.

He lifted his gaze to meet Sophia's.

She smiled.

Not with her lips . . . but with her eyes.

Wicked laughter danced in her eyes.

She cocked her hip to better lift her foot. He noted the subtle movement . . . he sensed it, too.

James firmed his lips. The toe stroked his inner thigh in a soft and sweeping gesture, making the blood pound in his cock.

He parted his legs even more.

Take what you want, sweetheart.

She stared at him—a hot and stabbing stare. She wanted to make him sweat. She wanted to seduce him, to make *him* beg.

Not in everlasting hell.

James twitched.

She pressed her slippered foot between his legs—and rubbed. In a slow and teasing manner she tickled his sensitive cods, making him gnash his teeth to quell the pulsing need growing in his belly.

He was pinned between prim and passionless matrons, stupid and spoiled chits. He was trapped—and the she-devil was tormenting him.

Let her.

He had endured far worse on the island. He had suffered even greater anguish then. Heart hard, he welcomed the pain she unleashed within him. He embraced the agony pouring through his veins.

Let her see.

Let her see he was unbreakable. Let her know he was able to bear far worse, that he would not submit to her—before she submitted to him!

James slipped his left hand beneath the white linen tablecloth and grabbed her ankle.

She stiffened.

He sensed her warm blood pulsing against his palm. One tug at her foot and she would tumble and fall. She would be exposed for the wild creature she was . . . but he wasn't after the woman's public ruination. He lusted after far more intimate revenge.

James stroked the bone at her ankle before he maneuvered her foot and pressed it against his cock. He watched her quiet. He watched her breastbone expand as she took in a big breath of air.

She attempted to pull back her foot, but he maintained a steady hold of her ankle as he resumed his meal with his right hand.

He thickened.

Sophia quieted even more. She stopped struggling.
That's it, sweetheart. Grow hungry for me.

He moved her heel against the tip of his swelling prick. She stared at her plate, the food untouched.

James was putting himself through hell. But he was putting her through hell, too. And he would suffer the torment. He would endure the pain if he made her sweat and ache and gasp for his touch, too.

Beg me.

"Is something the matter, Miss Dawson?" said Rosamond. "You haven't touched your food."

Sophia quickly picked up her fork. She stabbed at the roasted carrots on her plate and popped the vegetables into her mouth.

She chewed slowly. She still stared at her plate, but it was not the food she longed for in her mouth . . . it was he.

James sensed her arousal. It made him harder in return. He slipped a finger into her slim satin shoe, brushing the sensitive underside of her foot.

She shuddered. The quivers vibrated right down to her toes—and against his lengthening cock.

She fluttered her lashes. A dreamy look entered her eyes. She was chewing on her bottom lip now. If she wasn't vigilant, she might betray the lust ballooning in her belly with her wanton gestures.

A servant entered the room and approached the table with a silver tray. "A letter for Captain Hawkins."

James dropped Sophia's foot.

She gasped, stunned. Blood filled her cheeks. Quickly she glanced across the table.

Don't worry, sweetheart. I alone know what you were thinking . . . what you were feeling.

The servant rounded the table and served the tray.

James took the missive and shredded the seal. A snort from one of the haughty matrons cooled his fingers, and he opened the letter with more restraint. He scanned the epistle:

> *Come home.*
>
> —W

James glared at the tidy penmanship. Blood pounded in his head. He wanted to tear the blasted paper to pieces. He folded the succinct message and tucked it into his pocket instead.

He was stiff. Every bone and muscle throbbed inside him. He missed the warm touch of Sophia's foot against his cods. He missed the feel of her pulse pounding against his palm.

Curse William! James was so close to victory, so close to getting Sophia back into his bed—where she truly belonged. If he headed home now he would lose the passion he had stirred within her.

But William wouldn't pen such a curt note unless it was a matter of dire business—pirate business. It was too dangerous to expound on the matter in ink, for the letter might fall into the wrong hands. The Hawkins brothers always handled "family affairs" in person.

James beat back the dark desire growing inside him, tamped it into submission. There was only one thing to do.

He looked at Sophia.

This isn't over, sweetheart.

With every eye watching him, James returned to the meal. He would head home tonight—after supper. If he got up from the table now, he would create a spectacular stir . . . although the image of fainting matrons was an agreeable thought.

"I trust all is well, Captain?"

The nosy chit.

He responded to the vicious fire-eater coolly. "I'm afraid there is a matter of business that requires my attention, Lady Rosamond. I must return home after supper."

"Oh." The chit feigned a pout. "We are sorry to see you go, Captain."

She lied with such fierce spite; every fool in the room could tell she wasn't the least bit sorry . . . except for her brother.

"Yes, truly sorry," said the earl. He sounded genuinely aggrieved. "I've yet to extend my full hospitality."

"You've been most gracious, my lord," said James.

"Still, I can't help—I know! You must accompany us to the opera on Wednesday. My sister and I are escorting Miss Dawson to the last production of the season. Will you attend?"

Rosamond made a garish noise; she mewled as if a mouse were gnawing on her toe. "And you are welcome to come, Anastasia and Imogen."

"Yes, we will all go," said the earl. "We'll have a wonderful time."

"Oh, drat!" Anastasia frowned. "I can't attend. I'm leaving for the country."

Rosamond glanced at the other young woman with a pleading look in her eyes. "And you Imogen?"

"Thank you," the girl said quietly. "I have no other plans. I'd be honored to attend the opera."

Rosamond sighed. James ignored the malicious brat. He glanced at Sophia instead.

The witch was still blushing.

Good.

I wish you nothing but pain until we meet again, sweetheart.

"I would be delighted to attend the opera, too," said James.

"William!"

James kicked the door closed with the heel of his boot. It was shadowy inside the town house. A few oil lamps still burned throughout the space, beacons to guide the fledglings throughout the apartments, for Edmund and Quincy often staggered home in the wee hours of the morning.

James snatched one of the glowing glass orbs as he moved through the dark passageway, footfalls pounding.

He reached the study and entered the room. He slammed the door closed. It was stifling inside the small space. He set the lamp aside and rent the noose from his neck.

James tossed the scrap of fabric into the fireplace. There was no flame burning in the coal-fueled hearth; however, it pleased him to see the wretched cravat where it belonged—in hell.

There was a table with bottles beside the bookcase. Lamplight bounced off the shiny crystal decanters.

James grabbed the first bottle in reach. He dropped the stopper on the table. The sharp noise resounded in the quiet room. He filled a glass with liquor.

At the sound of the soft whistle of iron hinges, James turned around and confronted his brother. "I'm home."

"I heard."

William stepped inside the room and shut the door. He was dressed in trousers, feet and torso bare. He had a dark brow, heavy with sleep. And a peeved expression crossed his tired features, making him look like a surly brigand.

"How was the house party?" William yawned. "Or will I read all about it in the gossip papers?"

James bristled. Even his brother thought him a barbarian, incapable of keeping his temper and composure, wont to cause scandal wherever he went.

James dropped his head back and guzzled the fiery spirits, slaying the turmoil, the chill in his belly. "Why did you summon me home?"

William rubbed his eyes. "Are we going to do this now?"

"Why not?"

William looked at the timepiece on the mantle. "It's almost four o'clock in the morning."

James set the decanter aside and wiped his mouth. "I can't sleep."

He was restless. As soon as he had departed the earl's home, the blood in his veins had roiled in protest. Even now the stiffness in his joints was acute. He wanted Sophia. He wanted to be close to her. He had walked away from her in the middle of a heated battle of the senses. He had severed their intimate connection before either of them had had the satisfaction of a thorough bedding.

And now he was in pain, the separation from Sophia bleeding him. He had to wait two more days to see her again.

Wednesday.

At the opera.

Would she be engaged by then?

James reached for the spirits again. He tamped the nausea in his belly with another hearty swig.

What did it matter if she was affianced? He would still have his revenge. He would still have the woman in his bed. He would still hear her admit she needed him, she *craved* him. He would still have her disengage with the earl and come to him . . . before he walked away from her.

William's expression soured even more. "*You* can't sleep, so to hell with the rest of us?"

"Something like that."

James stared at the painting on the wall: a sea witch. Quincy had brought the infernal artwork home one night. It was his favorite piece. But James loathed it.

William approached the desk and cocked his hip against it. "Am I to assume the picnic didn't go so well?"

He turned away from the garish artwork. "Thanks to your interruption. Now what the devil is wrong?"

"What's wrong?" William folded his arms across his chest. "Our lives are in danger, that's what's wrong. And while you've been following the stirrings of your cock, we've been hunting the impostors pirating in our names."

James slammed the bottle against the table. "I'm here! So drop the righteous horseshit and tell me what's the matter!"

The door opened.

"Waz all the shouting about?"

Quincy entered the room, followed by Edmund's long figure. The two bucks looked bedraggled. Words slurred. Shirts rumpled. Hair mussed.

William frowned. "Are you two *just* getting in?"

The fledglings settled into two winged chairs positioned beside the fireplace. Edmund closed his eyes, disinterested in the goings-on around him. Quincy grinned, however.

"You told us to make sure it looked like we were having a good time," said the pup. He hiccupped. "So we did."

Aye, they'd had a good time. James had only to glance at them to see they were foxed. He ignored the rubbish about it "looking" like they'd had a good time. He assumed it was besotted drivel. He focused instead on the "good time" and turned to William with pointed regard.

"Aren't you going to preach to *them* about responsibility?"

"They were working," returned William.

"You mean whoring?" said James.

"I mean working." William set his eyes on Quincy again. "Well?"

Quincy flicked his fingers for dramatic emphasis. "We spread the news."

"Word should reach them soon," said Edmund, dozing.

There was a creeping chill that gripped James's bones. He sensed he was back at the house party. Once again he was barred from the conversation, barred from entry. Foxed and drowsy, the men still had a better grip on the conversation than he had—and he was sober and alert with all his faculties in place.

James curled his fingers into his palms. "I'm going to shoot each of you if you don't tell me what the hell is going on."

"We've set a trap for the impostors," said William.

James gathered his brow. "What sort of trap?"

William moved away from the desk and approached

the liquor table. He poured himself a small amount of spirits.

"Here." Quincy stretched out his hand. "Pass the rest o' the bottle to me."

William snorted. "You've had enough."

Edmund was breathing deeply, sound asleep.

William looked at James again. "We tried hunting the charlatans, but they're elusive. We figured we'd let them come to us instead."

Quincy chimed in with, "Eddie and I spread the word about our precious 'cargo' in port tonight."

"Is that why you're piss drunk?" demanded James.

The kid shrugged. "It's all Will's fault. He told us to make it look like we were having a gay ol' time before we let word slip about our valuable cargo. Less suspicious, you know?"

William clarified, "The impostors won't think it a trap then."

James glared at the lieutenant. "What cargo?"

But it was Quincy who blurted, "Diamonds."

"Blimey!" James blustered, "We're going to have *every* ship—pirate or not—hunting us now!"

Edmund started at the bellowed remark, blinked, then dropped back against the chair and closed his eyes.

"Quincy's teasing," William said in a calm manner.

James glared at the pup.

Quincy looked sheepish. "You'd think bedding a wench like Sophia would put you in a better mood."

William downed the spirits. "I don't think he bedded Sophia."

The pup's eyes rounded. "Oh, that'd put me in a foul temper, too."

"Fuck off," said James. "All of you."

William set the empty glass aside and returned to

the matter at hand. "We spread word we were hauling two hundred tons of sperm oil across the Atlantic. The booty will fetch a high price in America. It's sure to entice the impostors out of hiding."

"Aye." Another hiccup. "Eddie and I were 'foxed' and let the word leak."

"You are foxed," James growled, "and you're repeating yourself."

The kid looked confused. "Am I?"

"We're to set sail in two nights," informed William. Wednesday night.

James rubbed the back of his neck, so stiff. The trap coincided with the opera—and his revenge. But he refused to give up on Sophia. He refused to let the witch think she had chased him off with her wily ways, that she had won their battle of wills. He would attend the opera and still return in time to set sail with his brothers and crush the impostors.

"There's a lot of work to be done over the next two days," said William. "We need to prepare the ship and crew."

The ship and crew were already prepared, thought James. The men might have retired from piracy, but the fight in their blood was still strong. And the *Bonny Meg* was always equipped for a brutal sea battle, her guns in ideal condition. However, there were other provisions to amass, like food and gunpowder, more canvas, and medical supplies. Two days was plenty of time to gather the needed materials.

James sensed the spasms in his neck, the twisting muscles. His brethren had done everything without him. They had prepared a trap and set it in motion without advice or leadership from him. They had never done that before.

James fisted his palms as if to keep the authority, the control from slipping between his fingers. "Fine. We weigh anchor in two nights."

Quincy rambled, "And the *Bonny Meg* needs to be in good shape for our next venture, too."

"What venture?" snapped James.

The inebriated Quincy glanced at William with only one eye open. "You still haven't told him?"

James cut the lieutenant a sharp glance, too. "Told me what?"

William looked from one brother to the next, the room quiet except for Edmund's sound and steady breathing.

"Let's talk about it some other time, James. Get some sleep. We have a lot to do before we set sail."

The lieutenant was right. James was fagged, the spirits he had swallowed earlier taking hold of his senses and making him drowsy. Whatever shipping venture his brother had planned, let him deal with it. He always did.

William headed for the door. "I'll fetch Sophia and return her to your room."

Yes, Sophia.

James still had that island witch to seduce, and he needed all his faculties intact to bring about her downfall.

Chapter 12

⌒⌒⌒∽◯◯∽⌒⌒⌒

Sophia searched the crowd. The opera was scheduled to begin in a quarter of an hour, so the theater
was brimming with patrons. It was hard to see over so
many heads.

Where are you?

She pinched her eyes closed. A longing stemmed
from her toes. The appendages twitched at the memory
of his touch, his heat.

She huffed. Curse the blackguard! He possessed her
senses even now. He chained her thoughts, even her
will. For two days she had suffered in silence. For two
days she had languished without a touch or a word
from him. Lifeless. Even the earl had cooled his pursuit of her. The black devil had pressed him to be more
affectionate. Jealousy had goaded him to be more pos-
sessive. But as soon as the pirate lord had deserted the
country house, the earl had returned to the aloof yet
amiable gentleman that he was—sans proposal.

Sophia opened her eyes. She lifted them to the
vaulted ceiling. Stone columns and arched doorways
supported the grand structure. She was dizzy. She
lowered her gaze to the wide steps, carpeted in rich
red fabric. She placed her hand on the wood finial for

support. Traffic ascended the mighty staircase. The upper levels housed the private boxes. There was so much noise, so much color and movement.

Once more she searched the throng of spectators. She stepped onto the red carpet, seeking height—and the proverbial black locks that heralded *him*.

One look and she would be satisfied. She would ignore him the rest of the evening then . . . but the brigand had a way about him that disrupted her senses. Would a single look be enough to quiet her restless jitters?

"My dear, did you hear?"

Sophia grabbed the glossy banister, startled. "Hear what, Lady Lucas?"

The matron dabbed her brow with a kerchief. "It's most shocking!"

Sophia had parted from the party, looking for breath and quiet . . . and him. She wasn't privy to the goings-on that had transpired in her absence. But she had to wonder: What had happened in the past two minutes that was so shocking?

She eyed the woman closely. "What's wrong, Lady Lucas?"

"Well—"

"It's horrifying, Miss Dawson!"

Sophia glanced at Lady Rosamond, skirting toward her. The girl's cheeks boasted rich pigment, even her lips looked bright and plump with blood. And her eyes! Her eyes glowed and sparkled and burned with energy.

"It's all my fault." The earl was more ashen. He followed his sister like a sentry. "It's my duty to protect you, Mondie."

Sophia quickly descended a step. "What's happened? Are you hurt?"

Rosamond gasped for breath. "I've been corrupted!"

"Nonsense, Mondie!" cried the earl.

"I was very *nearly* corrupted . . . and by an acquaintance I trusted, Miss Dawson."

Lady Lucas was flushed, too.

Sophia's head throbbed. She whispered, "Who?"

"There she is!" Rosamond squeaked. "What is she doing here?"

Sophia whirled around. The horde still moved and laughed and chatted. However, the whispers started, too. The pointed looks.

Sophia followed the bloody trail of gossiping voices and disdainful expressions to the wounded creature in the center of the room.

Imogen.

"You invited her to the opera, Mondie," said the earl.

"Two days ago! I didn't know who she truly was then."

Sophia's heart cramped. "And who is she?"

"That's what I was trying to tell you, my dear." Lady Lucas whispered, "Miss Rayne is a fallen woman."

It was a hammer to the heart, the words. So hard and biting. Sophia watched the lone figure fidget. She listened to the ghastly murmurs, so much louder in her own head. They were like savage blows, the voices and looks. Her bones ached under the pressure of the beating. She wasn't even the unfortunate victim . . . but she sensed it. She sensed every brutal bash.

Sophia trembled. "Are you sure she's a fallen woman?"

"Oh yes," said Lady Lucas.

"It's all over Town." Rosamond hissed, "She lost her virtue to a Jew."

"Mondie!"

The chit composed her features, brimming with vim. "It's what I heard."

"You should not speak of such things," Maximilian chastised. "It's indelicate."

"Yes, very indelicate." Lady Lucas cupped the girl's hand. "Come, my dear. Let me take you away from such unsavory company."

The chit made a noise of protest as she was ushered up the steps by the matron. Sophia and the earl remained behind.

Sophia was in a dream. Nay, a nightmare. She stood vulnerable, naked. She gazed at herself in the mirror.

It was a wretched sight.

She whispered weakly, "How do you know she's a fallen woman?"

"I understand it happened this morning. Miss Rayne was spied in a compromising situation."

"And you believe the gossip?"

"I'm afraid I must, Miss Dawson. I must guard my sister's well-being."

So even the *hint* of scandal was enough to devastate a woman's position in the world?

Sophia shuddered.

"How could I have been so careless?" said the earl. "I never suspected Miss Rayne a deviant."

Sophia swallowed the sob in her throat. "It's not Miss Rayne's fault."

It was cruel. So very cruel. Imogen was in love. She wanted to pursue an honorable courtship. But her parents—society at large—forbade it, forcing her into an illicit affair.

Or was it an illicit affair? Imogen had insisted her beau was a respectable gentleman. Had she been deceived? Or was it true? Was he a respectable gentleman? Had the couple shared an innocent kiss? Was that the "compromising situation" everyone was talking about? And was it enough to ruin her forever?

"You're right, Miss Dawson. It's not Miss Rayne's fault. She is sweet and impressionable. I blame the Jew who tempted her into the affair. *He* led her astray."

Sophia's heart was heavy. The pressure squeezed her breast, taking her breath away. The gossip had spread so quickly. It had surprised even Imogen, it seemed. The woman had come to the opera with nary a thought about the spiteful words circling Town about her. Where was her chaperone? Had she vanished in a panic when the whispers had started?

The snipes and glares bounced off Imogen. Sophia flinched with each cutting remark and harsh eye that passed through the room. Jeers filled her head.

"A pity such a charming young lady is now ruined and not fit for good society," commiserated Maximilian.

A great pity.

Sophia trembled. What would happen to the girl now? What would society do with a "charming young lady" not fit for respectable company? Banish her to the country? Ship her to the continent?

Sophia gnashed her teeth. She wanted to reach out to the spooked young woman. But she pressed her fists at her sides instead. If she reached out to Imogen, she, too, would be sucked into the black vortex that was ignominy. And as distasteful as it was to admit the truth, Sophia wasn't prepared to suffer Imogen's fate—not again.

Imogen's wide eyes filled with tears. She was rooted to the spot. So was Sophia. It was easy to lose one's sense of balance, even poise in such a situation. Sophia remembered the garish laughter, the disgusting hoots and gestures on the island. She remembered feeling overwhelmed. Powerless. Desperate.

Their eyes met.

Help me, Sophia!

Sophia listened to the cries in her head . . . but she did not budge from the sturdy stone steps. The hard rock maintained her weight, her composure. It sheltered her from the wild and bloody storm that swirled around Imogen.

Sophia gasped for breath. Imogen was alone. Hurting. She was a woman of grace and compassion. She filled an awkward void in a conversation. She offered an arm in support or a smile in encouragement.

But no one offered her such assistance.

"Scandalous!"

"Barbarous!"

"Shameful!"

The ruthless mob emitted such vulgar judgment, Sophia's head smarted. She yearned for Imogen's well-being. She—

She wanted to shout with joy.

He cut through the rabble with quick, hard strides. He paused for no one. He allowed no one to step aside. Jump or be trampled. And he offered no apology if he treaded across a hem or a booted toe.

He was big and barbarous as charged. And the

room pulsed with energy as soon as he entered it. Sophia pulsed with energy as soon as he entered it, too.

James took Imogen by the hand.

She collapsed against him.

Sophia wanted to collapse, too. The tautness in her muscles eased as soon as he took charge of the girl and sheltered her.

The mob swarmed them.

Sophia twisted her throat, searching. But the couple had vanished. A gong resounded. Last call. The opera was about to begin.

"Come, Miss Dawson." The earl offered an arm. "Let us join the other ladies."

Sophia placed her clammy palm on the cuff of the earl's well-tailored coat. She mounted the steps, bemused. Her heart swelled. The pirate lord had saved Imogen. He had whisked her away from all the dreadful reproach.

Sophia's heart knocked. It rattled and raged against her breastbone. Fire welled in her belly, her bust. A dangerous fire . . . for him.

"I respect Captain Hawkins." Maximilian placed his fingers over her hand. "I would have escorted poor Miss Rayne from the theater myself if it wasn't for my sister. I must protect Mondie's reputation. I cannot associate with a woman of ill repute. You understand, don't you, Miss Dawson?"

"Yes, my lord."

She understood very well indeed. She understood she had to guard her scandalous past as the state guarded the crown jewels—or she would face Imogen's dreadful fate.

The earl steered her through the dark passageways: a labyrinth of tunnels and lush curtains protecting the lofty spectators within.

"Here we are," he said. "After you, Miss Dawson."

Sophia entered the private box. She was still in a daze, weak. She had a wicked headache. The disgust chained in her belly roiled. She wanted to let it out. She tamped the nausea instead. She had to maintain her composure. She had to keep her features cool.

"What happened?" demanded Rosamond. "Tell me!"

"Sit down, Mondie," ordered Maximilian. "Can't you see Miss Dawson is ill with grief?"

"Such a pity," said Lady Lucas. "A tragedy, really . . . Here, my dear. For the performance."

Sophia stared at the delicate opera glasses. She took them from the matron before she settled into the plush seat next to Lady Rosamond. So weak. Sophia was so weak. Restless, too.

"Where's Imogen?" the chit wondered. "Was she chased out of the theater?"

"Mondie!" The earl tsked. "I'm disappointed in you."

The girl pouted. "Why?"

"You have an unhealthy fascination with salacious tittle-tattle."

"Miss Rayne was my friend," she said defiantly. "What's become of her? I want to know!"

"I'm afraid nothing will ever become of her now," returned Lady Lucas in an authoritative manner.

Sophia's heart ached at the words. So true. So dreadfully true. She clutched the opera lenses in her hand, knuckles white.

The earl took the empty seat beside the matron. "Captain Hawkins escorted Miss Rayne out of the theater."

Rosamond gasped. "He did?"

"Yes," said Maximilian succinctly. "And we'll hear no more about the matter."

"But where is the captain?"

"I don't think he'll be joining us this evening, Mondie."

"But—"

"Mondie," the man said with warning.

The girl huffed. She glanced at Sophia and whispered, "What else happened, Miss Dawson?"

"Mondie!" from the earl.

"Ohh."

The girl sulked.

Applause resounded as the limelight dimmed and the main stage curtain parted. Sophia dismissed the lavish production from her mind. The dark theater offered her an opportunity to rest her stiff features, to let loose the anguish brimming inside her.

A maelstrom of feeling ravaged her breast. She gasped for breath to quell the misery filling her veins . . . the self-loathing.

She had forsaken a good woman, a friend. She had treated her with the same disdain and rejection others had once treated her with on the island.

Sophia's belly ached. She placed her hand over the stirring movements to stifle the nausea.

So cruel. Society was so cruel. But Sophia didn't want to change society. She just wanted to be a part of it. She *yearned* to be a part of it. It was so ignoble to be an outcast, to endure shame and aloneness. She wouldn't be a pariah anymore. It would devastate her.

The air was thick. She was going to be sick. She set aside the opera lenses and quietly excused herself from the private box.

The matron quickly followed her into the passage-way. "Are you all right, my dear?"

"Yes, I'm fine." Sophia circled a small spot. "I need fresh air, is all. Might I have a private moment?"

The matron eyed her warily. "Call if you need me."

"I will."

The older woman reluctantly returned to the private box. The murmurs started right away. Sophia listened to the hushed inquires:

"Is she all right, Lady Lucas?" from Rosamond.

"The poor dear is distressed," returned the matron.

"Yes, Miss Rayne's disgrace is distressing to us all," said the earl.

Sophia twisted her fingers together. She kneaded her palm with the pad of her thumb, pressing against the muscles, the veins.

She strutted away from the private box. She moved against the shadows in the passageway, searching for light.

There was an alcove. She spotted the lamp inside. She slipped between the walls. There was a bench and she settled against the cushioned pillows.

She breathed deep and hard to soothe the thrum-ming pulses that afflicted her senses. The islanders' jeers and lewd comments still resounded in her head. She closed her eyes and pressed her fingers against her head to quiet the vulgar tongues, the crude laughter.

"You really are like one of them."

She gasped. Something ugly, something vile churned in her belly at the cutting words. Slowly she opened her eyes and confronted the brigand's tower-ing figure. She flinched under the man's scorching glare.

"How is Imogen?" she whispered.

He rumbled, "Do you care?"

"Damn you, Black Hawk." She stood and confronted him. "You don't understand!"

He was a man. If he bedded a hundred women, *still* society would invite him to parties and balls. But she was a woman. She was chained. And she refused to discard the manacles that ensnared her. She wouldn't let them laugh and sneer at her again—as they had laughed and sneered at Imogen.

"I understand, sweetheart."

He approached her. She shuddered as he placed the pad of his thumb against her warm cheek. The tender strokes soothed her wild heartbeat like no other touch or word or balm.

"I understand you once had a heart . . . but now you're a cold bitch like the rest of them."

She slapped him.

His head veered to one side.

Slowly he looked at her again. "A little harder, sweetheart. You know I like it rough."

She slapped him again. Hard. Her fingers pulsed with pain.

The edge of his teeth cut across the inside of his cheek, drawing blood. He wiped the red drops from his mouth. "Was it worth it?"

She was shaking, sweating. The fire in her belly bounced and burned with renewed energy, the fleeting tranquillity quashed by his vicious taunt. "Striking you?"

He snorted softly. "You don't hurt me, Sophia." There was an icy sparkle in his deep blue eyes. "Not anymore."

She fisted her palms. She ached for his tender touch again. But he was a black-hearted devil. He stirred pain in her breast; he always would.

"Leaving the island?" he said coldly. "Was it worth it?"

And leaving me? Was it worth it?

She heard the words in her head.

He glowered at her. "Are you happy here? With *them*?"

"Yes," she hissed, the word quivering.

He offered her a dark look. It crushed her soul. "I have a ship to catch."

Slowly he walked away from her.

Sophia waited for the man's robust figure to round the corner before she crumpled against the bench seat, weak and alone.

Chapter 13

She was beautiful. Her wide belly rested in the still waters. Moonlight pierced her white sails, unfurled and heaving.

James longed to set foot on the sturdy deck. He headed for the three-masted schooner like a lover in need, wending through the bustling port. He ignored the rabble and thick movement of bodies. He dismissed the dockside wenches and sidestepped the grimy rats.

He fixed his eyes firmly on her: the *Bonny Meg*, mistress of the sea. She was everything right in the world. She was home.

Unlike Sophia.

He hardened. The spectacle at the opera house circled in his head. He listened to the derisive laughter and haughty snorts. He envisioned the poor girl trapped between so many cruel smirks, weak and defenseless.

It burned in his breast, the venomous treatment. It disgusted him, the abuse. But it dismayed him even more to know *she* was like one of the ruthless members of the peerage. She had warned him she had changed. He had not believed she had changed so much.

James crossed the pier and climbed the scaffolding.

He boarded the vessel. Boots hit wood. He was filled with renewed energy. There was harmony in his soul once more. Every muscle and bone shuddered with delight.

"Ahoy, Captain!"

He moved with the ship. In sync. In balance. He crossed the deck, saluted the tars in return. He approached the poop and mounted it. There the sea stretched before him. There the black and endless waves welcomed him.

Water lapped against the hull. It slapped and caressed the ship's belly. And James sensed every playful movement. He heard it, too. That seductive call, a siren's song.

He closed his eyes and breathed deep. He inhaled the rich and briny air. It was brimming with life, the gusting sea breeze. It filled his empty lungs and chased away the dark and stirring sentiments choking him.

"You're late."

William ascended the poop, too.

"I know." James stripped the noose, the coat from his body. "I was at the opera."

He frowned. "What were you doing at the opera?"

"Watching a tragedy."

William humphed. "We have to wait in queue."

"How long?"

"An hour maybe."

"Fine," returned James.

"Do you want to change?"

"Are you trying to get rid of me?"

The very idea sounded absurd. He was the captain. He commanded the vessel. She sailed under his word, bared her guns at his order. The *Bonny Meg* was more than a home, she was a part of him.

"You look like you're dressed for a funeral in that black suit," said William. "It makes the crew uneasy."

James snorted. "I'll be back in an hour then."

"Aye, Captain."

James swaggered off the poop and headed below-decks. He yanked the shirt up over his head, eager to be rid of the confining apparel.

"Easy there, Captain." Quincy strolled through the corridor, chuckling. "Anxious to get your breeches doused?"

James paused and glared after the kid. Was Quincy drunk? He'd clock the pup's head against the mast if he was. He knew damn well he wasn't supposed to tip the bottle before a mission.

James snarled and opened the cabin door. He stepped inside the refuge and tossed the disgusting garments aside before he reached for the buttons of his trousers.

He paused at the sound of tsking.

"Willy was right; you are in need of a good bedding."

James glanced up. Moonlight entered the cabin through the small window. There was enough light to make out the shadows in the room . . . and the sultry figure resting on the bed.

He sighed. "Cora."

The buxom wench slipped off the covers and approached him, hips swinging. She had painted eyes, so dark and seductive. Red lips, too. Even in the dimness he eyed the woman's plump and rosy mouth. The color matched the bright, scarlet locks that coiled across her ample breasts, thrust high in a tight, low-cut corset.

"You don't sound too happy to see me, Capt'n."

No, he wasn't. Not when the blood in his veins still screamed for an island witch. Even now the mark on his cheek pulsed with the imprint from her hand. His whole body pulsed, in truth.

Curse William! He had orchestrated the whole blasted affair, thinking a good fuck would put the captain's head to right . . . maybe it would.

"The ship is about to set sail, Cora."

"A quick tumble, then?" She pressed her big breasts against his belly and whispered hotly, "I've missed you."

He scoffed. "You've missed my money."

She smiled. "That, too."

She was honest. That's what James liked about her. She didn't pretend to be a lady. She didn't act with airs. She wanted a gold coin from him. That was all. She didn't want to depend on him or form a family with him. She offered no false expressions of love. She was cold. He liked that about her, too.

She cupped his cock. "I see you've missed me, too."

He gritted, "Easy, woman."

She winked. "Aren't I always?"

Slowly she dropped to her knees. James closed his eyes. He let the heat in his bones and muscles cool and settle as the woman deftly fingered the buttons of his trousers. She was strong. She could take a rough bedding. A good thing, too, for he needed one right now.

The cabin door opened.

James lifted his eyes, muscles seizing.

Sophia took one look at the prostrated wench—and snapped.

The knife glistened in the moonlight. Sophia had grabbed it from the sheath between her breasts so fast, he had nary a second to reach for the blade before it sliced at the mistress screaming at his feet—and his cods.

James roared, "Blimey!"

Sophia had almost nicked him.

Cora jumped on the bed, shrieking.

Sophia lunged after the other woman again.

James grabbed Sophia's wrist, her midriff. "Drop the knife!"

A hysterical Cora scrambled from the bed and dashed from the cabin.

Sophia was wild. She thrashed and slammed her body against James, disrupting his balance and sending him crashing into the wall. He then hit the ground with her in tow. He winced as he smashed his hip against the flooring.

"Damn you, woman!"

James wrestled with her. He pressed her against the planking and wedged his knee between her kicking legs. He then grabbed her wrist, squeezing.

She hissed.

The knife popped from her hand.

He reached for it before she scooped it back up again, and hurled it somewhere across the room.

"Hold still!" he barked.

He pinned her against the flooring. He clasped both her wrists, the threads of her reticule curled around his fingers, and stretched them high above her head before he pressed the rest of his weight against her belly.

She gasped for breath.

"Cease, Sophia!"

She stilled.

He was breathing hard, his hip throbbing. As soon as she quieted, he eased his belly away from hers; he offered her room to breathe.

"What the hell is the matter with you?" he growled.

She was panting. There was a feral look in her eyes. She had a jealous streak, even a violent one. But he had never seen the woman like this before.

"You're a bastard," she charged between heated breaths.

"And you're mad, sweetheart."

The heat in his bones and muscles returned. The pulsing pressure in his limbs surged. He was wrapped between her skirts, her legs. Trapped. It felt so bloody good.

He looked into her eyes, heart pounding. Such bewitching eyes. Even in the shadows, she snared his senses with that wicked look. The fire that burned in the dark brown pools scorched him, filled him with deep desire.

"What do you want from me?" she said, lips flushed.

He pressed his brow against hers, wet and hot. "*You* came looking for me, remember?"

"Damn you, James! What do you want? One last fuck good-bye? Take it! Take me! And then get the hell out of my life. I don't want to see you ever again!"

He gnashed his teeth at the brutal assault. She had used his name. She had said it after seven bloody years—only to dismiss him again, to cast him aside like soiled laundry.

James let go of her wrists and lifted to his feet. He fastened his trousers. Blood filled his head, making him dizzy; his hip still ached. "Get out."

She struggled to her feet as well. "Not before we finish this."

"I said get out!"

"No!"

He pressed his nose against hers. "This ship is about to set sail."

"Not for another hour. I heard William."

She was still wearing the same dress she had sported at the opera. It was a deep umber brown with a sweeping décolletage trimmed with lace. Another garish jewel marred her seamless bustline, an amber stone sheathed in gold. So fake. She looked ridiculous. He spotted her thick hair, the dark locks mussed after their heated roll across the floor. That was Sophia. Free. Wild. He ached for that spirited woman. He cursed her, too.

He still gasped for breath. "You were spying on me?"

"Eavesdropping."

"What's the difference?"

"I'm not going to report the conversation . . . unless you stay away from me."

"You witch." He chuckled darkly. "Is that why you're here? To make more threats? I thought you didn't flout convention anymore. What would the harridan think to know you were standing here?"

She was winded, too. "I'll see you hang, Black Hawk."

His nostrils flared. He was Black Hawk again, was he? "Not before I see you disgraced, sweetheart."

She fisted her palms. The veins that stretched from her fingers to her throat throbbed. "You're determined to ruin me anyway."

"The hell I am."

"That's what you wanted to do at the opera, isn't it?"

"Ruin *you*?"

"Torture me!"

He grabbed her by the arms and pushed her against the wall. "You torture yourself, sweetheart."

"I hate you."

The muscles in his cheek twitched. "I know."

She pounded against his chest. "Leave me alone!"

"The way you left Imogen alone?"

She stilled, weakened. She drew in a deep breath of air. He heard it pass through her nose. "I couldn't help her."

"Liar!"

She flinched. "What could I do?"

"You and the harridan, that idiot and his sister could have saved her."

"How?"

"You could have gathered around her. The four of you could have stood beside her and *killed* the rumors."

Fat tears filled her eyes. "It was impossible. She was ruined."

"Horseshit! If *respectable* members of society band together, the gossip ends. If *noble* lords and ladies associate with the girl, then others will associate with her, too."

"No."

"Yes! This is my world, Sophia. I know rumors can be squelched if enough people refuse to listen to them."

"I didn't know."

"No. *No!*" He let her go and walked away from her, his temples throbbing. "You didn't *want* to help her."

"She's my friend."

"Poor Imogen," he sneered. "Cursed with friends like you and your bloody fiancé."

"He's not my fiancé—yet."

She still wanted the saphead? Of course she did. She wanted him *because* he was a saphead. He was too daft to see past her frilly wardrobe and fancy jewels. The woman wanted to be a countess. And she needed a foolish lord to wed her.

"I want you to stay away from me, Black Hawk."

"Why? Do I upset you? Do I make you look at yourself; see yourself for who you really are? Does it disgust you?"

"*You* disgust me!"

He crossed the cabin again. He cupped her cheeks. "You and I are the same, sweetheart."

The woman's eyes widened.

It's true. You and I are one.

She clasped his wrists and tugged at them. She stepped away from him. "Will you promise to keep away from me?"

"No." He combed his fingers through his hair, disheveled. He pulled the leather cord away, let the locks fall free. "I've already vowed not to betray our past. If you want something more from me, you can take out the ivory and jade players and as soon as I return to shore. Now get off my ship."

She stared at him. He sensed her eyes drop and caress his naked belly, his ribs before she slowly lifted them again. "I hope you drown."

She crouched. She searched the shadows for her knife, he presumed.

James was hot and hard. The hairs on his arms, his chest stirred. She had stabbed him, cut him with her eyes. But she had ravished him, too. Heat pumped through his veins at her sultry admiration.

"I hope lightning strikes the rig," she griped.

She brandished her plump arse as she groped in the darkness. He stiffened even more. "There's no storm."

"A storm is coming."

"And how would you know that? Did you cast a spell, witch?"

She snorted. "Are you daft? Can't you feel the rough waves?"

"What rough waves?"

But the ship *was* shifting with more vim. James crossed the room and looked out the scuttle—the port lights flickered in the distance. "Shit."

She had found the knife. She dusted the luminous blade, winking in the moonlight, before she slipped it back into the sheath between her breasts. "What's the matter?"

"We're at sea."

She balked. "No."

She skirted across the cabin, shoved him aside and peered out the glass. "Damn you, Black Hawk!"

He growled, "I told you to get off the ship."

"But William said—"

"I know what William said." He swiped the shirt off the floor. "Wait here."

James slipped the white linen over his head and stalked the corridor. He ascended the steps. Once topside, he searched the deck for his brother.

"Lieutenant!"

A dark figure stirred. "Aye, Captain."

James eyed the shadow and headed for the helm. He dismissed the quartermaster. William took control of the vessel then.

"What the hell are we doing at sea, Lieutenant?"

William maneuvered the wheel. "Are you *still* in a foul mood? I told Cora to bed you well."

James fisted his palms. "I don't need you to tell me who to fuck . . . now answer me!"

William shrugged. "I gave the order to weigh anchor."

"*You* gave the order?"

"I've given orders before. I'm the lieutenant, remember?"

"*You* can give orders when I'm dead."

"Or incapacitated." William looked at him with reproach. "You've been distracted lately. Cora was supposed to help you focus again, but once she'd left the ship there was no reason to delay our departure. I gave the order to set sail."

"There was no queue?"

"I wanted to give you some time with the wench." He sighed. "Why didn't you spend the whole hour with her?"

"She's still belowdecks."

"The devil she is; I saw her skirt off."

"Not Cora."

"Then who?"

James hissed, "Sophia."

William also lowered his voice. "What is she doing here?"

"Never mind," he growled. "Head back for port."

"No."

James bristled. "What?"

"We're on a mission, Captain. If we come and go from port all night, the impostors will think something is amiss and *won't* follow us."

"She can't stay here!"

"You should have thought of that before you sneaked her onboard."

The muscle in his cheek twitched. "*She* sneaked onboard."

"Then keep her quiet and locked in your cabin."

James imagined Sophia locked in his cabin, naked in his bed. He imagined the ship undulating as he rocked between her thighs in harmony.

"Are you crazy?" James charged.

"Me? You have your mistress stored aboard ship. You're the one who's crazy."

"She is not my mistress."

"Then what is she?"

She was a witch. She haunted him. She tortured him. She made his life even more miserable than it already was, for the memory of their past, and heated, affair was always at the forefront of his mind.

"Don't tell the crew the woman's here. The men will think it bad luck." William was firm: "But we're not turning back."

"I am the captain."

"You're not acting like one."

James saw red. "I can put you in the brig for that insubordination."

"Go ahead. Put me in chains. Return to port. What will the crew think? The impostors?"

"I don't give a damn what anybody thinks!"

"That's your problem; that's always been your problem. A little conciliation can make your life a lot easier, James."

He hardened. "What did you call me?"

"I mean Captain. Damn it, we have a mission—"

"I know! But she's a woman. It's too dangerous for her to be here."

"She's familiar with a gun battle at sea. She once sailed aboard her father's pirate ship, remember? She'll be fine."

Blood pounded in James's skull. He wanted to crush something . . . like his brother's head.

James grabbed the wheel to prevent William from keeping control. "If you ever give an order without my approval again, I'll drop you into the brig with the rats and let you rot. Is that clear?"

"Aye, Captain," he said stiffly.

Chapter 14

Sophia sat on the bed.

Two days at sea. Two miserable days at sea. She wasn't nauseous from the swelling waters, but sick at heart. What was she going to do? How was she going to make things right back in England?

She pressed her legs against her breasts, set her chin on her knees. She was trapped aboard the *Bonny Meg*, secured in the captain's cabin. How long would the mission last? A fortnight? A month?

She should never have followed the black devil back to his ship. Curse him for riling her senses so! She wouldn't be in this mess then.

She sighed. Lady Lucas would have an apoplexy. Perhaps the matron had already had one. Had she summoned the authorities to search for her missing charge? Had she asked the earl for assistance?

The earl. What would he think to learn his intended bride was lost? That she was off gallivanting with a bloody cutthroat?

"Arrgh!"

Sophia slammed her fists against the bedding. She was restless. Bored. She wanted to swim back to

England, to make things right with the earl and Lady Lucas.

Sophia was determined to keep her misadventure a secret. No one would ever know what had transpired between her and Black Hawk. But what *would* they think about her disappearance?

Perhaps she was fretting too much. Lady Lucas was a savvy woman. She might tell the earl her charge was "ill" and recuperating, that she wasn't seeing visitors or attending parties. And surely the matron wouldn't summon the authorities, creating a stir? She would set about a clandestine search for her charge, wouldn't she?

The damage to Sophia's reputation might not be so great. A missing young woman was always cause for speculation. However, if Lady Lucas remained calm and didn't voice her worries in public, Sophia might come out of this mishap without social scars.

She curled her arms around her knees. There was only one real way to determine the damage to her reputation: she had to return to England and confront the *ton*.

She shuddered. Thoughts of Imogen filled her head. Gruesome thoughts. The memory of the woman's suffering, her cruel fate still swirled in her skull.

You could have saved her!

Unwelcome tears welled in her eyes and she blinked to keep them back. Could she have saved Imogen as the boorish captain had charged? She would never know. Fear had crippled her. And her own deep desire to be a countess had prevented her from even trying to offer the girl a saving hand.

And that haunted her.

The cabin door opened.

Black Hawk entered the space. He filled the room with his robust presence. He was dressed in a white shirt, the fabric at his collar parted. The laces dangled, revealing the tufts of dark hair smattered across his strapping chest.

She licked her lips. He had the shirt tucked into his black trousers. Tight trousers. The material hugged his thick legs, his hips . . .

The swelling muscle between his legs made her heart quiver with longing. She tamped the wild passion into the pit of her soul. He still bewitched her mind. He still stirred her blood. She hated him for it. She hated herself even more for having the feelings a'tall.

He paused to look at her. Blue eyes, so riveting, fixed firmly on her, making her hot and needful—of him.

Could he hear her thoughts? See into her heart? He looked at her as though he could. She felt exposed. She wasn't naked. She was dressed in a shift. She had removed the formal frock, the jewelry to keep the articles from being wrinkled or broken. But even the flimsy white shift seemed too heavy, too rough against her skin. She wanted to take off the chafing garment. She squirmed as she imagined the pirate lord's warm, wet body pressed against her sweaty flesh.

She closed her eyes and shuddered. The damnable rogue! She needed to cut out his eyes. The haunting blue pools always put her wits in disorder.

James closed the door and headed for the small table in the corner of the room. The top was slanted, the papers and charts pinned to the surface. He flipped through a few sheets; she heard the rustling.

She humphed. That was the other reason she wasn't wearing stiff and proper attire; she was alone. Why be uncomfortable? She didn't associate with the crew *or* the pirate lord. She spent most of her time milling around the captain's quarters. The blackguard ignored her. He stayed out of the cabin during the daylight hours. In the evening he returned to the room to sleep in the hammock while she stayed in the bed. He said not a word to her. He didn't touch her, either . . . He only looked at her with those seductive eyes.

"What did you do with Sophia?"

He glanced over his shoulder. "What?"

The man's voice was like a low boom in the small space. It made her shiver. "Sophia. The snake. I thought she didn't like to sleep alone. Did you give her to your sister?"

James snorted and looked back at the papers. "No. She sleeps with the butler when we're all at sea. Sometimes I even take her with me. She takes care of the rats aboard ship."

Sophia made a moue. She hated that damn snake. She wished it, too, would drown. But the snake could swim, she suspected. Curse it!

"Why are you crying?"

Was she crying? Sophia wiped her cheeks. There was a single tear there, a lone drop of moisture she had failed to stave off. She rubbed and rubbed until her skin ached. She wasn't the maudlin sort.

"I don't want to talk about it," she said.

He was quiet for a short while, mulling over papers. Then: "I didn't give the order to set sail with you onboard."

She humphed. "Aren't you the captain?"

He gripped the edge of the table. "I didn't give the order."

She looked at him. He was so big. He had so much energy. He had so much strength. The blood moving through his veins pulsed with life. A life she sensed. A life she had once craved on the island.

Once upon a time, she had longed for the man every night he was away at sea. She had rejoiced every time the *Bonny Meg* had moored—and he had come for her. It had been more than pleasure, their affair. It had been more than lust . . . for her. But he had only wanted an island mistress.

Whore.

She wasn't fit to be his wife then. Now he wanted to let her know he had not devastated her? That he had not set sail with her onboard to ruin her reputation? That he cared?

She snorted inwardly.

He stiffened.

He had sensed her cynicism. Lush lips thinned as he stared at her. Eyes slanted. The beautiful blue pools darkened—and burned.

He approached the bed.

She bristled.

A warmth seeped into her belly: a familiar heat. That look in his eyes! She remembered that look.

Hunger.

He was always so hungry after a long voyage at sea . . . hungry for her.

It's good to see you, sweetheart.

She shivered.

But the wily cutthroat paused next to the sturdy sea chest instead. He flipped the lid, the roof landing on the bed with a thump, and rummaged.

She glared at him, pinched her lips together. He had rattled her senses, tossed her wits about with that scorching look.

For naught.

He had wanted to upset her, was all.

Slowly she slipped her foot across the bedding and reached for the lid with her toes. It wasn't a very heavy sea chest. It was constructed from wicker with canvas stretched across the frame. Still it was cumbersome. She angled her toes just under the clasp—before she flicked her foot and sent the roof crashing.

"Blimey!"

James curled his fingers together, the appendages red and swelling.

He glared at her.

"Oops." She smiled. "Sorry about that . . . my foot slipped."

She started to retract her leg. He grabbed her by the ankle and yanked her roughly toward him.

Sophia gasped as her arse scraped across the linen. The friction warmed her buttocks. She stopped at the edge of the bed, heart pounding. Skirt rucked up to her belly, bottom hanging precariously, she was vulnerable and exposed.

The way he liked it.

The way she liked it.

"You bloody witch."

James pressed his knee against the sea chest and curled his heavy body over her like a storm cloud. She was captivated by the man's thunderous expression. It stirred her blood to see the heat in his eyes—for her.

He took her leg and wrapped it around his hip, pressing more and more of his weight against her quim as he settled between her legs.

Sophia gasped again. Blood thumped through her veins. She took in a deep breath. Then another. Quick and hard.

"Are you sure you want to break my fingers?" He

slowly licked her lips with the tip of his tongue. "Are you sure you want to cripple me, so I can never touch you again?"

Sophia moaned.

He cupped her breast. It filled his large palm. She was hungry for breath as he kneaded the sensitive mound. The strength, the heat in his hand was pure torture. He moved his fingers in harmony with the waves. It was a lazy caress. But, oh, what a caress! It dazzled her senses.

"Have you missed my touch?" he whispered hoarsely.

He ripped the shift. She stiffened, pulse pounding. She grabbed his wrist. But he still slipped his stalwart fingers into her bodice and plumped her breast.

Sophia whimpered. Cool air rushed over her nipple, taut and peeking through the hole. He darted his warm thumb across the hard nub and rubbed.

Yes! Like that!

She chewed her bottom lip as he stroked the nipple. It lengthened under his masterful touch. It ached. *She* ached. For him. So deep. So strong.

Sophia closed her eyes. She reached for him with her hands. She reached for him with her lips . . .

He pulled away from her.

Not again!

He was breathing hard. So was she. He was fighting . . . what? Her? He had a voracious sexual appetite. She remembered the wench prostrated at his feet. Sophia had interrupted him with his paramour. He was still unsatisfied. How much longer would he suffer? How much longer would he make *her* suffer?

James opened the chest again.

She seriously contemplated slamming the lid on his fingers once more.

"I don't have time for this," he said brusquely.

She almost choked. She scooted back across the bed, pulled her skirt over her knees and covered her breast. "And what the devil is so important—"

He yanked the Jolly Roger from the chest.

Sophia stared at the skull and crossbones, the hourglass warning prey that time was running out for them.

She blinked. "I thought you'd retired from piracy?"

"I have."

"Then what are you doing with the flag?"

He looked at her sharply. "There's a ship tailing us. We're about to be attacked."

Sophia wasn't alarmed. The man had a lusty appetite for sex—and a good fight. Perhaps he wanted the other ship to attack? Perhaps he wanted another thrilling raid at sea? Cravats and coattails didn't suit him.

"Is it a navy vessel?" she wondered. "Is she here to apprehend you?"

"No," he said succinctly.

"Are you going to rob her then?"

"I'm going to sink her."

"Why?"

He said darkly, "She's my enemy."

Sophia shivered. *She* was his enemy, too. Would he sink her one day?

"Why is she your enemy?" she said, breathless.

"Do you remember the account in the paper about the pirates?"

"Yes."

"She's been posing as the *Bonny Meg*, attacking other ships in my name. I can't let her do that anymore."

Sophia's eyes rounded. "You're not really delivering cargo to America, are you? This was all a trap to lure the impostors out to sea."

"That's right."

"So that's your mission?" Sophia stretched out her legs and crossed them at the ankles. She folded her arms across her chest, too. She had tasted the smoke and blood of a sea battle before. She had endured the cannon's wrath on her father's pirate ship. She wasn't worried about the skirmish, and with Black Hawk at the helm, she'd bet her fortune he'd come out the victor. So . . . "Why are you letting *her* chase you?"

He regarded her thoughtfully. He then gathered his features, hard and inscrutable. "I don't want to frighten her off. I want her to come closer before I hoist the flag and attack her. I want her to know the *real* Black Hawk destroyed her."

That was the coldhearted devil she remembered from the island. That was the vengeful brute she had encountered at the earl's picnic—the very barbarian who might destroy *her* one day, too.

He headed for the door. "Stay here, Sophia."

"I hope she sinks *you* first!"

He paused, muscles stiff. "If anything happens to me, William knows you're here. He'll keep you safe. He'll take you home."

James left the cabin without sparing her another glance.

Sophia humphed. She hoped the blackguard drowned. She hoped a cannonball smacked him straight in the belly; he deserved it.

She rolled onto her side and closed her eyes. She napped . . . a minute later she jumped from the bed and started to pace.

The cannons blasted. Footfalls pounded overhead. Men shouted for gunpowder. Smoke and sulfur seeped into the hull, drifting through the ship and into the cabin space.

Sophia sneezed. Water filled her eyes. She wasn't crying, but the sting from the sulfur pinched her eyes and afflicted her vision.

She had to squint to see the lock. She angled the blade through the keyhole, digging. "Open!"

The door obeyed.

The lock snapped.

Sophia blinked. But she quickly smothered her wonder and slipped the knife back between her breasts before she scrambled to her feet.

Slowly she opened the door and peeked into the corridor. Empty. Good. She didn't want another pirate to see her, to know she was onboard. If her reputation wasn't already ruined, one word uttered by a foxed tar in port would see to it that it was.

Sophia sneaked through the passageway, her belly in a knot. She wasn't seasick. She had sturdy sea legs. However, the muscles in her midriff ached. Ached with dread.

She braced her hand against the wall for support as the ship lolled perilously. There was a ringing sound in her ears. Crackling drumbeats. The blasts resounded. One after another. Boom. Boom. Boom.

Sophia reached the stairs. In the violent upheavals, she grabbed the steps and ascended them like a ladder to keep her balance.

She popped her head through the hatchway.

Topside, dark clouds of ash and soot rolled across the deck. She choked back the fumes. The smoke was thick. It was hard to breathe—and see.

Where is he?

She was positioned astern, the length of the *Bonny*

Meg stretching before her. She searched the deck. She searched for him.

"Rake her!"

Sophia's heart thundered. She shifted her eyes to starboard. He was alive! So alive! Pinched nerves eased. Warmth rushed through her veins. She trembled. She was so weak. She had wasted so much energy fretting. It had been for naught. He was alive. He was still alive.

James moved across the deck in harmony with the thrashing waves. He was one with the ship. Chaos stormed around him, but he ignored it. He cut through the smoke. He moved with confidence, avoiding hazards even with a wall of soot obstructing his view.

The *Bonny Meg* belonged to him. Sophia sensed he'd move across the vessel with the same assured gait if he was blindfolded. He knew the ship so well. He was comfortable with her, too. If she dipped, he arched his body in the opposite direction to compensate. He maintained his balance. He never lost his footing. He was strong and in control. He was in his element. And Sophia was captivated.

"She's getting away!" cried James.

The *Bonny Meg* maintained the weather gage, bearing down on the enemy ship. The other rig was desperate to escape, turning downwind. As she rolled, she exposed her hull.

"Aim for the belly!" James ordered.

At the same moment the enemy's cannons pointed up at the *Bonny Meg*'s sails. A series of blasts thundered through the heavens.

Sophia's heart was in her throat as splinters rained. She ducked. The shards of wood pierced the deck like daggers. The fore and mizzen masts remained untouched. The mainmast was crippled, but standing.

Sophia poked her head through the hatchway once more . . . but Black Hawk was gone.

The deep, quick raps of her heart filled her head as the pressure in her skull mounted and throbbed. Blinded by the dense smoke, she screamed, "James!"

A big shadow loomed. It was a dark and familiar silhouette. A gust of wind pushed the gray wall of fumes across the deck, revealing the pirate captain looking haggard.

But alive.

Sophia's heart quickened. The black devil was covered in soot. It was smeared across his features, too. The black smudges stressed the dark fire burning in his deep blue eyes as he glared at her.

"Get below!" he blustered.

He was hoarse. The shouting and smoke had ravaged his throat, deepened his voice . . . made it huskier, more seductive.

She shivered.

She glanced at his dirty shirt, ripped. The muscles underneath glistened in the sunlight, the flesh stained with gunpowder and sweat—and blood.

He was hurt.

But he was alive.

She might not be for too long, though. He looked murderous. But she didn't budge from the hatchway. She waited another minute for the other ship to take flight before she was sure the battle was over—and he was still alive.

Sophia descended the steps, coughing. She beat the air with her hand, shooing the smoke as she returned to the captain's cabin to wait for him.

Chapter 15

James grabbed the ratlines. He curled his arm around the coarse rope and clenched his teeth. Lungs heaving, he glared after the enemy vessel sailing away and cursed the craven crew. He had come so close to sinking the impostors.

"Shit!"

William approached him, looking bedraggled. "I second that." He wiped the dark smudges from his brow. "At least we frightened her. She might not venture out to sea in our name again."

James gritted, "She didn't even balk when we raised the flag."

"She got a good beating, though."

"Aye, but she'll recover from it . . . and set sail again. She's cheeky."

"We can always give chase."

James glanced at the mainmast. Sunlight bled through the pockets in the smoke. He squinted and observed the ravaged tip. "We're hit. It's too dangerous to give chase. See to the repairs, Lieutenant."

"Aye, Captain."

"And the crew?"

"No casualties," reported William. "A few broken

bones, though. Cuts and bruises, too. Quincy's tending to the injured. He's got a steady hand with a needle and thread . . . Do you want me to summon him?"

James glanced at the wound smarting at his breast: a long gash that cut across his pectoral. Not too deep, though.

"No," said James. "Let Quincy see to the other men first. I can wait."

James looked at the *Bonny Meg*. There was still smoke drifting through the rig, but a strong wind quickly pushed the heavy fumes out to sea.

He surveyed the damage for the first time: tattered ropes and sails, smashed planking. The capstan was missing a few bars. But the rig was still in good order. The repairs would take a few days. A week, perhaps. But the *Bonny Meg* had weathered worse storms and battles. She was strong.

"Set a course back to England," ordered James.

"And the impostors?"

"We'll get them yet, Lieutenant."

"Aye, Captain."

William walked away, shouting orders to the tars. There was rapid movement as the able-bodied men cleared the debris and set to work on the repairs.

James glanced at the hatchway. He imagined the ghostly image of Sophia—and stiffened. He *would* throttle the witch. But not now. Now he had to inspect the rest of the ship belowdecks, the crew. But later . . .

An hour later James opened the cabin door. The viper had busted the lock. There was nothing to protect her from the rest of the men. Not that the tars would hurt her; James trusted the crew. But she had risked her own precious reputation. Was she daft?

Sophia was sitting on the bed. She jumped to her feet as soon as he entered the room.

She was ragged. Shift stained with soot, cheeks with ash. He glared at her. He moved his eyes from her head to her bare toes. No blood. No bruises. She was all right.

James let out a loud and heavy breath. He sensed he had been holding it for the last hour.

"I told you to stay in the cabin," he said darkly.

"I don't take orders from you." She glanced at his chest. "You're hurt."

"I'm sorry to disappoint you, sweetheart . . . I know you wanted me dead."

She cut him a wry look. She crossed the rubble in the room and collected a canteen of fresh water from the floor. "Take off your shirt."

Muscles twitched. "Like hell."

She grabbed a small towel off the floor, too. The room was a mess after the stormy battle. She had to circle tossed linens and toppled chairs to get to him.

The long wisps of her dark brown hair hugged her torso like a thick and woolly blanket. Wild. Sophia. *That* was Sophia.

"Let me tend to the wound," she said, eyes alight.

"I don't need your bloody help," he returned stiffly. He would endure the pain, the filth. He would stomach the blood and the ash before he'd let her touch him with a kind hand. A deceptively kind hand. The woman was cold. She had ice for blood. No heart at all.

Sophia tucked the towel under her arm. She pinched her elbow against her rib to keep the linen in place. It rested against her breast, pressed against the tear in her shift.

He eyed the soft, creamy patch of flesh that peeked

through the tattered fabric. James fisted his palms. His fingertips pulsed with the memory of her plump breast in his hand, her nipple hardening and lengthening under his thumb's ministration.

He shuddered. She reached for him with her free hand—and yanked the scruffy garment off his shoulders.

"There," she said smugly. "Now we're even." She tossed the rags away. "Sit on the bed, Black Hawk."

He didn't budge. Every muscle was taut. Blood pumped through his veins and into his cock. He was fighting hard to keep the fire in his belly from burning through what was left of his clothes.

Sophia pushed him. She splayed her fingers and pressed her palm against his midriff. She was hot, too. The heat in her hand—her eyes—betrayed her true feelings.

He sat down with a grunt. He glared at her, trembled softly. He watched as she popped the cork and soaked the linen with the fresh water.

She set the canteen aside. She looked at him with beautiful, bay brown eyes. Mussed hair. Wild lips. Sophia. *That* was Sophia.

She stepped between his legs to better reach the wound; his thighs quivered.

Softly she dabbed at the gash across his chest. He was quiet, unmoving as she nursed him tenderly. Not Sophia. She was not Sophia now. Sophia wasn't kind. She wasn't tender.

She mopped the blood. He ached to the bone. He ached for her. Seven years ago he had engaged in a battle. As now. Seven years ago he had returned to the plantation house after the raid, needing her. As now. But she had vanished. She had deserted him.

She had killed him.

He slapped her wrist.

She dropped the towel. It landed on his boot.

"What was that for?" she demanded, bemused.

She had touched him too much. She had liked it too much. It was there in her eyes. But the past was dead. He wanted revenge.

He kicked the towel across the room. It smacked against the wall. "Keep your hands off me."

She pinched her lips. There was a dark fire burning in her eyes. "But you're hurt."

"I'll heal."

He got off the bed. He was sick. There was a heavy, almost crippling sentiment in his gut. It stifled his movements.

James headed for the door. "I have work to do."

He had a ship to look after, a crew to heal. He didn't have time to waste with the witch. Let her cast her spells on some other poor sap, like the earl.

"Wait!"

"What?" he barked.

She slipped between him and the door. There was longing . . . lust in her eyes.

Burn, sweetheart.

He rasped, "Move."

"James," she whispered weakly.

"Oh no." He caged her. He pressed his hands against the door and looked deeply into her wicked eyes. "You can scream my name, Sophia. It won't do any good. I'm not interested."

"Liar," she gritted.

She was breathing hard. He inhaled the woman's sweet musk. It thrilled him, set his bones shaking. She was making him weak with her arousal.

"What do you want, James?"

I want you to beg me.

She reached for him, hand trembling. "Please."

He cuffed her fingers. Blood pounded in his head. He wasn't sure he had heard the word. "What?"

She mouthed the word again. "Please."

He gnashed his teeth. "Louder."

"Please."

He pressed his lips softly against her mouth and whispered, "Louder."

"Please!"

The aching cry resounded in his throat. It was his undoing.

He crushed his mouth over hers. So soft. So hot. She tasted like the sea. She tasted like smoke. She tasted like Sophia.

Sophia!

Long, strong arms gripped him. She pinched his neck in need. Such savage need. She opened her mouth for him and let him ravish her. She took everything he gave her—and she still wanted more. He sensed it, the woman's insatiable desire.

James grabbed her and thrust her against the door; the planking shuddered. Blood throbbed through his veins. He reached between her breasts and removed the small knife. "Spread your legs."

She obeyed.

He bussed her sweet lips before he dropped to his knees. She wanted to sink to the ground, too, for her knees buckled.

"Hold still," he ordered.

She spread her fingers apart, bracing the door for support. She whimpered. He loved to hear her wanton whimpers.

Come for me, sweetheart.

James pierced the shift with the blade. In one swift stroke, he rent the garment. She gasped. He dropped the knife. He seized the two halves and split the skirt even more. He split the linen right to her navel.

Sophia groaned as he exposed the folds of her feminine flesh. He groaned, too. He was so hungry for her. It had been so long since he had tasted her.

He trembled as he slipped a finger inside her wet passage and watched the sweet fluid bleed from her womb and soak his hand.

That's it, sweetheart. Come. Come!

She cried out. She wanted him. She *needed* him. He sensed her every shameless thought, her every throbbing want.

He was one with her. And she with him. She filled the dark and empty places in his soul. Giving her pleasure, joy made him feel alive. *He* made her wet. *He* made her happy. He alone.

He wanted more.

James parted the dark curls at her apex and softly kissed the engorged and quivering flesh, tasting the dewy moisture on her nether lips.

She whimpered and trembled even more.

More!

He wanted more from her. He wanted to unleash every desire she had buried, every passion she had smothered inside her. He wanted her to ache and throb and weep for him. And him alone.

You can't live without me.

He slowly raked his fingers along her leg, tickled the hollow at her knee. He caressed her warm thigh, stroked her buttocks as he licked her quim. He thirsted for the heady juices.

She cried out in pleasure.

Louder!

She twisted his hair around her fingers, pinched his scalp. She pressed him harder against her core.

"Oh, James!"

That throaty cry; it made him burn. He gripped her buttocks with both his hands, kneaded the plump flesh as he feasted on her most sensitive part.

She lifted one leg and draped it over his shoulder, giving him greater entrance to her pulsing arousal. He could feel her belly heave and quiver against his sweating brow, each gasp a soft cry of bliss, urging him to work faster, harder to give her release.

He slipped his tongue into her quim, so hot.

"Yes," she screamed. "Yes!"

He was hard. So hard for her. He pulled back and licked his lips, still hungry for her. He grabbed her hips, twisted her around, and pressed her against the door.

"What are you doing," she demanded breathlessly.

"Trust me, sweetheart."

He grabbed the knife.

She stiffened.

He sliced the back of the shift. She gasped again. He stabbed the wall with the blade before he tore the rest of the garment, exposing her delicious arse. The cheeks so white and creamy, he grunted in pleasure.

He kissed her buttocks. Nibbled.

She writhed against the door. "James, *please!*"

He wrestled with the buttons at his trousers and parted the flap. He lifted to his feet. He was stiff and ready for her. "Open for me, sweetheart."

Sophia thrust out her arse. He was taller than she, so she had to stand on her toes, while he had to bend his knees. He grabbed her hips and guided her over his erection.

She sobbed with pleasure to feel that familiar thickness inside her again. The heat. The powerful heat.

Like no other.

"Tell me, sweetheart." He thrust once. Twice. Slowly. Deeply. "Does it feel good?"

She gasped. "Yes."

So good!

So very good!

James rocked against her buttocks. It took him a minute to find the right rhythm. Their rhythm. But once he had recovered it, he moved within her with purpose. Strong and steady thrusts.

Sophia pressed her cheek against the door. She let him take her. Fill her. Blood throbbed through her veins. Her breasts ached and swelled as she undulated against the barrier. The friction teased her nipples, so sensitive, and she reached for the cords at her bodice to relax the garment.

But James was there first. He slipped his robust hand along her midriff and cupped an aching breast, making her moan with delight before he gripped the lacing between his fingers and pulled.

The bodice stretched. He shoved his fingers inside the material and kneaded the sore and tender flesh.

"Yes!" she cried.

She placed her hand over his. Their fingers worked in harmony to give her the pleasure she longed for.

She had missed him. She had missed the man's intimate touch. He moved inside her the right way. She didn't need to tell him what she wanted or even how she wanted it. He knew. He just knew.

He let go of her breast. She made a grousing noise

before she cupped the raw flesh and kneaded it herself. But he'd had to let go. He grabbed her hips again. He needed both his hands to properly guide her over his erection, to keep the thrusts strong and steady.

He pressed his thumbs against her backside. The man's fingertips gripped her hipbones as he maintained control, pumping into her quim with measured strokes. Not too slow. Not too fast. He was teasing her senses. She cried out for more.

Take me.

The energy inside her welled and welled. It was ready to burst. She had held it in for so long, since the night of the ball. She had seen him for the first time in seven years that night. And slowly it had been building. Slowly the need had been working its way through her bones and muscles, her heart and mind. And now it was time. Now it was time to let go of all that energy and frustration.

Take me.

She clenched her quim.

He grunted to feel the tightness. He liked it tight. The man had control. He had the power to take her slowly—or swiftly. But she knew him, too. She knew how to get what she wanted out of him without a word.

"Tell me, James," she whispered hoarsely. "Does it feel good?"

He grunted again. The hard and raspy breathing, the guttural groans as he worked harder to get inside her, thrilled her. The burning pressure within her strengthened as she heard him making love. He was loud. She liked it loud. She liked to hear from his lips what she was doing to him.

Take me.

He thrust harder. Deeper. Swifter. He lifted her toes off the ground as he plunged into her. Again and again.

"Yes," she screamed. "Yes!"

He touched every sensitive part of her. He snagged her wits, her senses, and she responded to his every command.

Take me!

She surrendered to him. She gave him everything. He sensed the capitulation, for he undulated in quick and piercing strokes. It was a dance. A wild and quick dance. In sync. In harmony.

The orgasm came. Her muscles throbbed. So sweet and hot. She cried out as the energy poured through her veins and tears filled her eyes. Tears of joy. And satisfaction. The afterglow was intoxicating, the sated feelings so incredible, she started to weep.

Sophia cried freely as he grinded his hips against hers, seeking his own desperate release. And with a feral cry he found it. He poured himself into her, the moist heat filling her. She tightened her muscles again, giving him the friction he needed to come.

She was so weak. She had lost everything to him and she wanted to sink to the floor, but he maintained a sturdy hold of her hips.

"Oh, sweetheart."

He pressed his heavy chest against her sweating back and dropped his chin on her shoulder. The man's breath was loud and fierce beside her ear. She matched his savage gasps. Together they breathed. Together their hearts beat as one.

He kissed her cheek.

She shuddered.

He had a tender side. It was achingly soft at times,

but it was so well concealed. It was only in times of great peace that he dropped his iron front and let the tenderness show.

He wrapped a stout arm around her midriff, keeping her close. He circled his other fingers under her chin and guided her features to meet his.

She did as he silently bade. She pressed her cheek against his throat and lifted her mouth. He lowered his head and touched her lips, kissing her softly, gently . . . lovingly.

The tears came fresh. Not tears of satisfaction, but tears of pain. Such raw and aching pain, she sobbed.

"What's the matter, sweetheart?"

He stroked her chin, her trembling lips with his thumb. He kissed her temple, taking in the briny tear that had spilled from the corner of her eye.

Why? she screamed in her head. *Why wasn't I good enough for you all those years ago?*

"Let me go, James."

She bumped his hip, telling him to step aside. He curled both his arms around her instead. And squeezed. Tight.

Hold me.

She wanted to step inside him, to shed her skin and become one with him. He'd want her then. If she was a part of him, he'd care for her. She would be good enough for him then.

She jabbed her elbow into his gut. "I said let go!"

He didn't.

"I know who you really are, Sophia. You will never be happy in this world with anyone else but me. You are your true self only with me."

She gasped at the words, burning in her ears.

No!

"You want me," he said roughly. "You belong with me."

She wanted him privately, quietly, intimately. But not publicly. Never publicly. The pirate lord's whore? No! She would never be that again.

"I belong with the earl," she said defiantly. "I belong with anyone else but you!"

His belly ballooned against her back as he took in a sharp breath of air. He let her go. She pressed her body against the cold door for support.

He stepped back. The chill was biting. She didn't look at him, though. She didn't have to, for the man's brutal expression, his cold eyes were there in the air; they pierced her spine.

She pressed her face against the door and quietly cried.

Chapter 16

S ophia stared at the rows of boxes. The structures flanked the quiet street. Impressive. Uniform. But one town house stood out from the rest. A few months ago, it had needed repairs. Lady Lucas had been living in poverty for many years. But now it looked so officious and grand: a solid structure of grace and superiority. Sophia had funded the refurbishment. The edifice was three stories high, pristine white, and surrounded by a spiked iron fence.

Keep out.

She curled her fingers into her palms, staked her nails through the skin. The sharp pain eased the stress in her belly. Would she be welcome inside the abode? A grisly darkness enveloped the slumbering city. There was no one in the street to whisper snide comments or to offer sneering looks. Was she ruined? There was only one way to determine the truth: she had to confront Lady Lucas.

Sophia opened her fists and pulled in a deep breath. She was back on land, but she sensed the ground moving beneath her feet, making her woozy . . . She sensed the pirate lord's eyes on her, too.

James was part of the interminable darkness. He

lurked in the shadows. He waited for her to enter the house. She had asked him not to come with her. She had asked him to remain aboard the *Bonny Meg*. But the stoic captain had rebuffed her request. Not in words. He had uttered no words. He had simply followed her off the ship. She had sensed his presence throughout the cab ride to the city. And she felt him now. He remained elusive. She didn't see him. But he was there. She knew it.

You are your true self only with me.

The words danced in her head, resounded in her soul. Even now the snug accoutrements squeezed her lungs and she ached for breath.

Was that all there was in life? To breathe and be free? She didn't have to hold her tongue or purify her thoughts with James. She didn't need to wear pinching corsets—or anything at all—with James. She didn't need to act or stand or sit in an uncomfortable manner with James. But no one would respect her if she remained with the pirate lord. Not as his mistress. Not even as his wife, for the man was a pariah.

And yet her own social footing might be lost in England. She might already be a pariah, too . . . like poor Imogen.

Sophia swallowed the tart taste in her mouth. Freedom wasn't worth ostracism. She looked into the darkness.

Good-bye, James.

It was time to part from him for good. She would either leave England in disgrace or marry the earl. But she would not be with the pirate captain anymore.

It was finished.

Sophia once more fixed her eyes to the imposing town house before she crossed the stone street with shaky steps. She approached the cold iron gate. The door was silent, well oiled. She passed through it and mounted the front steps. The tall, black entranceway welcomed her like robed death. She slowly removed the key from her reticule. Fingers quivered as she unlocked the door and entered the dark hall. Faint light flickered at the end of a narrow passage. Lady Lucas was still awake.

Sophia closed the barrier and smoothed her skirt, ruffled but not crumpled. She touched her hair, twisted in a neat fashion. There was a mirror beside the door, but no reflection. It was too dim. She had to trust she looked presentable. She had put herself together aboard the pirate ship. She had styled her locks holding a small piece of glass that had shattered during the sea battle.

Sophia headed for the light. She treaded softly through the house, each step muffled by the long runner. She walked slowly: an unfortunate wretch trying to stave off doom. She had witnessed many hangings on the tropical island. A sluggish gait had never prevented an execution . . . yet she still maintained a leisurely pace.

Sophia's heart boomed in her head. She meshed her lips together and twisted her fingers around the threads of her reticule. She stopped in front of the parlor door. There was a line of candlelight that peeked through the gap between the wood barrier and the floor; it illuminated her shoes.

She watched as a shadow whisked across her leather-tipped toes. A figure paced inside the room. With a heavy breath she rapped on the wood.

The shadow stilled.

Swallowing the cold knot trapped in her throat, Sophia opened the door. "Lady Lucas?"

It was a small space, but the ceiling stretched for fourteen feet. At more than twice her height, the long walls loomed above her—so did the shadows. A low fire sputtered in the hearth, making the lanky darkness bounce and laugh.

The old woman in the middle of the room was wearing a white woolly wrapper, her hair pinned under a frilly nightcap. Gaunt and pale, she had dark smudges under her eyes. She looked like a scorned wraith, haunting the dwelling, waiting for the chance to terrorize an unwelcome intruder.

Sophia retreated, trembling. She set her hand against her belly to quiet the churning grief.

She loathes me.

Lady Lucas darted across the room. Sophia stiffened her muscles . . . but the woman hugged her. *"Where have you been?"*

Sophia gasped. The matron squeezed her so tight, she was strapped for words, for breath. The grief subsided, the roiling movements in her belly stilled, and she let the matron coddle her like a lost child.

Lady Lucas wasn't the motherly sort. She had no children of her own. She had always conducted herself and her duties with cool deportment. But now she had set aside her firm demeanor. Sophia didn't mind the maternal gesture. She ached for it, in truth. She had rarely known the comfort of a parent's embrace. She needed it now more than ever.

"You're thirteen years old and it's time you start earning your keep," Alvera said. *"I'm tired of half my hard-earned pay going to feed you."*

"I won't do it!"

"You'll do it or you'll be out in the streets."

"I'll look for my father. I'll go and live with him."

Alvera laughed. "That crazy pirate? He's sired at least a hundred bastards on the island. He won't care for you."

"He will! I'll make him!"

"Fine. You go make him. But he's loco. He lives in the mountains when he's not at sea. You'll never find him. He's a paranoid devil. He thinks everyone's out to steal his precious gold. He doesn't even have any treasure."

"Maybe he's buried it?"

"Don't be daft, girl. Pirates don't bury treasure. They spend it on drink and women, like me—and you."

"No. I won't. I won't do it!"

"You'll starve."

"I'd rather starve."

"You say that now because your belly's full, but as soon as your belly aches you'll be back."

But Sophia had never returned. She had parted from her mother that day. She had set out to search for her father's lair—and she had found it.

Sophia stared at the drunkard. He was sound asleep beside the ramshackle hut. He had never made it inside the house; he'd collapsed at the door. He was snoring loudly. He didn't smell good, either.

He *was* her father?

She reached for a stick. She didn't want to touch him, for he looked dirty. She poked him instead. The man came up swinging.

He had a bushy black beard, speckled with gray. A long scar stretched across his brow and nose. He looked at her with piercing black eyes. "Who the devil are you?"

"I'm your daughter, Sophia."

He didn't seem surprised to hear her confession. Mother had said he'd sired a hundred bastards like her, that he wouldn't give a damn about her.

"Bugger off, brat!"

He went back to sleep.

But Sophia wasn't going back to the whorehouse. She poked him again. He came up swinging.

He looked at her, eyes red with blood. Wild. "Who the devil are you?"

She sighed. "I'm your daughter, Sophia."

"Bugger off, brat!"

He curled back into a ball. He was crazy, wasn't he? But she would rather live with him than with her mother. If she wanted to be with her mother, she'd have to whore like the woman, too. And she refused to do that.

"I'm here to live with you," said Sophia.

He rolled over and opened his eyes. "Like bleedin' hell you are!"

"My mother sent me."

"Aye? And who's your mother?"

"Alvera—"

"You jezebel!" He staggered to his clumsy feet and slapped her. "Off with you, Alvera!"

Sophia grabbed her pulsing cheek. She munched on her bottom lip to fend off the tears. "I'm Sophia! So-phi-a! You need a bath. Are you hungry? I can cook."

She stepped around the haggard man and entered the hut. She set aside the bundle in her arms—all the belongings she had in the world—and looked at her new home. The house was a mess. But she would make it better. She would make him want her, too.

Sophia returned Lady Lucas's embrace. She yearned for the affectionate gesture: a gesture she had seldom known from her mother. Or her father.

Patrick Dawson had eventually accepted her as his daughter and caretaker, even though half the time he had called her Sophia, and half the time he had called her by her mother's name, Alvera. He had always railed at her for something, but she had learned to ignore his demented outbursts.

The man had loved her in his own way. Her mother had been wrong about that; he had cared. Her mother had been wrong about a great many things, including that pirates didn't bury their treasure. Dawson had. He had buried so much treasure, he couldn't remember where he had put most of it.

But over time, Sophia had gathered all the gold into one secret spot. And on the eve of his death, Dawson had asked her to take the wealth. He had stunned her with the reasonable request, for she had believed the man crazy enough to demand to be buried with his precious treasure—not that she would have honored the balmy request and interred him with the gold. But he had been lucid at the end of his life. And he had wanted her to be happy, to have the money. He had never once said, "I love you" in all their years together. But he had cared for her, she was sure.

"Why are you crying, my dear?" Lady Lucas wiped Sophia's cheeks. "Are you hurt? What happened at the opera? Where did you go? I thought you had been kidnapped, but then there was no ransom note. Oh, there's been such buzz!"

Sophia's head was buzzing, too. She had been gone for four days. Had she really believed no one would notice her disappearance? That there would be no "buzz"?

The jeers and slights resounded in her head, the *ton*'s sharp laughter and biting snubs. She saw the contorted faces, so cold: the faces from the opera house. She saw them laughing at her.

Whore!

The thought made her cringe. Her fingers trembled,

the nerves numb. She had caged her natural desires, evaded her dishonorable past. For naught. She was disgraced, her dreams shattered. And she had disgraced herself with her own reckless behavior. She had fretted over Black Hawk so much, she had failed to keep control of her own wild impulses.

She swallowed the heavy knob of tears in her throat. The mockery and searing looks resided in her head. She had been spared public disgrace . . . unlike poor Imogen. Perhaps Sophia deserved the ignominy? She had let a good friend fall. And the scandal she had unleashed with her own thoughtless conduct was fate's vengeance, she supposed.

At least Lady Lucas was still kind to her. She was not alone. The old woman's tender touch assuaged some of the grief that quashed Sophia's spirit. But she wouldn't admit she had been aboard the pirate lord's ship. She wouldn't let the old woman think ill of her even more. Instead, she confessed:

"I was so upset about Imogen. I wasn't thinking clearly and I—"

"I knew it!" The matron took her by the hand and dragged her across the room. "Sit, my dear."

Sophia sighed as she rested against the plush and embroidered cushions.

"You looked so pale and distraught at the opera house." The old woman settled beside her on the divan and squeezed her hand. "I suspected you had gone off to mourn your friend in private."

Sophia shuddered at the word. She had mourned the loss of her father. Was Imogen's shame akin to a physical death? If so . . . Sophia was dead, too.

"I'm sorry, Lady Lucas. I've ruined everything."

"You very *nearly* ruined everything, my dear."

Sophia was fagged. Her heart had folded and ballooned so many times, she was weary. She had assumed she was ruined. She had resigned herself to ignominy. But the word "nearly" poked her listless heart to life, filling it with vibrant energy.

"B-but the buzz, Lady Lucas?"

"The buzz isn't about your disappearance, my dear."

Sophia's head throbbed, her soul pulsed with renewed strength. "Then what—"

"You must never run off like that again!"

Lady Lucas huffed. Sophia offered the faint woman an opportunity to gather her breath. She had endured great distress. She had struggled for four days to keep her charge's disappearance a secret. The outburst was cathartic, Sophia suspected. And she allowed Lady Lucas a few moments to regain her composure, while she wallowed in remorse for having put the sage woman through the terrible ordeal.

"I know you've lived in the jungle, my dear."

Jamaica, Sophia thought.

"But young ladies—even wealthy and independent young ladies—*don't* run away when they're upset. They lock themselves in a room and cry, as is proper."

"Yes, Lady Lucas." Sophia grabbed her chest, it ached so much. "I'm sorry. But the buzz?"

"Yes. Yes. The buzz about you and the duchess."

The duchess? "What duchess?"

"The Duchess of Wembury!"

Sophia jumped to her feet, the soft cushions more like hot bricks against her backside. "Oh no!"

"Yes, the captain's sister! She put an immediate end to the twitter."

Sophia whirled around. "There was twitter?"

"At first, but the duchess put a stop to it."

"How?"

Why?

"Her Grace announced you had *not* disappeared, that you were visiting with her at Castle Wembury."

There was pressure on Sophia's breast. It was hard to breathe. She had never met James's sister. She doubted very much James had ever mentioned her name to the woman. So how had the duchess learned about her? And why would she do such a thing? Save her brother's mistress from the chomping lips of the gossipmongers? Had James put her up to it?

"After you'd vanished, I announced you were ill," said the old woman. "The earl suspected your 'illness' a front for grief, that you were mourning the loss of Imogen's friendship in private. I let him believe it, too. But after two days 'shut in your room,' he wondered if you really *were* ill or even injured. Then the twitter started. And that's when the letter arrived."

"The letter?"

"From the Duchess of Wembury, requesting your presence at the castle. Why didn't you tell me you were friends with Her Grace?" Lady Lucas bustled across the room and foraged through the papers neatly stacked on the writing desk. "Here." She handed the missive to Sophia. "A footman arrived in person to deliver the invitation."

Sophia moved closer to the fire and perused the swirling penmanship:

My dear Miss Dawson,

The Duke and I would like to invite you and your chaperone to Castle Wembury. I long to see you, Miss Dawson. Please accept our hospitality.

Yours sincerely,

Belle

Sophia stared at the note, confounded. What did the duchess want from her? Was it a trick? Was the woman acting under her devious brother's instruction?

Lady Lucas was on her toes, peeking over Sophia's shoulder. "Look at how she signed her name: Belle. How informal. Oh, my dear! You must be such good friends. *Why* didn't you tell me you were acquainted with Her Grace? And when did you befriend her?"

Sophia's thoughts swirled liked the penmanship. Friends with the duchess? Hardly. And yet the woman had saved her reputation. And that meant James had been right, Sophia could have saved Imogen's, too . . . if she had tried.

Sophia gasped for breath. Ghostly fingers circled her throat—and squeezed. She had forsaken Imogen. She had forsaken herself, for she was like Imogen. She, too, concealed dark secrets. She deserved to share in her comrade's fate. And yet she had been spared the misfortune. Bitter tears welled in her eyes.

"I, um . . ."

"Never mind," said the old woman. "I informed Her Grace you had gone off to mourn the loss of your friend in seclusion. I didn't know how long I could maintain your 'illness.' And the duchess was your intimate, so I assumed I could trust her . . ."

The matron faltered. Sophia sensed her misgiving, her dread that she had erred in some way and aggrieved her charge.

"You did the right thing, Lady Lucas."

But Sophia sounded much more assured than she really was. She only wanted to put the matron's fear to rest, to disabuse her of the thought that she would abandon her, disgusted with her incompetence, and leave her penniless—again. Sophia respected the woman far too much to ever abandon her.

Lady Lucas gathered her features and bounded for the door. "Hurry! We have to pack."

Sophia pinched her brows. "Where are we going?"

"To the castle, of course." She paused beside the door. "The duchess let word slip that you are both friends. The *ton* thinks you are staying with Her Grace, so you *must* be there."

Sophia was in a precarious position. If she wanted to protect her character, she had to accept the duchess's invitation . . . But what awaited her at Castle Wembury?

It was that enigmatic question that chilled her, set her heart pounding.

Sophia stared at the imposing wood doors with polished brass knockers. She peered into the reflective metal and watched her face metamorphose in the twisted alloy. The distortion made her shudder. She looked away. Slowly she lifted her eyes heavenward, but the castle's looming towers disappeared in the dazzling sunlight. She lowered her gaze. Bright spots bounced before her eyes, making her dizzy.

"Achoo!"

Sophia glanced at Lady Lucas. "Are you all right?"

"I'm fine." She dabbed a frilly kerchief under her nose and sniffed. "It's the dust off the road."

The sound of grinding iron soon filled Sophia's ears. One thick and heavy door rolled on its hinges. The ancient wood released a spurt of cool air from inside the castle that swirled around her in greeting. A stoic gentleman also appeared. The butler, Sophia assumed.

The matron tucked the kerchief into her sleeve before she handed the butler a calling card. "Lady Lucas and Miss Dawson to see the Duchess of Wembury."

The old man bowed. "Welcome, ladies."

Sophia entered the castle's dark belly; it swallowed her whole. She suspected the ancient blocks of stone might crumble and crush her, and she took an inadvertent step back. But she had to be there or she risked her reputation being sullied. There was still the chance she might secure the earl's favor and become the next Countess Baine . . . unless James had employed his sister in some wily scheme to thwart her plans?

"Please follow me, ladies."

Sophia treaded after Lady Lucas and the butler as two liveried footmen attended to the luggage, while another scuttled off to fetch the duchess.

Sophia lifted her eyes to better examine the tall corridor. The stones gave way to wood panels that covered the walls and the ceiling in a grid pattern. She passed through three sets of ornate doorframes designed to keep in the cool air in the summer and let the warm air circulate in the winter.

At the fourth and last set of doors, she was greeted by a lavish lintel with gold filigree. She dropped her gaze and skimmed her fingers along the carved wood. It reminded her of home on the island . . . of James.

Sophia dismissed the black devil from her mind. He might still be the reason she'd been summoned to the castle. But if he *was* the nefarious culprit behind the invitation, if he intended to out her publicly with his sister's support as an act of revenge for rejecting him aboard the *Bonny Meg*, he would suffer for the betrayal. She would crush him, too, expose him as Black Hawk.

The butler opened the door. Sophia gathered her composure. But as soon as she entered the warm parlor, her heart fluttered. There was a row of tall windows along the west wall, the glass arced at the tips. The archaic style suited the ancient fortress. Each pane was flanked by white and translucent drapes, allowing the brilliant, late-afternoon sunshine to fill the room. Shades of blue, green, and yellow colored glass trimmed the windows, the floral patterns splayed across the floor and furnishings in a vibrant array.

It was unearthly, soothing. The walls were papered in the softest blue. The elegant furniture curved at each corner, giving the space the illusion of waves . . . the sea.

There was a large portrait above the whitewashed fireplace. A lovely young woman of about five-and-twenty. Eyes a deep amber, locks a tawny gold. She had a warm smile. She looked mischievous, too, almost seductive. She slanted her lashes and shifted her gaze to one side, as if flirting with someone just beyond the canvas's frame.

"Please have a seat," said the butler. "The duchess will be with you shortly."

Sophia followed Lady Lucas to the divan upholstered in eggshell white linen. A parlor maid soon
bustled inside the room with a silver tray.

"Tea?" offered the butler.

"Thank you," returned Lady Lucas. She settled in
the seat and murmured, "Very respectable." As the
staff prepared the refreshments, the matron whispered
in Sophia's ear, "I'm surprised the duchess is feeling
well enough to greet us."

Sophia was still bewitched by the comforting surroundings. She looked away from the curious portrait
and returned quietly, "Why wouldn't she be well?"

"I understand there was a complication with the
birth of her last child, a son. That was two months ago.
She very nearly died."

Sophia frowned. James had mentioned his sister
was nursing a new babe, but he hadn't expounded on
the traumatic birth. He had suffered sorely if he had
refrained from talking about the matter, for he wasn't
the sort to confess to weakness, to feelings like pain
. . . or love.

Sophia mulled over the pirate lord's dogged claim
that he had to protect his sister's reputation from his
sinful past. He adored his sister, Mirabelle. All four of
her brothers had spoken warmly of her on the island.
If James had conspired with the duchess to lure Sophia
to the castle, it wasn't to betray her. The man would
never risk his sister's good name or threaten her happiness. And both would be dashed to bits if Sophia
outed him as Black Hawk in retribution. So *why* had
she been invited to the castle?

The door opened.

Lady Lucas quickly lifted to her feet. Sophia mim-
icked. She folded her hands together and twisted her

fingers to quell the slight vibration skirting along her spine. She peered over the matron's shoulder and looked at . . . the woman from the portrait.

Mirabelle stepped inside the room. She was handsome in a brown linen day dress with ruffled sleeves and full skirt. A matching shawl trimmed with lace was loosely draped over her wrists and sagging below her waistline. The castle air was cool, but Sophia suspected another reason for the woman's warm attire. The duchess was ashen. It was the fashion to maintain a sallow complexion; however, the woman lacked a certain bright glow in her cheeks that the artist had captured in her portrait. Her faint skin was no vogue: the duchess was recovering from near death.

Mirabelle crossed the wool rug striped with a blue and white harlequin pattern. She was almost as tall as Sophia at about five feet, seven inches. She paused—and smiled. "Miss Dawson, I'm so delighted to see you."

Sophia prepared to curtsy . . . but she was swallowed by a lace-trimmed mantle as the duchess hugged her.

Sophia glanced at Lady Lucas, unprepared for the informal greeting. She had been trained to respond to the peerage with strict decorum. What was she supposed to do now? But Lady Lucas looked pleased at the casual salutation. She believed her charge and the duchess friends, after all.

The duchess stepped away, simpering. She looked at Sophia, glanced over her with her golden eyes. The examination wasn't judgmental, though. Sophia had endured a lot of scrutiny since her arrival in England. She knew when she was being critiqued. The woman was . . . admiring her?

The duchess glanced at the matron next. "You must be Lady Lucas?"

The old woman bobbed. "Your Grace."

"Please have a seat, ladies."

Sophia and Lady Lucas returned to the divan as the duchess filled an opposite seat. She looked over her shoulder. "I will serve our guests, Jenkins."

"Yes, Your Grace."

The butler and maid quietly quit the room.

Sophia stared at her counterpart. She was everything Sophia was not: a respectable wife without a sordid past. Oh, she was a pirate's daughter, too. But her kin protected her from the scandalous secret. Sophia had no one to guard her from her own past transgressions. She had to protect herself. And that meant she had to resolve the mystery of her invitation. Why was the duchess so pleased to meet her brother's former mistress?

"Thank you for inviting us to the castle," said Lady Lucas. "We are honored."

"It's my pleasure."

The duchess looked at Sophia again, giddy.

Sophia shifted.

"How was your journey?" said Mirabelle. "Are you tired? I've prepared two of our best rooms. Would you like to rest? Refresh?"

Lady Lucas smiled. "You are too kind, Your Grace."

The door burst opened.

A four-year-old child with twirling gold locks bounced inside the room, waving a bonnet with green ribbon. "Look what I found, Mama!" She placed the frilly cap on her head, but it was too large for her. The headpiece slumped over her brow, covering her big blue eyes.

Lady Lucas frowned. "That's my bonnet."

"Oh no," Mirabelle groaned. "Alice!"

The sprite peeked at her mother from under the cap before she kicked up her feet and dashed from the parlor. Both the duchess and Lady Lucas chased after the girl, leaving Sophia alone in the room, staring blankly and listening to the ruckus as it unfolded in the passageway.

A few minutes later, the duchess returned—alone. She closed the door and shut her eyes. "That child will be the end of me."

Sophia pinched her lips. She would never know the headache of a household of noisy brats. She was glad about that.

The duchess sighed and moved away from the door. She headed for the serving dishes and poured two cups of steaming tea. "I'm afraid Lady Lucas is indisposed." She circled the furniture, petticoats swishing, and offered Sophia the light refreshment. "Alice got her fingers into the luggage. Lady Lucas is with the maids, tending to the mess."

Poor Lady Lucas.

But Sophia was in a similar bind. She now had to confront the duchess alone. The woman was soft-spoken and courteous when Lady Lucas was in the room, but now . . .

Sophia set the tea aside, feeling insecure about holding the dainty set of dishes. "Congratulations on the birth of your son."

"Thank you. Henry's a joy. He sleeps most of the time." A clatter resounded from the passageway. "He's quiet as a mouse."

Sophia looked at her hands. After a few silent moments, she wondered, "About the invitation . . ."

"Yes, I'm glad I have you alone, Sophia. May I call you Sophia?"

She nodded.

"You and I have always lived an ocean apart." Mirabelle smiled. "I'm glad we meet at last."

Why *was* she smiling?

"Are you well, Sophia? Oh, listen to me . . . I'm sorry about the loss of your friend. Lady Lucas informed me about the tragedy. How did the girl die?"

"She, um . . ."

"Forgive me. You don't want to talk about the ordeal, I understand. You're still feeling ill." She set her teacup aside and lifted to her feet before she took Sophia by the hand. "Come. I'll escort you to your room."

Sophia snatched her hand away.

Mirabelle frowned. "Is something the matter?"

"Forgive me, Your Grace."

She smiled and settled beside her on the divan. "Belle, please."

The sweet scent of citrus soap filled Sophia's nose. She took in a deep breath, for the tangy fragrance reminded her of the tasty fruits on the tropical island, and the thought of home always put her uneasy mind to rest.

"Why did you invite me to the castle, Belle?"

"You are Dawson's daughter."

Sophia looked at her, confounded. "What?"

"I love your father." She slipped her hand through Sophia's arm. "And so I love you, too. You are a part of him."

Her father was so fearsome. Mad. It was the first time someone had ever treated her *well* for being the man's offspring . . . That wasn't true. James had treated her well for being Dawson's daughter, too.

Sophia's thoughts swirled. "My father is dead."

"I know," said the duchess, her voice a soft inflection. "Word reached me through my brothers. I regret I never had the opportunity to tell him thank you in person. He saved my father from slavery. He allowed my father to return home. I can't express my gratitude to him anymore, but I can express it to you."

Sophia sighed. For a decade, Drake Hawkins had remained captive aboard a naval vessel, pressed into service. It was her father who had attacked the ship and offered the weary sailors an opportunity to join his pirate crew. Drake Hawkins had turned traitor. He had lived a brutal existence under a sadistic naval captain for far too long. He had no feeling of loyalty left for the crown, which had snatched him away from his home and kin. And so he had joined Dawson's crew, touring the Caribbean for another two years in servitude to her father.

It was the way of the sea: allegiance and duty. But soon Drake had befriended her father—she suspected it was Drake who'd befriended him, for her father wasn't the affable sort—and he was eventually set free with his fair share of the booty. Drake had returned home to his family after a twelve-year hiatus. And he'd captained his own pirate vessel then, the *Bonny Meg*. The Hawkins family had flourished. Mirabelle and her two younger brothers had come along. And it was all "thanks" to Sophia's father.

The duchess was simpering again.

Sophia's heart slowly shriveled. The duchess wanted to pamper her in place of her savior father. James had had nothing to do with the invitation to the castle. The woman didn't even know Sophia was her brother's former whore. She wouldn't be so kind to her then. She would be like all the others, dismayed and repulsed.

Sophia almost wished the woman *was* privy to the

truth, then Sophia wouldn't have to maintain the pretense. Now she had to conform to an image of Dawson's saintly daughter. And she had to keep her affair with Black Hawk an even firmer secret.

"As soon as I heard you were in the country, I wanted to meet you. I feel like we are sisters, you and I. Both pirates' daughters. Look!"

There was a thin gold chain at her bust and a ring. It looked familiar. Sophia examined it more closely. The emblem was a winged hourglass. It was a pirate symbol, sometimes a part of the pirate flag, warning ships—prey—that time was running out for them, that they were about to be attacked.

"It belonged to your father." Mirabelle stroked the bauble. "He gifted it to my father before the two parted ways. My father always loved the ring. It reminded him that time was precious. He presented it to me for my twentieth year . . . just before he died."

Sophia eyed the other woman thoughtfully. The ring linked them in kinship, she supposed. But being part of a family was a wistful sentiment, for Sophia had not enjoyed the succor of familial rapport since her time on the island with her father . . . and the Hawkins brothers. And that time was long since dead.

"Why didn't you write to tell me you were coming to England, Sophia? I would have sponsored your come-out."

She said stiffly, "We've never even met."

"We have now." Mirabelle cupped her hand. "If you need anything from me, you need only ask. My home is your home."

It was a thoughtful but misguided sentiment. Sophia didn't belong inside the castle. Not with the duchess: James's beloved sister. She dishonored the woman with her presence. James would think so. Sophia belonged with the earl. Then she would be on equal footing with the duchess.

Again the door opened.

Sophia's heart swelled as the dark and towering figure sauntered into the room.

James!

He looked dashing in a close-fitted vest and double-breasted, tailed coat. Strapped in snug trousers and high leather boots, he was dressed in black. Formidable. Respectable. Long locks fastened in a queue, there was a wayward tress that curled under his eye. That one imperfection shattered the visage. The loose and sooty hair testified to the wild beast that breathed beneath the thick apparel. He had just witnessed his mistress and his sister in the same room, holding hands.

He was angry.

Slowly Sophia lifted to her feet, pulse throbbing, and approached him. He had paused beside the door, bemused and furious. He now followed her every step with his deep blue eyes. He set her blood and skin on fire with that hard and hot-tempered glare. So smoldering. So profound. She itched to strike him. She stopped beside him instead.

His breathing was shallow. She heard the short and heavy drafts of air seep into his lungs. She felt the warmth of his breath, too. It smacked her cheeks.

Sophia's bones trembled as she struggled to keep the shame in her breast: the shame he compounded with his sinister regard.

"Go to hell, *sweetheart*," she whispered before she brushed past him and bustled from the room.

Chapter 17

⁓~⟡~⁓

The woman's venomous words seeped into James's blood and weakened him, made him numb.

What was *she* doing here?

"Do you know who that is, James?"

The tart inquiry punctured the thick and murky cloud in his head, and he glanced at his sister. "Do you?"

Mirabelle placed her arms akimbo. "It's Dawson's daughter, so why are you glowering?"

Dawson's devious and cold-blooded daughter.

I belong with anyone else but you!

He let out a slow, deep breath. The words resounded in his head, making his skull throb and his blood burn. She had tricked him. She had once made him believe he belonged with her. She had once accepted him for who he was. She had desired him for it. And he had desired her. For her independence and her refusal to submit to social convention. Free with her words, laughter, and body, she had concealed no pretenses. No false airs. But now the woman was a fraud. She wanted to be a countess. But *he* wasn't an earl. And she would stop at nothing to claim that infernal title, even threaten him . . .

James looked at his sister, so ashen. He imagined the blade pressed between Sophia's breasts. He imagined it pressed under his sister's throat and he thundered across the room. "Are you all right, Belle? Did Sophia hurt you?"

Mirabelle lifted a slender blond brow. "Are you daft, James?"

"What is Sophia doing here?" he demanded.

Was the witch looking for some way to snag the earl? Was she ruined and desperate and seeking support from his sister to reestablish her standing in society? She had put her treasured reputation in jeopardy by spending four days aboard the *Bonny Meg* with him. She would do anything to reclaim her cherished status, even brandish her knife. His sister wasn't privy to the woman's true, wicked nature. But he was; he still had the scar on his chin to prove it.

Mirabelle frowned. "I heard Sophia was in Town, so I invited her to the castle."

"Why?"

"In honor of Dawson, of course."

James swallowed the dread that had welled in his breast. Sophia had not come to the castle to seek favor from the duchess. She had come at the behest of his sister. She had come in lieu of her father: the man who'd curtailed the misery James had endured as a child.

You must help me, James. You must help me now that Papa is gone. I need you, James. I can't take care of you and William by myself. You will help Mama, won't you, James?

He shuddered at the haunting reflection. He had looked after his brother. He had labored for food. But he had not helped his mother. She had sobbed in loneliness every night for years. She had toiled every day as a milkmaid, apple seller, or scavenger to feed him and his kin. And as he and William had matured, so had their needs: the need for more clothing, more food. However much he'd worked to compensate for the burden, it had never been enough. She had depended on him for help and he had failed her.

"What are *you* doing here, James?"

He stared at his sister. She looked so much like their mother. She had the same golden curls and eyes as Megan Hawkins, while he and his brothers distinctly mirrored their father with their dark features and blue eyes.

Mirabelle was weary, her flesh fair, after the difficult birth of her son. And now that she was a mother, too, he wondered if she suffered under the same burden.

He bussed her pale brow. He wasn't the mawkish sort; the sentiment repulsed him. He had only ever kissed his sister once before . . . right before her near death. But the desire had welled inside him again, and he hadn't quashed it.

"Can't I visit with you, Belle?"

She quirked her brows. "Of course you can. But that's not why you're here, is it?"

The room soon filled with the rest of the Hawkins brood as his brothers entered the parlor and circled Mirabelle in greeting.

William hugged her. "It's good to see you again, Belle."

Edmund frowned. "Are you well? You don't look well."

"Aye, she's well." Quincy kissed her cheek. He brooked no argument that she was still ill. He refused to even contemplate the thought of losing her. "Where are the children?"

"Yes, I'm fine." Mirabelle welcomed each sibling in turn before she said, "Henry is asleep in the nursery, but I'm afraid Alice is terrorizing the household."

Quincy beamed as he dropped into the nearest seat and propped his boots on the furniture. "Still at odds with Squirt?"

"Yes!" She paled even more. "I need a governess."

"Sit, Belle," ordered James. "Rest."

What was she doing out of bed? Two months had passed since the birth of her son, but she still looked weak.

James remembered that wretched night. He remembered standing in the passageway just outside the birthing room, listening to her desperate wails. She had not delivered the afterbirth in a timely manner and they had all feared she would perish from the fever . . . but she had lived.

James suppressed the chill gripping his bones. He shrugged the icy fingers away and eyed his sister closely.

"I'm fine, really." She was naturally mulish. However, she heeded his advice this once and filled an empty seat. "What are all of you doing here?"

"We need to speak with your husband," said William.

She groaned. "I thought we agreed Damian is family. You can't kill him."

As soon as he was sure she was all right, James headed for a window and stopped beside the speckled pane of glass. The former "Duke of Rogues" wasn't worthy of his sister's hand. James would like nothing better than to see her widowed. But she adored the bastard, and that was cause enough for James to keep his fists at his sides.

"We don't want to hurt him, Belle," returned William.

Edmund snorted.

"We *won't* hurt him," the lieutenant clarified.

"Then what do you want with him?" she demanded.

Quincy crossed his ankles. "We need to speak with his brother, Adam Westmore."

"Why?"

William sighed. "We're in a bit of trouble, Belle."

She pinched her brows together. "What sort of trouble."

"Don't fret," said Quincy.

She raised her voice a notch. "About what?"

William folded his hands behind his back. "Have you read the paper in recent days?"

"No." She frowned. "Damian won't let me near any dreadful news or scandal. He hides the paper from me. Why? What did you do?"

"*We* didn't do anything," insisted Edmund.

Quincy quipped, "I like how you trust us, Belle."

She humphed. "Then what's in the paper?"

"News about a band of impostors," said William.

She made a moue. "Impostors?"

William hesitated. "Sailors posing as . . . us."

Mirabelle's eyes widened. "I was afraid this might happen one day!"

"Don't worry, Belle," he quickly assured her. "We'll find the impostors before word leaks out about our true identities and you're ruined."

"I'm not worried about *that*, but your necks."

"Do you need a drink?" wondered Edmund.

"I'm not an invalid," she snapped. "I won't faint." She huffed. The brothers quieted as she stewed for a few moments. "What do you want with my brother-in-law, Adam?"

James fingered the stained glass. He let the vibrant shades play across his hand. "Adam might know more about the impostors."

"He once hunted us in revenge, remember?" William rubbed his chin. "After the robbery at sea, Adam searched for us, but stumbled upon a band of bootleggers posing as pirates instead. We need to speak to him about the bootleggers. The men and our impostors might be one and the same."

She appeared thoughtful. "You don't have a very good rapport with the man. Do you think Adam will help you?"

"We're family now." Quincy grinned. "Of course he'll help us."

James wasn't so sure, though. Some sour feelings might still linger between the two clans. However, James had agreed to come to the castle, to try to gather more information about the impostors. William had staunchly promoted the idea, too, believing the excursion would get the captain's mind off Sophia. But nothing short of revenge would get the woman out of James's head, disentangle her icy fingers from his heart. And now he had another opportunity to obtain his revenge.

He slowly reached into his pocket and caressed the shattered timepiece.

May you rot in everlasting hell.

That biting inscription still hounded him, tortured him, strengthened his desire for revenge. Sophia had him in chains, the witch. She still enslaved him. But he would break the bonds keeping him shackled to the past.

He would break her.

"But we need to know where Adam lives," expounded Quincy. "He's hiding."

"He's not hiding." Mirabelle frowned. "I get regular letters from him and his wife."

"He lives in the wilderness, Belle."

"Rot, Quincy! The couple lives near the sea."

"There's no address," grumbled Edmund.

"Right." She sighed. "Very well, I'll have Damian note the directions to their home."

"Thank you, Belle," the brothers returned in unison.

"Hell's fire," she muttered. "You've all too many enemies."

William consoled her with "We'll have a few less as soon as we find the impostors."

"I'll have the staff prepare your usual rooms." She lifted from her seat. "But you have to behave during your stay at the castle."

Quincy grimaced. "Why?"

"I have company."

He griped and removed his dusty boots from the furniture. "You mean, I have to *behave*?"

"Who is it?" said William.

"Dawson's daughter."

The men quieted.

Quincy quickly propped his feet back on the furniture. "Oh, well, in that case."

Mirabelle looked at him sternly. "She might be a pirate's daughter, too, but you still have to behave, Quincy."

"Why? She's—"

"Quincy," James drawled in a low yet deadly voice. He didn't want Mirabelle to know about his former relationship with Dawson's daughter. It wasn't right for her to hear about such intimate things.

"She's my guest," returned Mirabelle sharply. "We all owe her father a great deal of gratitude. I want to offer her my hospitality and friendship, so be polite. No scandals!"

"Too late," said Quincy. "She's James's mistress."

James gnashed his teeth. "You miserable son of a—"

"She's *what*?" Mirabelle glared at James and crossed the room. She smacked him in the arm. "How dare you!"

He glowered. "What was that for?"

"That poor girl is trying to make her way through society and she's recently lost a dear friend. She's vulnerable. How dare you seduce her!"

Quincy snorted. "He seduced her eight years ago."

"*What?*"

"Shut up, Quincy!" James barked.

The Duke of Wembury strolled into the room, unruffled by all the customary familial noise. "Jenkins wants to know where to put the snake?"

Mirabelle blinked. "Snake?"

"Achoo!"

Sophia eyed the old woman in bed as she dabbed a cool compress across her wrinkled brow. "We should not have journeyed to the castle, Lady Lucas."

The matron had suffered great stress over the past few days, keeping her charge's disappearance a secret. The strain had weakened her, made her more susceptible to illness.

"Rubbish." She sniffed. "I'll be fine. All I need is Dr. Crombie to mesmerize me, then I'll be cured of the chill."

Sophia admired her grit and good cheer. She wasn't one to forsake her duty, not even for a cold. She would see her charge safely at the castle and ensure all whisper of scandal quashed before she'd confess to any discomfort.

"Would you like me to summon a physician, Lady Lucas?"

"For the sniffles? No, my dear."

"I'm sorry, Lady Lucas." Sophia stroked the woman's hand. "It's my fault you're sick."

"What tripe." The matron rubbed her nose with a kerchief. "It's the weather, I'm sure. Autumn is approaching. There's a chill in the air, I can feel it." She sighed. "I won't be with you for supper tonight, I'm afraid. But don't fret, my dear. The duchess will be there. She is respectable. You won't have to endure the barbarian's company alone."

Sophia set the compress aside, a thick darkness flowing through her veins and pumping into her heart. The shame still lingered in her breast. The black devil had made it clear she wasn't worthy to be in his sister's company. What would he do to her at supper? How else would he humiliate her? He had suffered scorn and ostracism at the earl's country house party. But now he was surrounded by his kin. Now he was in his element and *she* was the outsider. And she suspected he would make her feel it keenly.

"I would much rather stay here and take care of you, Lady Lucas."

"No, my dear. You must honor our host and hostess. Be strong. I know you dislike the captain's company, but be brave."

What *was* the pirate captain doing at the castle anyway? Had he followed her to the ancient keep?

Had he come to punish her for rejecting him aboard the *Bonny Meg*?

"It will look like the barbarian is courting you."

Sophia's heart quivered. "What?"

"Forgive me, my dear. I was thinking aloud." She meshed her pasty lips together. "The captain is visiting his sister, but it will look like the man is courting you once word reaches the *ton* that you are both at the castle. It's such a vexation. He isn't supposed to be here."

Sophia quieted the myriad fretful thoughts that besieged her with a deep and measured breath. No, he wasn't supposed to be at the castle. He wasn't supposed to be back in her life at all. But Providence had thought it a splendid jest to pair them together again.

"Perhaps all is not lost," said the matron, nose congested. "We might be able to use the situation to our advantage. The earl might still propose."

"Do you really think so?"

"Oh yes. Do you remember our talk about jealousy? As soon as you and the captain boarded that boat—"

"What boat?!"

"The rowboat at the picnic, my dear."

Sophia's pulse softened. She was dizzy. For a moment she had believed the matron was privy to her sojourn aboard the *Bonny Meg*. Now *that* report would ruin her for sure.

"As soon as you and the captain had boarded the boat," the old woman croaked, "the earl was positively green. What will he think to learn you are staying with the captain's sister?"

What would he think, indeed? All Sophia could think about was the trouble she had had in that rowboat . . . as the damnable pirate lord had aroused her senses to wretched want before he'd abandoned her, unfulfilled.

"Our trip to the castle might stir the earl's conviction to marry you," said Lady Lucas. "The man is wary. Or mulish. He thinks he can take his time proposing, that you will always be waiting for him. Perhaps our visit with the duchess will convince him otherwise—and encourage him to act before he loses you."

Sophia's heart pinched. "He won't lose me to the captain!"

The thought made her heart swell with gloomy memories. She had not been good enough for the captain seven years ago. And she still wasn't good enough for him. Not now. Not when he had a duchess for a sister. If the man ever married, he would wed a woman with pure blue blood. Not one with a pirate for a father and a wench for a mother.

"Marry the barbarian? Outrageous, my dear! But we can let the earl *think* he is losing you to the captain."

Sophia pressed her fingers against her breastbone and massaged the muscles, pulsing with vigor. "But the earl is an honorable man. You said so yourself, Lady Lucas. That he might step aside if he believes the captain is interested in me . . . or he might search elsewhere for a bride if he thinks I am attached to the captain."

"That was *before* the country house party. Now the earl knows—and likes—you better. He might not be so honorable anymore. He might fight for you, Miss Dawson. Men do that, you know?"

"With swords?"

"How uncivilized! No, my dear. I mean he will not be such a gentleman. He will not just step aside and let the captain have you. He will court you enthusiastically instead. Perhaps even propose."

Sophia was wary. The season was over and most of the peerage had settled in the country in preparation for the approaching winter. What if the earl resumed his courtship of her in the spring? Or not at all?

"You should go below, my dear."

"Yes, Lady Lucas."

Sophia left the woman's bedside and approached the tall mirror. She perused her reflection, eyeing the golden satin and lace. She touched her locks in lambent strokes to ensure the thick tresses firmly in place before she sighed wearily.

"You look lovely, my dear."

"Thank you, Lady Lucas." She glanced at the matron, so pale. "Are you sure you'll be all right?"

"A bit of rest will do me good." She fluttered her kerchief. "Now off with you."

Sophia sighed again. She offered the old woman a weak smile before she quietly quit the room and traversed the lonely causeway, her innards twisted in dread.

The elegant wall sconces illuminated her path, guiding her to the dining hall. She stayed on the lighted trail, peeking into the other dark passages that branched away from the main one. She wondered if Black Hawk was staying in one of the rooms draped in shadows. She wondered if he was staying in one of the other wings, far away from her.

Not far enough.

He was never far from her thoughts. He lived inside her head, it seemed. He lived under her skin for sure, for she sensed his burning eyes on her even now.

Sophia reached the top of the steps and paused. She stared at the waiting sentry stationed at the lower level, and hardened.

He stood at the base of the stairwell, blocking the route with his robust form—and commanding eyes. That set of hard blue eyes willed her to remain still as he perused her figure in thorough detail.

"Do I meet with your approval?" she gritted.

Slowly he lifted his eyes from her toes and stabbed her with another piercing stare, making her bones rattle. "Take off the diamonds."

Sophia touched the jewels at her throat. She fingered the cold stones as she descended the steps, gaze fixed firmly on the barbarian.

He was even bigger as she approached him, thick arms folded across his wide chest. The smell of the dust from the road, the vegetation from the wood still remained in his hair, lingered on his skin. She inhaled the heady and natural musk. She inhaled him. The man's scent swirled through her senses, lighting her blood and making her heart pound. She was accustomed to the treacherous desire of her flesh and bones. She had learned to accept the stirring want within her whenever he was near. She had learned to stand her ground despite it.

She stilled a step above him, at level with him. She delved into the dark blue pools of his eyes and searched for truth. He hated to see her in the jewels. Why?

He sensed her probing stare, and his eyes blackened even more, as if to shield her from the truth, to keep her from delving too deep into his soul.

He had once let her inside his heart. He had once let her see and hear his every thought and feeling. But now he cast her out of his inner being. And the chill was biting.

"I like the diamonds," she said tersely.

Slowly he inclined his head. She gasped as he set his lips so close to hers.

"The earl isn't here, Sophia." He brushed her lips with his warm mouth, ever so softly. "There is no one here to seduce."

She shuddered. "Not even you?"

He stiffened. "If you want to seduce me, take off the diamonds."

She was woozy. The black devil always played with her senses, manipulated her good thought. "I think I'll keep them, then."

The balmy look in his eyes singed her. He stepped away from the landing. She quickly skirted past him and headed through the unfamiliar causeway, searching for the dining hall.

He followed. "Where's the harridan?"

The looming shadow at her heels was hard to ignore. Worse, the searing look from his eyes, pressing into her spine, made each step a struggle.

She returned in a prim manner, "Lady Lucas will not be joining us for supper this evening."

"Oh?"

"She's ill."

"Pity."

Sophia gnashed her teeth at his terse response.

"Turn left," he said in a low timbre. "The dining hall is at the end of the passage."

She slowed, overwhelmed by the realization that she was walking straight into a den of lions.

He bumped into her backside, the touch of his hard muscles sizzling.

"What's the matter, sweetheart? Aren't you hungry?" He dropped his lips beside her bejeweled ear and whispered, "I know I am."

She shivered.

She closed her eyes and let the comforting heat from his torso warm her. She wasn't prepared to confront his family yet. She wasn't ready to be put on exhibit in front of *them*.

James was still behind her. He sensed her misgiving, but he didn't snipe or touch her. He remained at her backside. He let her feed off his strength, his energy. And she did. She was rooted to the spot. She stayed there until the unease drifted away from her bones.

Sophia opened her eyes. At the end of the passageway was a set of tall and elaborate arched doors. The room was bright with candlelight, and warm with the sound of familial laughter.

She sensed she was even more out of place, but she now had the vigor to move onward, to greet her host and hostess and the rest of the Hawkins brothers.

Sophia approached the entrance. She paused between the well-polished doors and bristled as the babble hushed and the occupants inside the room stared at her.

They know.

It was there in their eyes. The pirate brothers had known for a long time she was the captain's former mistress, but now the duke and duchess were privy to the truth about her scandalous past, too.

Sophia dropped her chin and whispered over her shoulder, "You told them, didn't you?"

But she didn't get a response. She didn't need one. The barbarian wanted to humiliate her with the truth. He wanted to see her quail.

She wouldn't give him *that* satisfaction.

Chapter 18

"**Y**ou told them, didn't you?"

She sounded betrayed.

James noted the way her breath shuddered. She quickly lost her voice, too. She only mouthed the last word, "you."

He was disarmed by the discomfort in his breast, a squeezing pressure on his heart and lungs. He quashed the feeble sentiment. What the hell was he feeling sorry about? He wasn't the one who had betrayed their past. That blame rested solely with his dim-witted brother, Quincy.

Sophia entered the room.

James admired her pluck. And yet he wasn't surprised by it. She wasn't a coward. Not at heart. She had let the posh and amoral ways of society pervert her spirit. The ridiculous taboos had stripped her of some mettle, molding her to be another mindless miss seeking preservation and status.

But she wasn't robbed of all grit just yet. And he relished the confident way she strutted across the room. Every muscle in him pulsed with delight to see her behaving like the old Sophia again: the woman who had once wandered the plantation house in the buff without a thought to superficial mores.

James followed her inside the hall. He watched the candlelight shimmer and bounce off the sensuous fabric of her evening gown, a delicious honey brown. There was a short train that trailed behind her like a siren's fin. He watched the supple material glide across the floor and round the furnishings as she approached the long dining table, festooned with burnished silverware.

"Good evening, Miss Dawson." Damian Westmore, the Duke of Wembury, welcomed Sophia with a courteous bow. "It's a pleasure to meet you."

James glared at the former "Duke of Rogues." The reprobate had a notorious disposition for a beautiful face. James was convinced the man made his sister a miserable husband, that he would never reform his philandering ways. But the duke was either a skilled thespian or he really cared for his wife, for the bastard was polite and maintained a thoughtful countenance. No licentious stares or wicked winks.

"Thank you, Your Grace," Sophia returned in a cool yet cordial manner.

A footman escorted her to an empty seat beside William. The lieutenant lifted to his feet in deference. Edmund and Quincy followed suit.

Sophia gracefully took the chair, her skirt swirling around her ankles and the furniture's legs.

The men resumed their seats, their expressions inscrutable. However, Quincy was simpering like a distasteful fop. James had a ruthless desire to grind his booted heel into the pup's toes.

The duchess was seated at the head of the table. She smiled in greeting. "How do you like your room, Sophia?"

James was escorted by another footman to the other end of the long table. It was a corner seat between Edmund and the duke, who was positioned opposite his wife at the other head of the lengthy table. James suspected his sister had orchestrated the place settings to keep him away from her guest, the "poor girl." But Mirabelle would be hard-pressed to quash his deep-rooted desire for revenge.

"I like my room very much," said Sophia. "Thank you, Belle."

Sophia was stiff in tone and posture. James noted the sheen across her brow. The moisture shimmered under the dappling candlelight, the roasting candlelight. The ball of fire was suspended above the table. The iron hands twisted together to form an intricate pattern of horns that carried dozens of white candles.

It was easy to assume the heat from the glowing aura warmed her features, but he sensed it was more than the flickering lights that made her skin glisten. She was uncomfortable. And he disliked seeing her ill-at-ease. He had no tender regard for the heartless woman; however, he resented the insinuation that his family was akin to the cold and brutal *ton*, that his kin ostracized or tormented a welcome guest. Sophia was putting herself through hell with her own distorted thoughts and twisted perceptions.

Let her.

Mirabelle glanced around the room. "And Lady Lucas?"

Sophia folded her hands together and placed them in her lap. She lowered her eyes, too. Was she hiding from the scrutiny?

He willed her to fight. If she thought she was being judged, he wanted her to confront her accusers with defiance, not bleed into the patterned paper and furnishings like a wallflower.

"I'm afraid Lady Lucas isn't feeling well and will not be joining us this evening," said Sophia.

"I'm sorry to hear that." Mirabelle frowned. "Would you like me to summon a physician?"

"It isn't necessary." Sophia returned, "It's just a chill."

"Very well, then." The duchess looked at the butler. "Jenkins, please prepare a meal for Lady Lucas and send it to her room."

"Yes, Your Grace."

The butler then signaled for the cuisine to be served. As a host of servants transferred the steaming platters and salvers from the buffet to the table, James resumed his vigil of Sophia. He observed her as she unfurled a pristine napkin and set it across her knees. She smoothed the material over her skirt with methodical strokes before she lifted her eyes—and glared at him.

The rich brown pools burrowed into him, and he was filled with the intense warmth of her bile. Now *that* was Sophia.

He smiled.

She looked away from him.

Soon each plate was stuffed with roasted fare, and the glasses filled with wine. The staff then vacated the hall, shutting the grand doors in customary fashion.

Sophia peeked at the secured doors, looking caged. She was likely accustomed to the servants remaining inside the room during the course of the meal, to offer assistance if needed. It ensured civil conversation, for one didn't discuss matters of an inappropriate nature during supper; the staff might overhear and gossip about it later.

But James's family didn't abide by social convention at home. They endured enough suffocating rules and customs in society. Supper at the castle was always an informal affair.

Sophia looked meek. Did she think they were going to hound her now? Rip her to pieces? As *they* had ripped him apart at the earl's dry and fastidious country house party?

He snorted softly. She was thinking like one of *them* already. She had condemned Imogen for her sins, and now she awaited the same fate to befall her. But no one would scorn her. Not here. His brothers liked her— Quincy liked her too much, he thought sourly—and Mirabelle adored her for being Dawson's daughter. The duke was wont to scandal himself, and so offered no moral judgment on others. In truth, she was seated at the table with equals. Every heart that pulsed in the room concealed a dark family secret. And if Sophia just shrugged off the unnatural manacles that caged her, she'd see it, too. She'd see she had no one to fear . . . except him.

Quincy dropped his fork as soon as the servants had departed from the hall. "I thought they'd never leave."

Mirabelle glared at him.

"You're not serious, Belle." Quincy gesticulated. "Lady Lucas isn't even here. We're all family!"

But Mirabelle was unmoved by her brother's reasonable cries. She glared at him until her cheeks flushed. A surly Quincy was forced to resume the proper supper accoutrements or risk being shot.

Mirabelle sighed in exasperation—and a whisper of mortification. But the pretension wasn't necessary for Sophia's sake, James thought. She was a pirate's daughter, too. She had witnessed far more scandalous behavior than a man eating with his fingers.

However, James remained quiet about the matter. He didn't want to upset his sister and ruffle her weak disposition even more. He still believed Mirabelle belonged in bed, resting. But she was too headstrong to heed the suggestion, he suspected.

"Edmund and I will set out tomorrow to take care of some business," said William as he sliced the roasted game.

James glanced at the lieutenant. Their "business" was to contact the duke's brother and gather whatever information they could about the bootleggers and potential impostors. James wasn't sure what sort of assistance the duke's brother would offer the retired pirates, though. There might still be buried resentment between the two families. But the hunt for the impostors had stalled, and it was worth the effort to make fresh inquiries into their whereabouts.

Quincy swallowed a mouthful of pheasant. "I'm staying here to visit with Squirt and Henry."

The table quieted as everyone reflected upon the same conclusion, that James was also staying behind to "visit" with Sophia. That wasn't true, not entirely. He and Quincy had resolved to remain at the castle, for years ago they had both robbed the duke's brother during a raid at sea. The men had agreed it was wiser for William and Edmund to make the seaside journey instead. James had intended to visit with his niece and nephew, too . . . however, now he had another houseguest to engage his interest.

James looked across the table at Sophia's profile. She pinkened. She had sensed the table's thoughts, too. He eyed the rosy pigment bleed through her cheek and jaw and even singe her earlobe. She never used to blush, he reflected. Very little had embarrassed her in the past. The only time he had ever seen her flush with color was after a vigorous bedding. But now the slightest indiscretion mortified her. She really had changed.

"The weather is cooling," said the duke. He filled the vacuous silence with his booming voice. "There was even dew on the ground this morning."

The table murmured in agreement.

"I can't wait for autumn," said Mirabelle. "I love it when the leaves change shade. Oh, Sophia! Have you ever seen the woods change color?"

"No," she said quietly.

"Then you've never seen snow, I imagine." The duke pressed onward: "Are you prepared for the winter, Miss Dawson?"

Sophia flicked her fingers behind her ear. Her thick tresses were knotted in a fashionable swirl. Every lock was neatly in place, and yet she still fidgeted with phantom loose curls. "Lady Lucas will prepare me for the winter, I'm sure."

"You should go ice-skating," suggested William.

Edmund smacked his lips at the tasty fare before he groused, "You should stay home beside the fire."

Quincy quipped, "There are other ways to keep warm."

The pup choked. Someone had kicked him under the table as punishment for the double entendre. James suspected it was his sister.

"She can purchase fur." Quincy made a moue. He reached under the table to rub his leg. "There's no reason for her to be trapped indoors."

The table quieted once more. James stirred the

food on his plate, thinking about Sophia and the coming winter. The duke was right; she had never seen snow. A profound longing welled inside James to be with her when she eyed the icy flakes for the first time or touched the frosty ground in wonder. The longing stripped him of the firm darkness holding his heart. For a moment, he yearned to forget about the past and his quest for revenge. For a moment, he yearned to be with Sophia again, to show her the wonders of his world as she had showed him the wonders of hers.

"I remember the first time Alice saw snow." Mirabelle smiled. "She tried to catch the puffs to take a closer look at them. She was so miffed when the flakes disappeared in her hand."

The duke and duchess exchanged fond glances. James was disturbed by the growing ache in his belly. He had to finally admit that the roguish bastard cared for his sister. Even worse, their affectionate exchange had made him ache for the same solidarity with Sophia.

But only for a moment.

He crushed the weak sentiment inside him. Sophia had deserted him. The tenderness they had shared on the island had been a manifestation in his head, a farce on her part. She had used him for her own erotic desires and then discarded him for loftier ambitions.

He was such an ass.

Sophia sensed the heat stemming from the pirate captain's torrid gaze. She fastened her eyes to the dishes on the table in a bid to ignore him, but she eventually surrendered to the treacherous impulse and eyed the black devil.

What was *he* looking so peeved about? She was the one trapped between his loyal kinfolk. She should be the one glowering at him.

She cut him a fierce stare before she returned to her meal, the fare cooling on her plate. She had lost her appetite even before she had entered the dining hall. The desire for food had deserted her the moment she had realized she would be sharing the castle with James.

She shuddered. She had shared the earl's country house with James, too. But the pirate lord was still a memory to her then: a memory of lost passion. After their intimate encounter aboard the *Bonny Meg*, the memory of lost passion was alive again, so vivid and palpable. So, too, was the hurt. It thrived in her breast and choked her breath at times.

"The season is over." Mirabelle glanced at her youngest brother. "I understand you attended a ball a few weeks ago. Did you enjoy yourself?"

"Always," said Quincy.

Edmund snorted.

Mirabelle frowned. She glared at Edmund for making the indelicate sound at the supper table, but he was too engrossed with the succulent fare to regard his sister's baleful expression.

Sophia, on the other hand, listened and observed every detail that transpired between the family, wretchedly aware that she was the outsider intruding upon their informal gathering. She waited for James to elaborate upon the earl's ball, where she and the pirate lord had reunited after seven years, but the brigand remained tactfully silent. He didn't even mention the end of the season or the dreadful truth that she was still unattached to the earl. She should probably be grateful for his quiet manner. She was not, however. The man's calm tended to unnerve her more than his blustering temper. He was honest when he fulminated. There was something insidious about his temperate nature.

Slowly the duchess returned her attention to Quincy. "And I trust you met many eligible ladies at the ball. Did you court any of them?"

"Many," the pup quipped, his mouth full of pheasant.

The woman's frown darkened. She whispered, "Don't be a pig."

Quincy looked at her askance. He then brandished the cutlery. "I'm not."

The duchess blushed.

Sophia glanced at her own plate again and mustered the will to partake in the fare before her hosts perceived something was amiss.

The table was quiet for a moment. But then Quincy said in a slapdash manner, "James's been having the most fun, though."

Sophia coughed.

Mirabelle twitched.

Quincy yelped. He reached under the table and massaged his leg. "Who keeps doing that?" He scowled. "I mean, James was at the ball *and* he went to a house party."

"He also attended the opera," William offered dryly.

"You've been busy, Captain Hawkins." The duke was blasé. "Whenever did you find the time to pirate a passenger vessel, too?"

Sophia looked across the table at James, who was glowering at William and his brother-in-law. But both the duke and the lieutenant were unmoved by the captain's ominous glare. Perhaps they were well acquainted with the black devil's hostility, for neither seemed perturbed by it.

"Yes, about the raid at sea." The duchess stared at her husband. "You read that report in the paper, didn't you?"

"I did," he returned primly.

She huffed. "Well, why didn't *you* mention it to me?"

"I didn't want to upset you."

"But the account was about my brothers."

He smiled. "Exactly."

The table quickly erupted in protest, the Hawkins brothers incensed at the insinuation that they aggrieved their sister with their scandalous ways.

Sophia sighed and quietly moved the food across her plate with her fork, thinking about the first time she had dined with the brigands and her father.

Quincy grimaced as he stared at his plate. "What is that?"

"It's Stinking Toes," returned Sophia. "It's an island delicacy."

Edmund slurped the sweet pulp from the fruit without protest.

James glared at the fastidious pup. "Eat it, Quincy."

"But—"

"Sophia prepared it," from William. "Eat it, Quincy."

"Aye, but—"

Patrick Dawson picked up the pistol beside his plate and aimed it at Quincy's head. "Eat it."

Sophia smiled at the warm memory. She had always enjoyed supper on the island with her father and the Hawkins brothers. Informal, even droll, at times, it had always been one of her favorite activities, for she had liked cooking for them and then sharing the meal with them. She missed the camaraderie, the familial rapport.

The table was still embroiled in a heated discussion. Sophia lifted her eyes and glanced at the pirate captain, who was watching her thoughtfully.

Her smile fell. She had let down her guard for a moment. After reflecting upon the past, she had relaxed about her present predicament. It was clear to her now that the duke and duchess, the Hawkins brothers had no desire to torment her or even make her feel uncomfortable. The family was irreverent, even cheeky. It was in their nature. She had nothing to worry about . . . except for James.

She had to protect her heart from the ruthless devil, for he was still out to make her suffer, she was sure.

Chapter 19

Sophia strolled along the pebbled walkway. It was a brisk morning. The sweltering heat of summer was slowly fading away. She wasn't accustomed to the cooling temperatures. She was wearing a spencer. The black velvet material protected her bust from the chill in the air, but the breeze still nipped at her nose.

Sophia explored the immaculate grounds. She searched for tranquillity in the manicured garden with its rows of trimmed hedges and late-blooming roses. The trilling birds offered sweet music as she perused the landscape, thinking about her encounter with the Hawkins brothers, the duke and duchess the other night.

After a few uncomfortable moments had passed, she had come to relax and enjoy the evening. The brothers had treated her well. Quincy had flirted with her. The duke had been kind, as had the duchess. If it wasn't for Black Hawk's company, she would have had a thoroughly gay time.

What's the matter, sweetheart? Aren't you hungry? . . . I know I am.

She shuddered. Throughout supper James had watched her, and whenever he had set his deep blue, hungry eyes on her, she had stilled. Every time he had looked at her, he had roused her blood and attracted her senses.

He had made her hungry, too.

Sophia dismissed the black devil from her mind. She heard a voice, a soft humming. She followed the faint sound to an ornate stone fountain in the center of the garden, where the duchess was resting with an infant in her arms.

Mirabelle patted the babe, wrapped in a white blanket. The small creature was perched on her shoulder, sound asleep.

Sophia admired the quiet couple for a moment. The duchess seemed so content, she thought. So at peace. She and Mirabelle shared a similar past, a common upbringing, and yet their present situations were so vastly singular.

Sophia didn't want to disturb the mother and child, and so she retreated; however, the duchess had spied her loitering.

"Good morning, Sophia." She smiled. "We missed you at breakfast."

Sophia returned the greeting and approached the woman. She settled beside her on the fountain's edge and peeked at the tiny, slumbering features poking through the warm woolly wrapper. The babe was handsome, she thought.

"I'm just taking Henry out for some fresh air while the weather's still warm."

Warm? thought Sophia. So what was the weather like when it was cold?

"How is Lady Lucas?" wondered Mirabelle.

Sophia wove her fingers together. "She's doing well."

"Good." She looked at her askance. "And you?"

Sophia burrowed her booted toes into the pebbled walkway. "I'm fine."

"You seem distracted. Is everything all right?"

"Everything is fine," she parried.

It was a centuries-old game: polite intrusion. The duchess was fishing for answers to questions about Sophia's affair with her brother. It was obvious to them both they were thinking about the same thing, but neither was being forthright about it.

"I know you're still grieving over the loss of your friend—"

"She's not dead."

"What?" The duchess pinched her brows. "But I thought . . . Lady Lucas mentioned in her letter you were in mourning."

"Yes, I suppose I am . . . I can't see her anymore."

"Why?"

"She's ruined."

"Oh, I see."

The duchess fell quiet.

Sophia shifted, the stone fountain uncomfortable even with the layers of fabric under her posterior. "So you see, I am in mourning. She's dead."

"She's not dead."

Sophia shrugged. "It's the same thing." She moved her foot across the rough pebbles, swirling her toes. "The rules of etiquette are strict."

"I understand the rules of etiquette are strict."

Sophia glanced at her sidelong. "But . . . ?"

"But I don't really like following the rules."

Sophia flicked her fingers across the lambent water behind her, the ripples shimmering. There was a time when she had not cared for the rules, either. She had flouted them, in truth. But she had paid for her folly. At times she wanted to defy convention again—to see Imogen, for instance—but always the memory of noisy heckles surfaced to haunt her and keep her in line.

Mirabelle rocked the babe. "Is my brother treating you well?"

What were the odds she was inquiring about her brother Quincy? Slim, Sophia reckoned. But Sophia dreaded talking about the past. It exposed her, made her vulnerable. Still, she decided to stop prevaricating. The duchess was already privy to her former relationship with James. If the woman was going to make a fuss about it, she would have done so already.

"You know who I am, don't you, Belle? Who I was to your brother, I mean?"

"Yes," she said thoughtfully. "Quincy told me."

"Quincy?"

"He doesn't have a feather on his tongue." She sighed. "He says whatever's on his mind, I'm afraid."

So it wasn't James who had betrayed their past? Sophia should have considered one of the other brothers as the culprit. But James was such a ruthless devil, it was so easy to blame him for the treachery. And yet he had already lost the chess game. He had already vowed to keep their island affair a secret. Besides, he would never have talked about her—his mistress— with his beloved sister. Sophia should have known that.

The babe started to fuss. Mirabelle shushed him with a few whispered words. "James doesn't talk much—about anything. I'm his sister, and yet I know so little about him."

Sophia was at a similar disadvantage. She had lived with James for a year before their affair had ended. She had developed a passionate attachment, an intimate bond with the man. She had come to know him. Or so she had thought. The pirate lord's true character was a mystery to her, as well. But she suspected the duchess still wanted to know more about the affair.

"What would you like to know, Belle?"

"Well . . . I've come to believe my brothers will remain bachelors forever, especially James. He's so stubborn sometimes." She grimaced. "All right, he's stubborn all the time. But now I learn there was a period in his life when he was happy with a woman. What happened?"

"I wanted to be married." She shrugged. "He did not."

"I see." Mirabelle was pensive. "I'm not sure if I should be surprised or not by that answer. I don't know my brother's heart very well, a'tall."

He had a small heart, thought Sophia. A black heart. There was room inside the gnarled muscle for his brothers and his sister. But no more. There was no space for her. There had never been any space for her.

Sophia rubbed her hands in her skirt, drying them. "I didn't think I would ever see him again."

"I suppose that's my fault. It was I who dragged him and the rest of my brothers into society. But I don't think James appreciates it. I don't think he's fitting into society."

Sophia snorted inwardly. How was a barbarian supposed to fit into society without polished manners, grace, or charm?

"But you seem to be doing well, Belle."

Mirabelle chuckled. "I am. At last!"

The duchess was also a pirate's daughter. She, too,

had a scandalous past. And yet she was wed and respected. Sophia admired her for the accomplishment. She intended to achieve the same feat herself one day. And there was no reason to suspect she wouldn't be just as content as the duchess.

What will you do when you're hungry, Sophia? What will you do when you're married and your bones throb in the dead of night? Who will you turn to?

Sophia shut her eyes tight and willed away the blackguard's taunts. She would endure the passionless marriage bed, the cordial bond with her husband. It was easier to bear than the ostracism and ridicule she was sure to confront as a fallen woman.

"And you are content, aren't you, Belle?"

"What do you mean?"

"Are you happy being a duchess?"

Mirabelle snorted.

"What's the matter, Belle? Is the duke a poor husband?"

"Not a'tall!" Mirabelle sounded aghast. "He's the best man I know, truly. And I love him dearly . . . I only wish sometimes he wasn't a duke."

Sophia was bewildered. "What?"

"It's such a bother, the pomp and presentation." She sighed. "I'd much rather live in a small and comfortable home, settled near my family and friends."

"And you can't have both?"

"No," she repined. "The demands placed upon me as duchess keep me busy and distracted. I spend very little time with my friends, and even less time with my brothers, who are often at sea. Although to hear my husband complain, you'd think my kin was at the castle *all* the time." She transferred the slumbering babe from one shoulder to the next. "It's just that after my mother died in childbirth to Quincy, and my siblings took to the sea, I lost a sense of family. I prefer an intimate, more homely upbringing for my own children."

That the duchess *had* a title and respectability—and didn't really want it—disarmed Sophia. She had struggled for so long to achieve her goal, she had never thought to wonder: Would she be happy elsewhere in the world? With someone other than the earl? . . . Like James?

Sophia mulled over the thought. But the memory of her affair with James on the tropical island tormented her. She had tried to live apart from social mores. The sensual and dreamy encounters she had shared with the pirate captain had lasted for only a year. It was impossible to evade the pressures from society, she had learned. Even the rebellious Black Hawk obeyed some social convention, for he had refused to marry his mistress.

"And James was *most* adamant I not become a duchess."

Sophia dismissed the longing in her breast, the longing to recapture and change the past, to inquire: "So he didn't want you to marry?" The brigand had made the opposite claim during the earl's country house party. Sophia remembered the words: *I approve of her marrying*. It was hard to forget the words, for they rankled her even now. "Ever?"

"Oh, James wanted me to wed. I was the biggest thorn in his side for years because I refused to marry and have babies and be a proper woman."

Sophia's heart pulsed with vigor. Was *that* what the barbarian considered proper for a woman: marriage and babies? He had denounced *both* on the island, the wretched, lying devil!

"But James loathed the duke, considered him an irredeemable rogue. I was determined to marry Damian, though. Title and all. I entered his world to be with him. And I dragged my brothers—and their enemies—into it, as well."

Sophia stilled her whirling thoughts. "Enemies? Like the impostors?"

Mirabelle lifted a brow. "You know about them?"

"Yes, James told me about the rogues raiding ships in his name."

"He trusted you well enough to tell you, did he?"

The woman sounded . . . pleased?

Sophia pressed onward: "Black Hawk is dead."

"What?"

"That's what James said."

"Oh. Yes. Metaphorically."

"And now there are a lot of smaller men out there, looking to claim the notorious title."

"I'm afraid so."

"And they're keeping Black Hawk's name alive."

"Unfortunately, yes." Mirabelle sighed in exasperation. "That's why James and the rest of my brothers are here. They've come to make inquiries into the identities of the impostors."

Sophia gathered her breath, temper still rankled. But she had learned one pressing piece of information: James wasn't staying at the castle to thwart her plans to marry the earl. He was staying at the castle because he was hunting the impostors. She didn't like the situation. However, she understood it better. And just as soon as Lady Lucas was recovered, she and Sophia would depart from the keep and resume her quest for a husband. A few days with the duchess was enough time to quiet any gossip about her and her "disappearance," she was sure. And then she would be rid of the barbarian for good.

A breathless figure approached, sprinting. "Your Grace!"

Mirabelle quickly lifted to her feet.

Sophia followed.

"What is it, Fanny?" The woman's words were clipped.

The maid kicked up the pebbles as she skidded to a stop, wheezing. "There's . . . a . . . snake."

"Where?" Mirabelle snapped. "In the nursery?"

"In the kitchen."

"Oh, Fanny."

Mirabelle sighed. The babe started to make mewling sounds, and the duchess bounced him on her shoulder.

"The garden snakes are everywhere this time of year," she said in a chastising voice. "They're looking for somewhere warm to hide for the winter. If one's slipped inside the kitchen, don't panic. The creature's harmless."

"No, Your Grace." The maid gasped for breath. "It's a *big* snake."

"Hell's fire." Mirabelle glanced at Sophia, frowning. "It'd slipped my mind. James brought a snake to the castle. He's had it for years. It's some sort of pet."

Sophia!

The babe was wailing. Mirabelle said in a raised voice, "It must have escaped its cage."

Sophia's heart throbbed. The loathing welled inside her until she tasted the bile in her throat. She looked at the maid. "Take me to the snake. I'll take care of it."

The maid balked.

Mirabelle looked confused.

"Don't worry, Belle." She winked. "I lived on a tropical island, remember? I know how to deal with snakes."

Sophia started for the castle.

The maid quickly scurried beside her. "Follow me, miss."

Sophia and Fanny moved briskly through the garden and approached the castle. Inside, Sophia centered her thoughts on the wicked reptile, her cursed namesake. She hated that bloody snake. She hated that James cared for it so much.

She curled her fingers into her palms, her fingertips numb as she traversed the stairs and entered the dark labyrinth in the keep's belly.

The kitchen was murky, but the window wells and lamps brightened most shadowy spots. Sophia scanned the main room. The great hearth was filled with steaming iron pots. There were long wood tables for food preparation, cupboards for dishes. So many places to look. So many places for a wily snake to hide.

Sophia grabbed a meat cleaver off one of the tables. "Where is it?"

Fanny was shaking. "There." She pointed to a chair. "Under the seat."

Slowly Sophia advanced. She breathed deep to keep her fingers steady and her heart firm. If she made too much movement or ruckus, she might frighten the snake away. She suspected the yellow boa too big and lazy to move swiftly, but she still didn't want to risk it getting away.

Sophia neared the chair. She spotted a tail curled around the furniture's leg.

She smiled. "Hullo, Sophia."

* * *

James thundered through the garden with long strides. He stomped the pebbled walkway and even some of the blooms as he rounded the sharp corners, searching for her.

He paused.

She was crouched beside a blossom, tenderly stroking the rich blue petals. It was her favorite color: deep sea blue. The long and fluffy material of her stark white skirt ballooned around her like a cloud. She was wearing a tight black spencer, and her thick, dark locks spilled over her back in lush waves.

She was so bloody beautiful, his heart ached.

"Witch!"

Slowly she glanced at him, her deep brown eyes spirited. "What's the matter, Black Hawk?"

He approached her, loomed above her, casting her in shadow. "You have a black heart, woman."

She lifted to her feet. There was a devilish slant in her fine dark brows. A wicked smile touched her plump and rosy lips. "Do I?"

The pressure mounted in his skull. "You lopped off its head!"

"It was terrorizing the household." She matched his smoldering glare. "What did you expect me to do?"

"It was asleep under a chair," he gritted. "Not terrorizing the household."

The tip of her tongue darted between her lips as she licked her mouth. "What are you so angry about? I didn't kill *your* precious snake."

He stared at her damnable mouth. That hot, plump, kissable mouth. "But you *thought* it was Sophia, admit it. You heard there was a big snake in the kitchen and you darted after it to kill it. Belle told me about your 'heroics.'"

"Yes, the maid's a fool. She said it was a 'big' snake." She huffed. "It was a long garden snake, is all."

"But you *thought* it was Sophia."

"Perhaps I did." The rich brown pools of her eyes burned like liquid bronze. She hissed, "I hate that snake."

I hate you, Black Hawk.

He grabbed her cheeks. He sensed the blooms in her hair, the mint leaves on her breath as she'd tasted the herbs from the garden. "Stay away from her."

Sophia showed her fangs. "You protect that snake like a besotted lover guarding his mistress from his jealous wife."

He pressed his nose against hers. "At least she's a faithful mistress."

Sophia took in a slow, deep breath. She slipped her hands across his breast and circled his throat. He shuddered. He let her touch him, even in that vile way, if only to feel her hands on him again.

Her breath quivered as her eyes darkened even more. In a broken voice, she whispered, "I hope one day she escapes from her cage, slithers into bed with you—and strangles you."

She let go of his neck and flounced off.

James stood quietly in the garden, blood pulsing through his head, his heart. He gathered a shaky breath and closed his eyes, tamping the wild cravings stirring in his breast.

She had him. She had him by the mind, the heart, the bloody cods. And she twisted his innards with such a vicious grip, he winced.

James opened his eyes and let out the breath he was keeping. He looked through the garden for her, but Sophia was gone.

He headed back for the castle, his steps measured, his thoughts sluggish.

He was supposed to have *her*, the witch. He was supposed to make her see she belonged with him.

"Blimey!"

He stopped and rubbed his brow. Memories flooded into his head. She had always belonged with him, ever since the first time he had set eyes on her.

James was greeted by the barrel of a pistol. But it wasn't the cold steel aimed at his nose that disarmed him, rather the pair of exotic brown eyes, trimmed with long, dark lashes, that peered at him suspiciously over the flintlock, mesmerizing him. The jungle mist reflected in the glossy pools of her eyes. She absorbed the gray and swirling light—drawing him into her, as well.

"Who is it, Sophia?" cried Dawson.

She recoiled the weapon and rested it over her shoulder, her lengthy, thick tresses like smooth cocoa, spilling over her generous bust in soft waves. "Black Hawk, I presume? My father's told me all about you." She stepped aside and welcomed him with a seductive smile. "Come in. Are you hungry?"

James closed his eyes again at the recollection. The hot and pulsing warmth that had seeped through his bones after he had first met Sophia welled inside him again. Their affair had lasted a year. But that year had filled him with such sweet life.

He gasped for breath, blood stirred. He resumed his slow march for the keep, struggling with the past, so warm at times . . . and so cold at others.

He had to make her remember the past. He had

to make her remember how good it used to be, then he would have her in his grip. He had to take back control and seduce the woman. Then she would admit she belonged with him. Then he would have his revenge.

James entered the castle, thoughts tangled. He wandered through the passageways without a destination in mind.

"No! No! No!"

James paused and listened to the rant before the parlor door burst opened—and Squirt stomped from the room.

"I hate you!" she cried, and pounded the wool runner.

James watched his niece skirt away in a huff. She stopped and looked at her feet, as if wondering why she wasn't making any noise. When she realized the runner muffled her footfalls, she crossed over to the wood floorboards and stamped her feet in a show of pique.

He lifted a brow. Slowly he approached the room and looked inside the vast space.

The whimpers captured his attention. There was a silhouette seated on a bench beside the window.

Mirabelle.

His heart cramped.

She glanced at him, eyes glassy with tears. "I'm a terrible mother."

He sighed. "No, you're not."

"I am." She sniffed. "I don't know what to do with Alice . . . and she hates me."

James rubbed his brow again; his head was crowded with predicaments. "Alice doesn't hate you."

"Yes, she does. She hates me. And I don't know what to do about it."

He loathed to see the woman in tears. She looked so much like Mother when she cried, her spirits crushed.

You must help me, James. You must help me now that Papa is gone. I need you, James. I can't take care of you and William by myself. You will help Mama, won't you, James?

James strangled the redundant voice in his head. "Stop crying, Belle."

She wiped her eyes. "I'm sorry. I'm just tired."

"You should rest."

He stroked his hair in a ragged manner, strapped for words, before he ambled across the room, the splayed light from the stained glass windows skimming his polished boots.

He knelt beside her. She looked so vulnerable. He wasn't accustomed to seeing her in such a manner. But ever since her brush with death two months ago, she seemed more delicate to him, mortal.

He cupped her hand. "You're a good mother, Belle."

And she was. She just didn't have all the maternal skills necessary to rear a willful child like Alice. She had lived without a mother's influence. Who was she supposed to emulate? Who was supposed to offer her advice?

He sighed. "Alice is just . . ."

"A brat?"

He chuckled. "I was going to say headstrong."

Mirabelle wiped her nose with her sleeve. He smiled at the unladylike gesture.

"I don't know why the girl is like that," she moaned. "I wasn't so troublesome at her age."

James glanced at the floor as he remembered the time Mirabelle had stuffed baby Quincy into a basket before she'd pushed him into the river for the faeries to take away.

"Alice must take after the duke," he said dryly. "Don't fret, Belle. It will get easier to rear the girl with time."

"You're lying." She offered him a crooked smile. "But thanks for lying."

He lifted off his haunches . . . and kissed her brow.

"What was that for?" she said, bewildered.

He shrugged. "You looked like you needed it."

He rubbed the back of his neck, feeling uncomfortable. Before he made an even bigger ass of himself, he turned on his heels and quit the room.

Sophia had really twisted his thoughts, unsettled his composure. But he would deal with her and her bewitching charm later. First, he had to attend to a familial affair.

James listened for the patter of little footfalls. The distant drumming resounded throughout the cavernous corridors, and he followed the echoes, rounding a corner.

Quincy was standing in the passageway, leaning against the stone wall in a lazy manner. He was smiling and staring after Squirt's small figure, as she dragged a blanket of toys and clothes across the floor.

James eyed the doll's hand peeking through the blanket. "What is she doing?"

"She's running away to Egypt," said Quincy.

He frowned. "Why Egypt?"

"Because that's where all the mummies are and she wants to get a new one."

James rolled his eyes and started after the girl. "Squirt!"

Alice bristled. Slowly she turned around, mouth agape. He had never raised his voice with her. He suspected she wasn't accustomed to being ordered about.

He hunkered and looked straight into her large blue eyes. "I think you owe Mama an apology."

She looked aghast.

"I want you to go back to the parlor with Uncle Quincy and tell Mama you're sorry about what you said."

She still glared at him like he was daft.

"Now."

She closed her mouth, confused. But she obeyed. She dropped the blanket and quietly strutted back down the corridor, where Quincy, chuckling, was waiting for her.

James shook his head as he lifted off his haunches. He sighed, almost witless with fatigue from all the drama he'd endured over past few days.

He stilled.

A shiver tickled the base of his spine. It shimmied up his back and caressed his ribs, his heart.

She stepped out of the dark passage, regarding him thoughtfully, arms folded under her breasts.

"I thought you disliked children?" she asked with suspicion.

"I do."

She eyed him with even greater suspicion. "But you love the brat?"

He scowled. "Of course I do. She's family."

"So there *is* more room in that black heart of yours."

Sophia's smoky glare set his blood thumping, his innards smoldering. She delved deep into his features, searching for truth. What had provoked her to make *that* inquiry?

"Where did you learn to do that?" she wondered next.

He frowned. "Do what?"

"Rear brats."

He shrugged. "I've raised three children." He said dryly, "Four if you include Will."

"Hmm." She approached him, making his muscles pulse. "And you don't want to be a father?"

"No," he returned succinctly.

"Or a husband?"

He bristled. "No."

She looked at him closely, hotly . . .

She humphed.

He remained rooted to the spot as she brushed past him and vanished through another causeway, leaving him bewildered, wondering what sort of game she was playing. But whatever the woman's scheme, it was doomed to fail, for he intended to be the victor in their battle of wills.

Chapter 20

~~~∽◯◯◯∽~~~

"*A choo!*"

Sophia rubbed her nose and sniffed. She snuggled under the coverlets to keep warm, for the room was drafty. It was a spacious bedchamber with tall ceilings. The furniture was fine. There was a dash of red pigment in the rosewood luster that matched the pink papered walls and apple crimson fabric. She cringed at the garish colors. She preferred the contrast of burnt sienna woods and milky white textiles. But the space was well manicured . . . if cold.

The low-burning flames in the hearth flickered as a soft zephyr moved through the room. Sophia searched over her shoulder for the source of the breeze. She eyed the black devil. He had entered the chamber and closed the door. He was watching her closely, hotly.

She shivered.

The man's dark trousers hugged his burly legs; the thick muscles thrummed with energy and strength. He was wearing a simple white shirt, tucked. The cravat was missing, the collar loose and low and exposing the center of his strapping chest.

She munched on her bottom lip as she met his

sexy blue eyes again, shadowed by black brows and thick, sooty lashes. The smoldering glow quickly warmed her.

"What are you doing here?" She glanced at the dagger on the small table beside the bed, comforted.

"You won't need it," he said sagely.

Slowly he rounded the bed, each laggardly step sensual. She wanted to bury her head under the coverlets. She was vulnerable. He sensed it. Something dark and playful kindled in his eyes . . . making her hunger.

"I've brought you some soup," he said in a deep timbre. The sound rattled her bones.

She glanced at the steaming bowl nestled between his large palms. As he moved, he stirred the air. The lamplight frolicked across his sturdy fingers. The bowl seemed so small in his wide hands.

"Did you make the soup?" she wondered.

"No." He pushed the dagger aside and set the dish on the table. "I took it from the kitchen. How are you feeling?"

She sniffed. "I'm fine."

She had inherited the matron's chill. However, she was hardier than Lady Lucas. She had no fever or muscle aches . . . well, parts of her ached.

James headed for the fire. He slowly hunkered, the strapping muscles at his thighs and calves supporting his bulky weight as he stoked the flames with the iron poker.

He had a tight arse, she thought. She imagined her fingers circling the firm flesh as she pushed him deep inside her quim.

Sophia shuddered.

She tossed the blankets. She was suddenly sweltering. The woolly sheets gathered at her waist, rucked.

She used her elbows to drag herself into a sitting position before she reached for the bowl of soup.

She sniffed the fare, but her nose was congested, so she couldn't identify the flavor.

"It's hare," he said as he lifted off his haunches.

He set the poker aside. There was a soft plunk as the tool rested against the stone hearth. He looked at her, eyes smoldering. He had his hair in a queue, so every angle of his masculine features were there for her to regard and absorb and dream about.

Sophia quelled the tremors that tormented her spine. She thought about more unsavory things. That he was inside her room . . . alone . . . at night.

She scratched that tempting image from her mind and contemplated a more disturbing thought: What if someone stumbled upon him in her room . . . late at night . . . alone . . . the household asleep.

Sophia sighed.

"You're wearing clothes."

"Of course I am," she snapped, dazed.

"You never used to wear clothes to bed."

She frowned and looked at her trim white night rail. "I do now."

James moved across the room. She followed his measured steps as he approached a chair and settled into the seat, folding his arms over the wide breadth of his chest. He was watching her closely. Waiting for her to . . . eat the soup?

She glanced at the broth. Was it poisoned?

"It's not poisoned," he said with a touch of dark wit.

She made a wry face that he had read her mind so easily before she set aside the spoon and lifted the bowl to her mouth.

She smacked her lips. "It's good."

"I'll tell Cook."

He was staring at her. It was hard to ignore such commanding eyes. What was he *really* doing here? He had cared for her in the past during bouts with illness. Once he had even boiled her a delicious stew. But the tenderness he was showing her now was suspect, and she eyed him warily as she sipped the potage.

He tapped the chess box on the table beside him. "Would you like to play a game?"

She choked. "A game?" She wiped the dribble from her lips. "What are we playing for?"

He shrugged. "Do we have to pay a forfeit? Can't we play for fun?"

She frowned. "No."

He chuckled. "No, I don't suppose we can. You and I always have to be at odds about something, don't we?"

She looked at him askance before she returned to the comforting meal.

"You can't sleep," he said with authority.

She glared at him and rebuked, "I can sleep just fine."

"No, you can't. You can't sleep when you're sick . . . I remember."

A quiver kissed her spine. "Is that why you're here? To . . . amuse me?"

He lifted a black brow. "Would you like me to 'amuse' you?"

She gasped. Not at the outrageous proposal . . . but at the pulsing want that so swiftly gripped her heart. "I'd like you to leave my room."

"All right."

"What? Wait!"

She wanted to bite her tongue as soon as she'd voiced the balmy command. He offered her a small yet wicked smile before he slowly slipped back into the seat.

Sophia set the bowl aside, the porcelain unsteady in her shaky grip. "I mean, you're right. I can't sleep. Let's play a game."

There was a devilish glimmer in his eyes. "What would you like to play for?"

She scowled. "I thought we didn't have to pay a forfeit?"

"I was wrong, remember? You and I must always be at odds."

She huffed. "Fine. We'll play for . . . sport. Winner takes all the accolades."

He snorted. "I was thinking about something a little more interesting."

She flushed. "Like what?"

"If I win . . . you must kiss me."

She took in a deep breath. The blackguard! He had already ensnared her senses with his sensual blue eyes and husky voice. What more did he want from her? Did he want to enslave her passions, too? Perhaps he was searching for a new mistress. She had chased off his last one, after all. Whatever the man's scheme, she was determined not to let him win their strife. She would not become his mistress—ever again! And while there was room in his heart for a family . . . there was no room in his heart for her. She had no future prospect with the man.

"Very well," she said tightly. "And if I win . . . you must give me Sophia."

The man's expression darkened.

Slowly she smiled, giddy at the thought that the vile

snake might soon belong to her. She imagined all sorts of grisly deaths for the reptile, and her disposition greatly improved.

"Do we agree on the terms, Black Hawk?"

He glared at her. She thought he might rebuff the dangerous request; he loved that damn snake. Instead he quietly collected the chess box from the table and approached the bed.

The man's considerable frame neared the furniture. She spied his stout physique. It moved toward her like a dark cloud, a storm. He was filled with power and zest. It tickled her senses, his robust form. Longing welled in her breast, and she squelched the deep desires stirring in her heart, distracting her.

She was determined to win the game.

James settled on the bed. The feather tick swagged. Blood rushed through her veins as she absorbed the weight, the strength he impressed.

He curled one thick leg across the coverlet and stretched forth the other, so one boot rested on the floor. He then opened the box that also converted into a chessboard, and meticulously arranged the jade and ivory players.

Sophia crossed her legs under the woolly blanket and watched him, transfixed. She watched the way his sturdy fingers nimbly assembled the pieces. She watched the lamplight shimmer across his polished black boots. She even watched the studious way he set his brow as he maneuvered the pawns and rooks.

"Ladies first," he said gruffly.

She smacked her lips together. She then examined the board closely before she selected a player and made the first move.

He followed suit. "How many lovers have you had since we parted ways seven years ago?"

Slowly she lifted her eyes. Was he trying to unnerve her again? Make her falter and lose? She had more gumption than that. "Do you really want to know?"

The man's expression hardened. "No."

"Then don't ask."

His features soured. She smiled inwardly. He had thought to distract her with the scandalous repartee, but he'd failed, blackening his own mood instead. But there was no reason for him to be jealous, for while she had searched for physical comfort when the need had come upon her, she had never formed another bond with a man. Not like the bond she had formed with James. But he didn't need to know that, of course. She preferred to keep him in high dudgeon. He was more likely to make an error and lose the game that way.

"I'm sorry, Black Hawk."

He glowered at her. "For what?"

"For spoiling the affair with your mistress."

The darkness in his eyes blackened even more. "Are you truly remorseful?"

"I didn't mean to chase her off like that. I was really angry with you, you know?"

The man let out a slow, deep breath through his nose. "And you're sure you chased her away? That she will not return to my bed?"

Sophia strangled the twinge of jealousy that had sprouted in her belly at the words "to my bed." She smiled wryly instead. "I'm sure."

He nabbed a pawn. "Why are you so sure?"

She frowned. "I'm a woman."

She stared at the chessboard, strategizing. She was

at a disadvantage, her head congested with a chill. She had to concentrate more on the game.

"Yes, I've noticed you're a woman," he said dryly.

She lifted a brow. "Well, as a woman, I can sense what another woman is thinking."

He looked at her pointedly.

She shivered under the man's piercing stare.

"And what was my mistress thinking?" he drawled.

"Your former mistress was thinking, 'I don't care how big his cock is, I ain't gonna fight the shrew for it.'"

The man's lips twitched.

Sophia suspected he'd smiled just before he'd smothered the impulse. A genuine smile. And for some absurd reason, she was pleased with the thought that she had made him cheerful.

He nabbed another player.

She scowled.

"No more talking," she said firmly.

He acquiesced.

In less than an hour, he had cornered her king, ending the battle.

"You lose, sweetheart."

Sophia gnashed her teeth. She had lost. But she was saddled with an illness, she thought, comforting herself. Had she possessed all her faculties, her wits, the game would have lasted much longer. She might even have been victorious.

James gathered the players and collapsed the chessboard. He set the box aside—and waited.

There was a sound throbbing in her head. Sweat gathered between her fingers as she fisted her palms. He looked so damn kissable. Curse him!

Slowly she crawled across the rumpled coverlet, heart booming in her breast. She was weak, shaky. He seemed so . . . hungry. She sensed the carnal thirst brewing within him. She was consumed by it herself. The man's tempting lips waited patiently for her, so lush and erotic and powerful. She ached deep inside to taste him . . . and hated him for it.

"I hope *you* get sick, too," she griped.

She closed her eyes . . . and pressed her mouth over his, flattened her lips. She imagined nothing. She stomped every stirring sentiment into the bowel of her soul as she ignored the steamy buss.

At last she pulled away.

He grabbed her by the back of the neck, wove his thick fingers through her mussed hair. "What the hell was that, woman?" He was holding her head tight. "I said *kiss* me."

Her heart fluttered. "I did."

"No," he said curtly. "Kiss me . . . kiss me until I'm satisfied."

She trembled. "I can't."

"You will."

She wanted to. Oh, how she wanted to! The very thought filled her with pulsing want. She yearned for a real kiss . . . she yearned for him.

He whispered, "Kiss me, Sophia."

She groaned.

She kissed him.

She wrapped her arms around him and straddled him, choking him with a deep and hungry and soul-ful kiss. She moved her mouth over him in desperate thrusts. She heard him gasp for breath. She heard him groan so deep in his belly. And then she kissed him even harder. She was hungry. So hungry for him. She had fasted for far too long. She needed him. He offered her breath and life. And she took both until she was sated. Almost sated.

He grunted. "Better."

She chewed on her bottom lip, swollen. She stroked his head, keeping back the whimper that welled in her throat.

"What's the matter, sweetheart?" He rubbed her spine. "Are you still hungry?"

She was breathless. "Yes."

The lamplight burned low, the shadows danced. But even in the darkened room, a flame glowed in his eyes, a ravenous look.

He pushed her against the bed. She shuddered with delight as he settled between her splayed thighs and cupped her lips in another gluttonous kiss.

"Oh, James." She searched for breath. She fumbled with his shirt, yanked the ends from his trousers. "Take off your clothes. I want to feel your skin."

He obeyed. He slipped the garment over his head and tossed it aside. When the wall of muscle pressed against her breasts, she moaned and circled his ribs in an avid hold.

The man's flesh was hot. It singed her fingertips. She opened her mouth and let him take her lips in insatiable want as she raked his fevered torso. She touched every muscle, every bone that throbbed beneath his skin. She marked him with her nails and sobbed in her soul to have him so intimately once more.

She reached for his waist and snagged her finger in his trousers. "Take everything off."

He looked into her eyes, scorched her heart. "*You* lost the game, sweetheart."

"Am I making too many demands?" She smiled. "*I*

lost the game. And I intended to kiss you until you're satisfied. Now take off your damn trousers."

He shuddered. The vibrations tickled her skin, arousing her even more. He pushed away from her, muscles taut, breath ragged. She gasped for air, too, as she watched him, mesmerized. He settled at the edge of the bed and removed his boots.

She raked her toes against his firm, moist back. He glanced at her, his long, black hair falling loose from the queue and shielding parts of his smoky eyes.

He lifted to his feet and unfastened the buttons of his trousers before he stripped the garment and revealed his naked splendor, whetting her appetite for him even more.

"You're beautiful," she said reverently.

He firmed at her words, every muscle stiffened. She explored the great expanse of his chest, the dark tufts of hair that gathered between his sculpted pectorals and tapered to his narrow waist . . . and to the throbbing erection that stretched between his thick thighs. She was wet with need at the sultry thought of him inside her, and she beckoned him back to the bed with her eyes.

He settled between her legs. She groaned. She opened for him, spread her legs wide apart. She watched him intently as he grabbed her night rail with shaky fingers and pushed the fabric up her belly. She lifted her bottom, allowing him to drag the flimsy shift off her back and up over her head.

Sophia shuddered at the contrast between the cool castle air and the balmy sweat that covered her limbs. Heart pounding, she was tight and greedy and aching for more of his touch.

Touch me, James.

"I've missed you, sweetheart."

He kissed her belly, dipped his tongue inside her navel, making her tight muscles bounce. She grabbed the leather cord still securing the last of his hair and yanked it through his locks.

"Everything." She breathed hard. "I want everything off."

The man's hair spilled forward and caressed her ribs as he licked her navel over and over again, whipping her arousal. She splayed her fingers and skimmed them across his scalp, finding a good and solid grip, and keeping his luscious mouth against her taut and thrumming flesh.

"You taste so damn good," he said hoarsely.

He moved across her midriff and bussed a hard nipple, making her shiver. The heat in her belly ballooned, the sweet pressure spiked between her warm legs as he parted his wicked lips and sucked her breast with both tenderness and force, drawing her deep into his mouth.

She hugged him, crushed him with a savage hold. "Lick me."

He let his long and lustful tongue slip between his teeth and swirl across the sensitive nub of flesh. The lanky strokes filled her with precious memories of heady tropical nights, slow seductions, and thoughtful intimacies, for he had always served her desires. Even if she had submitted to him, he had never let her walk away from a sexual encounter without feeling blissful satisfaction. And she sensed it deep inside her again, the knowledge that he would give her everything she craved for. That he would give her pleasure before he searched for it himself, that he would fill her with life and strength and renew her like no other.

"James," she cried, overwhelmed. "I want you inside me, so deep inside me."

He raised his heavy frame and captured her swelling lips in his mouth before he slipped his long erection into her aching quim.

Sophia sobbed with joy.

The woman's sob resounded in his head. James had waited so long to hear that lustful sound. The heady song confirmed Sophia's delight, and nothing stirred his soul like the knowledge that he had made her happy.

I intended to kiss you until you're satisfied.

The only satisfaction he received was in giving her joy—and she knew it.

He thrust deep inside her, filling her, stretching her. She quivered so greatly at the friction, he sensed her orgasm pinch the cusp of his erection.

"Don't you dare," he said roughly. "Don't you dare come yet."

She moaned as he rocked her. She grabbed his buttocks and pushed him deeper inside her body, ravenous.

James groaned as she burrowed her sharp nails into his arse, demanding more. He quickened the tempo, slaking her lust.

She let go of his arse and lifted her legs higher. She wrapped the limbs around his waist, crossing her ankles, holding him tight. So tight.

He searched for her lips again. He slipped his tongue into her hot mouth, penetrating her from the top and the bottom.

She circled his neck, pinched his airway. He gave her more. A deeper kiss. A deeper fuck. He wanted to give her everything she desired. He grabbed her hair and undulated against her tight, wet quim with quick, hard strokes.

She ensnared him, suffocated him. It was true passion. She needed him. And he needed to give her everything that he possessed, everything that he was. She wanted everything *off*. She wanted him. And him alone. No barriers. And he offered it to her. With every desperate breath and hard thrust, he gave her more and more of himself.

He was sweating. He tasted the salty sweat on her lips, too, the briny tears that had dropped from her lashes. She was so close to orgasm. She was so anxious to shed the suffocating guise and unnatural restrictions that had pressed her for so long.

"Don't you see how they crush you, sweetheart?" he rasped. "Take away your breath? Let me give you breath."

She sobbed even louder as he kissed her mouth. He moved within her with strong, firm thrusts, grinding his hips against hers.

"We belong together, Sophia."

She cried out. He sensed the sweet juices flowing and her muscles constricting, pulsing even, as she achieved climax.

She gasped for breath and shuddered violently before the spasms weakened. She was quivering, faint. He rocked her for a few moments more before the pressure in his cock reached a zenith and he pumped his hot seed into her wet womb with a feral groan.

James buried his face in Sophia's mussed hair. He hovered above her, still caged, for the woman had yet to relax her crossed limbs. But he was sated. He was at peace in her arms. He would endure eternity in her embrace.

"Achoo!"

He chuckled gruffly and kissed her cheek before he bumped her hips, shaking her loose. "And here I thought I'd cured you."

He rolled over, rested against the soft feathers, and sighed.

She sniffed and snuggled in the groove between his arm and ribs. "I do feel better."

"Good." He crooked his elbow and cupped her head. "I expect *you* to nurse me if I wake up with a chill tomorrow."

She smiled against him. He sensed the woman's lips move across his skin. Every part of him was still so sensitive. He closed his eyes and listened to the sound of her heavy breathing. Slowly the rhythmic respiration mellowed into a steadier tempo.

James sensed the soft caress. He opened his eyes. Sophia was stroking the mark on his chin, the scar.

He grabbed her wrist. "What are you doing?"

"I'm sorry I cut you."

He let go of her wrist.

She curled her arm across his chest and squeezed.

Pulses pounded in his head at her atonement. He remembered the night of the ball, the night she had sliced him. That she offered him words of contrition for such a paltry slight, and yet *no* words of repentance for what she had so cruelly done to him on the island, stirred his blood to boil.

James separated from the warm body pressed against him and slipped off the bed. He didn't need the woman's false tenderness. He would not let her hoodwink him into thinking she cared for him. She was grateful for the fuck, that was all. He would not let his heart get entangled with hers again. It would only distract him from his true purpose: revenge.

James walked around the furniture and picked up his scattered clothes.

"You're leaving?" she said softly, hurt.

A darkness filled his heart. The cheerless thought that he had enjoyed so many nights with her in the past—yet he never would again.

"I can't stay." He fastened his trousers and slipped on his boots. "What if a maid—or the harridan—finds me in here in the morning?"

She sighed. "I suppose you're right."

She sounded genuinely forlorn that he wouldn't be staying the evening with her. It compounded the pain in his breast. He looked at her. She was so lovely, tangled in the bed linens. Full breasts thrust in the air, hair mussed and scattered across the white sheets. She was wild. Free.

Sophia.

He crushed the maudlin sentiment. She had never really cared for him. He had to remember that. She had only ever cared for herself, for her own social desires and erotic pleasures.

He grabbed his shirt and pulled it over his head before he stalked toward the door. "Besides . . . Sophia doesn't like to sleep alone, remember?"

She glared at him, toffee brown eyes sharp—and dangerous.

"Good night, sweetheart."

He left the room and closed the door. Right away the knife, hurled through the air, struck the back of the door, the blade trapped in the wood.

He smiled.

Chapter 21

James stared at the high-back chair on the other side of the small, round table. He stared at it until the candlelight blurred and Sophia's ghostly figure appeared in the seat, clutching a fob watch. She dangled the timepiece, rocked it slowly back and forth, mesmerizing him.

May you rot in everlasting hell.

And so he rotted in hell, his innards twisted at the dark memory of her inscribed words, and the aloneness he had suffered the moment he had realized she had gone from the plantation house, never to return.

James shifted in the chair. He leaned his body to one side and made an L-shape with his thumb and forefinger, resting his chin in the groove.

But Sophia had returned, he thought, for she was again a part of his life. And soon she would know the wretched fires, too. Soon he would walk away from her—and have his revenge.

There was a rap at the door.

James ignored it. He was still recovering from his encounter with Sophia. Her scent and sweet juices still bathed his skin. He wanted to be alone in the shadowy room. He wanted to think about her—and machinate.

William entered the bedchamber. He wasn't aboard the *Bonny Meg* anymore, and so there was no reason for him to respect the captain's privacy.

James glared at his brother as he crossed the space in cool strides. William paused and knocked against the snake's glass prison, rousing the reptile before he filled the empty seat across from the captain, chasing off the phantom image of Sophia.

William stretched out his legs and crossed his ankles. "We've returned."

"I see that," he growled.

"Adam sends his regards."

"Horseshit." James scowled. "Well? What did you learn from him?"

He might as well hear what had transpired between the men, for his brother seemed determined to report the day's events. James suspected he wasn't going to get any quiet until the matter of the impostors was addressed.

The door opened once more, and Quincy and Edmund sauntered inside the room.

"Egypt?" Edmund frowned. "Why Egypt?"

"Because that's where all the mummies are—and she wanted to get a new one."

Edmund snorted.

William smiled.

"But James put a stop to it," said Quincy as he straddled a chair. "He ordered Squirt to make amends to her mother." He glanced at the captain. "And she did, you know?"

"Did what?" asked James.

"Apologize."

"Of course she did." James folded his arms across his chest. "I told her to do it."

The young bucks exchanged knowing glances.

"He gave her The Look, didn't he?" Edmund settled in the last of the four seats positioned around the small, round table. "I remember The Look."

Quincy grimaced. "I still get The Look."

James eyed the pup. "And yet it doesn't seem to have the same effect on you that it once had."

Quincy looked aghast. "I should hope not."

"Perhaps you should offer Belle some child-rearing advice?" William glanced at the captain. "It sounds like she needs it."

"Like hell. She's doing fine. I'm not going to play mother hen." Again! "Let's return to business, shall we? What happened with Adam?"

"Well, we discovered a few things," William said in a business-like manner. "It looks as though the bootleggers and impostors are one and the same. Their leader is a man named Hagley."

"It's just like we suspected." Edmund scratched his chin. "The men heard we were 'dead' and assumed our identities, testing the pirate waters first with bootlegging and then moving on to more dangerous pursuits, like raiding passenger vessels."

"So where is this Hagley and the rest of his cohorts?"

William shrugged. "We don't know."

James glowered. "So *what* was the purpose of the trip?"

"We discovered important information." The lieutenant counted off his fingers. "The leader's name. That we're chasing after one band of charlatans, not two."

Edmund nodded in accord with his brother. "It narrows our search."

"We can start making inquires about Hagley in port." William rested his forearms on the table. "Surely someone knows him by his real name."

"Like a scorned lover who'd like to see him hang," said Edmund, snickering.

"I volunteer for that mission." Quincy grinned in a rakish manner. "A scorned lover is always ripe for a bedding."

Edmund snorted. "I'm surprised you don't have the pox."

"You're just jealous, Eddie."

"Of *you*?"

"I'm charming, so I get all the ladies."

Edmund frowned. "I'm charming."

Edmund *was* a sour devil, thought James. Moody since boyhood. But James had never figured out the reason behind his younger brother's ill temperament. He supposed it was just his nature.

"You're both charming," said James, irritable. "Now what the hell are we going to do about the impostors if we don't find a scorned wench in port?"

"I suggest we set another trap."

"It won't work, Quincy." James was firm. "The impostors won't be duped a second time into chasing after the *Bonny Meg*."

"What if we offer them a harmless proposition?"

James stared at the pup. "What sort of proposition?"

"Well, we can spread word that Captain Hawkins is looking for a shipping partner, that he's interested in a joint business venture with Hagley because he's heard good things about the man. We won't mention the word 'pirate.' We won't spook him."

James scowled. He loathed waiting for the impostors to come to him—at sea or on land. It was so passive, so *un*like him. He'd rather hunt the miscreants. However, Quincy had a point. If James reached out his hand in amity, Hagley was much more likely to shake it. Otherwise, James risked frightening the impostors into deep hiding.

"Hagley might consent to the meet if only to hear the proposition, to see if it's worth his while," from William.

Edmund smirked. "And then he'll be ours."

"Fine." James sighed in reluctant agreement. "But what will we do if Hagley doesn't consent to the meet?"

The men quieted.

William looked at the captain. "There is one other option."

"What is it?"

"You *still* haven't told him, Will?" cried Quincy.

James glared at the lieutenant. "Told me what?"

William rubbed his jaw. "If we don't find Hagley and put an end to his piracy . . . we can always confess our true identities."

James glared at his brother. Was Sophia's cold already seeping into his brain, making him woozy? One of them wasn't making any sense.

"Are you drunk, Will?"

"Listen, James. There's always the threat of discovery hanging over our heads. Even if we find Hagley, there's no stopping another impostor from taking his place."

James stroked the bridge of his nose hard. The spot between his brows pulsed. "So you suggest we hang ourselves and get it over with?"

"No," William drawled. "I suggest we seek a pardon."

James scoffed. "The king will not grant us a pardon, even if we are the duke's brothers-in-law."

"But he might grant us the pardon if we . . . join the Royal Navy."

James hardened. The blood in his head throbbed like he was deep under water and his skull was about to implode from the pressure. "What?"

"The Royal Navy's African Squadron is undermanned and is searching for privateers to help hunt and capture slave ships." Edmund broached the matter carefully, his inflection steady. "If we enlist the *Bonny Meg*—"

"No."

James looked daggers at his brothers. A dark energy welled inside him, choking him. The old loathing for the Royal Navy burned his innards and scorched his throat.

"Listen, James," said William.

"No."

William sighed. "I know you hate the navy for pressing Father into service—we all do—but be reasonable. We have to protect ourselves. We have to protect Belle."

Curse his brother for using *her* against him! It was still raw in his belly, the grief James had suffered two months ago, believing his sister about to perish. He would do anything to keep her safe. William knew it, too. But James would find the impostors and crush them. He would *not* join the Royal Navy even if the devil himself offered him a pardon.

"We'll still have command of the *Bonny Meg*," William said in a sensible manner. "But we won't haul cargo across the Atlantic. We'll hunt slave ships instead."

James gritted, "I would sooner burn the *Bonny Meg* than see her serve the Royal Navy."

"James, think about it—"

He slammed his fist against the table, shaking the furniture. "I will *not* let the fucking navy have my ship!"

James jumped to his feet, the bile churning in his belly, the disgust filling his heart and head, making him sick with vertigo.

"*Your* ship?" William stood and grabbed the table's edge. "The *Bonny Meg* belongs to all of us."

Drake Hawkins had served as captain of the *Bonny Meg* for more than fifteen years before illness had weakened him. Chronic headaches and bleeding gums had sapped his burly strength, his robust energy. So as not to appear feeble in front of the crew, he had transferred command of the vessel to James in 1817 . . . the same year James had met Sophia.

He dismissed the thought from his mind, the peace he had found in her arms that year. He thought instead about the *Bonny Meg*. Drake Hawkins had died three years after giving James command of the vessel. The ship belonged to all of his siblings now, even Belle. But James had always considered the mighty schooner as his possession, his home. She was a loyal and steadfast companion. If he lost her, too . . .

"We've talked about this, James." William said slowly, "We've made a decision."

James stalked across the room and stopped beside the fireplace, encased in sturdy oak wood. He placed his hands against the protruding mantel and lowered his weight. "What decision?"

But it was Quincy who responded with "We want to seek a pardon. We want to be privateers."

James gripped the mantel until his knuckles turned white. He stared at the low-burning fire, listened to the hissing flames. The light reflected off his polished boots, laughing at him.

"We're not merchant sailors." Quincy sounded wistful. "We're pirates. It can never be like it was, we can never return to piracy. But we can be privateers. We can still know the taste of the hunt, the thrill of a battle."

James gasped for breath. He struggled to keep the demons caged in his head. He had sacrificed his blood. He had sacrificed *years* of his life to protect them, the wretched savages! But they were bored with being merchant sailors. And for that they were going to betray him?

"We'll have freedom, James," offered Edmund. "The threat of the noose won't hang over our heads anymore."

"Traitors," James hissed.

The chair legs scraped across the planked flooring as the last two brothers lifted to their feet.

"We are not traitors," the men said in unison.

Would they thrash him for the slight? It was more than he could bear. He had reared them, the ungrateful bastards! He had guided them through perilous waters, and wiped their arses when there had been no one else to care for them. And *this* was how they expressed their respect? By casting him aside like soiled laundry and stealing the *Bonny Meg*—his soul!—right out from under him?

"You're betraying Father's memory," James said quietly, darkly. The ruthless deserters might not give a damn about him anymore, but what about their father? "Drake would never have let the *Bonny Meg* sail under the navy's thumb." He had turned pirate, offering his own children freedom from servitude with the *Bonny Meg*. For what? So that in the end his sons could join and serve his former tormentors? "And what about Mother? The ship's named after her. It was a testament to the years she had suffered alone, while Father was held captive—tortured! How can you even *think* about joining the navy?" James smashed his fists against the mantel. "You have no shame!"

"And would our parents want us to hang at the end of a noose?"

William sounded so bloody calm, like it was a trifle that he and the other two mutinous cutthroats had shredded the captain to pieces.

James had always admired the lieutenant's unflappable, even dispassionate nature, for it had proved invaluable in the heat of battle. But now James wanted to piss on his brother's cool composure, his cold heart. He would rather William strike him, stab him. Anything! He wanted his brother to show *some* feeling for the brutal usurpation.

"Some things are worth dying for," James said through gnashed teeth.

"This isn't one of them," returned William. "The navy took away a part of Father's life, but they won't take anything away from us."

"No, we're going to give it to them," he sneered.

James trembled with repressed rage. He had thought it incomprehensible that his trusted brethren should betray him and dishonor their parents' memories. But he had been wrong. He had been wrong about a great many things. He had once believed Sophia incapable of the same treachery, the same deceit. But he had been wrong about her, too.

The flames from the fire singed his soul. James struggled for breath. He had suffered after his father had been pressed into service, too. He had endured the hardship and the hopelessness, the nights of endless toil alongside his mother. The Royal Navy had ruined his life. But it had not scarred his brothers as he had believed. William had not languished in dread with an older brother to look after him. And Edmund and Quincy had come along after their father had returned home, never having carried the crushing weight of responsibility—or the shame that had accompanied it when James had failed to save their mother from despair.

William grumbled, "I knew you'd hate the idea."

Blood pounded in James's skull. The darkness inside him threatened to shake him apart. How long had his brothers plotted the betrayal? Weeks? Months?

James should have suspected mutiny was afoot. A week ago, William had issued the order to set sail soon after the captain had boarded the *Bonny Meg*. He had usurped control even then, preparing for the day when he would head the *Bonny Meg* himself. But James had been too distracted by the island witch to detect the dangerous, telling signs.

"Get out," said James darkly.

Quincy had enough modesty to scratch his head in chagrin. "James—"

"Get the fuck out! All of you!"

The brothers remained firm, exchanging glances. But soon William nodded and the three quietly filed out the door.

Chapter 22

Dear Imogen . . .

Sophia stared at the two words and wondered what she would write next as she tapped the feather quill against her temple.

Her thoughts in a tizzy, she struggled with the letter's content. She wasn't skittish about penning the note. She had considered Imogen's fate for some time now. But Sophia had shied away from making the inquiries sooner, fearing her own precarious reputation would be tainted in some irreparable way if she contacted the "fallen woman."

Don't you see how they crush you, sweetheart? Take away your breath? Let me give you breath.

And so he had.

She closed her eyes and sighed at the warm memory of the man's stirring, provoking, spirit-freeing touch.

We belong together, Sophia.

Her heart throbbed with vim at the hot, firm words. Had he changed his mind about marriage the other night? Had he, too, realized it was kismet, that they were meant to be together?

There was an ache deep inside her to trust the brigand again, to be with him again. She dreaded going back inside her cage. She dreaded conforming, cramming, twisting her soul to fit into a thin and uncomfortable social mold.

She relished the freedom from timidity. She wanted to learn her comrade's lot in life. Sophia wasn't sure if the letter would ever reach the girl, but she was determined to compose it. She had to try to make amends. She had not treated Imogen like a true friend. But now she had the fortitude to break the rules, as the duchess had expressed. Now Sophia had the desire to do what was right . . . and not necessarily what was proper.

"What are you doing?"

Sophia looked at Lady Lucas, startled. The old woman had recovered from her illness. Sophia was feeling much better, too. She suspected her own swift recovery had stemmed from the uplifting truth that she belonged with James . . . allowing her to breathe.

The matron's glare was disquieting. Sophia's fingers trembled a tad. However, she maintained a firm grip on the quill—in her left hand.

"I'm writing a letter," she returned firmly.

Lady Lucas either ignored the faux pas or failed to see it, for she said nothing about the quill pen in her charge's left hand. Instead: "I see that. It's well after breakfast. Why are you still in your night rail? To whom are you writing?" She snatched the sheet and examined it. "*What* are you doing corresponding with Miss Rayne?"

Ghostly fingers circled Sophia's throat. She sensed the breathlessness. The feeling overwhelmed her whenever she heard a reprimand or anticipated censure. She struggled against the crushing sentiment. It was such a contrast to the healing, liberating intimacy she had shared with James the other night. A part of her bristled in defiance of the matron's reproach . . . while another part of her submitted to the older woman's authority and wisdom.

Lady Lucas ripped the paper apart and tossed the pieces into the low-burning fire. "I might admire your loyalty if the situation was different, Miss Dawson. But as it stands, you are still unwed and vulnerable. You mustn't do anything even remotely scandalous—especially now."

Sophia sighed and dropped the quill. "Why now?"

"Because the earl and his sister are here!"

The fingers at Sophia's throat tightened even more and her heart pounded in her breast. "What?"

"The siblings are below stairs with the duchess." The matron skirted across the room and opened the wardrobe. She fished through the heaps of fabric. "We must get you dressed."

Sophia gripped her temples, her mind a maelstrom of unsteady thoughts. "What is the earl doing here?"

"He's come to propose, of course."

"Here?"

"Lord Baine suspects he's about to lose you to Captain Hawkins." The older woman removed a simple white day dress from the wardrobe and eyed the flattering material. "Make haste, my dear!"

A few minutes later, Sophia and Lady Lucas were seated in the formal parlor with Maximilian Rex, the Earl of Baine; and his sister, Lady Rosamond.

The duchess engaged the earl's company as Sophia quietly sipped her tea and tamped the roiling movements in her weak belly. She had not visited with the earl and his kin for more than a sennight. It seemed to her a year had passed, the siblings more like strangers than acquaintances.

"So you are friends with the duchess?" whispered Rosamond in a peevish manner. Sophia suspected the girl disliked socializing with a woman of such high rank. It placed her own position of lady in a dimmer, and thus less attractive, light. "She is very civilized . . . unlike her brother."

Sophia cringed. "You dislike Captain Hawkins, don't you, Lady Rosamond?"

"I should think that was obvious, Miss Dawson."

It was, wretchedly so. Sophia glanced at the earl. He smiled. She returned the polite gesture, her lips trembling.

"Why do you dislike him?" Sophia asked in a hushed voice.

The girl pinched her brows together. "He treated me in a wicked manner at Max's ball."

Sophia remembered the night of the ball. She remembered meeting the dashing pirate lord after so many years apart. He had shattered her composure in an instant that night. He had beckoned every wild desire and dangerous passion to light once more. He had disturbed *her* in a wicked manner, not Rosamond.

"I don't understand, Lady Rosamond."

"Really, Miss Dawson." She huffed. "Don't you remember? He asked you to dance."

Sophia frowned. She remembered being put out by the brigand's request, nay, demand. But why would it have upset Rosamond?

"So?" said Sophia.

"He asked *you* to dance while *I* was standing beside you." Venom passed between the girl's lips. The poison was palpable. "*I* was the ranking eligible female. And *I* was the host's sister. He should have asked *me* to dance before you."

"And you wanted to dance with him?"

"Goodness, no! I intended to refuse him, of course. But he breached protocol."

"And protocol is everything?"

The chit sniffed. "That's right."

Sophia pondered that evening's circumstances. Was the girl really miffed because the captain had breached protocol? Or was she feeling slighted because James had not demonstrated an interest in her, the ranking— and supposedly more desirable—female?

"And you cannot forgive him his transgression?" Sophia sipped her tea, blanketing the distaste in her mouth. "Even after he saved you from falling?"

"Saved me?" She snorted softly. "I think not, Miss Dawson."

"You mean you fainted on purpose?"

"Yes."

Sophia glowered. Lady Lucas noted the scowl and quickly rubbed her own forehead, instructing her charge to smooth her wrinkled features. It was unladylike to frown.

Sophia glowered even more. "But why did you fake the vertigo?"

"To teach the captain a lesson, of course."

It struck Sophia soundly, the devious girl's true intentions. After she had feigned faintness, she had issued an invitation to the captain in "gratitude." She had wanted James to come to the country house party so she could humiliate him publicly—as he had "humiliated" her.

Sophia breathed through her nose in a steady manner, her heart thudding, her skull throbbing.

"The grounds here are so lovely, Your Grace," the

earl blandished. "Might I have the pleasure of taking a turn through the garden?"

"Yes, Lord Baine," returned the duchess. "I'll summon the head gardener to give you a tour."

"That isn't necessary, Your Grace . . . Perhaps Miss Dawson would be so kind as to accompany me? We are both avid horticulturists."

The earl simpered.

Sophia frowned.

The duchess offered Sophia an uneasy look. "Miss Dawson is recovering from a chill, my lord."

"But you look so well, Miss Dawson." Rosamond chirped, "And the air will do you good."

Lady Lucas nodded brusquely in encouragement.

"Besides," the chit whispered, "my brother is far better company than the barbarian."

Sophia gripped the porcelain cup and murmured, "He's not a barbarian."

James parted the white curtains. He glared at the two distant figures, festooned in lavish attire. The couple entered the grand barouche before the vehicle set off across the pebbled path.

The earl had come to propose.

James observed the cloud of dust as the peer and his wretched sister departed the castle grounds.

And James knew Sophia's answer.

He turned away from the window. He took the empty bottle beside the bed and caressed the spout with his thumb, moving his finger over the slick surface, circling the glass until his own head was spinning.

He pitched the bottle across the room.

The glass shattered.

"I see you're still in a foul mood."

Slowly James lifted his burning eyes and trained his weary gaze on William. The lieutenant was positioned beside the door, arms folded across his chest.

James slumped against the wall and gnashed his teeth. The darkness in his soul crippled him. Everything was gone. His brothers . . . Sophia.

"We're not taking anything away from you, James."

The sage lieutenant had guessed the captain's gloomy thoughts. The man sounded so bloody calm, even blasé, and that infuriated James even more. He looked daggers at his brother.

"Stop thinking with your heart, James. If Father wasn't pressed into service, would you still think joining the Royal Navy a poor idea?"

"It's called loyalty," he growled.

"To whom?"

"To Father."

"Father's dead."

James scoffed. "Yes, he is. And his memory is worth shit, I see."

"You son of a bitch." William stepped deeper inside the bedroom. "Do you think you're the only one who loved him? He was my father, too. But Quincy and Edmund are still fledglings, and I'm not going to see them swing from a noose. Not when I can save them." He gritted, "Father wouldn't want it to end that way."

James turned away from his brother, listless. "I'm going to find the impostors."

"Fine. We'll search for Hagley and his crew first, but then—"

"No." James looked back at his kin, glowering. "After I find the impostors, I'm going to keep the *Bonny*

Meg. You and Eddie and Quincy can rot alongside the Royal Navy."

William rubbed his lips, his chin. "You can't do this, James."

"I can. And I will." He rasped, "The tars are loyal to *me*. You'll never get your hands on the ship so long as I live."

William crossed the room and slammed his fist into James's cheek. "I don't *want* to take the ship from you!"

James didn't budge. Blood filled his mouth. He tasted the thick, warm fluid. It filled him, soothed him. At last the stoic lieutenant showed real feeling. And that was enough to pacify the demons raging inside James's skull.

"I want us *all* to be privateers," he blasted. "I want us *all* to sail aboard the *Bonny Meg*!"

James wiped the blood from his swollen lips. "Get your own damn ship."

William stepped away from the captain, combing his shaky fingers through his well-groomed hair. "You would cut us off?"

"I'm not the one cutting you off."

It was like a cutlass carving his innards, the betrayal. *He* was not the one who had walked away from the brotherhood and the *Bonny Meg* . . . and the plantation house.

"You're the one who's walking away," said James darkly. "You and Eddie and Quincy and Sophia."

William frowned. "Are you *still* pining after Dawson's daughter?"

He fingered his sore lips. "I'm not pining after her."

"You're still in love with Sophia, admit it."

James slammed his fists against the wall behind him. "I'm *not* in love with that witch!"

"Then what do you want from her?"

"Revenge."

William regarded him, confused. "What do you mean?"

"I want her to know pain." James gasped for breath. "I want her to feel the same fucking despair that I had to feel when *she* walked away from me."

But she would never know such bereavement. She would marry the earl, he thought bitterly. She would be a countess. And he would rot in everlasting hell.

"I didn't think you so small, James."

There it was again, that cold and passionless point of view. William might be levelheaded, but he was also aloof and indifferent. He suffered nothing, for he felt nothing. It was easy for him to walk away from the *Bonny Meg*. But it was not so easy for James to forget about the past.

"You have no soul, Will. You can't bleed. You don't even know love."

"Nor do you, it seems," he said quietly, glowering, before he walked out of the room.

James grabbed his head, still woozy with drink. He dismissed his brother's cavil as tedious gibberish and thought about Sophia instead. The witch was victorious. She had won their battle of wills. He appreciated her ruthlessness; it deserved applause. And so he would offer it. He wasn't small, as William had suggested. He would congratulate her on the triumph.

James vacated the bedchamber. He moved blindly through the passageways. He suspected she was in her room, crowing over her achievement, and so he instinctively traveled toward her quarters.

He opened the door without rapping on the wood first.

The blade sliced through the air and pierced the wall beside his head.

Slowly James looked at the hard steel. His bloodred eyes reflected in the luminous metal. He then glared at Sophia. "You missed, sweetheart."

She was wearing a simple white day dress. It was clean and crisp. No hideous jewelry marred her bust or ears. Even her hair was free of restraint and ornamentation, the long, thick locks flowing across her back in luxurious, cocoa brown waves.

The muscles in his midriff stiffened. She looked so damn lovely, yet she was so cold and unsightly inside.

"Damn you to hell, Black Hawk."

He smirked at her incisive insult. He entered the bedroom and closed the door. "I'll knock next time."

She was glowering, flushed. Had he ruined her private celebration by being there? He remained rooted to the spot. He wouldn't depart from the bedchamber. He wasn't feeling so magnanimous.

"Congratulations . . . Countess."

Her lips firmed. She skirted across the room and rummaged through the box of precious stones sitting on the vanity.

"What are you looking for?" he wondered sluggishly.

"Another knife," she said, words clipped.

He chuckled and rubbed his burning eyes. "You give no mercy, woman."

She sobbed in frustration before she scooped up the small chest and hurled it across the room.

The wood cracked against the wall; the shimmering jewels rained like falling stars.

He stared at the garish baubles. "Are you mad?"

"I'm not going to be a countess."

James looked at her, bewildered. He eyed her breasts, heaving. She bunched her fingers into fists and licked her lips in an almost frantic gesture.

"Don't lie," he said curtly. "The earl proposed, admit it."

"Yes, he did." Dark brown eyes filled with tears; the glossy pools reflected the firelight in the hearth and the bright sunshine coming in through the unmasked windows. "But I refused him."

He frowned. "Why?"

"Because I'm a fool."

He listened to the quick and shaky timbre in her voice. He listened to the woman's words, so perplexing. She had desired the earl's title, coveted the worthless name for months. Hell, *years*! She had deserted him for the blasted opportunity to gain a footing in posh society. And now that she had a chance to step into the aristocratic shithole she'd so earnestly longed for, she rebuffed it?

"I am such an idiot!" she shrieked, eyes wild. "Have you come to gloat?"

Was she daft? He had lost everything dear to him. *What* was there to gloat about? He said through gritted teeth, mouth bruised and tender, "I'm not here to gloat."

Fat tears soaked her cheeks. "No?"

James studied the woman's erratic mannerisms. He watched her as she scrubbed the briny moisture from her skin. She looked more and more savage as blood filled her features, so inflamed and irritated.

"What the devil is wrong with you?" he wondered gruffly, each pearled tear piercing his gut and making him feel uncomfortable. The woman was strong, unbreakable. Or so he had thought. He wasn't used to seeing her in such distress.

"Isn't this what you wanted? Well, here it is. Take it!"

"Take what?" he barked. "What are you talking about?"

"Despair!"

James took in a sharp breath. "You were eavesdropping?"

She had a nasty tendency to do that. She had listened to his conversation with William aboard the *Bonny Meg* before she had stowed away. And she had listened to it again at the castle . . .

James bristled. So she was privy to his desire for revenge? He had already cut out his heart for her once before. There was nothing left for her to maim.

"I heard every word." She trembled. She said weakly, "Was it all a lie?"

He looked at the bed, the sheets neat. He remembered the mussed bedding, stained with sweat. He remembered every sweet kiss and intimate embrace.

James stalked across the room, more memories filling his skull. He remembered every spirited laugh on the island. Every soft smile and wicked wink.

"Yes," he hissed. He looked deep into her watery eyes. "It was all a lie."

Every playful flirtation and beloved caress and cherished whisper. A lie! A sinful, ugly lie!

"Ugh!" she cried. "I said no. No! He asked me to be his wife and I said no. I waited for him to leave before I rushed upstairs to tell you. I am such a fool! You want pain?" She knocked him in the cheek with her knuckles. "Here's your despair!"

James was numb, stoic. He didn't feel the woman's assault at all. One pressing thought gripped him. "Why did you refuse him?"

"Because I wanted you!"

The cold and listless ice that had caged him slowly chipped away. A fire burned deep in his belly. A light. She had wanted him. Him! She had forsaken her desires and lofty ambitions to be with him. It was what he had struggled for: revenge. It was the perfect moment to walk away from her, to leave her in despair the way she had abandoned him.

And yet every dark and twisted desire to crush her had flitted away from his blood and bones. He stared at her swollen lips and puffy eyes. He listened to the aching sobs buried deep within her bosom. Perhaps he had never truly believed he would have his revenge. Perhaps he had always believed her too cold to feel angst. But confronted with her shattered dreams, he had no desire to devastate her even more.

She had a heart.

The truth stirred the hurt in his breast, making him gasp for breath. "Why? Why did you leave me all those years ago?"

He had believed her cruel, a witch. But she possessed feeling . . . so *why* had she deserted him?

"You refused to marry me," she said with scorn.

James sensed the blood in his brain humming. "You deserted me over a game?"

"Not the game. I only challenged you to the game to win the forfeit. I wanted to marry you!"

James rubbed the back of his throbbing head in slow and methodic strokes. "Why?"

"Because I was a stupid chit." She rucked her brow, lips quivering. "I wanted to be a proper wife."

"But you loathed convention." Free. Wild. Unabashed. *That* was Sophia. It was one of the reasons he had desired her so greatly. "You snubbed social mores."

"And so you assumed I'd never want to wed?"

"Yes!" He flared his nostrils. "I would've stayed with you—forever. There was no reason to get married. I would *not* have abandoned you."

She scoffed. "Yes, I know. I'd be your everlasting island whore."

James cringed. "What?"

"I was your island whore! I endured the ridicule and the cold snubs from the rest of the islanders. I was Black Hawk's mistress. And I was treated like it."

"Why didn't you tell me?" he demanded, pulse thumping loud and strong in his head.

"I asked you to marry me," she returned fiercely. "That would have silenced the islanders. But you refused; you reneged on the forfeit." She fisted her fingers. "I was nothing but a warm wench to you. I was the daughter of a pirate, a prostitute. I wasn't good enough to be your wife."

James grabbed her arms. He dragged her against his hard muscles. He inhaled the rich, citrus scent of her soapy flesh, and curled his fingers through her wild tresses. "You wretched witch." He hugged her tight. "I loved you more than breath. There was no woman in the world I wanted more."

"Liar."

He pressed his thumb against her cursed lips. "Damn you, Sophia."

"You didn't even want me to meet your sister," she said, words wobbling. "You were ashamed of me. You are still ashamed of me."

"Never." He delved deep into her lucid and be-witching eyes. "I was never ashamed of you, Sophia. Hell, *I'm* the son of a pirate. Do you think me such a hypocrite? But a man doesn't talk about such things with his sister, especially his innocent sister. And she *was* innocent then."

She struggled in his arms. "Then *why* didn't you marry me?"

"I didn't want you to depend on me."

She stilled. "What?"

James closed his eyes. The woman's warm breath bathed his features, quieted the haunting reflections that always hounded him.

He had headed the family since boyhood, but his mother had suffered great hardship during the twelve years his father was away. Drake's return had allowed James a respite from constant duty and obligation, but soon thereafter his mother had died, and once more James was thrust into the position of parent and guardian.

He had always fulfilled the role of either mother or father. And he had failed at both. Mother had toiled in wretched poverty for years without surcease or com-fort from him, for he had burdened her with his basic needs for food and shelter and attention. And he had failed to inspire his own brothers with a sense of loy-alty and respect, for the men had deserted him, too.

"I didn't want another family to look after." He opened his eyes and twisted his fingers deeper into her hair. "I didn't want you to depend on me for all your needs . . . and be disappointed."

"I don't need you to take care of me."

"I know." He snorted. "Why do you think I was so at-tracted to you? You didn't need me. If I'd died in a fiery raid at sea, you would've been fine. You were strong. You had nursed your father. You had wits and will. Money. There was nothing more I could give you."

"Except yourself."

"Yes," he said softly. "Except that."

"And yet you didn't give me that, James." She pushed him away. "That was the one thing in the world I wanted from you . . . and you didn't share it with me." She chewed on her bottom lip, her eyes cold. "I had a chance to become a respectable wife, a countess. No one would've ridiculed me ever again. And I gave it all away for you . . . for nothing."

She shuddered, breathless.

"Sophia—"

"Good-bye, James."

Chapter 23

James swigged the sweet rum.

Slowly he set the empty glass on the scuffed tabletop and signaled for a buxom barmaid to bring him another drink.

He was ensconced in a shadowy corner of the seaside pub. It afforded him an opportunity to observe the rowdy fishermen in an unobtrusive way as he awaited the pirate impostor, Hagley.

"Here ye are, sweetheart."

James bristled at the familiar endearment as the cockney-tongued wench set another glass on the table and rubbed his hand. It was a flat and worthless invitation, leaving him feeling cold.

"Anythin' else?"

He offered her a coin for the rum. "No."

She shrugged and skirted off.

James was numb. Not from the spirits. The drink was just a ruse. He had to make it look like he belonged inside the pub, hence the second, and last, glass of rum. He needed to keep his faculties sharp, to take down the miscreants with a clear, quick mind. But he was insensible to the rest of the world, especially his brothers.

James glanced across the crowded, hazy, and boisterous room. The lieutenant was seated at another table with Edmund and Quincy. James had said very little to his brothers over the past few days, their rapport awkward. This would be their final mission together before they parted ways for good. It was a bitter moment, knowing he wouldn't have his kin at his back anymore . . . or Sophia at his side.

James stared at the glass, stroking the cold, moist surface with his thumb. She had stormed from the castle for London, the harridan in tow, soon after their last heated exchange. He was still bemused, the woman's revelations ringing in his head. Seven years ago, she had wanted to wed him to be a respectable wife. Three days ago, she had wanted to wed him to be . . . just a wife. His wife. She had wanted him. Him! He had thought her heartless. But she had cared. She had cared for him. And the truth of it washed away the years of former misery . . . and yet the deeper truth compounded the fresh despair. She *had* cared for him. He had lost her again.

"Captain Hawkins?"

James smothered the fiery wound in his heart, as he had so many times in the past. He glanced at the burly figure towering above the gloomy table. "Are you Hagley?"

"I am."

James perused the dastardly knave in detail. He was fair, with a suave manner and a deep, rumbling voice, which James suspected was induced to make him sound more formidable. Bulky, but not as big as James, he had no other characteristics to suggest he was the notorious pirate leader Black Hawk. The impostor had unjustly seized his rightful title. And to

make matters even more deplorable, he wasn't doing
the epithet justice.

James scowled. "Have a seat." He then knocked the
glass on the table. Once. Twice. The informal gesture
signaled to his brothers, and a dozen other tars from
the *Bonny Meg*'s crew, scattered throughout the pub,
that the target had arrived.

Hagley stroked his curly brown locks. "I understand you're interested in doing business."

James still glared at the charlatan, who had caused
him so much vexation, and restrained the whim to
snap the blackguard's neck in full public view.

"Yes, I'm looking for a partner."

"Oh?" said the scoundrel.

"There's trouble at sea. Perhaps you've read the account in the papers?"

"The account?"

James downed the rum and wiped his mouth before
he slammed the empty glass against the wood surface.
"About pirates."

There was a flicker of trepidation in the scalawag's
eyes before he composed his features and returned
coolly, "Pirates, you say?"

Hagley's bravado was admirable, but James wasn't
at the pub to make friends with the devil—but to crush
him.

"Yes, I was nearly robbed of cargo a fortnight ago.
I'd like to take on a partner, divide shipments in the
future."

Hagley stroked his chin. "Ah, strength in
numbers."

"That's right." James glowered. "Shall we find a
more quiet setting to discuss the matter further?"

"I don't think so . . . Black Hawk."

James hardened. "What did you call me?"

"I'm honored, truly. It's a real pleasure to meet the notorious pirate captain. I thought you dead. Why did you give up piracy?"

The man's bravado wasn't bravado at all. James looked across the room. The patrons merrily drowned in ale and frolicked with wenches. He spotted his crew, still positioned at random tables throughout the pub, surrounding him. He had their support, but he sensed it inadequate. Hagley had far greater numbers skulking out of sight, he was sure.

"Well, I've enjoyed being you these last few months." Hagley grinned. "Quarry is so much more accommodating with their jewels and other valuables after I announce my—er, your name." He sighed. "I'll miss the notoriety, the respect. But I suppose it's time I step down from the title . . . and let the real Black Hawk have it back."

James fisted his palms. "Black Hawk is dead."

Hagley lifted from the chair and winked. "Aye, he very soon will be."

The room suddenly swelled with brutes.

"You see, I suspected it might be you hounding me," expounded the miscreant. "And I sent word to the authorities, informing them about the *real* Black Hawk's whereabouts. I can't have you—or them—on my tail forever."

The brutes approached. James eyed his brothers, the men already on their feet and reaching for their concealed weapons, and with a plain, sharp look ordered them all to stand down and not engage the advancing Bow Street Runners. Right now it was only James the authorities targeted. If the rest of the men remained quiet, they would get out of the pub alive and unmolested, for even the sorrow of their betrayal was not strong enough to erase James's need to protect them. He didn't want them to hang.

"You're a lot brighter than I'd thought you'd be, Hagley."

He chuckled. "Thank you, mate . . . and good luck to you."

"Why are you packing?"

Sophia stilled. She glanced at the matron. The woman was wearing a white woolly wrapper and ruffled nightcap, features grave. She entered the bedroom and closed the door.

"I'm leaving for Jamaica in two days." Sophia folded the dress and placed it inside the chest. "You know that, Lady Lucas."

"No, I mean why are *you* packing?"

"Oh." She reached for another garment, a deep shimmering bronze, the same dress she'd sported the night of the earl's ball, the night she had reunited with James. She caressed the fabric softly, wistfully. "I dismissed the maid to bed. I'm restless. I need to occupy my fingers."

Lady Lucas peeked inside the chest and wrinkled her nose at the creased attire. "Perhaps you should summon the maid to return to her duty?"

"It isn't necessary."

Sophia had no desire to preserve the outfits. What would she do with them in Jamaica? There'd be no formal suppers or prim picnics on the island. And she suspected the governor's wife would not welcome her inside her stylish house even if she was wearing the refined material.

"I don't like it, Miss Dawson. It's improper."

Sophia sighed. "I'll iron the fabric when I get—"

"No, my dear." She flicked her fingers. "I mean, it's improper for you to be traveling to the island alone."

"Don't fret, Lady Lucas." She tucked the dress inside the chest. "The captain will serve as chaperone. I will be under his protection throughout the voyage."

"I see." She twisted her bony fingers together. "I'm sorry, Miss Dawson."

Sophia dusted the matching satin slippers before she interred them, too. "There's no need to apologize, Lady Lucas. You've done nothing wrong."

"I've failed you."

Sophia's heart pinched. "No, I've failed *you*."

She whisked across the room, her heart thudding. The matron had labored arduously on her behalf, priming her and guiding her through social norms and customs, grooming her to be a countess. And Sophia had snubbed the woman's efforts with her willful refusal to wed the earl . . . and her foolish desire to wed the black devil instead.

Sophia collected the next batch of belongings scattered across the bed, seeking comfort from her troubled thoughts with her rushed movements.

"The barbarian bewitched you, didn't he, Miss Dawson? That's why you rejected the earl?"

Sophia set the items on the table beside the chest. She stuffed each corset, stocking, and petticoat inside the leather trunk, cramming the articles into the nooks and corners, working through her frustration.

"Yes, he bewitched me," she said stiffly. "But that isn't your fault."

It's mine.

She was the one who'd believed the man had changed his views about marriage, that there was finally a chance for them to share a future together.

"It is my fault, Miss Dawson. I failed to protect you."

Sophia paused. She looked at the frail woman and frowned. "I will honor our agreement, Lady Lucas. I will not leave you destitute."

"Thank you, my dear, but that's not why I'm so aggrieved . . . I failed in my duty. I've never failed in my duty, Miss Dawson."

Sophia delved into her chaperone's weary gray eyes. "You haven't failed, Lady Lucas . . . I just don't belong here."

Not in England. Not with James. She belonged on the island. It was home. She only wished she wasn't retuning to the tropical paradise in disgrace . . . and despair.

"Good night, Miss Dawson."

Sophia said quietly, "Good night, Lady Lucas."

The matron departed from the room, closing the door softly behind her.

Sophia stared at the barrier, thinking about the old woman who had served as teacher and chaperone and even mother for the past few months.

She sighed. She would miss the matron's companionship. Sophia would miss the friendship of others, as well. The duchess, for instance. Even the Hawkins brothers—well, three of the Hawkins brothers. She had learned that not every member of the peerage was a cutthroat . . . but that some cutthroats deserved the epithet. Some cutthroats truly carved the heart and sliced the soul.

She tamped down the bitterness that had welled in her breast. She resumed packing and reached for another bundle of clothing . . . when a warm hand slipped over her mouth and a strong arm circled her belly.

Blood throbbed in her veins and she thrashed mightily, kicking her feet and swinging her arms.

"It's me Sophia," he hissed. "Be still!"

Sophia listened to the familiar low timbre and sighed through her nose, muscles loosening.

He removed his hand from her lips. "I'm sorry I frightened you, but I didn't want you to scream and attract attention."

She whirled around and glared at William. "What are you doing here?"

"We need your help, Sophia."

She glanced at the other two brothers, unceremoniously rifling through her luggage. Quincy crooked his finger and lifted a silk stocking.

She snatched the legging. "What are you doing with that?"

"Where are you going?" the pup wondered.

"I'm leaving for Jamaica in two days." She huffed and stuffed the material back inside the chest. "Now *what* are you doing here?"

"It's about James," said William.

She bristled. "What about the black devil?"

William frowned, looking haggard. "He was apprehended by the authorities tonight."

Sophia took in a sharp breath. "The charge?"

"Piracy."

"No," she said succinctly.

Quincy balked. "What?"

"No, I won't help you," she returned tersely, and set about packing again, methodically moving through the room, gathering more property.

"But he'll hang!" cried Quincy.

"Good."

William touched her elbow. "I know you're angry with him, Sophia."

She shrugged and dumped the rest of her possessions into the chest without a thought to the wrinkles. "No, you don't know or you wouldn't be asking me to help you."

The lieutenant said softly, "You still care for him."

"Like hell I do!"

She slammed the cap over the brimming apparel and pinched her lips as she struggled with the gold clasps. Quincy sat on the lid, crushing the items inside, but sinking the closure, allowing her to snap the locks tight and fasten the belt buckles.

"Thank you, Quincy," she said curtly.

William persisted, "And he cares for you."

She glared at the lieutenant. "Liar."

"It's true." Quincy moved away from the chest. "He's a miserable brute, you know that, but the year he spent on the island with you was the one time in his life he was truly happy."

Sophia shuddered. She was overwhelmed with joyful memories—and sick with wretched echoes.

I want her to know pain. I want her to feel the same fucking despair that I had to feel when she walked away from me.

"Well, he doesn't care for me anymore." The tightness in her breast was suffocating. "He wants me to feel despair."

William looked at her thoughtfully. "He's angry with you for deserting him."

She cringed. The words stirred regret in her belly: an inkling of regret for walking away from the pirate captain in such a cruel fashion all those years ago.

I was never ashamed of you, Sophia.

She had believed the man deserved the cold fare-well for the way he had treated her . . . but if he hadn't treated her in an ill manner? If he hadn't been ashamed of her, as he'd claimed? Then perhaps she had been wrong, deserting him without a word of good-bye?

"I know he's furious," she retorted. "I was eaves-dropping."

"Then you also know you broke his heart when you walked away from him seven years ago."

She fisted her palms and gritted, "Well, now we're even."

The black devil had shattered her heart, too. What more did William want from her? Tears? Wails? It was over. Tit for tat. Let the blackguard rot!

"We have to save him, Sophia," said Edmund. "He's our brother."

"So save him!" she snapped.

"We need your help." Edmund, so temperamental, furrowed his brow. "Newgate is heavily guarded."

Sophia imagined James paraded to the gibbet, the crowd heckling, before a coarse noose was fastened over his hooded head.

She scowled. The vision had failed to bring her the pleasure she'd hoped for, the retribution she'd craved.

"Surely he won't hang tonight?" She placed her arms akimbo. "Before a trial?"

"No, a trial might even exonerate him." William slipped his hands over his hips. "We've already sent word to the castle for the duke to come to London to bear witness to James's character, to affirm his brother-in-law is *not* Black Hawk."

She brandished her fingers. "There, you see."

"And if the court rejects his testimony?" from Edmund.

"Why would they do such a thing?" She gathered her brows. "He's a *duke*."

"The authorities are desperate to hang someone for the crime," said William. "They might think the duke's testimony tainted because of his connection to our family."

"And it would be, but that's not the worst of it." Edmund glowered. "The duke might not even testify, considering his strife with James. He might let our brother hang!"

"Or James might incriminate himself," said Quincy.

Sophia balked. "What?"

"James ordered us not to save him." Quincy scratched the back of his head in an uncomfortable manner. "We intended to capture the leader of the impostors tonight, but it was a trap. James sacrificed himself so we could escape the authorities . . . but I don't think he cares whether he hangs or not. I wouldn't be surprised if he admitted in the Old Bailey courthouse to being Black Hawk."

"Why would he do that?" she demanded.

Had the notorious rogue lost his mind?

Quincy looked sheepish. "We had a falling out."

"What sort of a falling out?"

The pup glanced at the floor. "We want to join the navy as privateers . . . James isn't too keen on the idea."

Sophia lifted a brow. "I'm surprised you're still alive, that he didn't hang *you*."

Quincy sighed. "He thinks he's lost us . . . and you, too. I don't know if he's thinking with a clear head."

Sophia balled her fingers into fists and gnashed her teeth. The black devil was going to hang. And *she* had to save him? Curse him!

William looked grave. "We have to get to him before word leaks that he's been captured and the gaol is surrounded with spectators."

Quincy nodded. "Last time a woman hanged, forty thousand gathered at Newgate to witness the execution."

"Salacious criminals and infamous crimes draw spectators." Edmund frowned and crossed his arms across his chest. "How many do you think will come to Newgate once word spreads that Black Hawk's in the gaol? We'll never get inside the fortress then. We have to do this tonight!"

"Think of Belle," Quincy pleaded, eyes round and imploring in that charming—hoodwinking—fashion. "She almost died in childbirth two months ago. She's still recovering from the ordeal. The stress of James's execution might send her into regression."

"All right." Sophia lifted her hands in defeat. The pup had sensed her misgiving. He had offered her the one bit of sound reasoning she was willing to listen to: the duchess's good health. "I'll help you save James from the gallows for Belle's sake. What do you want me to do?"

Chapter 24

The walls of Newgate stood thick and craggy with soot.

Sophia stared at Debtors' Door: the ominous gateway that the condemned had to pass through on their short journey to the scaffolds. The hangman was already preparing the ropes for that morning's executions scheduled to commence at eight o'clock sharp. Simple wood coffins lined the platform, ready to protect the corpses from the rowdy mob seeking macabre souveniers and preserve them for the anatomists.

Sophia shuddered. She had a hard belly. She had witnessed many executions on the island. But knowing James was inside the sturdy stone walls, that soon he might stand on the gallows and take his place inside a dark coffin, chilled her.

"Where are they?" grumbled Edmund. "They're never late. It's every morning at half past seven, right?"

Quincy gesticulated with his hand. "Here they come!"

Sophia eyed the troupe of hooded ladies, dutifully bobbing along Old Bailey Street. The females turned the corner onto Newgate Street and headed south toward the prison gates.

Quincy pressed the basket into her hands. "Remember your guise?"

"I'm part of the woman's reform movement for the better treatment of convicts," she repeated the mantra, while Edmund lifted her hood.

William then grabbed her by the arms and looked firmly into her eyes. "Find him. Signal us when it's safe to enter. Don't go after him yourself. If you're captured aiding his escaping, you'll hang alongside him."

She nodded brusquely.

"We'll have you home in time for breakfast." He sighed. "Good luck, Sophia."

She snorted. Luck? She didn't believe in the rot. Sound wits, good instincts, and a flair with a dagger were all she needed.

Sophia stepped away from the protection of the shadows and scurried across the junction under the cover of dusk. She eyed the great dome of St. Paul's Cathedral, struck by the juxtaposition between eternal life and gruesome death, before she surreptitiously joined the line of females, pretending to be part of the charitable organization.

As she neared the gaol gates, she gripped the wicker handle with more vim. The looming structure was three stories high. There were two single doors at ground level, positioned under lintels, leading to the quarters for the turnkeys. The main entrance was raised and flanked by the lesser doors. Two sets of steps, one from the north, the other from the south, sloped at a steady elevation toward the center entranceway.

Sophia mounted the northern steps, gazing through

the double arched windows as she waited in formation, for each woman had to present the contents of her basket before she was permitted entry into the formidable gaol.

Sophia licked her lips as she reached the main door. She flicked her wrist and removed the white kerchief, revealing the bread and cheese.

The burly sentry prodded the contents with a fixed frown before he bobbed his head, granting her passage.

Sophia swallowed the sigh that had welled in her throat. She skirted after the other philanthropists, moving through the keeper's house and past the lodges for the turnkeys. The group cut through the chapel, located in the center of the gaol. William had offered her a printed map of the interior, and Sophia had memorized the layout of the prison.

She passed through the men's quadrangle, a vast stone courtyard. Female felons were housed to the south and debtors to the north. She had only a few minutes to peruse the male convicts, housed in the east wing, and locate James before the humanitarians moved on to the other inmates.

Sophia quietly tailed the ambitious matrons as the party entered the poorly lit men's ward. She quickly gasped as the putrid stench of sickness and unwashed bodies filled her lungs, making her choke, and she tamped the urge to vomit into the bowel of her belly. The floor was greasy, and the pitiful whimpers from the chained prisoners resounded throughout the tunnels.

Sophia shivered. She set to work, handing out the loaves of bread and cuts of cheese through the small rifle slots in the iron cell doors. The eager convicts—

men and boys alike—reached their grimy hands through the openings, fingers trembling with hunger.

Sophia was brimming with compassion. But she wasn't here to set all the wretches free . . . just one.

James.

He was in the dark hell, trapped. But where? She glanced through the tunnels, peered into the dank wards. How was she going to locate him in the labyrinth?

"Thank ye, miss."

Sophia glanced at the frail hand clutching the rye bread. It was a child's hand, and she crouched, peering through the square portal. "What is your crime, young man?"

A set of gloomy eyes observed her. "Pickin' pockets, miss."

Sophia sighed. "What is to become of you?"

"The colony, miss."

Australia, she thought grimly, patting the boy's hand in support, about to move off, when she thought to inquire in a whisper: "Is there a new prisoner? I have bread for him, too."

"Aye, miss." The lad stuffed his gaunt and sallow cheeks with the fare, mumbling, "He come through last night, thrashin' and hollerin'."

That sounded like James, she thought dryly.

"Did you see where the gaolers took him?"

The urchin pointed a sharp and bony finger through the portal. "There, miss. Up them steps."

She smiled. "Thank you."

Sophia lifted off her haunches and traversed the passageway. Curved steps spiraled between the two male wards—and one cantankerous-looking guard defended them.

James had to be secured apart from the other convicts; his notorious reputation warranted the segregation. But she had to be certain before she summoned the rest of his brothers inside the gaol. If she was wrong, if the brothers aimlessly fumbled through the prison looking for the captain—and were captured—it might mean *all* their necks in a noose.

Sophia meshed her lips together. She steadied her thumping heart with a few measured breaths before she coolly approached the sentry.

The surly devil moved to curtail her steps. He obstructed her ascent with his wide shoulders—and belligerent glare. "Where do you think you're going?"

Unflappably she lifted the basket. "I have food for the prisoner."

"No." The man's words clipped. "No food for this one."

"Yes, sir."

Sophia quickly retreated. If she pestered the gaoler, he might suspect something was amiss, and yet she was convinced James was secured upstairs. How to reach him and be sure?

Sophia spotted the hairy ball. It scuttled across the slick stone floor. She smirked, an idea popping into her head.

She tiptoed after the vermin, glanced from side to side, then scooped up the rat by the cool, slick tail, gently setting the wriggling rodent into the basket of a passing matron.

Sophia swiftly skirted off. She ensconced herself in the shadows . . . and observed as the woman reached inside her basket.

The scream bounced off the walls in the long and cavernous passage.

A whistle shrieked. Sentries circled the woman, perhaps convinced the convicts had accosted her, but the kerfuffle would last only a few seconds before the truth was revealed.

Sophia glanced at the stairwell. The stationed guard had abandoned his post to assist the philanthropist, just as Sophia had surmised. She slipped out of the shadows and briskly climbed the winding steps. On the second level, she found another ward. She whisked through the tunnel, past the empty cells, and headed for the one sealed door at the end of the passage.

Sophia hunkered. She opened the rifle slot and peeked inside the room. "James?"

A large, dark figure rested in the opposite corner, surrounded by dank-smelling straw.

"James?" she hissed, tongue parched. She licked her lips again and squinted, the portal small. "James, is that you?"

"What are *you* doing here?"

Something quivered in Sophia's belly at the sound of his raspy voice. It was a profound sentiment that stirred her blood and swelled in her veins, making her heart throb and her muscles clench.

"Shhh." She glanced over her shoulder, but the passage remained empty. "I'm going to fetch your brothers."

"No."

She huffed. "What?"

"Get out, Sophia. And stay out! Don't bring my brothers back here. Do you want us *all* to hang?"

She mulled that over. "You're right." She set aside the basket and reached for the small dagger tucked between her breasts. "I'll get you out myself."

"Sophia . . ."

She ignored the man's growl and slipped the shiny blade into the keyhole. She then yanked a hairpin from her bun and inserted it into the pin and tumbler device, counting the pins and judging their length. She pressed the knife against the shorter pins and . . .

"I've got it!"

Sophia tucked the dagger back into the sheath between her breasts. She grabbed the basket before she opened the cell door and slipped inside the chilly room.

Her heart seized.

The pirate captain squatted in the corner of the cell, ankles manacled, arms listless at his side. There was thick, dry blood smeared across his handsome features. Bruises scarred his cheeks and swelling lips.

Sophia closed the door. "They beat you?"

He grunted. "I'm not very well-liked."

"You mean Black Hawk isn't very well-liked?" She dashed across the cell and settled beside him. "You don't sound too incensed over the thrashing."

He shrugged. "I wanted to fight."

It was that one little word—"wanted"—that had her scowling. The man might be in a sour mood about the strife with his brothers, but he wasn't suicidal. A good duel with fisticuffs had cooled his frustrations.

"I think Quincy's feeling guilty about your strife." She set the basket aside and lowered her hood. "He was sure you were feeling melancholy, that you might even confess your true identity in court because you *wanted* to hang."

"Quincy's an ass."

With tender taps, she fingered his jaw. "Is it broken?"

He jerked his head away. "No."

"Well, you're welcome," she said tersely.

He glowered. "What are you doing here, Sophia?"

"Your brothers beseeched me for help."

"I'll kill them."

She snorted and reached for her knife again. "I can take care of myself." She examined the shackles. "I can't believe they chained you, too!"

But James ignored her peevish cavil. He pressed on with "They had no business placing you in harm's way."

She slipped the blade between her breasts again. The steel tip was too wide to fit inside the narrow keyhole. She burrowed through the lock parts with the hairpin instead.

"I placed myself in harm's way."

She stiffened. He stroked the loose curl at her temple, winding it around his bloody knuckle. The tender ministrations made her shiver, and she dismissed the growing ache that filled her belly and squeezed her heart.

She furrowed her brow in studious regard, jammed the hairpin . . .

The clip-clop of boots resounded.

She looked at Black Hawk, spooked.

He gnashed his teeth. "Get out!"

"It's too late," she whispered.

"Damn it, I told you—"

She placed her finger against his plump and battered lips. "Quiet."

Swiftly she crawled toward the door and wedged herself in the corner, hugging the basket against her breast.

She murmured, "Look miserable."

He scowled.

The footfalls rested beside the door.

Sophia stopped breathing.

She sensed the gaoler's eyes peering through the rifle slot, but she was hunched in the nook beside the door. It was impossible for the man to detect her presence at that angle . . . unless he discovered the door was unlocked—and stepped inside the cell.

One.

Two.

Three.

Four seconds later, the footfalls retreated.

Sophia sighed. Blood rushed into her head. To be sure it wasn't a ruse, she mouthed silently: *Is . . . he . . . gone?*

Slowly James nodded.

Sophia dropped the basket and scurried across the cell floor once more. She knelt at the captain's feet and inserted the hairpin in the manacle's lock.

James grabbed her wrist. "Get out, Sophia. Now!"

"I'm not leaving without you." She wrenched her fingers loose and defeated the first shackle. "Hold still!"

She fished for the right pins. As soon as the second lock snapped, James bounded to his feet. He grabbed her arm and hauled her toward the door.

She snatched the basket and trailed behind him, trapped in his robust grip. Even after the bloody scuffle, the pirate lord still possessed enough strength to secure her . . . and she resisted the impulse to let his vigor seep into her bones.

He was still the rogue who had shattered her heart. He was still the villain who had wanted her to suffer, to feel despair. That he'd bewitched her senses was moot, for he had also devastated her dreams. And she would not forgive him for that.

"There's a guard stationed at the bottom of the steps, James."

He looked at her sharply. "Stay here."

He vanished.

The "oomph" and muffled thud that followed seconds later snagged her attention, and she waited with bated breath as a figure mounted the stone steps.

But the hulking shadow was James. She recognized the man's stout form. He hauled the unconscious gaoler up the uneven steps, then dragged the limp body across the passageway and into the cell.

Sophia maintained a vigil, her heart in her throat. The din from the gathering rabble was growing more dense and vociferous. It was almost eight o'clock. It was almost time for the executions. If the mob discovered Black Hawk escaping . . . "Hurry!"

James snapped the manacles around the man's ankles and piled the straw next to his head, concealing his features. He then closed the cell, leaving the rifle slot opened. The gaoler carried no key on his person, for only the turnkeys possessed them, so the door remained unlocked. But the mock prisoner would offer them more time to escape, as no one would sound the alarm if they believed the pirate still secured and chained.

James clasped her by the wrist again, but she wriggled loose, taking his meaty hand instead. "Follow me. Your brothers are waiting."

He didn't protest. He followed her, let her guide him to safety.

"Why did you come, Sophia?"

She steered him through the passageways, careful to keep to the shadows and avoid the other gaolers roaming the causeways.

"I told you, your brothers asked me for my help."

"You could have told them to bugger off." He demanded fiercely, "Why did you come?"

She huffed. "I didn't want your hanging to upset your sister."

The man's black mood blackened even more, for he stiffened his fingers and clenched her palm.

Sophia disregarded the pressure on her hand. She also overlooked the growing pressure in her heart as she tried to convince herself she didn't give a damn about the pirate captain, that she was just saving his arse for Belle's sake. But the more she repeated that mantra in her head, the hollower it sounded.

She maneuvered James along the stone wall and toward the southernmost entrance, where she and the brothers had previously agreed to meet.

The couple slipped through the vacant turnkey's quarters. The ground floor door was farthest from the gallows, which was located at the northeast corner of the street. Even so, as soon as she unfastened the bolt and slipped through the door with James in tow, she was swarmed by myriad spectators.

Sophia gasped. The wall of energy, the dense thickness of limbs was suffocating. James shielded her from the crushing crowd with his weight. The mob hollered, anxious to witness the day's hangings. Ten wretches were already lined along the platform, awaiting death. Even the gaolers were too preoccupied with the frantic throng to detect their stealthy escape.

Swiftly a mantle smothered James. Edmund and Quincy had circled the captain, concealing him from public view. The rabble was too thick, too randy to recognize the captain's visage, but the precaution was wise, nonetheless.

William grabbed her. "You were supposed to come get us, Sophia."

The reprimand in his voice lifted her hackles, and she snapped, "The plan changed."

William glowered at her before he looked at the fledglings and ordered, "Take him to the ship."

But James resisted. "Sophia!"

"I'll take care of Sophia." William avowed, "I'll see her safely home. Now go!"

"Go, James," Sophia urged him, glaring at him. "Go before they find you missing or it will have been for nothing."

James stopped struggling against his kin. He let his brothers, and the swaying movement of the other bodies at large, determine his steps and steer him in the opposite direction from her.

Their eyes locked one last time as the bells tolled eight o'clock and the trapdoors parted, snapping the necks of the condemned.

Chapter 25

James stretched his booted toes toward the coal-burning fireplace and folded his hands across his midriff. He looked at the oil painting that Quincy had purchased, above the mantel and trimmed in an elaborate, baroque-style frame. The artwork illustrated a siren, clutching a rock plastered with algae and coral as the foamy sea battered her scaled fins.

He glowered at the piece.

A soft breeze whisked through the room as someone opened the study door.

James remained rooted in the wing chair. He listened to the clip-clop of footfalls behind him and recognized the familiar gait.

"What do you want, Quincy?"

The pup settled in the twin seat beside him, looking grave. "Will's pestering me about my latest pursuit, so I've come seeking refuge." He followed the captain's gaze to the canvas. "She's beautiful, isn't she?"

"I hate that picture."

"You have no appreciation for art, James."

Quincy rubbed his sluggish eyes, pupils constricted. "How are you feeling?"

James regarded the pup thoughtfully before he

stroked his chin, rife with stubble and bruises. "I'm fine."

James was back inside his town house. The charges against him had been dismissed. The Duke of Wembury had presented testimony in court that James was *not* the notorious pirate leader Black Hawk. The court was unwilling to hang a man so intimately connected with such a prestigious family. The accusation was deemed a misidentification—and James's escape from the gaol was overlooked.

"Will's also searching for his own ship to captain . . . but it won't be the same at sea without the *Bonny Meg*—or you, James."

He hardened. "Then don't join the navy."

Quincy sighed. "I wish it was that simple."

"It is."

"No, it isn't, James." He stretched his legs and crossed his feet at the ankles. "We need to be privateers."

The muscles in his jaw firmed. "We'll find the impostors. We don't need to seek a pardon."

That dastardly knave Hagley and his crew were still on the loose, but James intended to track the conniving bastards to hell. He intended to quash the impostors and put an end to his own infernal namesake once and for all.

"It's not just the impostors pushing us into a corner, James."

"Aye, you're bored," he said succinctly. "I know."

"Think about it, James. It's not easy going against one's true nature, even instinct. Being a privateer will give us the freedom we need to be ourselves."

James had once echoed similar claims . . . to Sophia.

Don't you see how they crush you, sweetheart? Take away your breath? Let me give you breath.

He closed his eyes. He was breathless, too. He had once commanded respect as the infamous pirate captain Black Hawk . . . now he was a barbarian, parading in fancy robes, like a sideshow carnival chimp, for the *ton*'s amusement.

Muscles stiff, James demanded, "And do you think it's easy for me to be a merchant sailor?"

Quincy snorted. "No, I'd wager the *Bonny Meg* you're miserable about the whole ordeal, too. But unlike you, I intend to change my circumstances."

"Well, I can't." James seethed. "The navy destroyed my life. You don't understand."

"I understand," he said quietly. "I know you regret the past. And I'm sorry."

James glanced at the pup, frowning. "For what?"

"For making your life so miserable."

Long-ago memories surfaced in James's head: Quincy's childhood antics, his rebellious, teenage stage—which he had yet to grow out of—and yet James wouldn't use the word "miserable" to describe the past twenty-one years he'd shared with the pup. It wasn't Quincy who'd made him so miserable, but the hardship of caring for him—for all of them. Even with his father's help in the latter years, much of the burden of parenthood had rested with James . . . perhaps a burden he had wittingly placed on his shoulders. He could have offered his siblings more freedom as they'd matured, but he had chosen not to.

James smelled the fumes stemming from Quincy's clothes. "You've been chasing the dragon again, haven't you?"

He shrugged. "It makes me forget."

"Forget what?"

"That I killed Mother . . . that I ruined your life."

James scowled. "What the hell are you talking about?"

"If I hadn't been born, Mother would still be alive and you wouldn't have wasted your life playing nursemaid."

There was a profound and biting sentiment in his belly as he imagined the past two decades without Quincy's foolery and charm.

"I know you loathe the navy for taking Father away, James. Why don't you loathe me for taking Mother away? . . . Or do you?"

"I don't hate you, you ass."

He chuckled. "Well, that's good to hear."

"Damn it, Quincy!" He slammed his fist against the armrest. "It isn't the same. The navy willfully kidnapped Father. You didn't intend Mother harm."

"Still—"

"Enough!"

Quiet settled between the brothers as the evening shadows skulked inside the room through the darkening windows.

"Sophia is sailing back to Jamaica tonight."

James stifled the bleeding sore in his soul. "I know."

"Aren't you going to go after her?"

"No."

"But you love her."

James rubbed his thrumming brow, struggled against the cold darkness slowly filling his heart. "She doesn't want anything to do with me."

"She's angry with you, but she loves you, too."

He scoffed. "And how do you know that?"

"She saved your life."

"She did that to protect Belle from humiliation and distress."

Quincy tsked. "You might be old and wise, James, but really . . ."

Slowly James lifted a single brow.

"Sophia wouldn't be so furious with you if she didn't love you," the pup said sagely. "She wouldn't be in such pain."

James looked away from his brother. He shut his eyes, his heart against the anguish stirring in his own mind and soul. "I'm not going after her."

"You'll regret it."

"Blast it, Quincy! Don't you have a wench to bed? Enlist in the navy?"

"Fine." He lifted from the chair, lethargic. "But let me ask you this, James: If you'd had the chance to make it right seven years ago, would you have done so?"

A piercing image raided his head, captured his senses:

"There was nothing more I could give you."

"Except yourself."

"Yes. Except that."

"And yet you didn't give me that, James. That was the one thing in the world I wanted from you . . . and you didn't share it with me."

The words tormented him. James reflected upon the past, the empty plantation house, the dastardly fob watch. If he'd had the chance to make it right then . . .

Sophia had wits and will. She had infiltrated the notorious Newgate Gaol and liberated him with a dagger and a hairpin. The woman was savvy and independent. She didn't need him . . . but if she desired him?

Quincy headed for the door. "Don't let another seven years pass before you make it right with Sophia. You don't need more regret."

* * *

Sophia stood at the poop. The captain had granted her permission to scale the officers' deck. She watched the frothing waves behind the *Titan*, the folds in the dark water as the mighty vessel cut through the tranquil sea.

He had not come for her.

Two days ago, she had departed from England. She had wished Lady Lucas a fond farewell, she had penned Imogen Rayne a conciliatory note, and she had expressed her sincere appreciation to the duke and duchess for their friendship and hospitality in another epistle. She had terminated all relationships . . . bar one.

He had not come for her.

Sophia had thought he might swoop into port. She had imagined the theatrical way she'd rebuff the black devil if he'd begged her to stay with him in England.

But he had not come for her.

And her revenge fantasy seemed trite and hollow now. She envisioned a far different outcome: a longing look . . . a word of contrition . . . a spirited kiss.

She sighed.

Loudly.

"Are you all right, Miss Dawson?"

Captain Higgins stepped beside her, thoughtful. At age sixty-six, he sported a white coif with fashionable curls and a studious countenance, befitting his rank and experience. She was under his protection during the two-month voyage home. He had proved a sage commander and an amiable supper companion.

"I'm fine, Captain."

He looked out to sea. "It's a lovely night."

Sophia gazed at the full moon, low in the starry heavens. The ethereal white light was so pure and bright. "Brilliant."

"Are you comfortable, Miss Dawson? Do you have everything that you need?"

No, not everything, she thought wistfully.

"I'm fond of my quarters. Thank you, Captain."

He offered her his arm. "I've come to escort you to supper."

She smiled and placed her hand on the white linen sleeve of his formal coat. "I'm famished."

Later that night, Sophia trolled her private cabin, restless. The rich fare was still anchored in her belly, and her head was still filled with rambunctious thoughts, making it difficult for her to fall asleep.

He had not come for her.

The blackguard had deserted her in port, leaving her hampered with so many tempestuous words. She was never going to get any rest so long as the bothersome reflections occupied her thoughts.

Sophia quit stalking the small space and rummaged through the top crate stacked at the foot of her bed. She grabbed the neatly folded letter-writing desk and sat on the soft feather tick, curling her legs together. She opened the slanted box with green felt upholstery, positioned a piece of paper across the hard, woolly surface, and dipped the quill into the small copper inkwell.

She had lost the opportunity to confess to him the brewing feelings inside her, so she intended to record them instead. She might mail the letter to him once she reached Jamaica. Or perhaps she might keep it as a token of her thoughts about the man. But for now, she scratched goose feather against paper, emptying her mind.

A blast shattered the stillness.

Sophia smeared the ink all over the paper and her

hand, her heart pumping in wild beats. She skirted across the cabin and peered through the scuttle, but there were only black, velvety waves and haunting moonlight. She moved into the passageway next. She was still dressed in her evening wear, and so mingled with the other passengers, who were all frightened and disoriented.

"What's happened?" demanded Sophia.

A young gentleman hugged his panicked wife. "There was an explosion."

"Are we sinking?" cried the other woman.

The myriad voices and cramped causeway offered Sophia little insight. She pushed through the throng of anxious passengers and scaled the steps, poking her head through the hatchway.

Smoke roiled across the wide deck.

Tars scattered in alarm.

Was there a mishap in the galley? Had the vessel rammed another ship at sea?

She coughed, the smoke stifling. Tears filled her eyes, the fumes biting . . . Sulfur. She sensed it now, the stinging stench.

She grabbed a desperate sailor. "Are we under attack?"

He bobbed his head. "Pirates!"

The impostors!

Sophia curled her fingers into fists. The bloody cutthroats! Quincy had mentioned the dastardly charlatans were still at large, that they had failed to apprehend them.

"Best get belowdecks, miss."

But Sophia was miffed. She stalked across the deck instead. She wasn't in any immediate danger. The impostors didn't want to sink the vessel. The cannon blast had served as a warning to stand down, to prepare to be boarded. The brigands wanted treasure.

Sophia eyed the sinister three-masted silhouette. Moonlight kissed its sails. It was positioned broadside, its cannons aimed at the *Titan*.

She heard the distinct footfalls of heavy boots as the pirates boarded the ship.

"Stand your ground, men," ordered Captain Higgins.

The crew stilled as the brigands slowly crossed the deck, hulking shadows cutting through the waft of smoke.

One thick figure moved through the fumes and headed for her. She reached for her dagger, prepared to cut the corsair's gullet . . . but she gasped as a set of dark and commanding eyes fixed on her.

Black Hawk!

Sophia's heart boomed. She was transfixed. What was *he* doing here? How was he even here? The man had forsaken piracy to protect his sister . . . and yet he looked like a pirate, so dark and dangerous, rough and wild. He had his hair in a queue, cheeks scratchy-looking with stubble, clothes coarse. No one aboard the vessel would recognize him as Captain Hawkins, the brother of a duchess. He was Black Hawk. And she pulsed with giddy energy at the wicked sight of him.

"Keep your wits, gentlemen." Quincy brandished a pistol. "Black Hawk won't harm you. He's just here to take your most valuable cargo." He grinned. "We understand there's an heiress onboard: a Miss Dawson. We've been following her for some time now."

All four brothers were on deck in disguise. Sophia recognized their voices and mannerisms . . . but it was the towering figure of James that mesmerized her the most, made her weak with vertigo.

James stopped in front in her, his thrumming strength so heady, she almost sighed with pleasure to see him again, to feel him so intimately.

He glanced at the dagger in her ink-stained hand and slowly lifted a brow . . . before he crouched and scooped her into his arms, dumping her over his wide shoulder.

Sophia didn't protest the jostling, too staggered to breathe a word.

Captain Higgins stormed after the pirate lord. "Vile vermin!"

"Don't start a fuss," William said sternly, curtailing the commander's heroics as he positioned his body between the man and his brother. "Consider the other passengers in your charge, Captain. Miss Dawson will remain unharmed, I assure you."

Captain Higgins blustered, "Liar!"

Sophia was lowered down the rope ladder and into the waiting rowboat. She gathered her scattered senses and shouted, "Don't fight them, Captain Higgins!"

She didn't want the good captain or the innocent crew and passengers to end up in a scuffle with the pirates. She wasn't in any real danger . . . she was sure.

"You heard the lady," from Edmund.

The brigands quickly retreated after the pirate captain and his "cargo."

"You'll hang for this!" Captain Higgins grabbed the starboard rail and vehemently proclaimed, "I'll see to it that the ransom is paid, Miss Dawson. Be brave!"

A few minutes later, Sophia found herself aboard the *Bonny Meg* . . . inside the captain's quarters.

James effortlessly set her on the ground. She staggered backward, woozy, thoughts whirling. "Are you mad?" She grabbed her midriff, gasped for breath. "You belong in Bedlam, not Newgate."

The rogue's smoldering glare bewitched her, and she sensed the thrilling shivers that caressed her spine as her body warmed.

He closed the door before he approached her in deliberate strides, his robust figure so full of vim. He reached for her, twirled a lock of her mussed hair around his long finger. "You boarded the ship."

The gentle touch disarmed her, summoning every wretched hurt and throbbing want to the forefront of her thoughts. She trembled with the burden of sensations.

"You didn't stop me." She was breathless. "You didn't come for me."

"Did you think I would?" The man's eyes glowed as the milky light from the full moon pierced the scuttle and bounced off the stormy pools. "Did you think I would beg you to stay with me?"

Sophia shuddered, her blood singing as he slowly dropped to his knees, keeping her ensnared with his commanding eyes the whole time. A strangled cry seeped from her lips as he circled his burly arms around her arse and buried his face into her belly, rousing every fine hair on her body to sensitive life.

He breathed deep.

Sophia's muscles capered at the man's hot sigh, sinking through her apparel and branding her taut skin. She fingered his dark tresses, wove her shaky fingers through the tight queue.

"Do you want me to beg, sweetheart?"

The pulsing rhythm in her breast now pounded in her ears. "No."

She closed her eyes. She let the bounder's crushing hold and sinful lips torment her senses. She had no desire to hear him beg, the way she had begged for him inside the very same cabin. As soon as he had dropped to his knees, he had begged her in silence. And that was enough.

"You should have told me." He bussed her midriff. "You should have told me all those years ago you were unhappy on the island."

Her lips quivered, her heart throbbed. "You're right." She squeezed his long tresses between her fingers. "I made a mistake. I shouldn't have deserted you. I should have told you what was wrong. I'm sorry I hurt you . . . but you still want me to feel pain, *despair*."

He stroked her backside in slow and tender regard, spreading his large fingers apart, warming her posterior, her innards with his powerful touch. "I was angry then. Vengeful. But I'm not anymore. Forgive me."

Sophia swallowed a sob. There was something about those heartfelt words that cut through the thick and putrid layers of hate and hurt, making her rich with a pounding warmth. The sentiment stirred her blood and warmed her belly and eased the pressure in her aching head.

"Marry me, Sophia."

The words. He had said the words she had longed to hear from a man for so long. But it was not the words that moved her anymore, but that the words had come from him.

She sniffed. "I'm going to make you miserable for the rest of your life, Black Hawk."

"I know." He lifted his sexy eyes, the surrounding skin still bruised from the gaolers' thrashing. "But I'll be far more miserable without you, sweetheart."

She snorted. But a smile touched her trembling lips, too, and she stroked his temples in a soft and lazy manner, her heart booming with the words she had yearned to express since the first day she had met him on the island. "I love you, James."

He shuddered. She sensed the vibrations ripple across her belly and along her legs. His eyes glossy, he said roughly, "I love you, Sophia."

She took in a shaky breath, smiling. She was brimming with brilliant light and comforting heat and familiar desire.

She cupped his coarse cheeks and caged his features firmly between her palms as she lowered her mouth and captured his lips in a long and sensuous kiss.

She was free. Free from dogma and fear. Free to be the woman she desired to be . . . in the arms of the man she desired.

Sophia pushed him against the floor and straddled him, hot passion burring in her belly, making her weak—and hungry.

She pinned his arms above his head and pressed her torso against his strapping chest. "I'll marry you, James . . . but under one condition."

He lifted a smoky brow.

"Kill the snake."

He chuckled, a hoarse and sensual sound.

"I'm serious, James." She glowered. "I won't have it in our house."

"I know you're serious." The man's chest shuddered with laughter. "How about if I give her to William instead?"

Sophia mulled over the proposition. "Deal."

She then scooped his wicked lips into her mouth and kissed him until they were both breathless, their hunger quenched.

Epilogue

"**C**ongratulations, Black Hawk."

James hardened at the epithet. "Black Hawk is dead."

The duke extended his arm in a gesture of felicitation. "Only in my dreams."

He took in a slow, deep breath before he accepted the handshake. "Thank you for your help in court."

"Hmm . . . next time I'll let you hang."

Damian smirked before he strolled off. James followed his exasperating kinsman with his eyes . . . but as soon as he lighted on Sophia, the displeasure in his breast withered away.

The woman's smile and gaiety were infectious. She thanked the duke for his well-wishes, then embraced Mirabelle in a sisterly fashion.

A warm and pulsing sentiment gathered in James's belly. He observed his bride-to-be in admiration, for the woman was beyond lovely in a brilliant bronze dress of lustrous satin with short puffed sleeves that hugged her delectable shoulders. She had forsaken the garish baubles, her full and tempting bust smooth and luscious. Even her dark hair, curled and pinned, was loose in its arrangement, so soft tresses cuddled her ears and caressed her throat.

James ignored the merry din in the castle as the engagement party was well under way, content to observe his fiancée instead. She had vowed to make his life miserable . . . but he was determined to make hers wonderful.

William approached him with a glass of champagne in his hand. "Congratulations, James."

"Thank you, Captain."

Captain William Hawkins looked flustered at the appellation. That made James smile even more. His brother was now in command of his own vessel. He would have to grow accustomed to the term of respect . . . and the burden of responsibility that accompanied it.

"When do you set sail?" said James.

"In a fortnight."

He nodded. "I have a gift for you, Will."

He lifted a brow. "You do?"

"To commemorate the event of your maiden voyage . . . I'll give it to you after the wedding, though."

William shrugged.

A moment of quiet passed between the two men.

James regarded his brother thoughtfully. "Good luck, Will."

"Thank you, James." There was a silent understanding that their strife was over. "I'm going to need it with Eddie and Quincy serving onboard."

It was time the brothers parted ways. James would always be there to support his kin, however he would not serve under the Royal Navy. If the men needed to be privateers and explore the world without him, then he wished them wisdom and sweet winds . . . at least the brothers needn't worry about the impostors anymore.

Quincy entered the parlor. "I've got it!"

Alice bounded across the room and hugged her uncle Quincy's leg. "You got what?"

"You've got what?" corrected her mother.

Squirt screwed up her face. "I don't have anything."

Mirabelle rolled her eyes.

Quincy chuckled and ruffled the chit's curly locks. "I have the paper." He cleared his throat. "The headline reads: *Black Hawk Is Dead!*" He wagged his brows. "Memorable, eh?"

"Well?" said Edmund, frowning. "How does the rest of it read?"

Quincy rustled the pages. *"The infamous pirate leader Black Hawk is dead, the crew drowned! The notorious villain tempted fate with his heinous conduct, kidnapping the wealthy Miss Sophia Dawson for ransom. The young lady's fiancé, the valiant Captain James Hawkins, hunted the surly devil at sea, and in a dance with death, defeated the wretched pirate lord, rescuing the damsel and sending the cutthroats to the bottom of the sea. The water is free at last from the wicked corsair and his motley crew of scalawags."* Quincy twisted his lips. "Scalawags?" He sniffed. *"The sea is once more the domain of our nation's great navy. Rejoice, good reader! Rule Britannia!"*

"Hurrah!" Squirt danced on her toes. "I hate pirates."

The room erupted in guffaws, for Alice wasn't privy to her uncles' notorious reputations. James wondered what the squirt would think to learn she was standing in the same room with the infamous villains.

James moved off and settled beside a window,

the sunset casting the crisp, autumn landscape in a fiery glow of brilliant russet reds and bright golden yellows.

Black Hawk was dead. James had "killed" the brigand at sea, and as a result, he didn't have to chase after the impostors anymore. The knave Hagley and his cheeky crew could pillage the waters all they liked . . . under another pseudonym. No one would ever take the legendary title away from James again, and that meant the brothers needn't seek a pardon for their wicked ways, their pasts secured. William, Edmund, and Quincy had enlisted under the Royal Navy's African Squadron as privateers without censure, scandal, or legal delicacies.

"Good evening . . . valiant Captain James Hawkins."

He quirked a wry smile at her smoky drawl and showmanship.

"Good evening, sweetheart."

She slipped her arms around his waist and rested her warm cheek against his breast, making him shudder. He closed his eyes and embraced her, his soul quiet as she snuggled against him, chasing away the last remaining shadows in his heart.

"I received a letter from Imogen today."

"Oh?" He bussed the top of her head, the sweet scent of bay rum shampoo filling his nose, his lungs. "How is she?"

"*Mrs.* Lewis is doing very well. She and her husband are coming to the wedding."

"I'm glad to hear it."

James was pleased to know the girl was fit and in good spirits, that her beau had proved honorable and faithful, whisking her away from scandal and wedding her proper.

"Lady Lucas will attend our wedding, as well."

James's good mood soured.

"I think you'll find her much more agreeable, James."

He frowned.

"You are the valiant Captain James Hawkins, after all."

He sighed at that, Sophia chuckling.

"Alice, put that down!"

James and Sophia glanced across the room—and witnessed Squirt inspecting a dainty dish.

"I was just looking at it, Mama," she said peevishly.

"You might break it, Alice. Put it down!"

The spiteful chit glanced at the dish . . . then at her mother . . . then dropped the porcelain.

"Alice!"

She scurried into her uncle Quincy's protective arms. "It was an accident, Mama!"

Sophia groaned in sympathy with the duchess. "I think it's time Belle hired a governess."

"I think you're right," he said grimly.

She offered him a sassy smile. "Are you sure you won't regret not having offspring of your own?"

"Bite your tongue, woman."

She chuckled and rested her chin against his breastbone. "I have something for you."

He looked down into her bewitching, cocoa brown eyes and shuddered at the smoldering expression in the deep, dark pools. "You do?"

Slowly she gathered her slender brows in a seductive, nay, mischievous fashion.

James watched as her thin fingers sensuously slipped into her bodice and stirred in the pocket between her breasts. With a wicked grin, she removed a small, black velvet pouch with golden cords from her corset.

"No knife?" he asked.

"No knife." She handed him the mysterious parcel. "I thought you might like a new one . . . to replace the old."

He furrowed his brow at the enigmatic clue before he took the weighty gift from her fingers and stretched the threaded cords. He turned the satchel upside-down.

A fob watch slipped out of the bag.

James took in a sharp breath. His heart thumped hard as he fingered the timepiece, rubbed his thumb across the smooth glass surface and solid gold underside.

"Read the inscription," she said softly.

He gazed into her lovely eyes, so mesmerizing, before he lifted the watch toward the window, the bauble shimmering in the splayed light, and read:

May you rot in everlasting matrimony.

Fingers quivered, then his lips. He whispered, "Witch."

"Aye, I am." She kissed his breast, stirring his blood, his bones, his heart to pulsing life. "But it's no worse than you deserve, you infamous rogue."

If you've enjoyed reading
THE INFAMOUS ROGUE,
look for Alexandra Benedict's ebook novella
MISTRESS OF PARADISE,
to find out how Sophia Dawson and
Captain James Hawkins
first fell in love.

Available now at *www.harpercollinsebooks.com*
And wherever ebooks are sold.

Next month, don't miss these exciting new love stories only from Avon Books

Never Marry a Stranger by Gayle Callen

After being presumed dead in battle, Captain Matthew Leland gives the *ton* quite the shock when he arrives in Madingley Court. But no one is surprised more than Matthew, because waiting for him at home is a bewitching beauty—and she claims to be his wife!

Passion Untamed by Pamela Palmer

Though the Mage witch Skye has a gentle heart, demonic forces have enslaved her, forcing her to kidnap Paenther, a powerful and dangerous immortal. Even chained and naked, he is a cunning prisoner who seduces her, turning captive into captor.

The Seduction of Sara by Karen Hawkins

Lady Sara Carrington's brothers want to marry her off to some stodgy old man to curb her wildness, so she's determined to find her own husband. Yet the man she picks is England's most notorious rake and has sworn never to marry . . . will Sara's plan of seduction succeed?

To Wed a Wicked Earl by Olivia Parker

Adam Faramond, Earl of Rothbury, needs to find a wife—immediately!—or his beloved grandmother will leave him penniless. But Adam, an unrepentant rake, would reform for only one woman, the woman he's lusted after—and loved—for years. But would she ever consent to be the blushing bride of a rogue?

At Avon Books, we know your passion for romance—once you finish one of our novels, you find yourself wanting more.

May we tempt you with . . .

- **Excerpts** from our upcoming releases.

- Entertaining **extras**, including authors' personal photo albums and book lists.

- Behind-the-scenes **scoop** on your favorite characters and series.

- **Sweepstakes** for the chance to win free books, romantic getaways, and other fun prizes.

- Writing **tips** from our authors and editors.

- **Blog** with our authors and find out why they love to write romance.

- **Exclusive content** that's not contained within the pages of our novels.

Join us at
www.avonbooks.com

AVON *An Imprint of* HarperCollins*Publishers*
www.avonromance.com

Available wherever books are sold or please call 1-800-331-3761 to order.

FTH 0708